American Skin

Novels by Peter Viertel

THE CANYON
LINE OF DEPARTURE
WHITE HUNTER, BLACK HEART
LOVE LIES BLEEDING
BICYCLE ON THE BEACH
AMERICAN SKIN

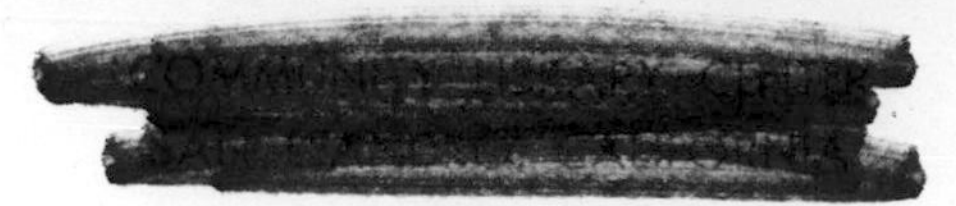

Peter Viertel

AMERICAN SKIN

HOUGHTON MIFFLIN COMPANY BOSTON
1984

Library of Congress Cataloging in Publication Data

Viertel, Peter.
American skin.

I. Title.
PS3543.I326A8 1983 813′.52 83-12587
ISBN 0-395-34647-9

Printed in the United States of America

S 10 9 8 7 6 5 4 3 2 1

For Irwin, Marian, and Adam
"¡ Que nos quiten lo bailado!"

I, so far as I can sense the pattern of my mind,
write of the wish that comes true, for some reason
a terrifying concept, at least to my imagination.

— James M. Cain, August 6, 1949

Part One

Brandt stood with his back to the Mediterranean and looked up and down the Paseo Marítimo as if he had never been there before in his life. The name of the place he was trying to find was El Faro. He was sure of that much, as he had had breakfast there every morning for a month only a few years ago. There had been a lighthouse a block down the street, from which the restaurant had obviously derived its name, a small, brown, rectangular house with a white tower at its far end that had served as a landmark for the fishing boats that worked a few miles out during the night. Now there was a long row of high apartment buildings facing the water, and the first of the skyscrapers, the ground floor of which had housed the restaurant, was lost in the crowd. It seemed incredible to Brandt that the town could have changed that much in so short a time, and for a moment he thought he had come down the wrong street. Yet the old port was there, although the sea wall protecting the yacht harbor had been extended. It stretched out over four blocks, and Brandt realized that he would have to walk the whole length of it in order to locate El Faro and keep his appointment with Guy Manning.

He glanced at his watch. It was a quarter to eight, and except for an old man fishing, there was not a soul in sight whom he could ask. If the restaurant had gone out of business, Guy would certainly not have agreed to meet him there when they made their date on the telephone the previous night. The morning sun was already quite hot on his back, giving promise of a sweltering summer day. The breeze was from the east. *Levante,* Brandt said to himself, remembering that you lived by the wind on that coast, and that the east wind was the most benign of the prevailing winds, and the least dangerous.

He started slowly up the street, occasionally checking the buildings on his right. The view to his left was a more pleasing one, with the long line of pleasure boats moored along the gray cement sea wall, their pennants fluttering lazily. There was a graffito visible behind the masts of a dilapidated old schooner. *¡Viva Tejero!* it read in tribute to the hero of the comic-opera coup d'état of the previous winter. *¡Fascistas! ¡Hijos de putas!* another spray-can artist had squirted in reply a little farther along. The handwriting on the wall, Brandt thought, the lunatic fringes of the extreme right and left giving their warnings that another upheaval might soon mar Spain's future.

He may have come back at just the wrong moment, Brandt reflected. It had all changed so much. It was no longer the pleasant little white town it had been when he and Pamela had come there five or six years ago. La Fonda, the hotel at which they had stayed, was a restaurant now, one of the most expensive in the town. It had been a charming little Andalusian inn with about thirty rooms that looked down on a series of patios decorated with bougainvillaea and potted palm trees, each room furnished in a different style. They had slept in an antique bed of iron bars with brass knobs; they had been happy there. Well, everything changes for the worse, he thought; the whole world is getting uglier day by day.

He heard a shout from behind him, and looking over his shoulder he saw Guy waving to him from in front of a reddish-brown building that Brandt hadn't even bothered to look at. In his mind's eye the wall above the plate-glass windows of El Faro had been white. That was how he remembered it: the white town, the blue sea.

"Where the hell were you going?" Guy asked once they had greeted each other. "You walked right past here. I was sitting inside watching you."

"I was busy reading the slogans on the wall, and looking for the old lighthouse. I suppose they've knocked that down."

"No. It's over there, where it's always been," Guy Manning said, and pointed a nicotine-stained finger down the street.

"Somebody must have moved it," Brandt said. "I could have sworn it was only half a block away."

"Memory is a tricky thing, old boy," Manning said, and Brandt thought, rather uncharitably, that despite his friend's slightly seedy looks, he had managed to retain his upper-class accent. "How've you been? I was surprised when you called. I didn't think you were ever coming back."

"It was probably a mistake," Brandt said, grinning.

"Well, yes. It's changed an awful lot in the last few years. And now the Arabs have arrived. That certainly hasn't done the town any good. And the hordes of tourists in the summer! It's like Miami Beach, isn't it? Are you and Pamela still together?"

Brandt noticed that the important question had been saved for the end of Manning's little speech. Pamela had been Guy's favorite; he had always preferred her company, had made no secret of it. But then that was to be expected, as they were both Brits, and Pamela was beautiful in that special English way, clear skin, blond hair, and a strong, erect figure that, even if it was not perfect in every detail, was nothing you could "crab her for," as her friends said.

Brandt said: "No. Pam has joined another regiment. She has a new commanding officer now."

"I *am* sorry," Manning said. "It must have been quite a blow for you, David."

"I could see it coming, and that helped a little," Brandt replied. "Shall we go inside and have a little breakfast? I don't like to talk about my personal disasters on an empty stomach."

The interior of the restaurant hadn't been altered. The same wooden tables and chairs still stood on the worn tiled floor, with the bar in the back of the room, near the side entrance. The only new features were the brown fishing nets that decorated the walls and, instead of Franco, the King's photograph in a lacquered frame. He was dressed in a white naval officer's uniform, fittingly enough, and he appeared to be staring out to sea, with a look of uncharacteristic solemnity. The same barman was there in his stained black trousers and creased white shirt, although he had put on a little weight around the middle. He patted Brandt on the back with his thick hand, a shy version of the usual embrace.

Manning ordered an anis seco with his coffee but refused Brandt's offer of something to eat, as he'd already had his breakfast at home. "Marie insists on getting up and making me a cooked breakfast," he explained, "so I have to eat it, whether I'm hungry or not."

"Have you seen Freddy Weaver around?" Brandt asked, before Guy could begin questioning him about Pamela. That was one of the reasons he had come back to the coast, to forget Pamela and find his old friend. Weaver, one of the "early settlers," had been partly responsible for Brandt's first visit to the coast in the sixties. In London the rumor had been that Weaver had smoked himself into a state of oblivion and had gone off to Morocco, where hash was easier to come by.

"I can't say that I have," Manning replied. "But then I haven't been to Daphne's for months. Was he a good chum of yours?"

"I used to see quite a lot of him here and in London," Brandt said. "Then last year I was told he'd gone back to the States, but that turned out to be just another rumor."

"Tangier's more like it. Freddy was never one of my favorites. Too damned unreliable for my taste. A drifter. Anyway, I've had enough troubles of my own." He paused and sipped his anis, then drank his coffee in one gulp. "I told you on the blower last night that I had to charter my boat. That's why I wanted to talk to you as soon as possible, in case you might be interested."

"I thought you never did that," Brandt said.

"There are a lot of things you wind up having to do in life that you thought you never would have to," Manning said, and frowned. "Chartering your boat to a friend is probably one of the least painful." He watched Brandt spread marmalade on his piece of toast, then produced a package of Spanish cigarettes, which he put down on the table. "Do you mind?" he asked, about to light up.

"No. Go ahead. The air in here is fairly polluted as it is." A small group of sailors had come into the restaurant for their morning coffee. They were standing at the bar, smoking and talking.

"How did you manage to lose a girl like Pam?" Manning asked, exhaling an acrid cloud.

"The usual way," Brandt said. "By taking her too much for granted. Somebody else came along who didn't."

"Perhaps you should have gotten married."

"She didn't want to, and neither did I. Who was it said that only priests and faggots think of getting married nowadays? A French lady writer, I believe."

"I don't think it matters," Manning said, and smiled sourly. "It's not really true. So now you've decided to come down here to fornicate and forget. Lie in the sun all day, and sleep with a different Swedish girl every night. That's how this place is advertised, isn't it?"

"I suppose so, although that's not quite my plan," Brandt replied. "I felt I needed a vacation, and a friend of mine in London suggested I might do a little work for his company if I felt like staying on. They've bought a hotel with a good deal of land, and they're building an Andalusian village. Since I speak the language and know the country, he thought I could be of help to them. So what the hell, it meant a change of scenery and maybe even a chance to make some money."

"Well, if you're going to be a high-powered real estate hustler, a boat will come in handy," Manning said, with a note of sarcasm in his voice. "Take your prospective buyers out for a ride. You used to enjoy the sea, I recall."

"I still do," Brandt said warily. "I remember that the beach wasn't very pleasant," he added.

The Englishman nodded. "That's about the only feature of the town that hasn't changed," he said. "The godawful beach. So you might as well charter my old tub. I'll let you have her cheap."

"I'd like to think about it."

"Come and look at her," Manning said. He seemed most anxious to make a deal.

Brandt stood waiting on the dock while Manning removed the tarpaulin that covered the back of the wheelhouse of *Lulubelle II.*

Her home port, painted in small golden letters under her name, was Southampton. It was hard to believe that she had made the journey across the Bay of Biscay and down the Portuguese coast on her own steam, but then the English were capable of all kinds of follies, especially when it came to boats, and Manning was quite obviously an expert sailor, judging by the way he moved around the cramped space of the afterdeck that the tightly stretched canvas left available for his movements.

He was a thin man, a little over six feet tall, in his early fifties, with gray hair and parched skin. His worn jeans and faded navy blue shirt hung loosely from his body. The heat was making Brandt sweat a little as he stood there in the morning sun, yet Manning appeared not to be bothered by it. He was folding the tarpaulin now that he had disengaged it from the various hooks and pressure buttons by which it had been attached, and Brandt started down the worn gangplank in order to give him a hand.

"Permission to come aboard, sir?"

"Permission granted."

Brandt gave a mock salute to the faded Union Jack in the stern, kicked off his sneakers, and stepped into the cockpit. Manning dropped his end of the tarpaulin and unlocked the door to the main cabin. Then, picking up the folded canvas again, he tossed it onto the cockpit. "What's her overall length?" Brandt asked. He hadn't planned to charter a boat, but it was probably not a bad idea, he thought now, if the price was right.

"About thirty-five feet, if you count the swimming platform in the stern. The hull's ten meters exactly. She draws about twenty-eight inches of water, but it's best to reckon three feet if you're running in close to the beach."

"Have you ever owned a sailboat?" Brandt asked. Manning was not the type of man who went in for stinkpots.

"That's all I've ever had. But for this coast a sailboat's a waste of time. There's no place to go, no sheltered harbors, so all you really want is a swimming platform, something to take you away from the pestilential waters along the shore." He pulled open the windows on both sides of the wheelhouse and backed down the ladder into the cabin. "Well, here we are," he said as Brandt joined him in the cabin. "A place to lay your head and a few of your friends."

It was an old American joke that Guy had probably collected from some expatriate yachtsman who had retired to a small villa on a dry hillside.

"It's a nice cabin," Brandt commented. He didn't feel like encouraging sex talk or being reminded that he had come there to "fornicate and forget."

"Do you ever spend the night on board?" he asked.

"Not very often. Once a year or so, when I take her to Gib in order to stock up on paint and booze. Would you like a lager?" Manning fished two bottles of San Miguel out of the plastic container and opened them. He made room for his guest on the L-shaped bench behind the varnished table and took a swig from his bottle. "A boat makes all the difference in the summer," Manning said. "You can get away from the heat of the day, and swim in clean water. A boat helps catch the birds, too," Manning added with a wink. "You know, you shouldn't let Pamela's going off get to you. I know a chap whose wife left him, and it really left its mark on him. Sad. He only goes out now with eighteen-year-olds. As if he has to prove something."

"You're making my mouth water," Brandt said, and was gratified to see that he had managed to get a genuine laugh out of the man facing him. "Anyway, let's not worry about what effect being single again will have on me. How much would it cost to hire your boat for the month of July?"

"Well, a boat like this is worth about two hundred and fifty thousand pesetas during the summer months. But as she's of British registry, I don't have the right to charter her, so I'll take seventy-five. You buy the fuel and pay the sailor who washes her down after you've come in. I insist that whoever charters from me doesn't take her to Gib, because I don't want trouble with the police. I'll throw in what's left of June as a part of the deal."

"Well, that certainly sounds fair," Brandt said. Seventy-five thousand pesetas was about seven hundred and fifty dollars at the present exchange rate, Brandt calculated. It was cheap at twice the price.

They took *Lulubelle II* out for a trial run. Manning said he wanted to show Brandt how the boat handled and to see how he handled her. He would never charter a boat without finding out for himself if the customer was not just another *marinero de Córdoba,* a local joke that could be freely translated as a sailor from Kansas City. Brandt reminded Guy that he had served in the U.S. Navy, as well as having crewed for various friends in his youth in Southern California. The run to Catalina was perhaps not the greatest test of a man's seamanship, but compared to the waters off the Costa del Sol, the Med was "a walk in the park." More boats had been lost in the Catalina channel in the last twenty years than had been lost in a century or two in the western reaches of the Mediterranean.

"She cruises at about sixteen hundred revs," the Englishman shouted above the roar of the Ford diesels. "Does twelve to thirteen knots. If you want to save fuel, and not have your lady friends shivering in the breeze, keep her at about fourteen hundred. That's fast enough if you're not going anywhere."

Brandt nodded and took over the wheel. Then as they swung southwest along the coast, he stood listening to Guy's tale of woe while keeping an eye out for logs and floating debris.

Manning had come out there with his wife and all his savings, having sold marine insurance for most of his life for a London firm of brokers. They had bought a villa cheaply enough in the hills overlooking San Pedro de Alcántara, and then out of boredom, and because of the swiftly sinking pound sterling, they had opened a small restaurant near Marbella. It had gone well for a while, but in the years immediately following Franco's demise, business had turned sour. The waiters and the cook had joined the local union, and although their salaries had not increased all that much, the social security payments had added to the cost of running the restaurant. Manning had raised the prices on the menu and had lost customers. Finally, seeing that they were running at a loss during the winter months, he and his wife decided to sell the place. The new owner had not been able to make the promised payments, and now they were involved in a lawsuit, the restaurant was closed, and the Mannings were eating up their capital. Marie, Guy's wife, had gotten a tumor in her breast, and the hospital bills and the surgeon's fee had really brought the wolf to the door.

It was a fairly typical story of the coast. Brandt had heard a few worse ones, but had never had to listen to them being shouted above the roar of twin diesels. He pulled back the Morse controls and shut off the engine.

"How about a swim?" he asked Manning. "We don't have to anchor, just take a quick dip."

"I don't have a bathing costume."

"Well, I won't look, if you don't."

Manning smiled, showing an uneven set of yellow teeth. "You're on," he said.

They peeled off their clothes and dove into the clear water. The temperature was perfect: invigorating, yet fairly warm once you were used to it. "This is what it's all about, isn't it? That's why the tourists still keep coming to this place," he said to Guy as they floated, toes up, near the stern of the *Lulubelle.* "It's certainly not for the scenery or the food."

"The sun and the señoritas, dear boy. Don't forget either one of those."

There were no towels on board, and so they sat on the plastic cushions and let the breeze dry their bodies.

"Have you ever read Gerald Brenan?" Manning asked. "*South from Granada* or *The Spanish Labyrinth*?"

"I have. I'm not totally uncultured, even though I do come from Southern California." Brandt noticed that Manning had a workingman's suntan: his arms were brown to where his sleeves stopped, and he had a tanned circle around his neck. He had probably not had time to take a swim or lie in the sun this year, the poor bastard. "He's a wonderful writer," Brandt said. "Why do you ask?"

"Well, Brenan wrote in one of his books that the first people who settled this coast, many, many centuries ago, came from the British Isles," Manning said quietly. "It would be ironic if they would be the first to be squeezed out in the present day."

"They won't be," Brandt said. "The people I may be working for will see to that. Time-ownership is their answer. They're aiming their effort at the British market."

"Yeah, and they'll bugger up the place even more. Just look over at the coast. See all those skyscrapers standing in the morning mist? Hell, we might as well be in Fort Lauderdale or San Diego."

"But there are not as many gringos."

Manning laughed. "Yes, that's true," he replied. "I'm glad *you* said it. But they're better than the Arabs; there's that to be said for your lot."

He got up and slipped on his jeans. Then he went below and reappeared with two more lagers. "I'm glad you decided to come back to these shores, David," he said, handing Brandt an open bottle of Aguila. "You cheer me up no end." He took a long drink. "You know why they call camels ships of the desert? Because they're full of Arab seamen." He laughed heartily at his own joke, and Brandt felt obliged to smile.

"They don't bother people much around here, do they?" he asked. "They keep pretty much to themselves."

"Yes, but they raise the price of everything, the buggers. And they're a dirty lot. They've built a mosque right outside town. Took them six months and cost the earth. You'd think they'd build a decent hospital first."

"They fly back to London or Geneva when they get sick."

"That's about right," Manning said. He got up, having finished his second beer. "Might as well go back, don't you think? You've probably got plenty to do to get organized." He started the engines without waiting for an answer. He was used to doing as he pleased on board *Lulubelle;* that much was quite obvious.

Brandt put on his shorts and his khaki slacks. Manning swung the boat around, then headed west. The Rock was not visible. It was hidden in a mist. Secretly solid, Brandt thought to himself. "Why don't you want her taken to Gib?" he asked Manning. "What's the harm, if people don't try to smuggle anything ashore?"

"Well, the registered owner is supposed to be on board going into a foreign port. Then, the marina there is a toilet out of place. You get the hull all dirty, and we've just cleaned her up for the season. It costs about a hundred quid to pull her out of the water and put her back in again. Anyway, there's nothing much to buy. And the Spaniards don't like it. So that's one of the conditions I put on the charter."

"That makes sense," Brandt shouted above the roar of the engines as they started to pick up speed.

They ran for a brief while with the Sealog indicating eighteen knots, and then Manning pulled back on the controls and resumed a more normal speed. "What about Pamela?" Manning asked. "Do you think she might change her mind?"

"No, I don't think so," Brandt replied. "We'd about had it, anyway. The relationship wasn't what it should have been. That's how she felt, and there was no point in arguing with her. Of course, there was somebody else in the picture, but I didn't know it until we'd busted up. We exchanged the usual unpleasant phone calls, and that was it."

"You don't like to talk about it, do you?"

"I don't particularly enjoy it. It still hurts a little. Especially in the late evening."

"Well, you'll find a lot of ladies to comfort you on this coast," Manning said. "You won't find anyone like her, though, I'd be willing to wager."

"I'm not going to look," Brandt told him. "I want to get straightened out with myself first."

It was eleven-thirty by the time he was ready to leave the hotel again, having showered and changed his clothes. He didn't want to make his first appearance at the Sun and Sea Realty Company looking like a beachcomber. He had met Richard Grey, the man in charge, several times in London, and had a fairly good idea of what kind of man he was. Grey was tall and conventionally handsome, with a lean body and an unlined face, the kind of upper-class Englishman who was always impeccably dressed, and who undoubtedly judged his fellow men by their outward appearance. He had made a fortune as a young man in the commodity market before branching out into real estate, and was well known in both the City and the frivolous society that frequented Annabel's and the more exclusive clubs of Mayfair. He rode to hounds, was a member of White's, and had at one time held a safe Conservative seat at Westminster. Property was his main interest now, and Brandt wondered once again, as he drove through the heavy traffic of the small Spanish town, how, despite the crippling tax laws of Great Britain, Grey had managed to amass such a large fortune. Knowing how to make money was apparently only part of the game; knowing how to circumvent the law was equally important. Well, *he* hadn't really managed to do either, Brandt reflected.

It was suffocatingly hot inside the Seat 850 he had rented at the hotel on the previous evening. It was an uncomfortable little shoe box of a car, and Brandt resolved to take it back to the car-rental people as soon as possible and get a bigger one. The traffic on the four-lane highway that ran along the coast was even worse than he remembered it, the number of maniacal drivers having increased rather than diminished. There seemed to be some strange, illogical behavior pattern that all Europeans were prone to once they got behind the steering wheel of a car. It had always been that way in France and Italy and Germany, but not in Spain, where owning a car had been restricted to the privileged few. However, with the prosperity that had come during the last ten years, that had changed. Now rich and poor alike were out to slaughter each other seven days a week.

The chief vice of the Spanish driver was tailgating. A plump, suntanned woman with a small child clinging to the back of her seat was following Brandt at that moment, and he was tempted to frighten her by touching his brakes. But after studying her face in the rearview mirror, he decided that she would probably plow into him and then accuse him of reckless driving. He pulled over into the right-hand lane and waved her on. "The road's all yours, you silly bitch," he called out to her as she roared past.

"She can't hear you . . . only I can." Pamela's voice came to him out of the past. "So why shout at her?"

And he could hear himself answering: "I shout because I'm pleading for my life. I'm not like you, controlled and sensible and British." Although, in the end she hadn't been all that controlled and sensible either; their last quarrel had been a fairly violent one. But that had probably been his own fault. Before deciding to share the same flat, they had agreed to be honest and direct in their personal relationship, and when he had discovered that she had become involved with someone else and had hidden the fact from him, he had not behaved as well as he might have, had even pleaded with her to come back to him and start all over again, which was something he had thought he would never do.

Don't think about all that now, pal, he counseled himself grimly. Fornicate and forget.

Once again, for although forgetting was not all that easy, he realized that Pamela remained there beside him as he drove on, and only when he turned off the main road, after a quarter of an hour's drive, did she leave him, temporarily anyway. He parked the little red car in the shade of a grove of eucalyptus trees and walked up a curving path of red tiles to the entrance of the small modern office bungalow that had, by the look of it, only recently been built. There was a pine forest beyond it, with the glistening sea barely visible in the distance. A billboard of modest dimensions told him that he had come to the right place, and he paused for a moment in the shade of the entrance before making his way through the glass doors, wiped his hands and face with his handkerchief so as to appear normally confident and not too eager for the job that might be offered him.

The receptionist had bluish-black hair and was decidedly overweight, with at least half a dozen rings on her fat fingers. She was on the telephone to her boyfriend, but she interrupted her conversation to inquire what it was Brandt wanted. When he told her that he was there to see Señor Grey, she put her boyfriend on hold and pushed several buttons in order to inform someone called Penny that there was someone out in front to see her boss.

Penny was Australian, to judge by her accent, with a good figure and a friendly smile. "Mr. Grey will be with you in a few minutes," she told him, and led him into her own office, a small cubicle with a desk and two leather armchairs. "Have you just come over from London?" she asked him once he was seated.

"Yesterday evening," he told her.

"And how's the dear old town? Cold and wet as usual?"

"It hasn't been too bad this year," Brandt replied. "Not like this, needless to say."

"Someday I'm going back there," the girl said. "When I've had enough of the sun and the tourists. Of course, I've been saying that for three years." There was the sound of a buzzer, and she got to her feet. "Richard will see you now; Mr. Grey, that is," she added with a giggle.

Grey looked up from the letter he was reading and indicated a chair in front of his desk. "We *have* met, I believe," he said, rising to shake Brandt's hand. Despite the heat, Grey was wearing a beige polka-dot stock tie inside his monogrammed silk shirt, the trademark of the upper-class Englishman, as if to prove that only the lower orders were incapable of enduring a tropical climate, and as a result bared their chests.

"I think we have," Brandt said, recalling at least two occasions when they had been introduced at Les Ambassadeurs.

"Probably with Amir Rajawi. He's a great chum of yours, isn't he?"

"Yes, we're friends. We play a lot of tennis together." Amir was one of the few Iranian refugees who had left his country prior to the fall of the Shah, because his father had been opposed to the Pahlevi regime, although he always hastened to add that the present regime was probably worse.

"As you know, he's one of our partners. He wrote me that you were coming down here and that you might make a most useful member of our team. You're well acquainted with Spain, I believe. Speak the language, and all that."

"I was in Madrid in the sixties," Brandt said. "In the movie business."

"Yes, well I don't know much about films. Never go to them, as a matter of fact, unless I'm forced to. You were in a management position, I believe," he added, glancing at the letter in front of him.

"I was a production manager," Brandt said. "I worked for Bronston until his company folded."

Grey appeared not to be interested. "We're hoping to do something quite out of the ordinary on this coast," he said. "If time doesn't run out on us and the entire country collapses. Amir probably told you that we've acquired a four-star hotel, and about two hundred and fifty acres of land. It was part of another deal," he added with a secretive smile, "that our chairman made in Paris last year. The sweetener, you might call it. We've renovated the hotel and have started building several apartment houses, as well as a few luxury villas. We consider this coast a high-risk area, which is why we want to presell as many of the apartments we're constructing as possible. I presume you've heard of the time-ownership plan?"

"I know something about it," Brandt said. "The sucker buys

three or four weeks' holiday time in a villa or an apartment, and shares the ownership with whoever buys the same space for the rest of the year."

Grey smiled briefly to show that he was not lacking in a sense of humor. "The word 'sucker' implies dishonesty, and so is inaccurate, to say the least," he replied.

"It was said in jest."

"I realize that. Still, it's not a word we use around here. We've invested four million pounds in the hotel, and we are investing at least another four million in new construction. So we're not a fly-by-night, get-rich-quick corporation. We employ a lot of Spanish labor, and we have a right to expect a profit," Grey continued. "Capital investment is what this country needs right now. Their own bankers and high-rollers are running for the hills at the present time. The hotels in New York are full of them, the expensive hotels, that is," he added pointedly. "The money we're bringing in is a blessing as far as Spain is concerned."

"Is it Arab money?"

"Some of it is. Some of it is Lebanese, some of it British, and some of it, as you know, Iranian. Why do you ask?"

"Just curious. I like to know who I'm working for."

"Money doesn't fly a flag," Grey said evenly. "If our large Jewish clientele doesn't have any objections, I don't see why it should worry you." He got up from his desk and sauntered over to a framed aerial map on the wall. It was marked with thick blue lines that obviously showed the land that the corporation had acquired. "Here's a bird's-eye view of our development," Grey said. "Incidentally, we're a British corporation, and if you join us, you'll be paid in England. That is, if you're interested."

"I am or I wouldn't be here," Brandt replied, going over to the map. The interview wasn't going well, but he didn't really care. He didn't need a job. He had come there for a month's holiday. It had been Amir's idea that he look in on Grey. "I've never been a salesman," he added. "It may be a little late to start now."

"I don't know about that. It's not difficult to sell something that gives value for money. And we're doing just that. More than most of the other land developers in town." He indicated the map. "This is one of the best locations on the coast. And we're not about to spoil it. I can assure you of that."

It was always the same story, Brandt thought. If you were not too eager for a job, they always wanted you more. "Just what would I be doing if I joined the firm?" he asked Grey once they were both seated again and facing each other.

"Well, we were hoping you could take charge of our public relations. We need to make a big splash in the press, in England *and* the States, if possible. Amir tells me you're an expert at that. And that you know how to operate in Spain."

"I lived here for a while," Brandt replied, disregarding the compliment. "What's your budget for advertising?"

"You mean what does the job pay?"

"That's part of my question. Up front I like to know what I have to work with."

Grey smiled wryly. "Our overall budget is three million pesetas for the first phase of the venture. That's approximately thirty thousand dollars. Your fee would be about five percent of that, plus an apartment and a car. For the next six weeks, that is. After that we could talk again." He paused. "I know that's not the kind of money you've been making in London, but this is less than a full-time job . . ."

Brandt said: "The money's all right. I'm more worried about the overall budget. Amir said that you were planning to give a party for the opening of the hotel and wanted to invite a few celebrities. That's expensive, you know."

"Well, we're not absolutely fixed on that sum. If necessary, we could increase it. It rather depends on the kind of celebrities you come up with."

"Fair enough," Brandt said. "I presume you don't expect me to produce members of the British royal family."

"Hardly," Grey replied. They shook hands across the desk. "I seem to recall now that we met in one of the more select gaming dens of Mayfair," he said as they both got to their feet. "I can't quite remember which one it was, but there were a good many brown-skinned chaps about."

"It doesn't really matter." They both laughed. "I'd better have a look at that apartment," Brandt said. He didn't feel exactly exhilarated, but he was pleased. Chartering *Lulubelle* was no longer an extravagance. And he had never enjoyed a pointless vacation. "I'll do my best for you," he told Grey.

"I'm sure you will, David." Grey patted him gently on the back, a final, somewhat patronizing gesture.

"Do you know why they call camels ships of the desert?" Brandt asked as they stopped near the door.

"No. Why?"

Brandt gave him the punch line of the joke and was surprised to see that the Englishman laughed heartily. Even if he had heard it before, he was obviously making an effort to be a nice guy.

The first apartment that was available turned out to be a few kilometers past the office on the Málaga side of the town. Brandt was tempted, as he followed the young woman in charge of rentals in her red Mini, to turn back and ask her to show him something nearer the port. But once they had arrived at the block of apartments, he decided at least to have a look at the place, as the building was on the beach side of the main road. That in itself was an advantage, he decided, because he would be able to go for a swim before breakfast. He parked the Peugeot he had exchanged for the Seat 850 and followed the young woman into the building.

Her name was Esperanza. She had a trim figure and a pleasant-enough face, despite her dyed hair. Her wrists, he noticed, were hung with the usual golden chains and charms, and she sported a gold and stainless steel Rolex, the model that served as a kind of caste mark in Spain. Esperanza probably belonged to a good middle-class family, or she had a rich lover who lavished expensive presents on her. As Brandt stood beside her in the small elevator, the odor of her perfume permeated the air around them. It was a scent that Pamela had worn occasionally when they had first met.

There seemed to be days when it was impossible to escape the past, he thought, as he stood waiting for Esperanza to open the door of Apartment 11. She was trying various keys, and finally she inserted the right one and opened the door with a sigh of relief. The place seemed too small at first glance, but once she opened the shutters, the view of the sea reconciled him to the size of the living room. There wasn't a great deal of furniture, but the sofa and the two matching armchairs were obviously new. There was a double bed in the bedroom, and a chest of drawers, as well as a closet filled with a score of bent wire hangers. That was always the way with a rented apartment. Pamela and he had bought hangers all over southern Europe and left them behind for the next occupants.

The hangers were the only used furnishings in the place. That appealed to him. It was like starting all over again. The bathroom was newly tiled, and there was even a shower, which was a rarity in this part of the world. Esperanza glanced at herself in the mirror and made an adjustment to her hair. Brandt said, "We should be quite comfortable here," and the young woman smiled at him and led the way back to the living room.

"There's a telephone," she said in her heavily accented English. "It is the only apartment I can show you that has one."

"That settles it. Is there a kitchen?"

"Of course." She crossed the living room in her high-heeled espadrilles and opened the door for him to have a look. The kitchen was tiny by any standard, but there was a refrigerator and a gas stove that looked equally new and unused.

"We won't be able to give any big dinner parties," Brandt said, "but we won't starve to death, either."

"Menos mal," Esperanza replied, and laughed.

"We'll eat out tonight. You can choose the restaurant."

"I'm sorry I won't be able to join you," she said in Spanish, "but I have to cook for my family in the evening."

"You have children?"

"Three," she said, "and a husband who is always hungry. The maid comes in at eleven in the morning. She is paid fifteen thousand a month."

"That seems reasonable enough."

After Esperanza had left him, he moved the furniture around a little and went down to get his luggage out of the Peugeot. He would go to the flea market that was open every Saturday in front of the *plaza de toros* and buy a few cheap watercolors and maybe a small table, he decided. That was also true of every place he had ever rented: there was never a good reading lamp or a table on which to write even a letter. The people who spent their vacations in the sun were probably too burned-out to open a book or write anything more than a postcard, so only the most basic furniture was required: a bed in which to sleep and copulate, and a few easy chairs to sprawl in after an exhausting day on the beach.

The afternoon light had turned the sea a hazy light gray by the time he had finished unpacking, and he lay down on the double bed to relax for a minute or two. The cover smelled slightly musty, probably because the apartment had never been lived in. He got up and hung it on the balcony railing. As he crossed back to the bed, the telephone rang. It startled him, since he was not expecting anyone to call. It was probably a wrong number, and he remembered that this was a common occurrence in this country, where the dial telephone worked about as capriciously as it did in England. But when he picked up the receiver and said hello, he recognized Manning's voice on the other end of the line.

"Sorry to bother you, old man, but I wonder if you could come by the marina tomorrow morning at ten and meet Manolo, the man who will look after you."

"Okay. I'll be there," he said. "By the way, how did you get my number?"

"I called the Sun and Sea people. They seem like quite an efficient lot. Well, I'll see you in the morning."

"Fine. At ten o'clock."

"By the way," Manning said, "I've asked a few people about Freddy Weaver, and nobody seems to know what's happened to him. They all seem to think he's living in Tangier now."

"That's all right. He'll probably turn up."

"Yes. He probably will." Manning paused briefly. "I had a little run-in with him, so he's not apt to come looking for me. I didn't mention it this morning, because that's all past history."

"A run-in? What about?"

"Nothing important. I'll let him tell you. I'll be waiting for you at El Faro," he added, and hung up.

After that he didn't feel like a nap anymore, and so he took a shower and shaved. The supply of hot water was limited, he noticed as he rinsed off his face, and he thought that it was just as well Pamela wasn't with him, or anyone else for that matter, or he would be taking cold showers during his occupancy.

He put on a clean shirt and a light pair of trousers and took a sweater along, knowing that the nights were generally cool early in the summer. He had decided that he would go to the Puerto Banús, the main yacht harbor, six miles out of town, to see if there was anyone around he might know, and then have a little dinner and go to bed early. He felt a little tired. He hadn't done all that much, but the change of climate was taking its toll on his body; the heat and the moist, mild air took a few days of getting used to after England.

Instead of taking the elevator, he walked down the narrow stairs to the street. There was the smell of urine on the last landing. Obviously some of the building's occupants had been in a hurry to relieve themselves and had not made it back to their apartments, or they had children who, in true European fashion, were allowed to pee wherever and whenever they felt like it. He would use the elevator, from now on, he decided, as he crossed the street to where he had left the Peugeot.

He rolled down the front windows and started the engine. The battery sounded rather weak, and he glanced at his watch to see if it was too late to take it back to the car-rental people before dinner. But it was a quarter to eight, and their office would be closed by the time he made it into town. Well, the drive to the Puerto Banús would charge up the battery, and if not, he would have to find somebody to help him jump-start it. It wasn't all that easy to live in an underdeveloped country, he thought to himself, and for the second time that day he wondered what the hell he was doing there, if it wasn't time for him to go back to where he belonged, to California, where everybody else in Europe who could afford it was buying a house or an apartment. He didn't have much capital to invest, but at least he had the right passport, for whatever that was worth.

He'd forgotten how beautiful the evenings were. The warm air and the sky full of stars always made up for the heat of the day and the dust that the wind had churned up. It was not surprising that the natives kept such absurd hours, that they ate their dinners at ten-thirty or eleven o'clock at night, and that the people who came down from Madrid to spend the summer exceeded even this ridiculous timetable. Very often, when he had dined with Spanish friends, they had not arrived at the restaurant of their choice until midnight, and then had gone on to a bar or a discothèque for a drink. The flamencos that took place during August never got under way until three o'clock in the morning, and even if you were dog tired, the *palmas,* the complicated, staccato clapping of hands, soon woke you up. During the last years of the Franco regime they had tried to enforce a law that required restaurants to close by midnight, and it was virtually the only law that had been quickly abandoned by the Caudillo and his council of ministers.

Brandt wandered through the port, amazed at the many new bars and restaurants that had sprung up and at the mass of people moving along the street in front of the whitewashed buildings. The yacht harbor was only fifteen years old, and already it looked as if it had always been there. Nearly all the slips were occupied, an armada of pleasure craft sitting on the surface of the shimmering water, which seemed to give the lie to all the news of economic disaster that filled the newspapers. Men were still killing each other at the far end of this pleasant sea, but here there was evidence only of man's desire to play in the sun during the day and to couple at night.

A voice called Brandt's name from one of the tables of Menchu's Bar. It was Lewis Safire. He was dressed in white trousers and a blue blazer, with a golden chain around his neck, from which hung an antique, golden crucifix. His narrow face looked slightly battered by time, swollen and sunken in a few of the wrong places, as well it should be, for Safire, Brandt calculated quickly, was certainly in his early seventies. He looked damned good, considering everything he had been through, Hollywood, and India during the war, three wives, one of them a well-known actress, two different careers (he had been a producer as well as an agent), and enough food and drink to destroy any man not born with a Herculean body. Safire had been one of the few agents who was considered socially acceptable before the standards of Tinseltown were relaxed, and even in the old Hollywood he had always been invited to the best parties.

Brandt crossed the narrow street in order to be embraced and kissed by a man he had known for twenty-five years or more, but whose presence here on the coast he had completely forgotten about.

"David! My dear friend!"

"How are you, Lew! It's good to see you," Brandt said, as if they were meeting on Beverly Drive.

"I didn't know you'd arrived, baby. Why didn't you call me? How's Pam?"

"She's not with me," Brandt said, and turned to the others at the table to be introduced.

Safire had trouble with the names of several of his companions, which didn't seem to matter to them. They obviously made allowances for his failing memory, for an old man who had been around too many bars and had met too many people in a long and varied lifetime.

"Sit down and have a drink," one of them, a gray-haired gentleman in navy blue trousers and a pink shirt, said courteously, and beckoned to one of the hovering waiters.

"I'll just stay a minute," Brandt said, and ordered a vodka and tonic. He caught a glimpse of Menchu, standing at the bar inside, and waved to her. She blew him a kiss. Brandt noted that she hadn't changed much since he had last seen her, that she still had the look of a Mediterranean siren, with her reddish hair and easy smile, an aging Lorelei hovering at the side of a land-locked sea.

Safire was patting his knee and going on about how happy he was to see him, disregarding the others, who were continuing with their conversations now, small talk about the weather on the coast this year, the heat that had come too early, and the lack of rain. Brandt realized that they were all residents, senior-citizen expatriates.

"Come to dinner tomorrow night," Safire whispered to him. "I'll cook you some delicious Chinese food, we can talk, and you can tell me everything there is to tell."

"All right. What time?"

"Oh, nine-thirty, quarter to ten. You want to bring a girl, or should I invite one for you?"

"I don't know any girls," Brandt said. "I just got here. What about Wilma? Are you two still married?"

"Of course," Safire said vehemently. "She wanted to stay home tonight and rest. Can you blame her?" he added with a grin.

The vodka and tonic arrived. One of the ladies, a handsome

woman with gray hair, asked if they were ever going to eat, and Brandt sipped his drink and looked out at the crowd in the street passing by, the sunburned Brits and Germans with their bright red arms and faces, showing off their seared flesh, and the young Spanish couples walking arm in arm. Then he saw the pasty-faced man with the lion cub approaching, along with his associate, the thin photographer with the unwashed blond hair. Brandt had read somewhere that the lion cubs that were handed to the tourists, so that they could have their pictures taken, rarely lived more than six months, and of all the hustlers that worked the port, the innocent-looking kids who sold the bunches of roses to the ladies, and the man with the chimpanzee that smelled of stale urine, he disliked the two men with the lion cub the most, and one night, when they had insisted that Pamela take the small, sleepy cub in her arms, had almost had a fight with them. They had seen him, too, and went quickly on to the restaurant next door.

Brandt got up and excused himself. "Where you going, baby?" Safire asked. "Christ, it's early."

"I have to meet some friends at the club," Brandt told him. "I'll see you tomorrow."

"Don't be late," Lew Safire warned. "I'm still the most temperamental cook in town."

"*¡Ay, qué calor!*" It was a familiar complaint, and yet Brandt couldn't help wondering why the natives were so upset by the heat. He said as much to the maid, and she told him quite acidly that people who had to work for a living suffered under the high temperatures, not the ones who spent their days lying in the sun and bathing in the sea.

Her name was Carmen. She had a golden front tooth and, although she looked to be no more than thirty-five, the kind of ample bust that Brandt suspected was sure to collapse once the artificial supports were removed. She had a deep, somewhat hoarse voice, the one Spanish female characteristic that knew no boundaries of class or education. She wanted twenty thousand pesetas a month instead of the fifteen Esperanza had mentioned, because the bus fare had gone up, as well as the monthly social security payments, not to mention the soaring price of food, which indeed she did, in great detail. But she seemed to be quite a cheerful woman, and with the dollar soaring daily against the peseta, Brandt reckoned he could afford to pay her twenty thousand if she was willing to do his laundry.

He was already well prepared for the inflationary rise in wages, because he had met Manolo, Manning's *marinero,* earlier that morning. Manolo was anything but cheerful. He was a short, stocky man, with thick black hair that he wore in a crew cut. He had asked for fifteen thousand pesetas a month, as it was a temporary job, and Brandt had agreed. Manning had looked slightly irritated and was about to intervene, but Brandt told him that fifteen was all right and not to worry about it.

He had gone straight to the office from the port, where he found a message from Grey to take the day off, since they were cleaning out a cubicle for his use, and it wouldn't be ready until the next day. The east wind had come up to about force four by noon, so Brandt went to the beach in front of his house and body-surfed the small waves. He had lunch at the local *chiringuito,* one of the small, temporary restaurants that sprang up all along the beach in the summer, and then took a long nap that left him feeling rested and refreshed. Inspecting himself in the mirror after he had shaved and showered, he was pleased to see that his first day on the beach had already had a beneficial effect on his face and body. He didn't even think about Pamela until he was dressed and ready to go to the Safires' for dinner.

The evening was always the bad time, he remembered from the last few months he had spent in London. To be alone during the day hadn't bothered him, as he had his job to do and the people at the office to keep him company. But going out at night presented a different problem. He had invited a few women to dinner during the first month of his newly found bachelorhood, but he soon discovered that it was an effort to make conversation, and no matter how attractive the lady across the table had appeared to be a few months ago, he found his thoughts returning with monotonous regularity to Pamela.

That was a habit he would have to kick, he told himself as he rode down in the elevator and found his car. It started on the first try, the battery, too, having recovered its strength. When he got to the main road, he stopped and waited for a break in the traffic. A steady stream of fast-moving vehicles was heading toward the intersection, as if the plague had broken out in Torremolinos or Fuengirola. Then he looked to the left and saw a tall blond girl in a white dress walking toward him. "You go to Marbella?" she asked with a thick German accent.

He didn't like picking up people, and never stopped once he was on the road, since he could make the excuse to himself that it was dangerous. But he was stopped now, and the girl looked to be quite pretty at first glance, tall and tanned, and for a second he flirted with the idea of taking her to dinner with him at the Safires'. But that, he reckoned, would probably turn out to be a mistake. He said, "Sure. Get in." Then, as he reached across to unlock the door on the passenger side of the car, he saw her wave, and two more girls appeared, blond and tanned as well. He was annoyed with himself for falling for such an obvious ploy, but thought: What the hell, they're not going to hog-tie and rape me. The girls all said their *Dankeschöns* and giggled among themselves, congratulating each other on their good fortune.

"*Lieber Gott,* it is hot," the leader of the troupe moaned as she rolled up the window on her side.

"It's warm," Brandt agreed. "So why shut the window?"

"*Unsere Haare,*" the girl said. "Our hair. You do not mind?"

"I don't mind," Brandt said, although he did, for now the car was filled with an odor of perfume that was lightly laced with perspiration. "Where are you girls going?" he asked, glancing at the two in the back.

"Banús. *Der Hafen,*" the one on the driver's side of the car told him. She was the prettiest of the trio, and also the most aggressive.

"I'm not going quite that far, but I'll drop you off near the Marbella Club."

"The Marbella Club iss fine," his new co-pilot said. She adjusted her skirt over her brown legs and reached inside her handbag for a cigarette. "You smoke?" she asked, offering him a battered package of Winstons.

"No, thanks."

"It is all right if I do?"

"It's all right," Brandt said, thinking that the cigarette would counteract the smell of cheap perfume that had infested the car. "Where are you ladies from?" he asked after he had turned out onto the main road.

"Hamburg," his co-pilot said. "And you?"

"California."

"Ah, California!" the girl said wistfully. "That is where we all want to go."

"Tonight?"

"No, not tonight," the girl said, and laughed. "But someday, maybe. You come from San Francisco?"

"No. The south."

"But San Francisco is nicer, no?"

"I like Los Angeles better," Brandt said.

"Los Angeles would be all right, too."

"Schwatz nicht so viel, und lass ihn fahren," the girl directly behind him said.

It would discourage conversation, Brandt thought, if he kept his scant knowledge of German to himself. In his younger days he might well have exchanged names and telephone numbers, but he was beyond all that now, did not have the patience to make the small talk that would be required for even a brief conquest. And except for the tough-looking one, they weren't all that attractive. Anyway, he was late, and Safire had warned him that he was a temperamental cook.

He turned off the main highway after he had dropped off his passengers, and took one of the narrow secondary roads that led up into the hills. He was uncertain at first that he had taken the correct turning, but he soon recognized the rusting green street lamps on his left that were partly hidden by the pine trees that grew in this area. The street lamps were not really a good landmark, as they were one of the first features of every real estate development on the coast, but combined with the pine trees, they reassured Brandt that he was on the right road. They had never served as a source of light, he noticed, but that wasn't particularly surprising either, because only a few urbanizations had so far managed to fulfill their promise of well-lighted streets, especially in the remote areas of the foothills.

Safire, too, Brandt remembered, had been one of the town's "pilgrim fathers," had bought an old Andalusian farmhouse with thick walls and a roofline that could easily have inspired a Miró painting. At the time he purchased the place and rebuilt it, late in the fifties, it had been an adventurous step to take, since there were virtually no other houses nearby. Now there were any number of small residences on both sides of the road, and as Brandt continued on toward the Sierra Blanca, he noticed that he was passing quite a few large estates surrounded by high, white walls decorated with bougainvillaea and geraniums. Through the iron grillwork of their imposing entrance gates, he caught glimpses of vast, well-tended lawns leading to spacious villas, the names of which left no doubt as to the nationality of their owners. As a young man, Brandt had read somewhere that the powerful Arab families that had been forced to leave Spain at the end of the fifteenth century had handed down, from generation to generation, the keys to their houses in Granada as symbols of their resolve to return someday. Well, they were back now, in strength, not in Granada perhaps, but on the Costa del Sol.

He turned left at a fork in the road where a new villa was in the process of being built. The untended groves of pine gave way to a stretch of open country that reminded Brandt of the hills above the San Fernando Valley, at least the way he remembered them from his youth. The weeds in the fields were a golden brown, and there was a smell of summer in the air. He passed an old, crippled peasant, supported by an almost equally aged woman, limping slowly along the edge of the road. Was that the purpose of the high white walls, he wondered, to hide the misery that still existed in this country from the eyes of their rich owners? In California things were better organized. The very poor lived too far away from the big houses in Bel Air and Brentwood and the Pacific Palisades so that no one was ever disturbed by the sight of an old couple in rags limping past.

There was a sign with an arrow marked Las Golondrinas, and Brandt turned down the graveled drive that led to the old house. Las Golondrinas, the Swallows, had been the name of Safire's place in Brentwood, too, although it had not been as prominently displayed. There had been a mailbox with his name on it, and the figure of a darky dressed as a jockey standing beside it; in those days it was not considered offensive, at least not by its Caucasian owner. There was no cast-iron black in view here, and Brandt parked his car near the main gate, behind a Mercedes sedan, and rang the bell.

He heard a woman's voice call, "Come in," and recognized it as belonging to Wilma Safire, so he stepped through the gate into a dimly lit patio. There was a small triangle of lawn and two large fig trees, and beyond them the old house with its long covered porch. On the walls, under the overhanging roof, were several varnished bullfight posters and a foresheet for a film Safire had produced in the early days of his career, a romantic saga of the Foreign Legion, to judge by the three men in white képis facing a distant horizon under the title of the movie.

He didn't see Wilma Safire at first, and only when she spoke did he realize that she was standing behind one of the fig trees in the patio, near the front door. She had gained weight, to judge by her face. Her body was hidden in the folds of a white Moroccan gown. Her hair was gray, but she still had about her the look of beauty that had been so startling when she was young. She smiled vaguely. She seemed to be having trouble recognizing him, but finally she said: "David. David Brandt. How nice to see you."

"Didn't you know I was coming?" Brandt asked.

"Yes. Of course, I did. But the light's so bad here, I didn't recognize you at first. How are you?"

"I'm fine," he said, and kissed her cheeks.

"You look fine," she replied. "A little pale, but thin. And that's what counts, isn't it? Never too rich and never too thin."

"Only the bums are always tanned. That's what they used to say at the studio."

She laughed. "I guess so, I don't remember. I'm sorry about you and Pamela. She was such a sweet girl."

"She still is," Brandt said. "People don't die because they leave you."

"No, but *you* must have died a little, you poor darling," she said. "Well, we won't talk about it."

"Right. No mention of casualties in the mess." He followed her through the open door into the living room, impressed, as he had always been, by the charm of the old house, the timbered ceiling and the recessed windows and the stone fireplace, filled with cushions now that it was summer. "And Don Luis?" Brandt asked. "Where is he hiding?"

"In the kitchen, where else? Showing off to your date." She pointed to a swinging door with her cigarette holder, and then led the way through it. "More guests, honey," she said in her deep voice, for they had arrived in the pantry, and the kitchen was beyond it through another paneled door.

Safire turned away from the stove, where he had been stirring a sauce, and waved to Brandt with a wooden spoon. "Ah, you've arrived, baby. I was getting worried that I was going to have to take care of these two ladies by myself. Because I'm getting a little old for that there crap," he added. "One at a time is all I can manage. And only once a week."

"I don't believe it for a minute," Brandt said. "You look as if you could handlc half a dozen." Under the white apron, Safire was at his usual elegant best, in bright red slacks with a pink silk shirt that was partly unbuttoned, after the local fashion. In Hollywood, and in London after that, where Brandt had seen him occasionally, Safire had been a little more hesitant about showing off his well-preserved body. Living on the Costa del Sol had obviously liberated him. Or maybe now that he had turned into the home stretch, he had decided that he might as well flaunt his manliness as long as he could.

A dark-haired young woman had appeared behind him, had stepped out of the maid's room, it seemed to Brandt, although she was certainly not the maid. He noticed her tanned arms and legs and her thick, well-groomed dark hair even before he saw her face. For a moment he thought she might be Spanish, but then he knew at once she was American by the shape of her limbs. There was some special look about them that Brandt recognized, the influence of court games, and the mixture of races, and the food, maybe; European girls weren't built that way.

She was no longer a kid; he noticed that as well, although he couldn't really guess her age. She might even be forty, he thought to himself. But she was pretty; healthy-looking. That was the descriptive phrase that came to his mind. She was not beautiful, but her features were pleasant. Her lips were rouged, and as Safire introduced them, she smiled, showing even white teeth that further confirmed her nationality. "This is Hope Clarendon," Safire said and, waving his spoon once again in Brandt's direction, "Meet David Brandt, one of my oldest friends. A word of warning," he added. "Don't trust the son of a bitch."

"Ah, another Esperanza," Brandt said, sounding foolish to himself as he did so. "That makes two I've met in the last few days."

"No. My name is Hope," the woman said, pointedly. "I'm not Spanish. I'm American."

"Forgive the bad joke."

"You're forgiven. What will you have to drink? I'm tending bar tonight. Isn't that right, Lew?"

"Yes, baby. Anything you say. Just be nice to David. He's not quite as nasty as he looks."

"I'll have a vodka and tonic," Brandt said, "with very little vodka and lots of ice and tonic." He followed Hope Clarendon to the antique chest of drawers, on the far side of the fireplace, that served as a bar. She was dressed in a white skirt and a navy blue sweater, with blue and white shoes; conservatively elegant, nothing gaudy, Brandt remarked to himself. She wore around her neck a golden chain with thick links, a replica of an anchor chain, as well as a couple of golden bracelets on her wrists and a wide, gold wedding ring on her left hand, enough of the precious metal to help her survive a lasting currency crisis, Brandt reckoned, should one come along.

She took an empty glass from the bar and turned to face him, the vodka bottle poised for pouring. "Tell me how strong you like it." He noticed that she had more of a bosom than he might have guessed after looking her over from behind.

"Just cover the bottom of the glass. That's fine."

"But you won't even taste the vodka," she said. "Why bother to drink?"

"Because I'm thirsty."

"I'll let you make it then," she said, and handed him the glass. He watched her as she wandered off in the direction of the stereo set. "What do you want to hear, Wilma?" she called out in the direction of the pantry door.

"Something old and sad," came the reply. "Old Blue Eyes, or Nat King Cole, or Lena. They're all there."

"How about a little flamenco?" Brandt asked.

She made a face. "You like that?"

"Yes. It's invigorating."

"I can't stand it. All that wailing. It's depressing. That's why I never turn on the radio or the television. If I could get Gib, I might."

"Why do you live here?" Brandt asked.

"Because I like it. Isn't that a good enough reason? I like the sun. I don't have to like the music, do I?"

"No. Certainly not," Brandt said. He and Mrs. Clarendon were not getting off to a good start. He had finished making his drink, and moved across the room toward her now as she fiddled with the stereo. Sinatra's voice filled the room, and she smiled again, pleased with her choice. She had a nice mouth.

"Do you live here?" she asked him in a cool, disinterested voice.

"No. But I'm thinking about it."

"Where *do* you live then?"

"In London. Or at least that's where I've been living up to about a week ago."

"And you're thinking about settling down here?"

"I don't know about settling down. But I wouldn't mind staying for a while. I like the people *and* the music. And the sun. Although I'm still thinking about going back home."

"Where's that?"

"California."

"I was brought up on the West Coast," she said, "but I don't want to go back. All those cars and the smog. I like Europe."

"I like Europe, too," Brandt said drily. "But I don't think it's going to last."

"Well, if it blows up, then there'll still be plenty of time to go back to the States. And anyway, the rest of the world will blow up, too."

"I suppose so."

"There's no use running away from things," she said. "At least, I don't think there is."

"Well, that attitude goes well with your name."

"What have you got against Hope?" she asked.

"Nothing, really. I was kidding you, that's all."

Safire came out of the kitchen carrying a bowl of chop suey. Wilma was right behind him with the vegetables and the salad. "Food, my darlings," he announced, looking pleased with himself.

All through dinner they talked of Hollywood in the old days. The "old days" as far as Safire was concerned went back as far as the middle thirties, but as that period provided no common ground, he didn't dwell on it. Apparently he didn't want to bask alone in his nostalgia. He wanted company on his journey into the past, and so the late forties and early fifties, he seemed to realize almost at once, were more acceptable to his audience. At least Brandt was able to corroborate Lew Safire's opinion about the people they had both known, the good guys, the jerks, the assholes, and of course the many beautiful women they had come in contact with in the line of duty. Despite the fact that Safire had been married during those years (not to Wilma), he had had a good many love affairs, and like an old hunter going over his trophies, he enjoyed boasting a little about his conquests, now that he was far removed from the chase.

Was he showing off for the benefit of Mrs. Clarendon, Brandt wondered as he sat listening to his host. Had the lady really been invited for his benefit, or did Safire have designs on her? Brandt couldn't be sure, nor did it matter all that much to him. Nor did Wilma seem particularly concerned. She drank her wine and ate the excellent chop suey, and only once in a long while did she correct her husband when his memory erred, or when he wandered too far afield down the memory lanes of Tinseltown. When he went out into the kitchen to replenish the dish of Chinese vegetables, she remarked briefly to Hope that she had been in New York "having a good time on my own. Lew and I didn't meet until 1958," she said.

"You were an actress, weren't you?" Hope Clarendon asked.

"Yes. For a while. But not a very good one. I did a little designing, too, and got married to the wrong guy. A Reno divorce straightened me out, and then I went to California to start all over again."

"And that's where it all happened," Safire put in, as he entered the room with a replenished dish of bamboo shoots and peas. "And you haven't looked at another fella since."

"I haven't had time," Wilma said. "I was always too busy checking up on you."

Safire laughed contentedly. "I wouldn't exchange what we had for anything in the world," he said. "I wouldn't want to be twenty now, or forty, even."

"How about fifty, darling?" his wife asked, sipping her wine.

"Fifty, maybe yes."

"I wouldn't mind being thirty again," Brandt said.

"What would you do differently, baby?" Safire wanted to know.

"I'd try to make some serious bread," Brandt said. "I wouldn't have come to Europe just because it looked like more fun."

Hope Clarendon turned to him for the first time since they had sat down to dinner. "What did *you* do in Hollywood?" she asked.

"I started in the Publicity Department at Warner's," Brandt said. "I wanted to be a director, but I got sidetracked."

"It's never too late to start, baby," Safire interrupted. "They let almost anybody direct a picture nowadays. Just as long as you're under thirty."

"Yeah, but you've really got to want it," Brandt said. "And I don't anymore. Once, I almost got a chance to take over a spaghetti Western in Almería when the Italian director in charge had a fight with the leading man. But they made up in the end, and I lost out. It was a lousy script, so I didn't feel too bad."

"Well, I did it all," Safire said, "until I discovered that the people who always wound up making the most money were the agents. Now, they're running the studios, God help us. You know, you can say what you like about the old bosses. They were tyrants and bastards, but they loved the movies. They weren't interested in spin-offs and mergers. They made pictures people wanted to see." He was off again, recounting anecdotes about Zanuck and Harry Cohn and old man Mayer, his many confrontations with the czars of the business when he was a producer and an agent, his quarrels, his triumphs, and his ultimate withdrawal to the hills of southern Spain.

"I think we should have coffee in front of the fire," Wilma Safire said pointedly, making an effort to stop her husband's flood of reminiscences.

"What about dessert?" Safire asked his wife. "I've made the most beautiful lemon sherbet, and there are raspberries galore to cover it. God Almighty, you're not going to pass that up, are you, darling?" he said, turning to Hope.

"No, of course not."

"You've bored the bejesus out of her with all that nostalgia, Lew, so the least you can do is let her make up her own mind about dessert."

"That's exactly what I plan to do," Safire said. "All right, everybody change places for the last act! Your host and his lady will clean up the mess."

Brandt found himself alone for a moment with his dinner partner. She seemed a little more friendly than she had been at the start of the evening. She said: "I think if you went back to California, you'd find it very changed. I was there during the winter. The prices have gone sky-high, and everybody is frightened to death of getting mugged."

"It's bad here, too, they tell me," Brandt replied. "Some of the girls carry spray cans in their handbags, and quite a few villas have been robbed."

"Almost everybody I know," Hope Clarendon said quickly. "Spain is no longer different." She smiled sarcastically. "The advantages of democracy. That's why I rarely go out for dinner. I'm scared to go home by myself at night. I don't have servants who live in, and coming back to an empty house is no fun."

"I'll follow you when we leave here," Brandt said politely, "and have a look around so you won't have to worry."

She smiled and said, "You can't follow me home every night."

"No. That's true. But at least tonight you won't have to be nervous."

"I live quite a long way away."

"I don't mind. Unless you're worried about me as well."

She laughed. "I think I can defend myself against one of my fellow citizens," she said. "But I don't want to trouble you."

"No trouble at all." He didn't want to give her the impression that he was planning to make a pass at her. Wilma arrived with the sherbet, and Safire with the berries, and they both dropped the subject of Brandt's seeing her home a little self-consciously.

They had their dessert, followed by coffee, and the conversation turned to life on the coast, the prices the Arabs were paying for the big houses, and the summer invasion of tourists, which promised to be worse than ever that year. It was after midnight when Brandt got up to leave. He followed Safire into the kitchen to say thank you and goodbye. For an instant they were alone with the dishwasher and the pile of pots and pans that were left over from dinner. "She's a nice woman," Safire said to Brandt in a low voice. "And a great lay. One of the greatest."

Brandt was embarrassed. He always was at moments like this. He hadn't expected that kind of a remark from his host, was totally unprepared for it. "Yes. Well, that's nice," he replied lamely.

"I'm past all that," Safire went on. "But an old man is entitled to his memories."

"Absolutely. You're a great cook, even if you've stopped being a great lover."

"That's what happens, baby. But we still go on trying to please the girls the best way we know how. You'll get there someday. Wait and see."

As they pulled out of the Safires' parking area, he noticed that the Mercedes in front of him had Monaco license plates. He made a mental note to ask Hope Clarendon about that. She had made no mention of living in Monte Carlo. Her husband probably kept a small apartment there for tax reasons. She was rich; he had guessed that earlier in the evening by looking at her jewelry. Her skirt and sweater, too, were not the kind of items you picked up at some little shop in the port. They had the stamp of Paris or Rome. That also explained her attitude toward Europe. If you were really rich, you could afford to lose your villa in the south of Spain and move back to God's country, to Long Island or Santa Barbara. And trust the fallout wouldn't seep into your bomb shelter.

She turned right on the main road, and Brandt followed her taillights, although he had to cut in ahead of a truck in order not to lose her. The driver gave him a blast of his air horn, and Brandt nodded to himself. The man was absolutely right. It had been a dangerous maneuver. But he had had no choice. He had no idea of where she was leading him; she had told him only that she lived on the other side of San Pedro de Alcántara, so if he lost contact, his gallant gesture would have come to naught. Apparently, she hadn't noticed that he was driving a small Peugeot either, for she was gunning her car down the center lane at just under eighty miles an hour. Was she showing off for his benefit, he wondered, or was she just in a hurry to get home for a late date? From what Safire had said to him before leaving, that, too, was a distinct possibility.

He pulled up alongside of the Mercedes at the stop light in San Pedro and rolled down his window. He could hear the stereo inside her car blasting out rock music.

"Where's the fire?" he shouted in order to make himself heard above the din.

She turned down the volume and said: "What? I couldn't hear you."

"I was just wondering if you were going to a fire?"

The light changed, and she smiled and waved, and they were off again, but at a more reasonable pace. She led the way past Guadalmina and, after a few more kilometers, turned off onto an unpaved road that led down to the sea. There was a field of sugar cane on the left, and then the road led through a gateway of two white pillars supporting a tiled arch, and they pulled up in front of the house. It was not Brandt's favorite style of architecture; Bermuda-modern was probably the best name for it. The shutters were white, as were the walls, and even the tiled roof looked as if it had been whitewashed. The circular turnaround in front of the main entrance was covered with the kind of gravel that is produced by crushing white marble. The light over the front door was on, and there were garden lights under the olive trees at each of the far corners of the villa. A bad place to mislay your sunglasses, Brandt thought to himself as he got out of his car.

"Well, at least you'll see who you're getting mugged by," he said, moving across the gravel toward the front door.

"I'd rather not see," Hope Clarendon replied. "I'd rather get bopped on the head and wake up when it's all over." She was struggling with the lock, and Brandt noticed that she carried a key ring like the head keeper of the Tower of London, or Mrs. Danvers. There was something Manderley-like about the place, despite the fact that everything was white. The proximity of the sea, probably, and the feeling of isolation, although the sea was flat as a mill pond at that moment. Brandt had caught a glimpse of it after passing the field of sugar cane. "This damned door," Hope Clarendon muttered. "They promised they'd come and fix it two weeks ago."

"Spain, dear lady."

"Yes, Spain and everyplace else. You can't get anything done anywhere." The lock gave way to the key. "Ah, I've got it," she said, and after inserting a second key in a second lock, she pushed open the door. "Come in. Would you like a drink?"

"No, thanks."

"Not even a nightcap? A cold beer or a whiskey?"

"All right. I'll split a beer with you. I'll look around first. Be kind of funny if you got robbed while we were sitting here having a lager."

"The bedrooms are down that way. I'll go get us our drinks."

His theory that the lady had a late date was definitely wrong, Brandt decided as he wandered down the white marble floor of the hallway. Mrs. Clarendon had planned nothing for the early hours of the morning except sleep. He stuck his head into the first room on the left. Here, surprisingly enough, the color scheme had been violated by the designer. The walls of this, the guest bedroom, were a Mediterranean ochre. There was a desk facing a shuttered window, a double bed of normal size, and a brown suede armchair. The husband's quarters, no doubt. The room looked as if it hadn't been used for quite a while. Brandt was about to close the door when a painting on the wall caught his eye. It was a portrait of Hope Clarendon, or whatever her maiden name was, as a young woman.

The style of the painting was rather stark, and Brandt searched the right corner of the canvas to discover whether Peter Hurd had painted the portrait, but the signature was a vague scrawl. He thought of Hurd because the subject was seated on a white timber fence, and behind her the hills of a Western landscape might well have been Arizona or New Mexico. Hope was dressed in jeans and a white blouse under a denim jacket. Her hair was tied in a bun at the back of her head, which gave her an Indian look that was accentuated by a silver Indian belt. The artist had painted the hills in the background the same color as his subject's hair, a vivid dark brown, while above the hills there were scattered clouds.

There was something angelic about the girl in the picture. She looked pure, as yet untouched by the problems and complications of life, although her eyes were already hard. Not cruel, but hard, ready to look any disappointment straight in the face, ready to deal with any disaster. Of course the disasters at that time and in that place were probably not very serious ones. A colt with the colic, or a dog that had gotten caught in a coyote trap. Nothing worse, no doubt. Certainly no worries about paying the rent.

Brandt closed the door of the room, regretting that he had not met the lady in those carefree days. Then he opened the adjoining guest bathroom and saw at a glance that it was empty. Satisfied, he proceeded down the hall to the master bedroom. It had white walls, as he expected it would have, a king-sized double bed, a white armchair, and a dressing table with lights recessed in the mirrors. There were two paintings on the wall that Brandt recognized as having been painted by Vincente Viudes, the Marbella painter who was very much in vogue. Viudes painted in vivid blues and greens; landscapes and the corners of summer gardens that were decoratively pleasing. They certainly helped relieve the virginal glow of the room, Brandt mused briefly, and they were worth whatever price the owner of the house may have paid for them.

He heard his hostess's footsteps on the marble floor of the hallway. "Have you looked under all the beds?" she asked with a smile.

"Just about."

"The study?" she asked, opening a door facing the entrance of the bedroom. "My den," she explained, "which now serves as my private movie theater."

She touched a light switch, and Brandt found himself facing a rectangular chamber, the walls of which were covered in a light blue material that looked like raw silk. At the far end of it there was one of the new projection television sets with an enormous curved screen. There was a card table off to one side as well, and a variety of armchairs facing the screen.

"Nobody lurking in here with evil intentions," Brandt said. "Is that it?"

"There are some servants' rooms on the other side of the house, but they're not in use. They're locked, anyway."

He followed her down the hallway into the living room, noticing as he entered it that she had placed a silver tray with two bottles of beer and glasses on the low wooden coffee table in front of the circular couch facing the fireplace. She went to the French doors that looked out onto the lawn, opened them, and began to struggle with the white metal grill that sealed off the terrace.

"I thought it would be pleasant to have our nightcap in the fresh air," she said, "but I can't seem to open this damned grill."

"Here. I'll do it." He pushed hard and stepped outside. There was a lawn, and a lighted swimming pool, and beyond it the sea. In the distance, bobbing up and down on the surface of the water, were the fishing boats that were always present on mild, windless nights.

"You ought to have a dog, a big one," Brandt said when the woman joined him.

"I have one," she replied, putting the tray with the beer down on a table surrounded by deck chairs. "But he's at the vet's."

"Is there a phone?"

"Yes. But it's temporarily out of order," she said with a laugh. "I know. Spain! They've been promising me they'll come to fix it for a week now. *'Mañana, señora,'* " she said, mimicking the girl at the telephone office in Málaga.

"And the servants?"

"They live down the road in their own little house. I prefer it that way. I don't like to have them around all the time."

"Well, I'm not surprised you're worried about coming back home alone at night."

"I'm all right once I'm inside."

"Well, you're brave."

"Not really," she said. "Anyway, it's worth it, isn't it? Don't you approve of the view?"

"Yeah, on a clear day you can see Catalina."

"Or forever," she added, and laughed.

They sipped their drinks. There was the distant sound of the lapping of waves and the chugging of the engines of the fishing boats.

"How long have you known Lew?" she asked.

"About a hundred years. My father was a cameraman. He shot one of Lew's early pictures. I met him on the set when I came to visit my old man. Lew wanted to use me as a child actor in the film, but I froze when I got in front of the camera. I was seven at the time."

"What a shame."

"Yeah, I guess so. But my dad didn't mind. He said it was enough having one whore in the family."

"Why did he say that?" She was amused, anxious to hear more, Brandt sensed, as he watched her press the rim of her cold glass against her tanned forehead.

"He wanted to photograph the plight of mankind instead of worrying about getting the key light focused on some pampered actress's cheekbones. He died on the next movie he was hired out to make. It was a Western, and they shot it in Pendleton, Oregon, in the summer. He had a heart attack, and they couldn't get him in from the location on time. He was forty-three, one year older than I am now."

"How awful."

Brandt shrugged. He could remember that forty-three had seemed like a ripe old age to him at the time. Although he had felt deprived, not having a father. He got up. He didn't enjoy talking about himself to someone he hardly knew, a rich lady with a big house who didn't like to have her servants around during the night. "Maybe we can have dinner some night," he said.

"I'd like that."

"When are you free?"

"Any time. Tomorrow. The next day. You name it."

"All right. Tomorrow. I'll pick you up, so you won't have to worry about driving home alone."

"Fine," she said, and got up to accompany him to the front door. "Nine-thirty?"

"It's a date."

She was friendly but distant, Brandt thought to himself. He wished Safire hadn't made that gross remark to him about her sexual talents. It was probably a lie, anyway.

"I'll be ready," she said, and held out her hand.

He leaned forward to kiss her good night. In Europe you kissed all your women friends, when you met them and when you dropped them off. There was nothing to it. He wasn't trying to come on with her, but he noticed that she stiffened visibly, and so he pulled back. "Don't forget to double-lock your doors," he said, and moved off across the gleaming white gravel.

He felt strangely elated as he drove home through the warm night. Outside the door of his apartment, he encountered a small black cat. It looked starved, and miaowed pathetically. "I have nothing to give you," he told the little animal. *"No tengo nada,"* he added in Spanish, since it was undoubtedly a local. He made a mental note to go to the market to shop for himself or whatever other lost soul might drop in to see him. He felt certain that he would be staying on for at least a month or two.

But once he was in bed and had turned out the light, he found himself thinking about Pamela again. The familiar features, the auburn hair, the startlingly blue eyes, and the pale skin crept back into his mind. And strangely enough, it was always the last days of their relationship that he found himself reliving, the inflicting of wounds. Instead of memories of the good times they had had together. There was no use struggling against this painful reminiscence. The pictures and scenes never varied, no matter how hard he tried to alter them.

She had gone to Paris on a business trip, or at least that was what she had told him, and was staying in a small hotel on the Rue Chambiges, where they had often stayed together. That had made it worse, somehow, as he knew the place so well, had taken her there. He knew the room clerk, who was also the switchboard operator, and the widowed Frenchwoman who owned the place, as well as the night porter, and they all knew that Pamela belonged to him. Whenever she had gone there on her own, he had called her regularly early in the morning, because part of her job with the London shop she worked for was visiting the various collections, the *prêts-à-porter* and the others, so that she was always out late, and the morning call from London was by way of being a small ritual.

But that particular night he hadn't been able to sleep, and it was one o'clock when he suddenly decided to call her. She wasn't in, the night clerk informed him. And so he had called at one-thirty and then at two. He took a sleeping pill, but it had had no effect on him. So he had continued calling her all night, at half-hour intervals. At five o'clock in the morning he had at last dropped off to sleep, but he awakened at eight and called her again, to no avail. Mademoiselle had not come in yet, the girl who had taken over the switchboard informed him.

He had finally reached her that afternoon. By the sound of her voice he knew immediately that something was wrong, that she was lying to him. She had spent the night with a girlfriend, she had told him. Why? Because they had finished the evening in a discothèque, and, as it was late, she had decided it was easier to stay with her friend, a retired model, than to go home. He reminded her coldly that they had agreed long ago that they would always be honest with each other, no matter what happened, and now she was lying, and lying badly. If there was someone else, he said, he had a right to know.

She had denied it at first, but under his persistent questioning, she had finally admitted that, yes, she had stayed out late, yes, there was someone else. He had demanded to know who it was, angry now, and unreasonable. But she had refused to tell him, had said that it didn't concern him, and tired and furious after his sleepless night, he had said, fine, okay, forget it, goodbye, and had hung up. To hell with her, he had thought, to hell with the lying bitch.

But his moment of strong resolve had lasted only twenty minutes, and then he had called her again. By that time she had left her room, and although he had asked to be connected with the concièrge, he hadn't been able to reach her. He hadn't been able to reach her that night either, although he called half a dozen times. Then he decided he would catch the next plane to Paris in order to have it out with her, but after he had made his reservation on Air France, he called her again. Mademoiselle had moved out of the hotel, the clerk informed him. No, she had said nothing about going back to London, had left no forwarding address. So he canceled his ticket. He had known, by then, that it was over, that going off to look for her would only make it all the more painful and, even worse, undignified.

Instead, he had packed up his belongings and had moved out of the flat they shared, had gone to a small hotel in Chelsea, thinking that a decisive act on his part might bring her back. Although he wasn't sure that he wanted her back. Yes, he wanted her. He felt lost without her, lonely. But she had not reappeared. Not for two weeks, and when she returned to London from the south of France, where she had gone with her new beau, she had called him at his office to say that she was sorry, that she knew she hadn't behaved very well, and that she hoped they could remain friends.

Her saying that had made him laugh, and he could sense that he had offended her, for her voice changed noticeably. "I know it sounds corny," she had told him. "It's not that," he had replied. "It's just that I have enough friends as it is."

The brief sequence out of his past made going to sleep a difficult task. It had always had that effect on him, so he got up and mixed himself a weak Scotch and water and went to sit for a while on the terrace and watch the distant lights of the fishing boats, his favorite seascape.

He drove into town early the next morning. At the first traffic light, where the road turned off to the fishermen's port, he caught sight of the village idiot. He remembered him from many years past, a husky boy, with an eternally crimson face, who always stood at this intersection clapping his swollen hands, *tocando las palmas,* as it was called when it was part of a flamenco. The complicated rhythms were an art in themselves, and you had to be born in Andalucía, and preferably have Gypsy blood in your veins, in order to capture the exact beat.

The village idiot was not concerned with that aspect of southern folklore. He beat his hands together throughout the day, while trucks brushed past him, and tourists stared at his red face and arms, beating out his own tragic rhythm, shouting some incoherent song that welled up out of his retarded brain. Occasionally someone warned him not to stray too near the macadam, and he would stare at them and move back a yard or two without varying his beat.

Brandt remembered that someone had told him that the boy had two brothers who were also retarded, and two sisters who were normal. The family was poor, and as the boy was harmless, they allowed him to go every day to the side of the highway, as if it were his place of work. In some ways, Brandt thought grimly to himself, he represented the spirit of the town, and perhaps even that of some of the better families of the land, although the new generation that had grown up in the sixties was more dedicated to work than to *la juerga,* the continual binge that the upper classes had always been addicted to.

The poor bastard must be in his early thirties now, Brandt reckoned. The skyscrapers had grown up around the town while he had clapped away the days. There was a Ford agency fifty yards away from the intersection that had been built, for some obscure reason, on a prime site facing the sea, and a Mercedes agency farther on. There was also the unfinished skeleton of a high-rise apartment house that still stood at the entrance of the town, an eyesore to shock the new arrivals.

The light changed, and he drove on. There was almost no wind. The sea looked like a grayish-blue slate, flat as far as the eye could see, all the way to the horizon. He would take the boat out that afternoon, he decided, and take advantage of the fine weather.

The bank hadn't changed, although now it was a branch of one of the biggest banking operations in Spain. And the same faces were still around, the friendly, pretty girls with their lighted cigarettes always within easy reach on a littered ashtray, and the serious young men seated in front of their calculators. The cashier who counted out the money was as unpleasant as ever. That was one of the basic operational procedures of their banking system, Brandt had figured out long ago. Everybody was courteous and pleasant except the man who actually paid out the money. He never smiled, or spoke even, thus giving constant proof that he had no friends, which was important in a country where friendship opened all doors.

The dollar was up, Brandt noticed. The grumpy teller paid out ninety-eight pesetas for every greenback he pushed onto the plastic turntable. Then he went on to the market and bought provisions for his new place of residence.

"Richard has gone to Madrid for the day," Penny, the good-natured Australian, informed him after she had ushered him into his new office. It was a small cell with windows looking out onto a minute patio, but there was a desk and a telephone and two leather chairs. "He suggested that you work on your tan while he's gone."

"Was that really what he said?" Brandt asked the girl.

"Yes. I'm not kidding. He'll be back tomorrow. I believe your friend Amir will be coming with him. I have to stay and answer the telephone, or I'd go down to the beach with you," she added.

"You've already got your tan," he told the girl.

"So I have," she said, inspecting her bare arms and shoulders. "Would you like a cup of coffee before you leave for the beach?"

"If you're making some."

He sat for a while at his bare desk, staring out the window at a lonely cactus that was growing in a corner of the tiny patio. It would be ironic if he wound up as a real estate salesman in this remote corner of the world, he found himself thinking. Well, he could do worse, at least for a couple of years. The movie business was going through a bad patch once again, and if he could make some money, this job might turn out to be a good stopgap. The Costa del Sol was not a bad place to kill some time for a couple of years. The climate was pleasant, and for a bachelor it was a rewarding environment, as his first few evenings out had proved. Anyway, nothing was forever. And in the past his life had often taken strange turnings, had often been influenced by chance meetings with people like Amir.

Their friendship had started under rather comical circumstances. The club secretary at Queen's had introduced them one afternoon when Brandt was looking for a game. Amir was tall and sturdily built, with thick black hair and a permanently surprised expression on his rather handsome face. When Brandt asked him his nationality, he had hesitated, explaining that if he told him the truth, Brandt would probably not want to play with him. "Because I'm an Iranian," he had finally confessed. "As long as you don't beat me six-love, six-love, I don't care what you are," Brandt had replied.

From that moment on they had been good friends. Amir had introduced him to the Persian colony, or at least to that part of it that he approved of, the wealthier refugees, a good many of whom had fled the country after the Shah's downfall. There seemed to be hundreds of Iranians living in London. Amir knew them all, the ones who had been part of the Pahlevi regime, as well as those who had been in the opposition, but were not connected to the Mullahs. They appeared to be a cheerful group, despite the tragic events that were taking place in Teheran. Or at least they tried to put a good face on the circumstances of their exile. There was often talk of the executions that were taking place in Iran, a brief mention of friends who had been shot or who had recently been jailed. Many of them were obviously wealthy, for there was seldom any talk of money, at least not among those who played tennis at Queen's or the other English tennis clubs near London. They made light of the fact that they were unpopular at home and abroad, and once Brandt had gained their confidence, they discussed the mistakes of their past lives with a candor that was most disarming.

Amir was apparently a shrewd businessman. He had lived in England quite a few years, having married an English girl after finishing university at Cambridge. He had been impressed by the fact that Brandt was well connected in the world of show business, and had suggested he help launch a new restaurant that he and some of his Iranian friends were starting. Then when that project had fallen through, he had suggested Brandt join the property-development company Amir had invested in a few years earlier.

Penny reappeared with his coffee on a small tray. "It's our best instant," she informed him. "Sorry about that. Our coffee machine is on the blink. It's Spanish, and it will be repaired tomorrow."

She left him to drink it on his own and to continue pondering life's ironies. Well, tennis had helped him with his career quite often in the past, in Hollywood and the Navy, and now in London, from where it had led him back to the Costa del Sol.

He was folding up the tarpaulin on the stern of *Lulubelle* when Manning appeared. He was wearing the same shirt and trousers as on the day they had met, Brandt noticed, and he didn't look any healthier. They exchanged heavily accented *Buenos díases,* and Manning came on board. "Going out alone?" he asked.

"Yes. I thought I'd take a little swim and work on my tan. My new boss feels that's important. Seems to help convince the customers they're buying a home in the right place. Want to come along?"

"I can't," Manning said. "Have to take the wife to the doctor in Málaga for a checkup." He paused. "I also don't believe in chartering my boat and then inflicting myself as a guest."

"I haven't paid you yet," Brandt said.

"I'm not worried. However, I don't think it's a good idea to go out by yourself too often."

"Why not? I'll be careful."

"Yes, I know. Just as long as you watch the weather. If the *poniente* comes up, it comes up fast." He raised one of the floorboards and turned the battery switches on. Then he stepped into the cockpit and started the engines. "Always warm up the engines before you drop your mooring. The starboard motor is apt to stall when it's cold."

"I'll remember that."

"And don't forget to anchor before you dive overboard."

"I won't."

"I sound like an old woman, I know, but a lot of people get careless. It looks like a lake, the Med, but it can change fast."

"I'm aware of that. She's insured, isn't she?" Brandt asked.

"Third-party risk, that's all. The premiums are too high for full coverage."

"That's bad news," Brandt said. "Why don't you take out full coverage for the summer? That can't be too expensive."

"It would cost two hundred and fifty pounds for a short-term policy, and I can't handle that," Manning said. "Anyway, I'm not going to sue you if you write her off."

Someone called his name from the dock before Brandt could answer. It was a French girl he had known in Paris, but he couldn't remember her name. She was standing in a bikini at the foot of the gangway, with a tall young man who looked as if he had put on his underwear that morning instead of a bathing suit. They were both deeply tanned, and the man carried a straw basket filled with their clothes and a couple of towels.

"I told Joel that I was sure it was you, David," the girl said. "You haven't changed at all."

"How long has it been since we've seen each other?" Brandt asked, stalling for time. Manning was blocking the narrow gangway, so he had no choice but to introduce him. "This is Guy Manning. So help me God, I've forgotten your name, honey."

"Denise Sorel. Don't you remember, I work in the Paramount office in Paris."

"Of course. I'm sorry. What are you doing down here?"

"*Vacances, vacances,*" the girl said, flashing a very prominent set of white teeth. "We're at the Club Méditerranée. I was supposed to meet a friend at the port. Are you going to Banús, by any chance?"

"I could, easily enough. You want a lift?"

"Yes, please."

They came down the gangway and shook hands with Manning. Brandt was relieved to see that they removed their espadrilles once they were on board. "You feel reassured?" he asked Guy. "At least I won't be facing the dangers of this sea single-handed."

"I wasn't really worried," Manning said. "Enjoy yourselves," he said to the sunbathers, and went ashore.

Denise took off the top of her bathing suit as soon as they were out of the harbor, and exposed a well-formed pair of breasts to the sun. Brandt had not bothered to put out the mattress that was made to cover the roof of the forward cabin, as it meant lashing the thing down. That did not seem to bother the girl and her escort. They lay spread-eagled on the recently painted roof as if they had fallen from the sky. The joys of yachting, Brandt thought to himself. Mademoiselle Sorel might have asked if he minded her exposing her tits. Perhaps his was an old-fashioned attitude, but then she might have taken the trouble to make a few minutes of polite conversation. He was not running a water-taxi service.

His brief talk with Manning disturbed him more. To charter an uninsured boat was not his idea of how to enhance the enjoyment of his stay on the coast. He had a good mind to back out of the deal or force Guy to take out a policy. It was hot inside the wheelhouse.

He knocked on the glass of the windshield in order to warn the sunbathers that he was going to open the center section of the glass. He didn't want Denise to cut her face if she suddenly sat up. It wasn't the best part of her, but it was functionally important. Especially the teeth.

The girl didn't understand his warning knock, but her escort explained it to her, and they moved forward. The cool air made Brandt feel better. He swung out a little farther to sea in order to avoid the muck in the water, the brownish foam, seaweed mixed with sewage, which floated in a curving line on the surface. In the distance he could see the tower of the Puerto Banús, and he steered a course for it. Then he checked the temperature gauges on the two engines, confirmed that they were both approaching seventy degrees Celsius, and pushed the throttles forward until the rev counters read sixteen hundred revolutions a minute. *Lulubelle II*, he noticed, rose slightly out of the water, and then put her bow down. The motors had a pleasant hum that confirmed that they were healthy. One thing was in Manning's favor. He maintained a faultless ship. And it *would* make a difference, Brandt thought, having *Lulubelle* at his disposal. If he was careful, there was no reason to worry about her not being insured. There were never so many boats out in July that a collision was even a remote possibility. And if he kept her well away from the beach, there was little danger of running aground.

When he was about a mile and a half away from Banús, he pulled back on the throttles and let the boat glide to a stop. The engines ticked over at idling speed. He noticed that there were tiny traces of grayish-blue smoke coming out of both exhausts. He would ask Manning if he had checked the injectors lately. "Want to take a dip?" he called out to his passengers.

"What a good idea," Denise replied enthusiastically. She said something in French to her companion, but he shook his head. He was lying face down on the cabin roof, toasting his pimpled back. "Joel says it's too cold, but I'd love a swim. Is it difficult to get back up on the boat?"

"No problem. There's a permanent swimming ladder in the stern."

The girl nodded and made her way aft on the port side. Her face was not visible as she passed Brandt. Only her torso appeared outside the wheelhouse for an instant, and Brandt felt a familiar stirring within him. It had been a long time since he had been that close to a naked female body. Two months, maybe more. Well, he was getting over the shock of Pamela's defection at last, he thought to himself, and shut off the diesels. Denise was standing in the stern, fussing with her hair. She had a nice body, a slim waist and long legs, but there was something unused about her figure. Her back was smooth and unmuscled.

"It looks cold, the water," she said.

"It's not too bad. At least it's clean." He took a deep breath and dove in, thinking that if he should have a heart attack, it would make for an interesting afternoon for the young Adonis in the bow. He had probably never conned a boat of any kind in his life.

But he didn't have a heart attack. He swam out a few strokes and turned back. The girl dove in after him. She gasped a little, but she didn't scream.

"I like your boat," she said, treading water beside him. Her brown breasts were facing him, her wet hair matted down on her head. "I hope you'll take me out again sometime."

"Be a pleasure," Brandt told her.

"Call me at the Don Miguel," she said. "I'm in Room 101."

Hope Clarendon's place looked even bigger in the daylight. There was a white wall down to the edge of the beach, and on the western border of the property there was a grove of eucalyptus trees that separated the garden from the rough, brush-covered land beyond it. The grounds contained at least ten thousand meters, Brandt calculated, if not more. He had noticed a For Sale sign when he had turned off the main road, and he could only guess that the land behind the property had gone up so much in value that Clarendon had not wanted to buy it. There was also a small white house in the field next to the wall, with a small vegetable garden behind it, which was probably the servants' cottage.

As Brandt crossed the white gravel in front of the house, he noticed that the wind had changed direction. That explained the clear horizon and the very dark blue color of the water. He stopped for a moment to ascertain the direction of the small waves that were falling gently on the beach. It was definitely the start of a westerly. In the extreme distance, beyond the curve of the coastline, he could make out the shape of Gibraltar, the Rock, as the Brits called it. The concrete water shed stood out against the pink of the sky like a snowfield covering a glacier in the Alps.

There was the sound of high heels on marble, and Hope Clarendon opened the door. She was dressed all in white, in a skirt and sweater with the sleeves pushed up above her elbows, either because the sweater was too warm, or because she had to make room for her collection of gold bracelets and chains. Brandt wanted to ask her if all that precious metal didn't weigh down her arms, but perhaps that was the point of wearing it. You exercised your pectoral muscles every waking hour. You didn't have to bother with weights or dumbbells. But she was ready to go out. That much was definitely in her favor. He wouldn't have to spend twenty minutes or more wandering around the house while she put the finishing touches to her make-up, which was the standard procedure with all the Spanish ladies he had known.

"You have a nice place here, ma'am," he said with a mock Southern accent. "Don't see no darkies laboring in the fields, but I guess they all done gone home now."

"That's right," she said. "They've all gone back to their cabins." She held the door open for him. "Would you like a drink?" she asked.

"Sounds like a good idea." He noticed that she locked the door behind him, even though it was still daylight. They crossed the hallway and went out on the terrace. A tray with glasses and bottles was on the table in the shade of the overhanging roof, which showed that she had prepared for his arrival.

"I'm having the usual," she said. "A vodka and tonic. What would you like?"

"The same would be fine."

He gazed out at the well-cut lawn and the glistening sea beyond it. He could understand that she didn't particularly want to leave this part of the world. He would be quite content to live in a house like this, away from the heat and the dust of the town. But for how long? That was the sixty-four-thousand-dollar question. He was not quite ready, as yet, to settle for a life of backgammon, golf, and adultery, no matter how benign the climate, or how profitable his association with the Sun and Sea Realty Company might turn out to be.

After she had poured him a drink, they sat in silence for a little while, enjoying the evening light. It was nine-thirty-five, but the sun was still quite high above the horizon.

Brandt said: "I still find it strange that you don't have anybody living in here. The way things are today."

"I've had people around me all of my life. Servants and children. So when we built this house, we fixed up the cottage down the road for the staff. Max didn't think it was such a good idea in the beginning, either."

"Max?"

"My husband," she said with a note of surprise in her voice, as if she expected Brandt to know all about her.

"And where is he now?"

"London or New York or Monte Carlo. I never know until he calls."

"When your telephone is not out of order."

"I have friends he can ring when that happens. We've lived in Spain quite a while. If there's a problem, he leaves a message that he wants to talk to me at a given time, and then I go to their house and wait for the call."

"That seems like a complicated arrangement."

"It is. But living here, you have to be prepared for anything. They usually get around to fixing the telephone sooner or later." She paused to sip her drink. "If somebody wants to rob or kidnap you, they manage to do so whether you have a bodyguard or servants or a phone. Anyway, I'm a fatalist."

"I suppose you're right," Brandt said. "What about dinner? Where would you like to go?"

"Anywhere you say. You decide. I'm never very hungry in the evening."

"The port in Estepona? You like fish?"

"Of course I do. If you live by the sea, you've got to like fish."

"I know a general in the Spanish Air Force who won't eat anything that flies. Chickens, pheasant, quail."

She laughed and said: "I have no hang-ups. You'll find that out when you get to know me."

She told him a great deal more about Max during dinner. She didn't complain about him. She spoke dispassionately. Brandt was used to listening to women describe their husbands' failings, but he had seldom heard a wife speaking so calmly about her spouse. But then Max Clarendon was an Englishman, and it was quite possible that some of his British objectivity had rubbed off on his American wife. He was, according to her, an exceedingly restless man. He had made a lot of money after the war in the aviation industry, during the brief period of time when England was still in the forefront of technical development. Then, in the early sixties, he had sold out, thinking that he might retire. That was when they had acquired the land on which they built the house.

The construction of the villa had taken two years, and he had thrown all of his energy into supervising the job. He had two children from a previous marriage, and he had thought that he was providing a summer home for them. But it turned out that they didn't like Spain, preferred to spend their summers in Monte Carlo, where Max had an apartment and a small yacht. They had gone to school in Switzerland, and French was almost their first language. Also, most of their friends were there. So the house in the north of Spain had become Hope's domain, "stepmother country" was how she put it.

After the villa was completed, Max had become restless. He played golf, and they went to all the parties, but that wasn't enough for him, she said, quite understandably. He was in his late forties, and he couldn't face the idea of merely vegetating in holiday resorts, skiing in the winter in Zermatt and living the rest of the year between Monaco and the south of Spain. So he got involved in real estate. That was her vague description of his activities, which Brandt realized were on a multimillion-dollar scale. Max had set up an office in England, although he had to be careful not to spend more than three months a year there, for tax reasons. He had bought a mews house in Belgravia, which was in the company's name, and a flat in Manhattan, so that now he was on the airplane a good part of the time, moving back and forth between the United States and Europe.

For a while she had accompanied him, but she had tired of the constant traveling, grew to hate cities, which was an attitude Brandt could sympathize with. She was raised in Southern California. Her family came from Santa Barbara. "We weren't poor, but we certainly weren't rich. My father owned a small drugstore, and he did pretty well. But that was before the California boom, so I went to work as a model in L.A. It wasn't a city then, and it isn't really a city now. I loved the climate, and the Costa del Sol reminded me of California. So after I met Max, settling down here seemed like a good solution. I found friends. I wasn't ever lonely. And when I had enough of the sun, I could always go to London or New York."

"It doesn't sound like a hard life," Brandt said.

She smiled at him. Her face changed completely when she smiled, he noted, lost the slightly defensive look that it had in repose. "It isn't," she said. "I'm happy when I'm on my own."

"You mean when Max isn't here?"

She fell silent. It seemed as if she didn't want to go beyond that particular statement, did not want to reveal any more about herself than was necessary. She said: "Unfortunately we've grown apart. I know that sounds corny, but he's totally involved in what he's doing, and I am too, I suppose, totally involved in my own life."

"Gardening and lying in the sun and playing golf?"

"Well, I don't garden," she said. "I'm not the type."

"Will you have coffee?" he asked her. They had finished their grilled sole, and the bottle of white wine he had ordered was empty.

"Yes. *Con leche,*" she replied, addressing the waiter, who had come to clear the table.

"I'll have an anis seco," Brandt told the man.

"If you're going to sin, I will, too," she said, smiling her pretty smile again.

"I don't want to lead you astray."

"Why not?" she asked. "Somebody has to."

It was the first inkling Brandt had that she liked him even slightly, or that she had some mild idea of flirting with him. Up until that moment she had been quite impersonal, friendly but distant. "Do you like your anis with ice in a big glass," he asked her, "or straight?"

She said, "I'll have it the way you do."

He was relieved to hear that she didn't want to go dancing. He didn't like Régine's, and she agreed with him that it was too noisy, too glittering. She said it was like sitting in a showcase at Tiffany's, with canned music blasting out your eardrums. She also agreed with him that they would both have to spend quite a few evenings there once the crowd from Madrid began to arrive, so why bite the bullet before you had to? Pepe Moreno's was for the very young and was slightly tacky. And the Mau-Mau, the place they both preferred, wasn't open yet.

Brandt said, "I've always thought it strange, naming a dance hall after the most evil terrorist group of our time."

"Maybe it's because they torture you there, too," she said.

It was a mild joke, but the first one that she had ventured to make. "You think that's how they decided on the name?" he asked her.

"Perhaps it had something to do with the kind of music they play."

"I prefer your previous explanation."

"Why don't we just go home," she said.

"That's all right with me. I'm not much of a dancer. The twist put me out of business." He paid the bill, and they walked in silence to his car. Brandt was conscious of the sound of straining mooring lines and the insistent banging of metal stays against wooden masts as he unlocked the doors of the Peugeot. The wind had come up several points while they had dined. He only hoped that the taciturn Manolo had moored *Lulubelle* securely after washing her down. "I've chartered a boat," he told Hope. "Maybe you'd like to come out for lunch and a swim someday."

"Yes. But not tomorrow."

"No, tomorrow won't be a boating day." They drove past the bull ring and through the town. The streets were crowded, and at one end of the municipal gardens, on the Paseo Marítimo, a Dodge-Em car park had been set up under a big tent. There was a long queue of customers waiting for their turn. "This is where they teach them to drive," Brandt said.

"I seem to detect that you're a little down on Spain."

"No. That's not true. I'm happier here now than I've been for quite a while. When I first arrived, I asked myself: What the hell am I doing here? Has that ever happened to you?"

"Only when I go home."

"To Santa Barbara?"

"We live in Carpinteria now; my family, that is. And I'm usually quite happy to visit them. It's arriving at Los Angeles Airport that puts me off. All those rows of houses, each with its own swimming pool. And the cars on the freeway. And the smog. And the hideousness of it all."

"Arriving at Málaga airport isn't much better. Every time I see Torremolinos I get depressed."

"Don't look at it," she said. "Never look out the window of the taxi until you can see the Sierra Blanca."

"I'll remember that."

They drove in silence until they reached the turnoff that led to her house. Beyond the field of sugar cane he could make out the lights of her garden.

"What's your house called?" he asked.

"Miramar. It's not a very original name, but the farm that was there when we bought the land was called that. And it's easy for my friends to remember."

He parked the Peugeot behind her Mercedes, and they went inside. He noticed that she locked the front door behind them, and then he made his little tour of all the rooms as a security measure. When he joined her again, she was standing in front of the bar in the living room. "I'm afraid I have no anis," she said.

"Well, then I guess we'd better go back to our vodka and tonics."

She nodded and made their drinks. "Very light on the vodka, I know," she said. She put the two glasses on a silver tray and crossed to the glass doors that led onto the terrace. She opened one of them, and the wind blew the white curtains back into the room like a spinnaker. "It's too breezy out there, I'm afraid," she said. "Would you like to see a movie?"

"I don't know. What have you got?"

"I don't have a big selection, because I just sent back some of the tapes I rented. Come and see." She led the way down the hallway to "her den" and crossed over to the stereo. "Have you seen *Marathon Man*?" she asked.

"No. But I've read the book."

"Well, what does that have to do with it?" she asked with a little laugh. "The movie version is never like the novel it's based on."

"Sad words, but true."

"So do you want to see it? I don't mind seeing it again."

He thought to himself: That's what's wrong with our culture. Because of all the new gadgets, we're satisfied to watch the same junk several times over.

"We can always turn it off if we get bored." She was busy fiddling with the stereo set. The curved screen was suddenly full of black and white dots and dashes, a static signal that hurt the eyes.

Brandt wandered around the room, observing the details of it that he had passed over on his security check. There were the usual silver-framed photographs, and he studied them briefly. Two of them held the pictures of her daughters, pleasant-looking teenaged girls with good teeth and clear skin. They hadn't quite inherited their mother's looks, her high cheekbones and her narrow face. "Are these your girls?" he asked her.

"My stepdaughters."

"Of course. I forgot that you and Max haven't been blessed by any progeny."

"I had a boy, but he died at birth."

"I'm sorry."

She didn't reply, and he turned to the next photograph, this one in a more elaborate frame of antique silver. A broad-shouldered man in shorts was standing on a pier beside a big marlin that hung from a hoist. The man had a handsome, sunburned face. He looked like a young football coach, or a rugby player in his prime, Brandt thought to himself, remembering that Max was English. For it was Max, there was no doubt about that. There was no one else's photograph she would have placed there.

"He's a handsome man, your husband."

"Yes, he is," she said quietly.

"How long ago was the picture taken?"

"Oh, about ten, twelve years ago. We went fishing in Baja California. He used to enjoy that. We went to Cabo Blanco in Peru one year, and then Baja three years running."

"Did you fish, too?"

"No, I used to go along to admire him. That's what a good wife is supposed to do, isn't it?"

"I don't know. My marriage didn't last long enough for me to find out."

"That's a shame."

"I don't think so. I never wanted kids. And that's about the only reason to get married, isn't it?"

"What about the ladies you were attached to?" she asked.

"They learned to do without."

He noticed that she made a face, looked slightly disapproving. Then she turned back to the machine in front of her, and a few seconds later the title music filled the room. It indicated that you were about to see a suspense movie. The screen was filled with hazy images, which took Brandt back over many years to screening rooms on the West Coast, when it had been his job to see movies before they were released and try to figure out how best to sell them.

"Where do you want me to sit?" he asked his hostess.

"Next to me. Where else?"

"So that I can hold your hands in the scary parts?"

"If you find that reassuring."

"I think I might." He found it refreshingly easy to be with someone who spoke his language, and it wasn't only that she was American. She was like the women he had known in his youth, in California, who used the same banter to disguise their feelings and intentions. And although her intentions weren't clear, he sensed in himself the same nervousness he had always felt before any sexual encounter. Or was she really merely inviting him to see a movie just to pass the time?

He watched her as she collected her cigarettes off the table next to the video set, picked up an ashtray, and then kicked off her shoes before curling up on the chair next to him. He heard the click of her cigarette lighter, and by its flame he caught a glimpse of her face. She appeared to be calm and composed, as if she were seated in a Beverly Hills living room at just the magic moment when the screen is lowered by an electric motor, and the Matisse or the Van Gogh is removed to make way for the windows of the projection booth. Maybe she really did want to see *Marathon Man* again? It wasn't supposed to be a particularly good movie, from what Brandt had heard.

She glanced over at him. "You're not watching the movie," she said.

"I prefer looking at you."

She laughed self-consciously. "It's an interesting picture."

"Yes? Tell me more." He put out his hand and rested it on her forearm. Her skin was smooth and cool, he discovered. American skin. It was a phrase that suddenly came to him, a romantic notion, perhaps, that his memories of home had inspired. He found her hand with his hand and brought it up to his lips. She tightened her grip on his fingers and turned her head to glance over at him. He kissed her. For an instant she resisted him, then responded to his mouth. She tasted slightly of tobacco, but not for long. He tried to pull her closer to him, but the arms of both of their chairs were in the way.

"If we're going to do this, we might as well do it right," she said, and got to her feet.

She took his hand and led him across the hall into the bedroom. Without hesitating, she pulled the covers off the bed, then turned to face him.

"Aren't you going to turn off the machine?" he asked, indicating the room they had just left.

"No, I think I'll leave it on," she said.

"Why? What for?"

"Don't ask so many questions," she said, and pulled him toward the bed. It didn't take her very long to shed her clothes. In the reflected light from the hallway he could see that, despite her slim build, she had a well-formed body, with firm breasts that belied her age. There were no white lines from a bathing suit, Brandt noticed, an obvious result of living by herself away from the town.

He pulled off his shirt and slipped out of his trousers. "All that music and dialogue doesn't bother you?" he asked.

"Not really. And in case the servants walk by and see your car, they'll think we're watching a movie."

"I see."

Her brown body stood out against the sheet of the bed. They made love fiercely, with great intensity. She pulled him over on his back and sat astride his body. After a while he pulled her down and rolled over on top of her. Then after it was over they lay with their bodies still locked in an embrace, their hearts pounding.

He said, "That's the best movie I've seen for years."

"I thought you'd like it," she said.

The small of her back was moist from her exertions, and he started to pull away from her. "Don't go away yet," she pleaded with him.

He obeyed, but finally pulled free. "Where's the bathroom?" he asked.

"The door on the right," she said. "You're very American, aren't you? A nice, clean American boy. Bring me a towel while you're up, will you?"

"Yes, ma'am."

When he returned from the bathroom he saw that she had pulled the sheet over her body, and he lay down on top of the flowered pattern and kissed her cheeks and her neck. "I want a cigarette now," she said. "I know you don't approve and that it's bad for me, but so are a lot of other things."

"This isn't. Or it wasn't, or whatever is right."

"I'm not so sure," she said slowly.

He thought of Safire and his ungentlemanly remark. Well, bad taste or not, he hadn't exaggerated. "I'm thirsty," he said to the woman beside him. "Aren't you?"

While they talked, the movie ran on in the next room. When she had finished her cigarette, Hope got out of bed, slipped on a negligée, and went to the kitchen for some ice water. Brandt lay back against the padded bedstead, listening to the music and the distant voices. He could remember the work that went into the writing of a script from his days in the Publicity Department at Warner's, because a few of the poor slaves in the Writers' Building had become his friends. They were constantly complaining about the changes the producers and directors required them to make, called themselves "highly paid stenographers." Well, despite the bigger credits the Writers' Guild had negotiated for them, they would still be overlooked in the near future, when half the nation would be watching movies at home, before or after fornication.

Hope came back into the room with two glasses of ice water on a tray. She slipped out of her robe and joined him in bed. She was obviously quite proud of her body, and well she might be, Brandt thought. She had the figure of a young woman, despite a few telltale wrinkles around the buttocks. They sipped their water and kissed. She tasted of tobacco again, cold tobacco, but Brandt did not complain. "You know, I worry about you, locked up in your white castle by the sea," he said.

"Why? Nothing's ever happened here. Spain *is* different, really."

"Not anymore. You said so yourself."

"Sure, there have been a lot of robberies, but nobody's been raped on this coast since the Civil War."

"Times are changing," he said. "There are millions of unemployed. And all the wealth that's flaunted here, forty miles from Málaga, one of the worst centers of economic distress in Spain."

"I can look after myself."

"Yes? How?"

"I have a gun. I'll show you." She turned on the lamp at the side of the bed and crawled across his body in order to open a drawer in the bedside table. An instant later she held up a shiny, bluish-gray revolver.

Brandt saw that it was loaded with lead-tipped bullets, and experienced a tightening inside his stomach. Hope held the gun in the palm of her hand for an instant, then dropped it back into the drawer. "Have you got a license for that thing?" he asked her.

"No, I don't," she said cheerfully.

"Where did you get it?"

"A friend of mine brought it over from the States. I know how to use it, too," she added.

"Not as well as the crook who might bust in here."

"I've heard that theory," she said. "That if you have a gun, the other guy might be tempted to shoot first."

"And suppose you kill an unarmed robber? Without a gun license?"

"I don't think they'd put me in jail for long," she said. "And anyway, I prefer going to jail for a few months to getting raped or robbed in my own home."

"You wouldn't feel upset about killing a man?"

"No, I wouldn't," she said with her most charming smile.

"And what does Max think about the revolver in your night table?"

"Max doesn't know I have it. I hide it when he's here."

"Who's the friend who gave it to you?"

"A friend."

"A lover?"

"I don't remember."

"What about Lew?" he asked before he could stop himself. "Was he your lover, too?"

"No. Why do you ask?"

"You're right. It's none of my business."

"It isn't, as a matter of fact. But did Lew say something that made you ask that?"

"No, of course not."

"You're lying!"

"Look, Lew's an old friend of mine. And I can't really remember *what* he said. Anyway, I'm indebted to him for introducing us."

"Yes. I suppose I am, too. But if he suggested that he'd been to bed with me, then he's a shit and a liar."

"Absolutely. I agree with you."

"I'm going to have another cigarette," she said defiantly.

"Every time you reach for one, I'm going to make love to you," he told her.

"You are? Then I'm going to smoke all the time," she said. She appeared to have forgotten all about Safire's boast. Maybe he really hadn't been to bed with her, and was just showing off, Brandt thought. Old libertines were inclined to say that sort of thing. The fact that the lady kept a loaded revolver in her night table drawer worried him more than her amorous past.

* * *

Amir said: "Well, this is very pleasant. I'm glad Richard could persuade you to become a member of our team. Those are his words, mind you. He always uses American slang when dealing with Wogs or colonials. It's his way of showing he's superior." They were seated under an umbrella on the terrace of the Beach Club, overlooking the sea. Less than twenty feet away, a varied array of naked bodies were roasting in the sun, well oiled from head to foot.

"Does that bother you?" Brandt asked the young Iranian.

"No. Because I own more shares in the company than he does," Amir replied, and laughed happily, showing his pink gums and strong white teeth. "I hope you're pleased," he added.

"I am, as a matter of fact. There'd be a mild, poetic justice in my making a lot of money out of my only Iranian friend."

"With," Amir corrected him. "That would be nice, wouldn't it? But even if we don't, you haven't lost anything. As a matter of fact, you already look better than you did in London. What have you been doing with yourself, besides lying in the sun?" He dried his glistening forehead, careful not to disturb his carefully brushed hair. "Have you found a kind lady to share the warm tropical nights with you?"

"No. But I'm working on it."

"That's good. That's number one priority. If there's no one around you care about, everything tastes flat. The food, making money, even sex. Ask Richard if that isn't true."

"Why should I ask Richard?" Brandt asked.

"Because the English always have everything figured out. And because he should be here any minute now." Amir glanced at the thin gold watch buried in the black hair on his wrist. "You know, he's not going to stay on here for very long. His wife hates the place, and he's got other fish to fry. So if you enjoy the work, who knows, you might be running the office in a few months."

"You're getting ahead of yourself, pal," Brandt said. "I'm not the executive type."

Amir grinned. "I know. You're a free soul. That's what I like about you." He patted Brandt's knee. "Maybe I am rushing things a little," he said. "That's the trouble with us Iranians. We get overenthusiastic. I was just thinking it would be nice if you took over down here. It would make my visits more pleasant. And there's a lot of money to be made on this coast. The most difficult thing about any business is personnel. Finding the right man to do any given job." He glanced over at the people at the adjoining tables. There were quite a few Arabs seated around the pool, corpulent men with dark skins, some of them with their wives and others accompanied by the rather tarty-looking women who were in evidence in all of the expensive restaurants and clubs. "Not a very distinguished-looking group," Amir added, and stirred his drink with his finger.

"It's like what a friend of mine said about Hollywood years ago. Every year the people get worse, and this year we have next year's people."

Amir leaned back in his chair and roared with laughter. "That's very good. I like that," he said. "Holds true of most places, too. Teheran, Cannes, Paris. Now what about some tennis this afternoon? I've brought my gear with me . . ."

"Sure. Where do you want to play?"

"What about our hotel? We've just put in a new manager. I could check on him and introduce you at the same time. Unless you're getting ready to quit on your third day."

"I won't quit," Brandt said. "Not for a while, anyway. Not until the competition offers me a better job."

Richard Grey had come down the stone steps leading to the pool and the restaurant. He shaded his eyes against the glare of the sun and then, once he had seen them, made his way over to their table.

"How can you concentrate on work in these surroundings?" he asked, and sat down in the shade of the umbrella, facing them. "Or maybe you're not talking about business at all?"

"We're not, as a matter of fact," Amir said in his best Cambridge University accent. "We were talking about *tits.* We were trying to decide what it is about them that turns you on in the sanctity of the boudoir, and turns you off when you see them exposed en masse like this."

"Too much of anything is a mistake," Grey replied. "Have you ever been to a chocolate factory?"

Brandt found himself only half-listening to them. He was thinking about Hope Clarendon, wondering what she was doing at that moment. He probably should have sent her flowers, he thought, as it was impossible to reach her on the telephone. He wanted to reassure her that as far as he was concerned, it had not been a one-night stand. He was eager to see her again. They had made a date for that evening, but he remembered that she had asked him for his telephone number in case she was unable to keep it. The thought troubled him.

"I think we should order," Richard Grey was saying with sudden impatience. "I hate these Spanish hours. Lunch at three-thirty in the afternoon is ridiculous!"

But when he arrived at the villa in the orange light of the setting sun, she was waiting in the rose garden in front of the house. She told him that she had cooked dinner, warning him that it was "a typical American meal," and that they could still go out if he preferred not to take a chance on her cooking. It turned out to be meat loaf, with baked potatoes and mixed carrots and peas that had the Technicolor look of frozen vegetables. He kidded her about it when she lifted the top of the Pyrex dish in which they were being kept warm. "You don't have to eat the vegetables," she said, and opened the oven door and let him look briefly at a freshly baked apple pie. "As American as the Stars and Stripes," she told him, "so that should make you happy."

"And violence, isn't that right?" he asked her. "No, that's cherry pie. Apple pie is what they give you down on the farm where things are still peaceful."

"I wouldn't know about that. I'm a California girl."

"They don't have farms in California?"

"I'm sure they do, but I never lived on one. I'm a product of the urban sprawl."

They went for a walk on the beach after dinner, because it was a moonlit night and they could avoid the rocks the west wind had laid bare. The *levante,* the east wind, he explained to her, always covered the shore with a fine, grayish sand, and the wind from the Atlantic carried it away.

"Where do you get all these fascinating facts?" she asked him mischievously.

"I'm a nature boy."

"So I've noticed."

They had gone a mile or so away from her house and were walking west toward the path of moonlight that covered the tranquil surface of the sea. She was carrying the tennis shoes she had put on to cross the beach, and she looked up at him, her face hard and suspicious, as it could be at times. "What exactly did Lew say about me?" she asked.

"Nothing important. Forget it."

"I'm not going to forget it. You were the one who brought it up."

"I merely asked you if he'd been your lover."

"Well, you had a reason to ask me that."

"Not necessarily."

"Oh, come on. If you're going to lie, don't be so clumsy about it. What did he say to you?"

"What difference does it make? It wasn't unflattering."

"*What* did he say?"

"Why do you want to know?"

"Because he's supposed to be a friend of mine."

"Well, he is."

"What did he say?" She sounded angry, angrier than the night before.

"He hinted that you had certain talents."

"Don't mince words."

"I don't want you to be upset."

"I already am. I want to know exactly how he put it."

"What for?"

"Because I want to know!"

Brandt realized that he was trapped. He was annoyed with himself for having broached the subject. It had been totally unnecessary, prompted by his own vanity. He said, "I'll tell you if you promise never to mention it to him."

"I'm not going to promise anything."

"Hope! For God's sake! Relax. Men say things about women that are ungentlemanly, but who cares?"

"*I* care."

"All right. If you want to know, I'll tell you. But if you make a big thing of it with him, you'll only cause trouble for me."

"I'll take that chance."

"You're a hard lady."

"I'm not. But I *can* be. What did he say?"

"He suggested that you were good in bed."

"That I was a great lay? Is that it?"

"Yeah, I guess so. I don't remember the exact words."

"What a swine he is," she said with uncontrolled fury. "Even if it were true, it would be an unforgivable thing to say. God, men are shits!"

"Women talk too, you know."

"Well, *I* don't."

"I feel reassured."

"You're probably just as much of a shit as all the others," she said. "You hide it a little better, that's all. So far, anyway."

"Why does it bug you that much if it's a lie?"

"You really think he was my lover?"

"I believe you," he said. He took her arm, trying to calm her. "I just don't see why you should be so angry."

"Because I thought he was my friend. He tried once, of course, and I told him no. As nicely and gently as was possible. I didn't want to hurt his silly male pride. He was supposed to be Max's friend, too, and I reminded him of that."

"He didn't like to be turned down. That's probably all there is to it. There's nothing as vengeful as a woman scorned, they say. Or a man. We're not all that different. Or maybe he was playing Cupid."

"I don't think you're very amusing," she said. "Let's go back and go to bed. That's really the only place I truly enjoy your company." She pulled her arm free and started off down the beach. A gust of wind blew her hair away from her face, lifted the fringe she had so carefully prepared, along with the dinner, the meat loaf and the apple pie.

"Look, don't stir things up," he told her. "Especially if he's Max's friend."

"I'll be discreet," she said evenly. "But I'll settle his hash the next chance I get. Now how the hell can I put my sneakers on with all this sand on my feet?"

"You wash them off in the sea. How long has it been since you went walking on the beach with a beau?"

"A hundred years. My father bought a yacht when I was five."

"Yeah? He must have done all right with his drugstore," Brandt said, and she laughed. The crisis was over, he thought to himself. For the moment, anyway.

Lew Safire called him early the next morning. "How you doing, baby?" he asked.

"Okay. Hanging in there."

"And your love life?"

"Memories, Lew. Memories, that's all."

"Shake hands with a millionaire," Safire said. He sounded disappointed. For the tip, Brandt reckoned, he had expected to hear in detail about the winnings.

"What's new with you and Wilma?"

"Not very much. We're going to Madrid for a couple of days. I've got to see my dentist, and Wilma wants to pick up a few clothes."

"A Spanish dentist?"

"He's terrific, baby. He studied at U.S.C."

"The movie school?"

"No, I'm not kidding. He's the best man who's ever put his hand in my delicate mouth. And that's saying a lot. I've been to Vidal in Paris and Montgomery on the coast, and this guy is every bit as good."

"Well, I want to know his name. In case of an emergency."

"I'll write it down for you. My address book's in the other room. Have you seen our mutual friend lately?"

Brandt decided to play it dumb. "Which friend? Who are you talking about?"

"Hope is a thing with feathers."

"No, I haven't seen her," Brandt said. "I don't know how to get in touch with her. Her telephone seems to be out of order."

"Well, just saddle up and ride out to her ranch. You know where that is. You followed her home the other night."

"I don't like to drop in on people, and I don't like people dropping in on me."

"Oh, you've changed, baby. You used to drop in on us all the time. Remember when we lived on Stone Canyon Road?"

"You had a tennis court," Brandt said.

"Yeah. Well, that's true," Safire replied. "Anyway, I'll call you when we get back from the big city. Have fun."

"You too. And don't let them file your teeth down too low."

"I won't," Safire said. "Work hard."

"That's exactly what I'm preparing to do right this minute," Brandt said, which was another lie.

He wanted to take Hope out in the boat, but it was still too windy. There were whitecaps a mile out to sea, and the multinational flags at the port were already snapping in the breeze. They played golf instead, which was not Brandt's best game. He had shot for a while in the nineties, but golf had taken too much of his time, and so he had returned to his first passion, tennis.

Hope, as he might have expected, played a steady game of fairly short drives, which she made up for by being accurate with her irons. On the greens she putted like Jack Nicklaus, or so he told her after he had lost five thousand pesetas to her at the end of the first nine.

"You get to buy me dinner tonight," he said, after she had begged off playing the second half of the course.

"Am I seeing you again?" she asked. "Don't you have any other friends on the coast?"

"Well, the Safires, but they're off to Madrid."

"That shit," she said, and pulled off her golf glove with a violence that surprised the caddy holding her bag. She tipped the boy and told him to put her bag in her car.

"A drink?" Brandt asked her.

"No drink."

"Lunch?"

"Not if I'm going to see you tonight. We'll run out of conversation before the week's over."

"All right. Then I'll look in at the office."

"That's probably not a bad idea."

"Don't be bad-tempered."

"I'm not. You owe me five thousand pesetas."

He took out his wallet and paid her. When he tried to kiss her on the cheek to say goodbye, she pulled back from him. "What's the matter?" he asked. "Don't tell me you're a bad winner?"

"No. I'm a married woman. And I know everybody around here, from the caddy master up and down."

"I'm sorry."

"You needn't be. Just be more careful. People talk."

"I'll do my best."

She looked back at him as she followed the caddy off in the direction of the parking lot, looked back for just a fraction of a second to smile her friendly smile. It was an afterthought, because she knew she had been rough on him. Brandt thought, The guy who falls in love with that lady is not in for an easy time. Fortunately *he* was not in any real danger as yet. Pamela still hovered in the bruised outer layers of his mind. And he knew better than to let his heart run away with him when it came to ladies with quick tempers, especially those who kept loaded revolvers in their night tables. *¿Enamorado? No,* he said to himself. *¿Encoñado? Quizás.* What a superior language Spanish was when it came to the gentler emotions! The word *encoñado* was untranslatable. *"Encunted"* was a nasty-sounding substitute, and really didn't mean anything. Perhaps in his own country no one had ever bothered to classify the difference, because by the time they were aware of it, they were already divorced. A thought for the day! He picked up his golf bag and lugged it back to the Peugeot, which stood waiting for him in the blazing sun.

That night Hope took him to a new restaurant that had just opened a few miles west of her house off the main road. Brandt was skeptical about going there, because he remembered that amateur cooks were the bane of eating-out on the coast. There was always a new place opening up, usually financed by the life's savings of someone who wanted to stay on in the sun instead of going back to England or France or Belgium. Like the Mannings, they would lease a restaurant that had closed down, redecorate it, and then try to make a go of it themselves, with the wife cooking, and the husband acting as a maître d'hôtel. The food was usually too complicated, with sauces to cover the stringy meat, and all kinds of fancy salads that reminded Brandt of the health-food restaurants in Southern California.

He said: "What was it Oscar Wilde wrote? The theater and prostitution, two of the world's oldest professions, spoiled by the amateurs. Well, you can add *la cuisine* to those two."

"Don't be difficult. I'm paying, so I get to choose."

"All right. Have it your own way."

But the place was charming, he had to admit once they had arrived. There was an orchard of fig trees leading up to an old farmhouse, and the covered terrace looked out onto the distant lights of Estepona. The couple who ran the restaurant came from the French Basque country, which endeared them to Brandt at once, since that had been his favorite part of the world before it became overcrowded. They knew all of the places he had gone to almost every summer, Saint Jean de Luz, Ascain, Guétary, Urrugne. They had owned a bistro in Ciboure, but out of season there had not been enough business to survive, and so they had decided to move south and try their luck.

After a long talk with the wife, Brandt decided to take a chance on the *plat du jour,* which was poulet basquaise. Hope ordered a steak au poivre, as a friend of hers had raved about the quality of the meat when he had recommended the restaurant to her. They sat on the virtually empty terrace, because only two tables in the main dining room were occupied, and these seemed to be overflowing with noisy children.

Hope sighed and lit a cigarette. "It's very nice here," she said. "Cool, and not too many people yet."

"Well, you're two up on the day."

"What'll that get me?"

There was something in the tone of her voice that made Brandt glance over at her. The hard look, as he had come to think of it, was on her face, that slightly aggressive tilt of her chin, the cold blue color of her eyes, which were, as always, perfectly made up. "Why are you always so uptight at the start of an evening?" he asked. "What's your problem?"

"Am I?" she asked. "I thought I was being quite normally pleasant. Maybe it's because I don't know what you're after, what you want from me."

Astonished at her answer, he said: "I don't want anything. I just want to have a pleasant time. I enjoy your company, aside from everything else. I'm not after your money, and I'm not anxious to have you fall madly in love with me . . ."

"Maybe that's it," she interrupted him. "In the beginning of the evening it all seems so mundane, a convenient arrangement that two civilized people have secretly agreed upon. Your heart doesn't seem to beat any faster until we've fucked."

"That's not a very attractive way to put it."

"No. But it's accurate."

"Clinical, I'd say."

"Well, all right. You can quibble about the words. But there's a certain truth to them. If Lew hadn't recommended my services, would you have bothered to ask me out?"

"Of course."

"Why? There are thousands of single girls here."

"I don't know that many. And you're a compatriot."

"What does that have to do with it?"

"I don't know," he said, trying to figure it out himself. "I was happy to be with someone who speaks the same language, knows the same jokes."

"And who had a husband who was out of town!"

"Well, that must have been true of some of your other lovers, too."

"Maybe it was. But it didn't seem so obvious a few years ago. Maybe I'm just tired today. But I hate casual relationships. 'I'm going out with my steady lay tonight,' " she added in a slangy voice. "Doesn't that sound awful to you?"

"It does. But those words hadn't really crossed my mind."

"No? Perhaps you put it more gracefully."

Encoñado, Brandt thought guiltily to himself. "Listen," he said. "I enjoy being with you. You make me feel better about life. I also dig your skin. Sue me if that doesn't sit right."

She laughed and said: "You're not rich. You told me so yourself. What good would suing you do?"

"Future earnings," he said. "You can enslave me for life."

"I may just do that," she said, getting to her feet, as the head waiter was bowing to them from the entrance of the main dining room.

"A mundane relationship is sometimes better than no relationship at all," Brandt said in a low voice as he followed her across the tiles of the empty terrace.

"You forget I have my video, David." It was one of the rare times that she had used his name.

"Yes, and Max turns up now and then."

"I'd rather not talk about that."

"What shall we discuss over my poulet basquaise, and your steak au poivre?"

"Oh, there's lots to talk about, especially for compatriots. Reagan, the new regime in Spain, the price of gold against the price of the dollar, will there be a war this year or next?"

"Okay. If that's the desired agenda, I'm well prepared," he told her, and pushed in her chair for her, noticing the pleasant roundness of her behind.

"We don't really have to talk at all," she replied, and smiled a little more gently than was her habit. From the next table, three small French children were staring at them as if they were creatures from another world. Hope raised her right arm and waved to their audience. "*Bonjour,*" she said with an American accent.

"*Bonsoir,*" he corrected her, and added: "Don't encourage them. You'll have one of them sitting on your lap before the dinner's over."

But inevitably they did talk about Max. By the time the subject came up, they were friends again. It seemed to take her an hour or so in order to settle some inward problem of her own and to accept him at face value, dispel her resentments or whatever it was that was bothering her. She bloomed in the late evening, so it seemed to Brandt, like the white flowers that grew on the coast, and that he had seen only recently again in the Safires' garden, flowers that opened slowly right in front of your eyes at sunset and then wilted the following day. He asked her if she knew what they were called.

"You mean *damas de noche?*"

"No, not *dames de noche.* Some people call them moon flowers, but that's not the right name for them, either."

"Well, then I can't help you. I think I know the kind you mean. But why do you suddenly ask me about that? Are you planning to plant some on your balcony?"

"No. I asked you about the flowers that bloom when the sun goes down, because you're like that. It takes a little while for you to open up and spread your petals."

"Are they pretty, these moon flowers that are not called moon flowers?"

"Very pretty. And sensitive to atmosphere, to light, to the right amount of warmth; not too much and not too little."

"And where do they grow?"

"Only here. At least, this is the only place I've ever come across them."

"Well, that's where the resemblance ends. I blossom out in quite a few other places. New York in November, the Alps in the winter, and the Costa del Sol in the spring and summer. But occasionally I wither."

"When does that happen?"

"Oh, I don't know. When I'm not with the right person."

"When Max appears?"

"Oh, why do you have to bring him up?" she asked.

"Because he's part of your life, and I'm interested in you. Is that so surprising?"

She fell silent for a moment. Then she said: "I don't wither when he appears. I'm a different person, that's all."

"A wife?"

"Yes. A wife. Or a woman who's been married more than fifteen years."

"A Spanish friend of mine said that she doesn't know if marriage is *bueno* or *malo,* good or bad, but she does know it's *largo,* long."

She laughed. "That's very true," she said.

"When you do think he'll turn up, your husband?"

"I never know."

"You mean he might arrive tonight, with the last plane?"

"No. I always get plenty of warning."

"Is Max possessive?"

"Yes. I'm one of his properties, I guess."

"Maybe he's still in love with you."

She shrugged. "I suppose he is, in his own way."

"Are you still in love with him?"

"No, I'm not," she said without hesitation. "I like him. I suppose, at times, I'm frightened of him, too. He's a strange man. He never discusses anything with me, never asks any questions. He never tells me what he's doing, either."

"Do you think he's involved with somebody else?"

"I don't know. He's away so much of the time that I have to assume he has girls."

"Is he a passionate man?"

"He was. He is, I guess. I don't encourage that side of our relationship."

"And why do you stay together?"

She shrugged. "There's really no reason not to," she said. "There was at one time, a little while back. But it didn't work out."

"For you, or for the other man."

"For me," she said. "I realized that I was about to make a big mistake."

"Did Max know about all this?"

She shook her head and said: "No, he didn't, thank God. He's not the kind of man to take things like that lightly. We don't have an open marriage."

"Does he spy on you?"

"I don't really know. I don't think he's ever hired a detective, or anything sordid like that. But he always asks where I've been and what I've been doing."

"Is that why you were so uptight at the golf club?"

"That was part of the reason. I also don't like people gossiping about me."

"But then wouldn't it be better for you to be on your own?"

"No, I don't think so. I know a lot of women who are divorced, and even those who have plenty of money appear to be quite unhappy. Certainly worse off than I am. Human beings were meant to live in pairs."

"I agree. But if one of the pair is always off on his own, what happens then?"

"Being a pair is a state of mind."

"I suppose so," Brandt said. "Would you like some dessert?"

"No, thank you. I'll have some coffee, that's all. I'm tired. I'd like to go home."

"And watch a movie?"

"No movie. Just sleep. A quick look-around to see that all's well at the castle, a good-night kiss, and *hasta luego,* you all."

"It seems a shame to waste a night, now that I know I'm living on borrowed time."

"Don't you ever get tired?"

"Sometimes."

"Well, *I'm* tired tonight. I'm sorry."

They drove back to her house in silence. He checked all of the rooms, wondering what he'd do if someone stepped out of a dark corner and challenged him. Submit to the worst, I guess, he said to himself. Give up my money and my girl. Or maybe he would put up a fight. That was what the lover was supposed to do.

She was waiting for him on the terrace, a lighted cigarette in her hand. He kissed her on the mouth and gathered her up in his arms. She pulled away from him. "You don't believe that I'm tired, do you?" she asked.

"I'd like to prove to you that you're not. It's nice that way sometimes."

And so in the end she agreed. In the semidarkness of the bedroom she gave herself to him slowly and somewhat hesitantly at first, and then with greater intensity than ever before.

"You were right," she told him when their hearts had stopped their wild pounding and they could speak. "I must tell Safire about you. That you're really a great lay, no matter what anyone has ever said."

"That would be most helpful. For my reputation."

She smiled and reached for her cigarettes, which were lying on top of the night table on his side of the bed, where he now knew the revolver was hidden in the second drawer. "I do love you just a little bit, too," she said.

"I like you a lot, too."

"And that's all?"

"That's all I'm willing to own up to. For now."

She slipped on her negligée and took him to the door. She was strangely silent as he stepped past her and started out into the warm night. Then he turned back and kissed her gently on both cheeks. "Thank you for flying American," he said in a guarded voice, conscious of the sounds of the crickets and the sea.

She sighed and shook her head. "Drive carefully, David," she said. "I'll call you in the morning when I get to the market."

"I'll be at the office by ten," he told her. "I have to make a go of my new job. In case I decide to stay on here a little while longer."

He slept well in the little apartment. It was cool, and the only noise early in the morning was that of the fishing boats returning to port. It was a pleasant sound to awaken to with the first light of day, and very often he turned over and went back to sleep for an hour or two more. Of course he probably would have slept well anywhere, he thought to himself as he squeezed his grapefruit juice. Making love had always had that effect on him, especially as a regular routine. Although it didn't inspire him to start the day like a young world-beater and come into the office full of energy and high spirits. But then the early morning at Sun and Sea Realty Company was not exactly a high-pressure scene. The two salesmen and the secretaries, everyone with the possible exception of Richard Grey, came tottering into the building like the survivors of Stalingrad. Even Penny, the "sporty Aussie," would stagger a bit on her high heels as she crossed the waxed tiles of the entry hall. They had all adopted Spanish habits. They dined at ten or ten-thirty, and then usually sat around an outdoor bar or went briefly to a discothèque to dance. *La juerga,* as the Spaniards called it, was an important part of everyone's life on the coast, so it didn't really matter if he, too, appeared at ten-fifteen.

He would surprise them today, Brandt thought, for he had finished his coffee and toast by nine o'clock. As he was running short of grapefruit and bread, he stopped at the market after breakfast. The dark-eyed girl at the fruit stand smiled at him and asked what made him such an early riser, and after he had gotten what he needed for the next few days' breakfast, he purchased a melon and a kilo of peaches, because he was hoping to go out on the boat.

At the entrance of the fish market, where the trucks were still unloading the morning's catch, he bought four tenths of a lottery ticket that ended with the numbers one, three, and five, which was how his Navy serial number had ended. Those were the numbers he had always played at roulette in Biarritz, with varying success. Although he had never won a lot of money, he had remained ahead of the game, which was enough of an accomplishment for a nongambler. He tipped the man a hundred pesetas, and was wished *suerte,* luck, and told to go with God, all for a little less than a dollar.

What would he do, he wondered, if he happened to win? Go back to California? But eighty thousand dollars, plus the money he had saved, wouldn't mean much in L.A. He could make the down payment on a small house in the valley, but with the interest rates what they were, he would have to find a job right away in order to keep up the monthly payments. Well, he hadn't won *el gordo,* the fat one, as yet, so there was no use worrying about what he was going to do with the money.

He drove to the office on the back road. The sea was flat, and there was no wind. The sun beat down on the dry hills, and there was a big fat cloud hanging over the summit of the sierra. He arrived at his desk at quarter past ten and was given a cup of instant coffee by Esmeralda, the overweight receptionist. "*¡Ay, qué calor!*" she complained, just not to be different.

"It's summer," he told her. And if it wasn't hot, nobody would be buying real estate.

That was true, she admitted, fanning herself with a small cardboard fan. Señor Ricardo had arrived, she informed him, with Señor Amir.

Brandt sauntered into Grey's office. He and Amir were having coffee and eating churros, the fried early-morning pastry that is popular all over Spain. Amir offered him some, but Brandt declined. "Have one," Amir insisted; "they'll do wonders for your backhand." Large circles of sweat already marked the armpits of his silk shirt.

"God, you live clean," Grey said, shaking his head. "Do you do your setting-up exercises every morning?"

"Only on Sundays. During the week I don't have time. I have to prepare myself mentally for my work."

Amir grinned and chewed noisily. "He's a very serious fellow, our David," he said.

"In that regard," Grey said, "I think you should prepare a guest list for the opening night of our hotel. I think it would be a good idea to invite a couple of press people from London. That chap who writes a gossip column for the *Evening Standard,* and maybe one or two others. I'm getting someone in to help you with the local invitations and the Madrid crowd."

"You said you wanted to invite some celebrities. Is that still on?" Brandt asked.

"I don't know," Grey said. "I'd like to think about it. Air fares run into a lot of money. Maybe you can find out if there is anyone of interest in Madrid. Movie people. They help dress up a party."

"Give me a day or two on that," Brandt said. "I'll make a few calls and see if there's anyone around."

"There's no hurry. Monday will be fine."

"Would you like to go out on the boat for an hour or so before lunch?" he asked.

"We can't," Grey said. "We have a business lunch with the former owners of the hotel. They had all kinds of connections with the old regime, and although they're not in power anymore, we still have to be polite. Just in case."

"In case of another coup?"

"That's most unlikely," Grey said. "But in this crazy country you never know what might happen. Have to be prepared for every contingency. Be polite to everybody."

"Even the Socialists?"

"Definitely," Amir said. "When they come to power, they'll still need the tourists. And us." He wiped his face with his monogrammed handkerchief.

Brandt went back to his cubicle. He opened his address book and began to make a list of all his Spanish friends, the ones who were apt to be on the coast in July and August. In all probability, not one of them would ever have dinner at the hotel again, since it was at the wrong end of the town. But their names sounded good, and as most of them were fairly young, they would help decorate the inaugural fiesta. Brandt felt certain that if they were invited in time, they would attend; a big party was always an event, and people liked to be seen.

Hope called from a pay telephone in San Pedro de Alcántara. They were cut off twice, which was the normal procedure, as nearly all of the pay booths were constantly being vandalized. "What's happening at the office?" she asked, once she had found a telephone that worked.

"Nothing very interesting. What are you up to?"

"Well, I've done all the shopping, so I'm free," she said.

"Why don't you come out on the boat?" Brandt asked her. "The sea is a piece of glass."

"Are you taking anyone else?" she asked, warily.

"No. Not today."

"Are you sure?"

"Absolutely. Why? Are you ashamed to be seen with me?"

"No. It isn't that. You know the reason. If you've invited other people, I'll stay home."

"I assure you, we'll be on our own."

Still, she hesitated. "All right," she said finally. "And how do I find your yacht?"

"I'll pick you up at twelve-thirty," he said.

Hope hesitated once again. "No, I think it would be better if I met you at the port," she said.

"All right. It's the old port, don't forget. At one. Berth thirty-nine. The name of the boat is *Lulubelle*."

"That's easy enough to remember. Shall I bring anything?"

"Just yourself, and maybe some sandwiches. I'll get the drinks and the ice."

"I'll be there," she said, and hung up.

Brandt finished making his list and drove into town. At the first traffic light an old man with a small herd of goats crossed the highway. His weatherbeaten face had the look of pride and nobility that Brandt had so often seen on the faces of peasants in Castille, a look that many years of enduring the harsh climate and living off the poor land had stamped on them. The goatherder's wife, a heavyset woman in black, followed at the rear of the procession, leading a mongrel dog on a piece of string. Brandt vaguely remembered having seen the couple before, crossing the road at this same intersection. Seeing them had always made him feel guilty. Eternal Spain, he thought to himself. Away from the big cities and the tourist centers the struggle to eke out a meager living still continued.

The light changed and he drove on, but the image of the old man and his wife stayed with him as he passed through the town. The sidewalk cafés were filled with sunburned foreigners, and as he turned off in the direction of the port, he still felt uneasy because his life had been such an easy one.

But he didn't feel guilty for very long. It was too nice a day. A slight breeze had come up, but there was not enough wind to put the excursion in doubt. It was hot in the port, and by the time he had cast off the stiff mooring lines, his shirt was clinging to his body, and rivers of sweat were running down the sides of his face. He started the engines and went below to change into his bathing suit. He waited for a few minutes in the shade of the wheelhouse, and then Hope arrived. She was wearing a white sun hat and dark glasses, and he didn't recognize her for an instant. She was carrying a straw basket and an orange plastic container.

He helped her on board, and together they stowed the food she had brought in the small refrigerator under the sink. "Did you remember to get some ice?" she asked him.

"No, damn it. I forgot."

She nodded and said, "I thought you might, so I brought some." The plastic container was full of sparkling ice cubes, packed in around two bottles of white wine.

"You see," he said, "I can't live without you." He showed her how to walk the bowline aft, and then called out to her to drop the marker buoy in the water so that he could retrieve it easily. Setting the throttles at idling speed, he steered the boat out of the harbor. It was much cooler once they were out in the open sea, although the sun beat straight down out of a cloudless sky. There was nothing for either of them to do now except enjoy the view of the coast. He said, "If you want to lie in the sun, grab a couple of those faded blue pillows and go up front."

"No, I'd rather sit with you for a while," she replied.

"That's very nice of you."

"Well, don't sound so surprised."

"You're not usually this friendly in the morning," he told her. "At least not on the golf course."

"The morning is when I'm at my best," she said. "You see, I'm an optimist." She lit a cigarette. She was seated on the navigator's seat on the port side of the wheelhouse, her naked feet resting on the handrail in front of her. Brandt admired her painted toenails and her narrow, tanned feet. He thought: She has never served as a beast of burden, or followed her husband up a winding dusty trail to some pasture where their goats could graze. "What's this thing?" she asked, pointing her right foot to the canvas-covered instrument below the handrail.

"A call radio for emergencies."

"Do you know how it works?"

"No, but I'm pretty sure I could figure it out. Not that there's anybody to call. I suppose you might get the tower at the Puerto Banús, but whether they'd come out to look for you is another matter."

"What about the Coast Guard? Or don't they have one in Spain?"

"No, but they have a Navy. There's usually a destroyer lying in Málaga harbor, but I think they've got other things on their mind besides rescuing gringos. The best thing to do is stick close to the shore."

"That sounds reasonable." She got up and went below. When she reappeared, she was dressed in a bikini. Brandt had never seen her body in the daylight, and he found himself studying her slim figure. She had had a child, she had told him, but there were no marks where the skin had been stretched by pregnancy, only a small scar that hadn't tanned quite as smoothly as the rest of her stomach. "What are you staring at?" she asked him.

"You. That's not against the rules, is it?"

She shrugged. "It's not the first time you've seen me undressed. Do I pass inspection, Captain?"

"You do, Lieutenant. Definitely."

"Well, that's good news," she said. "I want to stay on this ship. By the way, where are we going?"

"Up the coast a few miles. To look for cleaner water. If that's all right with you."

"Why don't we anchor off the villa? It's the servants' afternoon off, and the gardener leaves around four. I don't like to leave the place unguarded for too long."

"We can do that," Brandt said. "Where are you supposed to be today, in case anyone asks?"

"I said I was going to play golf. I had Juanito, the houseman, put my clubs in the back of the Mercedes. To make it look right."

"And the ice bucket and the sandwiches?"

"I said I was going to picnic on the beach with some friends first." She stood up and leaned out of the wheelhouse to study the narrow companionway she would have to follow in order to get to the sun mattress Manolo had lashed securely in place on the roof of the cabin. Then she collected her towel from the straw basket and made her way forward.

Brandt watched her as she spread the towel out on the starboard side and lay down on her stomach, with her head resting on her hands. For a while she remained in that position, then she turned her head and lay looking back through the windshield at him. Brandt smiled at her, but she didn't smile back. She seemed to be studying him. It made Brandt feel self-conscious.

He glanced down at the rev counters as though he were intent on some mechanical problem. When he looked up, he saw that her expression hadn't changed. He made a face, attempting to make her laugh or at least smile, but she buried her face in the crook of her arm as if she had decided to take a nap in the warm breeze. Something was obviously troubling her. Maybe Max had called to announce his imminent return. It was a mistake to get involved with someone else's wife. He had always stayed clear of complications of that kind. Or tried to, anyway. But Pamela's defection had had an effect on his judgment, to say the least. What the hell, he thought, don't let's spoil this fabulous day.

He pushed the throttles forward and ran along for a while at eighteen hundred revolutions a minute. They passed the Puerto Banús, and he set his course for the farthest point of land ahead. The water was cleaner, he noticed. There were no longer any doubtful trails of yellow weed or the muck that he suspected was thrown up into the sea by some underground pipe from a shore-based sewer. There were fewer buildings, too, and about three miles beyond San Pedro de Alcántara he saw a long stretch of deserted beach. The sand was gray, as it was all along the coast, but at least the shore was deserted. There was a ruined Moorish tower and a shack built of sugar cane fronds, and when he was within three hundred yards of the land he cut the engines and let *Lulubelle II* slide slowly to a halt, settling lower in the water and then rolling slightly in the waves of her own wake.

There was no current, and only a slight breeze, so it wasn't necessary to drop the anchor. He went below and found himself one of the blue pillows, but when he came up on deck there was no sign of his passenger on the sun mattress. Nor was she in the cockpit. He looked out the window on the port side, but she wasn't in the water there, either. He walked quickly aft and saw that she was holding on to the swimming ladder in the stern.

"You had me worried there for a while," he said. "I didn't hear you jump in."

"No Hope," she replied. "I guess that's enough to worry anyone."

"You can say that again." He dove in, making sure to land well clear of her, as he sensed that she was in no mood for being splashed. When he surfaced beside her, he saw that she had her head back and was wetting her hair evenly so that it would be clear of her brow. He watched her, admiring her body, as she climbed up the swimming ladder. He said: "May I suggest that you're not required by the regulations to wear a bathing suit on this ship, once we're out of port?"

"Oh, really? Well, I'm not the bare-assed type. I like a little mystery in the hard light of day."

"I'm not crazy about swimming in the nude, either. I just know that some ladies are. Wear your bikini, and wear it in good health."

"I will." She moved back to her place on the sun mattress once again. Brandt pulled himself up on the swimming platform and, after he had shed some of the sea water, went forward to lie down beside her. She had her eyes closed, and he leaned over her and kissed her on the neck.

"Would you like a drink?"

"No, thank you."

"Passion?"

"Certainly not. I don't like copulating in public. Anyway, I'm taking the sun." She turned over and lay on her stomach. He watched her as she undid the halter of her bikini.

"What about the other side? When does that get roasted?"

"In private," she said. "At the side of my pool."

"A time and a place for everything," he said. It was too hot in the sun, and so he moved aft and started the engines. He pushed the throttles forward and set them at fourteen hundred revolutions. There was no automatic pilot on *Lulubelle.* That was the one convenience that Manning had neglected to equip his boat with. Brandt also noticed that he had to stand at the wheel in order to steer. When seated, he couldn't see the water directly in front of the bow, and there was always the risk of hitting a floating piece of wood or a log that was near the shore. A helicopter passed overhead with the markings of the U.S. Navy on the fuselage. Good duty, he thought to himself. To be stationed in Rota, the naval base north of Cádiz, was better than being assigned to the Sixth Fleet somewhere in the Persian Gulf.

After a quarter of an hour or so, he saw the white wall and the grove of eucalyptus trees of the Villa Miramar off the starboard bow. He throttled back a little, checked the flat sea in front of him for obstacles, then made his way forward along the catwalk until his torso cast a shadow on Hope's brown shoulders. He said: "This is your captain speaking. We're approaching Clarendon country."

She raised her head and glanced toward the shore. "So we are," she replied. "You've made good time, Captain."

"Always try to please our passengers." He reckoned that they were running about four hundred yards out from the gray beach, but he knew that it was difficult to judge distance accurately on the water. "What's the bottom like outside your front yard?" he asked her.

"Rocky in places, but well over your head at high tide. Even at low tide there's about five feet of water."

"Well, we'd better not go in too close. *Lulubelle* is only insured for third-party risks."

"What does that mean?"

"The damage we do unto others, not the damage we do unto ourselves." He moved back and stood at the window outside the wheel and steered the boat a little closer to the beach without altering its speed. Below him he could see dark rock formations along the bottom, with occasional patches of undulating sand. The water was clear and a very rich color of blue. "Is there a reef?" he called out to Hope.

"Not really a reef," she said, sitting up and closing the halter of her bikini. "There are rocks, but they never break the surface unless there's a big swell."

"I don't want to foul the anchor if I can avoid doing so," he told her, and climbed back inside the wheelhouse. He pulled the Morse controls back to the neutral position, and then back some more into reverse until the movement of the boat had stopped. Then he brought them up to neutral again and went forward to drop the anchor. Hope was kneeling on the canvas mattress, shading her eyes while she looked off toward the shore.

"What time is it?" she asked. "I can't see the gardener anywhere."

"It's about two-thirty. He's probably on the other side of the house. There's a pair of binoculars below. On one of the shelves of the port side."

"I'll find them," she said.

He lowered the anchor slowly into the water, then let the nylon rope slide through his hands. There was a slight current from the west, and he allowed the boat to drift back thirty yards or so before securing the line. Then he stood watching for a moment or two to make certain that the anchor held them in place. Hope was standing in the cockpit with the glasses, studying the villa on the shore. Brandt went inside the wheelhouse and shut off the engines.

"What bliss," she said when the noise had ceased.

The silence engulfed them. A single gull hovered above them in the sky. The breeze from the land smelled of summer hay. "I wonder what the poor people are doing today," Brandt said.

"Yes. I wonder." She put the binoculars down, stepped gingerly up onto the gunwale in the stern, and dove into the clear water. Once she had surfaced, she smiled at him. "I can forget everything on a day like this," she said. "All my responsibilities, all my problems."

"That's why people have yachts," Brandt told her.

The movement of the sea woke him. They had taken another dip after lunch, and then had lain down on the sun mattress to dry off. It was probably the wine Hope had brought along that had made him drowsy, and swimming in the cold water. He looked off in the direction of the horizon in the east and noticed the swell that had come up. There were long, smooth waves now, and a hundred yards to his right he could see a line of white water where they broke occasionally across the shallow part of the rocky shelf beyond which they were anchored. He knew there was no reason for alarm as long as the waves did not increase in size, so he closed his eyes again. But Hope was awake now, too, and she reached out for the binoculars lying between them. He watched her drowsily as she sat looking off at the distant villa. "The shutters in my bedroom are open," she said. "That's rather strange, isn't it?"

"Is it? I don't know. Maybe the servants forgot to close them before they left."

"What time is it?"

"A quarter past five."

Hope had gotten to her feet and was standing in the bow, with the binoculars trained on the shore.

"The gardener's still not there. I'm going to swim in and find out what's going on."

"It's a long swim, honey."

"I can make it." She moved toward him and put the binoculars down in the center of the mattress.

"I'm not going to let you go alone," he said. "Anyway, if the shelf of rocks is to our right, as you say it is, I can move *Lulubelle* in a little closer. Or we can go back and get your car. Either one."

"It'll take us an hour to reach the port, and at least another half-hour to drive back up here. And as you say, maybe it's nothing to worry about. So why spoil the rest of the afternoon?"

He looked off to where a wave was breaking across the shallows. He didn't like the idea of leaving *Lulubelle* riding alone at anchor, but he liked the idea of her swimming in on her own even less, and so he went forward and began pulling in the line, which slanted forward in the clear water. It would have been better to start the engines first, he told himself, as he had been taught, but they were still quite far out, so it didn't matter too much. He brought up the anchor and put it down gently near the railing in the bow. Then he went back and took his place behind the wheel.

Both engines started at once. He put his head out over the gunwale and tried to judge the depth of the water as the boat moved ahead. Manning would have a shit hemorrhage if he could see him now, he thought to himself, and was surprised at how he reverted to Navy talk whenever he was nervous. Although in the Navy he had never really been frightened very often, except maybe as a boot.

They were passing over a large sandy area, and by the color of the water, he judged the depth to be about ten feet. When he looked off toward the beach, he saw that he had cut the distance to the house down considerably, that he could make out the edge of the swimming pool quite clearly, as well as the white table and chairs standing on the terrace. There was probably a strip of shallow water near the beach, so the distance they would have to swim was less than a hundred and fifty yards. Still, he kept *Lulubelle* on course at idling speed. Hope was poised on the companionway outside the wheelhouse on the starboard side.

"You look worried," she said.

"It's not my boat," he said. A swell lifted *Lulubelle* and increased her forward speed.

"I can make it easily from here."

"I'm not sure I can," he said, and pulled the throttles back. Then very gently he swung *Lulubelle* around so that her bow faced out to sea. Once the boat was in the position he wanted it to be in, he moved forward and eased the anchor into the water. As soon as it was lying on the sandy bottom, he tested the force of the swell by pulling on the rope to make sure *Lulubelle* wouldn't drift nearer the shore. The villa looked dangerously close. He could see the open shutter of the bedroom window swinging back and forth in the light breeze. "Do you know how to shut down the engines?" he asked Hope.

She said, "I think so," and climbed in through the open window on her side of the wheelhouse. Brandt watched her pull back on the stop levers on both diesels and then turn off the starter switches.

"Good girl."

She didn't reply. She had hung the binoculars around her neck before climbing through the window, and she was studying the house again through the glasses. Then she pulled the leather strap back over her head and tossed the binoculars onto the padded bench inside the cabin. "All set to go," she said.

"Pull the keys out of the ignition and stow them below," Brandt told her. "Just don't forget where you've hidden them."

"Aye, aye, sir."

"Have you got the keys to your house?"

She shook her head. "I'll go get them," she said.

"That's probably not a bad idea." He felt tense. Leaving *Lulubelle* anchored that close to the shore was still worrying him, and he wondered if he should let Hope swim in alone now that they were within fifty yards of the front lawn.

She joined him on the small triangle of deck in the bow an instant later. "My bikini doesn't have a pocket," she said. "Can you take the keys?"

He took the key ring she handed him and zipped it into the small front pocket of his bathing trunks. Then he tested the anchor line again with his foot. *Lulubelle II* seemed fairly well moored to the bottom. The waves were getting smaller, although he couldn't be sure. "Don't try to break any records swimming in," he said. "Just remember that we have to swim back out again."

"You really must think I'm an idiot," she said.

"No, I don't. But I don't know you well enough to rely on your common sense."

She made a face at him and jumped into the water. He watched her slim body as it rose to the surface, then dove in after her. The sea was much warmer now that they were nearer the land. He looked back at the boat. A big wave coming in from the east lifted her well out of the water. He could see the red antifouling paint on *Lulubelle*'s bottom looking bright and fresh, unmarked as yet by any marine growth. As he started swimming toward the beach, he was conscious of a certain discomfort at the back of his mind, and he couldn't help wondering if they had made the right decision. It would probably have been better to go back to the port and collect the cars, he reckoned. There would have been no maneuvering of the boat or swimming to shore, so it wouldn't have taken them much longer to reach the villa.

The last fifteen yards through the shallow water were the most difficult part of their ship-to-shore operation. There was a belt of sharp rocks that made it impossible to walk upright, and they both moved painfully on all fours, with the small waves breaking intermittently on top of their backs. Then, at last, they were on dry land. "I don't think much of your beach," Brandt said, inspecting his feet for cuts.

"It changes all the time," she said, mimicking his voice. "The west wind exposes the rocks, and the east wind covers them with sand. Haven't you heard?"

"Well, it's an easterly wind now."

"Yes, but it hasn't really started to blow."

"I hope it doesn't for a while," he said, looking out at *Lulubelle* again.

"Be careful," Hope warned him. "There are brambles ahead, over there where the dirt path leads up to the lawn."

"I'll follow you."

She nodded and led the way across the narrow strip of sand, stepping carefully over the high-tide line, which was filled with small particles of tar. Then she ran quickly up the cement steps and crossed the lawn. Brandt felt the sun burning the back of his neck. He noticed that Hope went straight past the swimming pool to the bedroom window with the telltale shutter and that she stood staring at it without moving. When he had joined her, he saw at once that the white steel grill inside the shutters was bent in the middle and that a pane of glass in the window behind it was broken. He said, "I don't see how a fully grown person could have squeezed through there."

"Somebody did, though."

"Maybe not. Maybe they just wanted to look inside for future reference."

She said, "Give me my keys," in a flat voice, and he unzipped the small pocket of his bathing suit and handed them to her.

She took them without a word and hurried around the side of the villa, past a small rose garden, following a gravel path that led past the back of the garage. They both had to walk more slowly once they had reached the white gravel of the parking space, which now lay in the shadow of the villa, because the fine chips of marble hurt their feet. He caught up with her before she reached the steps leading to the front door, watched her insert the house key and open it.

She said, "They've been here, all right."

"How do you know?"

"Because Juanito always locks both locks," she said, pointing to a small metal opening higher up on the door that was obviously a keyhole for a security lock.

"Maybe he forgot."

He followed her inside. She went straight to her bedroom and stood for a moment in the doorway. The room looked to Brandt to be in perfect order. The bed with its white bedspread and the small night table looked no different from the way he remembered them on his previous visits. But he didn't have time to look at everything very closely; Hope had crossed to the walk-in closet. She pulled open the door and uttered a startled cry. Brandt thought at first that she had come upon someone hiding there, but when he got within a few feet of her, he saw that it was the disorder inside the closet that had startled her.

There were clothes lying everywhere in a heap, a bright pile of a variety of garments that had been pulled off their hangers and dumped on the floor. Apparently she had waded across them, because she stood facing a small wooden cabinet, the front door of which had been broken open. There was a row of sliding drawers behind the door. The top one hung open at a strange angle, like a broken arm. Brandt caught a glimpse of colored silk, a scarf probably, that had been of no interest to the thief. For by that time there was no doubt in his mind as to what had happened.

Hope stepped back and said, "Oh, no," in a stricken voice. She swayed slightly, and dropped down on one knee. Brandt put his hand on her arm and tried to help her back up, but she shook her head and pulled free of his grasp. "I'm all right," she said, and got slowly to her feet.

They stood there for a while in silence, still moist from their swim. Brandt was conscious of the extreme heat inside the closet, and Hope must have noticed it, too, for she straightened suddenly and turned to face him. Her face was wet with perspiration, and her eyes had the look of an animal that has been wounded or frightened. "The air-conditioning isn't on," she said. "They must have turned off the main switch so the alarm wouldn't ring." She stepped past him into the bedroom, and then stopped abruptly again. He saw at once what had brought her to a halt. On the middle of the bed, sunken into the white lace cover of the bedspread, lay the revolver.

He said, "Don't touch it," for she had made a move toward the bed. "Don't touch anything," he warned her, and he thought to himself that it wasn't for nothing that he had spent so many years of his life watching detective movies. He glanced at his watch. "If the gardener left at four or four-thirty," he said, "they couldn't have been here very long ago. It's just after six now. If we call the police . . ." He stopped. He felt a little ridiculous, inadequate. If that was all he could come up with, he might as well have remained on board *Lulubelle.*

Hope sat down slowly on the edge of the bed and rested her head in her right hand. A strand of hair fell forward, and she combed it back with her fingers. Brandt noticed that her hand was shaking visibly. "How far is it to the servants' house?" he asked. "Didn't you say they live quite near here?"

"About half a mile down the road," she replied in a low voice.

"Do they have a phone?"

"No, of course not."

"And there's no restaurant or filling station nearby?"

"There's a filling station five miles away, but there's no telephone there, either." She sounded defeated. It seemed almost an effort for her to speak.

It occurred to Brandt that they could use the emergency call radio on the boat, and then he remembered that in all likelihood it would be impossible from where they were anchored to get through to the tower at the port. "Maybe we'd better get back to the boat," he said. "We can be in town in an hour."

She nodded and said, "All right." But she didn't move.

"What did they take?" he asked her.

She made a sound like a groan, but it was perhaps a sarcastic laugh; he couldn't be sure. "What did they take?" she said, repeating his question. "Why, just everything I had, that's all."

"What do you mean?"

"All my jewelry. Everything I've ever had that was worth keeping."

"Was it insured?"

She shook her head. "Max didn't want to pay the high premiums," she said. "He wanted me to put it in a safe at his bank. But what's the use of having jewelry if you can't wear it?"

"How much was it worth?" It wasn't any of his business, but it seemed the obvious thing for him to ask.

"*I* don't know. About half a million dollars, I suppose. That's the sum Max talked about when I asked him to find out what the insurance would cost us at Lloyd's." She looked up for a brief moment. Brandt saw that there were tears in her eyes. "He was going to talk it over with a broker the next time he was in London. That would be about now," she added, with a dry laugh. "A little late, wouldn't you say? Will you get me a tissue from the bathroom?"

He brought her the whole box. She blew her nose and dried the corners of her eyes. "We'd better go," Brandt said. "The more time we waste now, the harder it will be for the police to act with any kind of efficiency. There's always a chance they'll get your things back for you."

"You think so?" she asked. "They haven't managed to get anyone else's jewels back on this coast as far as I know. They've recovered a couple of paintings, but that's easier. You can't break a painting up and sell the pieces." She paused to blow her nose again. "It's funny, but you never think it's going to happen to you. At least, I didn't. There are so many much bigger houses around. Rich Arabs and Germans." She looked over at the revolver lying on the white bed cover. "They must have gone through every drawer in this room," she said. "Or how else would they have found the gun?"

"They probably started with the night table. That's where people usually keep their cash."

She got to her feet, pulled a couple of tissues out of the box, and crossed to the chest of drawers, on which more of the silver-framed photographs were still standing undisturbed. She wrapped the tissues around the gilded handle of the uppermost drawer on the right and pulled it open. "My money is still here," she said in a flat voice, and held up a small stack of five-thousand-peseta notes. "They obviously knew what they were after and where to look."

"Then why did they make such a mess of the closet? And the revolver? Why did they leave it lying on the bed? It looks to me as if it was someone who knew the house," he added. He crossed to the broken window and looked out across the lawn to see if the boat was still riding safely at anchor. It was there, just the way they had left it, but the waves breaking on the shore seemed bigger. "What about the servants?" he asked. "How long have they been with you?"

"Oh, for years and years. I don't think they had anything to do with this."

"You never know. Somebody might have gotten to them."

"I suppose anything is possible," she said, and before he could stop her, she had crossed to the bed again and had picked up the revolver.

"What the hell are you doing?"

"I told you that I don't have a permit for this thing," she said, "so I'm going to hide it before the police find it."

"Where?"

"I don't know." There was a note of panic in her voice.

He started toward her, wanting to take her in his arms. But before he could reach her, there was the sound of insistent knocking on the front door. Hope turned in alarm, with the revolver still in her hand, although she was pointing it down at the floor. "Maybe they've come back?" she said.

"Don't be ridiculous," he said. "You think they'd knock? And what the hell would make them come back? They got what they came for."

"What shall I do?"

"Put the gun back in the drawer and go see who it is."

"Alone?"

"I'll go with you, if you like. Whoever it is knows you're here because they've seen the boat." He took the revolver out of her hand and dropped it back into the night table drawer. Then he took her by both arms and pulled her to him. He said: "Come on. Get yourself together."

She nodded, but she didn't respond to his embrace. Then she followed him out of the room without a word of protest. But he knew that she would have preferred to stay there and do nothing. He could tell by her face that the shock of what had happened was beginning to set in, that she was no longer able to think rationally. He wasn't sure that answering the door was the best thing to do, either, but he felt the need to act. If they stayed there and waited for whoever was at the door to go away, they might well be trapped inside the house for quite a long time. If whoever it was knew the telephone was out of order, he or she could just decide to sit outside the front door and wait.

They both stopped in the middle of the entrance hall, under the Moroccan chandelier, and stood waiting. A man's voice was demanding to know if there was anybody home. "Who is it?" Brandt whispered to Hope, as if they were children playing hide-and-seek or some guessing game.

She said, "It's Yves Brouyère," and went to the door to draw the brass bar of the safety lock.

Later on he realized that there had been some other alternatives left open to them. He could have gone out to the beach, or even the pool, and that way Brouyère would have seen him only from a distance, thus avoiding the introduction that became unavoidable once she had opened the door. But he hadn't been thinking that clearly and had felt pressured by her nervousness as well as his own. The whole thing had been a mistake, coming to the beach in front of the villa, and then swimming in when it would have been much simpler to go back to the port and return by car. But that was all hindsight and as useless as wishing that he had made himself scarce before she had opened the front door, Brandt thought, as he stood facing a tall, half-naked man dressed in khaki shorts and dirty tennis shoes.

Brouyère was in his middle fifties, to judge by his lined face. His body was that of a much younger man, slim and tanned, with the muscled legs of a runner. He had blondish-gray hair that was as bleached by the sun as the rest of him, and that gave him the look of a typical beachcomber, one of those aging French nature boys that one was apt to run into at any Mediterranean resort. He said: "Where in God's name were you? I've been ringing that bell for hours." And before Hope could answer, two dogs appeared and dashed past him into the house. They were boxers, and they didn't look particularly friendly. Brandt stood watching them as they made a quick tour of the living room, the hallway, and the kitchen.

"Your dogs, Yves," Hope said, reproachfully. "You know that Max doesn't like them coming into the house."

"Max isn't here," Brouyère replied with a grin. "But since you brought it up, he'll be arriving at ten o'clock tomorrow morning. He called around noon. He said that it would be nice if *you* picked him up at the airport instead of Juanito. For a change." Then, as if Brandt had been invisible up until that moment, he stepped forward and held out his hand. "My name's Brouyère," he said. "What did you say your name was?"

"I haven't had a chance to say anything," Brandt replied. The dogs, he noticed, had circled back, and one of them was sniffing his crotch with a wet nose.

"Hector!" Brouyère said sharply, and the dog went over to him and stood looking up at its master while a pool of spittle spread on the marble floor beside the soiled tennis shoes.

"This is David Brandt," Hope said in a low voice.

"Brent?" Brouyère asked.

"No. Brandt."

"How do you spell it?"

Brandt obliged the Frenchman, thinking that it might have been wiser if Hope had invented a name on the spur of the moment.

"Ah, yes. My name's Brouyère, Yves to you. And this is Hector and Hercules," he added, indicating the dogs, which had both come to heel beside their master's bare legs.

Brandt shook hands with the man, conscious of his own moist palm. "We've just come up from the beach," he said apologetically.

"Is that your boat?" Brouyère asked and, without waiting for an answer, turned to Hope. "I didn't see your car," he said, "but I was sure you were here, because one of the shutters was open and because the boat was out there."

Brandt thought: So he's made a tour of the house. It didn't seem possible that he had had time to walk around the back, but he had obviously done so, because he'd seen the open shutter. "We came from Banús," Brandt said. It was better that Brouyère shouldn't know too much about him. If he had seen the name of the boat and decided to check on him, it seemed preferable not to tell him where she was berthed.

"Ah, that explains the riddle," Brouyère said. "No car, nobody home. That's always been the rule in the past. But I had to deliver Max's message, you see, and I was playing golf this morning. I was going to leave a note if nobody answered." He smiled, pleased with himself, as if he were a thin Gallic Charlie Chan. "Didn't you hear the doorbell?" he asked.

"The electricity is off," Brandt said.

"Well, that happens quite frequently," Brouyère replied.

Hope was just standing there, watching them both. Her face was moist with perspiration, although there was a cool draft coming in through the open front door. "What flight is he on, Yves?" she asked after a long wait.

"The same flight as usual. He's coming from London. British Airways, I suppose. Isn't that what he always does? Arrives with thc early plane?"

"Yes. As a rule."

"He didn't say anything else. Just that he was arriving at ten, and would you go to pick him up instead of sending the servant."

"All right. I'll be there," Hope said dully. "Would you like a drink, Yves?"

"No, no. I'll be off. Have to feed the dogs," he told Brandt with a smile. "They get rambunctious if they're not fed on time. Might eat one of the neighbor's goats, or even one of his children." He turned and started off in the direction of the drive.

Hope went to the door and waved listlessly. One of the dogs came back to sniff at her legs. Brouyère called out its name. It was Hector who was the disobedient one, or the more inquisitive of the pair. Hope gave him a gentle kick with her naked foot. She obviously knew them well, Brandt thought; was an old friend of their master.

"You said nobody could get through that small space between the bars on the window."

"They did, though. They probably used an ordinary jack from a car to bend them."

"And how did they leave? The kitchen door was chained and locked."

"They went out the front. They must have had some kind of a passkey that worked on the main bolt. That's a possibility, anyway. Because if they had a duplicate set of keys, they wouldn't have broken into your bedroom."

"I don't want to talk about it anymore," she said. "I want to forget it happened for a while."

Brandt nodded. "Still, I think it's a mistake to lie to the police," he said. They were back on board *Lulubelle*, with the evening sun slanting into the wheelhouse, now that they were heading east. It warmed their bodies and dried their skin. The swim out to the boat through the surf had been surprisingly easy, as had raising the anchor and getting under way.

"Why is it a mistake?" Hope asked defiantly. "Everybody else lies to them."

"Yeah, and that's why they drag their feet so much of the time. Then it can cause trouble later on. If you tell them you didn't discover the robbery until evening, and if for one reason or another they question Brouyère, he'll tell them he saw you at the house during the afternoon."

"Why would they question *him*?"

"I don't know. He's a friend, he knows the place, and he was there the same day. He might go to them on his own when he hears about the burglary."

"You're not convincing me," she said. "Anyway, I can still maintain I didn't discover that they'd broken in until after Yves left. It might have happened that way, you know, if he'd come half an hour earlier."

"What about Max? What are you going to tell him?"

She didn't answer at once. She was standing beside him, grasping the handrail as they plowed through the easterly swells. "I don't know what I'm going to tell Max," she said after a while. "I'm certainly not going to tell him I went out alone with you on your boat. You don't know Max. He'd probably jump to the right conclusion. And I don't want to go to the police. I'd rather wait until he comes home tomorrow. I don't want to go back to the house tonight at all."

"But that's crazy," Brandt said. "Nobody waits a whole night before reporting that they've been robbed of a half a million dollars' worth of jewelry. Anyway, what's the point?"

"I want to stay with you tonight," she said, "and think the whole thing out. I have a friend who'll front for me. I'll tell Max that I was afraid to stay at the house alone, and that I spent the night with her."

"What about the revolver?"

She frowned. She had obviously forgotten about the gun. "We'll go back together before dinner and get it," she said. "I'll call my friend Phyllis Dexter from the port and warn her that I'm supposed to be staying with her. She'll cover for me."

"What are you going to do about Brouyère? He'll tell Max you weren't alone when he delivered his message. Brouyère might even remember my name. He made sure what it was by asking me to spell it."

"I can handle Yves," she said.

"You can?" Brandt asked. "I thought he was one of Max's closest friends."

"He's more a friend of mine."

"Like Lew Safire? Or even more so?"

She glanced quickly over at Brandt. "Everybody has a past," she said. "I'm sure you've had hundreds of girls. We're not kids, either one of us. All right, I had an affair with one of my husband's friends. So what? Who else would I meet? I can't pick up people in bars. I'm not built that way. As it is, I think I've behaved pretty well for most of my life."

"I'm sure you have," Brandt said. In the distance he could make out the white apartment building on the beach at Guadalmina. He felt relieved. In less than an hour they would be safely back in port.

Hope said, "If you don't want me to stay with you, just say so."

"Don't be ridiculous. Of course I do. I'm just worried, that's all. You'll have to tell your girlfriend about the robbery, and that's one more person who'll know we were together at the house. Then, too, the longer you wait before you notify the Guardia Civil, the less chance you'll have to get your stuff back."

"I'll never get it back, anyway. It's gone. I know it is." She was staring out through the spray that was collecting on the windshield as *Lulubelle* plowed through the smooth swells, which were growing bigger as the wind gained in force. Her face had taken on a determined look, as if she had made up her mind that whatever pain she had felt at that first moment of discovering her loss, she was not going to allow herself to feel it again. As he stood watching her, a passage from a book by Nelson Algren, one of his favorites, passed through his mind: "Never eat at a place called Ma's, never play poker with a man called Doc, and never go to bed with a woman who has more problems than you have." Well, that was good advice, but it was too late for him to heed it now.

He opened his eyes and stared up at the ceiling. A small lizard clung to the white plaster directly above his head, upside-down and motionless, waiting to swallow its prey, or perhaps hoping to escape the notice of an imagined assailant who might rise up from the double bed. Brandt watched the lizard with vague interest. He felt weary. He hadn't slept well, even though he and Hope had made love with almost more than their usual intensity. He had been too conscious of her body lying beside him. Then, too, he had been worried about disturbing her sleep each time he had awakened, and had lain there in a semiconscious state, with the events of the previous afternoon running through his mind like a montage in an old-fashioned movie.

It always started with the white shutter moving in the breeze, and *Lulubelle* lying at anchor too near the shore, and the shiny revolver resting on the bed cover, and Hope on her knees in the closet fighting back her tears. Then there was Brouyère standing in the doorway of the villa in his khaki shorts, and the two dogs circling the living room like the lead hounds of some mythical, Gallic dog pack, and then all at once he was standing with Hope in the darkness, and they had just returned to the villa by car and were trying to decide what to do with the gun. She wanted to keep it, not hurl it into the sea, as he had suggested, and they were arguing fiercely for the first time, their nerves frayed by the exasperating events of the afternoon. The montage always ended with their stuffing the revolver into a trunk full of old clothes that stood on a shelf at the back of the garage, and once they had locked it shut, they had driven back into town in her Mercedes.

There had been a lot of traffic, a steady stream of cars moving in the direction of Málaga, tourists for the most part, to judge by their license plates, with a few Spanish cars from Cádiz and Algeciras, most of them on their way to the port or the town for an evening out, while he and Hope hadn't even had time to shower, had merely pulled their clothes on over their bathing suits. Brandt had driven carefully, knowing that if they were stopped by the police for a minor infraction, it might complicate things more. They had put their seat belts on, which neither one of them ever did, they agreed, just to be completely within the law. "I feel as if I had just robbed a house," Hope had said as they passed through Nueva Andalucía, which had broken the tension between them.

She had relaxed then, and after he had stopped to buy her a package of cigarettes, her mood had improved even more. It was as if she had suddenly been able to put the loss of her possessions out of her mind, and coming into Marbella she had commented humorously on all of the landmarks, the neon signs of the many banks that had established branches on the main boulevard, the blue lips that turned to an inviting crimson, flashing every few seconds to advertise KISS, one of the oldest nightclubs in the town, as well as all of the expensive shops that had opened in the last few years, where you could buy antique furniture or the most modern kitchen equipment for a price that twenty years ago would have bought a villa. She had confessed to Brandt that she didn't mind the change that had come over the place, that she preferred the present-day Marbella to the small fishing village it had once been.

"I don't," he had told her. "I liked it better the way it was."

"That's because you're hopelessly nostalgic," she had replied. "You long for the past, for the California of your youth, and the Spain of Franco."

"No. Now you've gone too far," he had said with a self-conscious laugh. But there was some truth in her accusation, he thought, as they drove past the old park, with the sidewalk cafés facing it full of people having a drink before dinner, and tapas, the delicious snacks that Spaniards so enjoyed eating at all hours of the day. It made her feel hungry, she had told him, and so they had ultimately stopped at a roadside restaurant. Although the hamburgers were only remotely similar to what they were both used to, they ate everything on their plates, including the soggy French fries served on the side, and the sour pickles.

She stirred in her sleep now. Brandt glanced over at the tousled head on the pillow next to his, and the curved back in the T-shirt he had loaned her, as in their haste to leave the Villa Miramar she had forgotten to take along her nightgown and toothbrush. He reached out with his left hand and touched her shoulder. She turned over on her back.

"It can't be time yet," she said. "It's hardly light."

"That's because the shutters are closed."

"What a shame," she said. "I was having such a wonderful dream."

"What was it?"

"I don't remember, but it was nice. We were about to make love again."

"We did that last night."

"I know. But in my dream you were younger and stronger."

"Are you sure you weren't with one of your other lovers?"

She sat up and said: "Yes, I'm sure. You know, in my dream you were actually quite charming."

He laughed and got quickly out of bed. The apartment looked small and bare to him, but less depressing than it had looked on the previous night when they had arrived there. He slipped on his undershorts and went to open the shutters. It was a bright, sunshiny day. The sea was flat. The wind had died out. About two miles out a freighter was steaming steadily toward the Straits of Gibraltar, cutting through the glassy sea, leaving no wake. He stood watching it intently, until he heard the bed creak behind him, and an instant later he felt her body pressing against his back, which was still warm from yesterday's sun.

"What are you thinking about?" she asked.

"You really want to know?"

"Of course I do. That's why I asked."

"I was thinking how nice it would be if we were both on board that ship, heading for the States."

"You were?" She sounded surprised.

"Yeah. Is that so strange?"

"Well no, not really. Where do you wish we were going? To anchor in Santa Monica Bay?"

"No. No special place. Just back where we belong. To start all over again."

She put her arms around his waist and drew him closer to her. "You mean a small apartment where I do the cooking and the housework and wait for you to come home every night?" She laughed quietly. "It's too late for all that," she said. "I'm too old to put up with being poor again. And I'm a lot poorer this morning than ever before, remember?"

"We wouldn't be poverty-stricken," Brandt said. "I've got a little money saved up. Not a lot, but enough to keep us in hamburgers. Then you could sell the house, and with your half of it you'd have some mad money, in case you got pissed-off at me someday and decided to split. Some Arab would probably pay a bundle for it."

"The house belongs to Max," she said, and released her hold on him. "The house and the car and everything else."

He turned around to face her. "But you own half, you're his wife," he said, not liking the sound of the word.

"I'm not Max's wife. He already had one when we met, and he couldn't get a divorce, or didn't want to. So to make things simpler, I changed my name." She bit her lip. "We're only married in the eyes of God."

"Poor God," Brandt said.

"What do you mean by that?"

"Nothing. Just that He has to keep His eye on a lot of things I'm sure He'd rather not see." He put out his hand, and touched her cheek. "We can still take the boat," he said, "if I win *el gordo* in the lottery, or make a killing in real estate."

She said, "I won't hold my breath," and smiled. "Do you mind if I shower first?"

"No. Go ahead. I'll make breakfast. You're in a bigger hurry than I am. I don't have to be at the office until ten." He watched her move off in the direction of the bathroom. Her tanned legs looked even slimmer than they usually did, because of the T-shirt that hung down below her knees. She turned on the shower, hoping to regulate the temperature of the water before stepping behind the plastic curtain. "How long will Max be staying?" he called out to her.

"A week or two, I suppose." She pulled off the T-shirt and glanced at herself in the mirror over the wash basin. The glass was beginning to cloud over, so she had to clear a space with her right hand. Their eyes met for an instant, and she smiled at him, a tender, slightly defeated smile. "I'll call you the moment he leaves," she said, and sighed deeply. Then she took a hand towel and wrapped it around her hair.

"Don't forget," Brandt replied. "I don't like to be kept waiting." She didn't respond. Perhaps she hadn't heard him, he thought, since she had already stepped into the shower. Not that it mattered. He had noticed before that she was given to sudden silences, the result, no doubt, of living for years with someone she no longer loved. Something like that.

They had breakfast on the small terrace, as if they were starting out on a holiday. Brandt had cooked bacon and eggs for them both, and he was surprised to see that she ate almost everything he put on her plate. She didn't seem depressed. On the contrary, she appeared to be quite cheerful. She made no mention of the events of the previous day, nor did she say anything about what she felt at that moment, on the eve of Max's arrival. She ate her food and drank the coffee he poured for her, complimenting him on being well organized after only a week of occupancy. "You probably *would* make somebody a wonderful husband," she said lightheartedly.

"Or lover, even."

"I suppose so." She sat looking quietly out at the sea. There were no ships in sight; only a few small fishing boats returning to port with the night's catch. After a brief while she looked at her watch. "I must go," she said.

"The plane might be late. Don't you want to call the airport to check?"

"No, I don't think so. It'll only be more painful if we both sit here for half an hour more. The last few minutes of any goodbye are always a bore. Even if it's a temporary goodbye."

"I agree with you there."

She got up and picked up her small handbag. She was dressed in the same clothes in which she had arrived on the pier the previous afternoon, but she looked as fresh and well turned out as if she had gotten up in her own house.

"I'll take you down to your car."

"No. I'd rather you didn't." She turned to go, and then stopped suddenly. "What about your 'wheels'?" she asked. "I forgot you left the Peugeot at the port."

"I'll call a taxi. Don't worry."

"It's late now, or I'd take you."

"Please. Don't give it a thought." He followed her to the door. She looked quickly around the room before exiting to see if she had left anything behind. Then she faced him with rather a sad smile, he thought, mocking him a little, or at least that was the way it seemed to him.

"I don't expect you to wait," she said. "But I'll be pleased if you do."

"You can count on it," Brandt said. "Call me, if you can. And good luck with the police."

"Oh, the police! I don't expect anything from them. Goodbye," she added quickly, and turned her face toward him to be kissed. "*Hasta luego.*"

"Yes. *Hasta luego,*" he said, and kissed her gently on both cheeks. "And *suerte.* Lots of good luck."

"Yes, a little luck would come in handy," she replied.

After he had watched her move quickly down the hallway, he went to the kitchen window, thinking he might be able to watch her get into the Mercedes and drive off, but when he had at last managed to open it, he realized that the parking lot was not included in the view and that the last picture he would have of her for the days to come was of her walking away from him across the tiled floor without looking back.

He went out to collect the breakfast dishes from the table on the terrace that stood as a reminder of their brief conjugality, and he discovered, strangely enough, that he felt slightly relieved. There was no use denying it. He was glad to be on his own again. For how long, he wondered, and opened the hot-water tap to fill the kitchen sink.

PART TWO

He was awakened by the telephone. It was not so much the sound that aroused him as his fear of missing the call. He had closed the shutters before going to bed, so the bedroom was still in darkness, and he reached out and picked up the receiver as if it were a precious and fragile object. With any luck, he would hear Hope's slightly surly voice bidding him good morning.

But all that he heard was a coin dropping into a distant box, and then the busy signal that followed when a pay station had been vandalized. He replaced the receiver and glanced at his wrist watch. It was a quarter to seven. That ruled out Hope as a possible caller. He lay back, knowing that whoever had tried to call would probably call back. It could still turn out to be Hope, he thought; she might have quarreled with Max and left the house in a fury. Another fantasy, he realized, like the many he had indulged in since her departure. For the feeling of relief at seeing her go that morning, more than a week ago, had not lasted very long. Just one hour later, while waiting for the taxi to take him to the port to retrieve his car, he had had the unpleasant sensation of having been abandoned yet once again.

Then that same evening, by mistake, he had put on the T-shirt he had lent her, and her perfume had produced instant insomnia, and he had lain in bed, fantasizing what it would be like if she suddenly returned and told him that Max hadn't been on the plane, that he was arriving a few days later; and in his fantasy she had gotten into bed with him and they had made love. After that, sleep had been out of the question, and he had put on his bathing trunks and gone down to the beach, thinking that a moonlight swim would relax his body, and walking in the mild night air across the debris-strewn sand, he had decided that Nelson Algren's maxims were perhaps not always to be followed, that the late novelist might have been right about not eating at a place called Ma's and not playing poker with a man called Doc, but that he was all wrong about not going to bed with a woman who had more troubles than you have, because going to bed alone was an even greater mistake, especially on a balmy summer night.

It hadn't been a good week for him. He hadn't felt like going out alone, nor had he wanted to look up people he had known from his previous visits to the coast. His Spanish friends had not as yet started to arrive from Madrid, and to get involved again with some of the permanent residents had seemed like too much of an effort. They were older than he was, for the most part, and they were Pamela's friends rather than his. Seeing them would call for a great many explanations, which he was anxious to avoid, and so he had dined alone every night and had gone to bed before midnight.

Unaccustomed to such a virtuous life, he had awakened early and had gone for a run on the beach and a swim before making his breakfast, a program that made him feel virile and extraordinarily healthy, qualities that under normal circumstances would have been most welcome. But not all that good for the Lone Ranger, which was how he was beginning to think of himself. "Human beings were meant to live in pairs," he could remember Hope saying, and she was probably right, although he could also recall that she had added that being a pair was a state of mind. That didn't, however, help you fall asleep.

The telephone rang again, and the same procedure as before was repeated: the coin dropping in the box, followed by the busy signal. He shouted *"¡Digame!"* a few times above the beep-beep-beep of the busy signal before hanging up. Then he cursed the Spanish telephone company, which he had always maintained was one of the greatest arguments against government ownership, and swung his body out of bed. It couldn't be anyone very intelligent calling, or they would certainly have moved on to a different pay booth. Perhaps it was Carmen, the maid, calling to say that she wasn't coming that day, that her mother was sick, which was the usual excuse. But it was just about as unlikely that she would be up at seven o'clock in the morning as that Hope had quarreled with Max and left the Villa Miramar at the crack of dawn.

It was quite possible that she would never call, he thought as he brushed his teeth in front of the faulted mirror. There was a good chance that he had merely fulfilled her temporary physical needs, had been a one-night stand that she had allowed to go on for a few extra days. There had been girls in his past whom he had treated that way, and although he didn't believe in any theory of mystical retribution, he did believe that life had a way of paying you back in the long run. He had certainly not brought her much luck, yet she had said that she would like him to wait for her. That could have been a polite remark she had felt was necessary for her to make at that moment. That was one theory. That it had all gone by so quickly, the events following their discovery of the burglary, that she had not even had time to tell him she felt there wasn't any future for them.

There hadn't even been a convenient moment to ask any of the questions he had wanted to ask her, the basic ones. Then, too, she had changed after the moment of discovery while he had stood watching her helplessly in the doorway of the bedroom closet. After her initial outburst of tears she had apparently come to some kind of a decision about herself, a decision she had not felt like sharing with him. He, too, had realized at that instant that they were strangers, that he was an outsider who had wandered by chance with her into intimacy. He was her physical partner for the act of love, more than anything else. "Your heart doesn't seem to beat any faster until we've fucked," she had complained, a comment that had shocked him but had intrigued him, too, as it revealed a greater sensitivity than he had thought was there.

After the robbery she might well have come to the conclusion that she was now dependent on Max more than ever before, Max, who was rich and powerful and who had looked after her for many years, so that it didn't really matter whether she was his mistress or his wife.

He heard the telephone and spat out the mouthful of toothpaste, then hurriedly rinsed his mouth. Whoever was trying to call him was fairly insistent, he thought. This time there was no busy signal after the coin had dropped. Instead he recognized Freddy Weaver's nasal drawl. "Christ, what a country," Weaver said. "I've had to change telephones twice before I finally found one that worked. How the hell are you?"

"I'm fine, Freddy. How are *you*?"

"All right, I guess. Winding up a long night." He didn't sound as if he were entirely sober. He was speaking more slowly than ever, choosing his words with great care. "Somebody told me that you were back and that you were looking for me."

"Guy Manning, probably."

"No, it wasn't Guy. It was his wife, Marie, as a matter of fact. When am I going to see you?"

"Any time. In half an hour. As soon as I get dressed. Where are you calling from?"

"From Banús," Weaver said thickly. "But maybe I should get some sleep first. I'm not at my best right now."

"Well, suit yourself. I could meet you at El Faro in thirty-five minutes."

"El Faro? Where the hell's that?"

"The café opposite the old port. You remember."

"Yeah, I guess maybe I do. You think they're open?"

"Sure they are. Don't get lost."

"I'll try not to," Weaver said. He sounded drugged rather than drunk. That tallied with what Brandt had heard about him in London, that Weaver spent most of his days in a hash-filled haze.

"You want to meet later?" Brandt asked, but Weaver had hung up. The advantages of our free and enlightened society, Brandt thought. A man could study to be a lawyer, build up a good practice in Beverly Hills, make money helping the rich avoid taxes, and then suddenly drop out of the picture. What had caused the change, Brandt wondered as he spread shaving cream on his face. Boredom, probably. Weaver was about forty-five years old, had been married twice, had a couple of kids, was what was considered normal in almost every way. Yet he had always seemed to be haunted by some kind of quiet despair, a feeling of emptiness that had turned him into what Manning, with true British superiority, had labeled a drifter.

He put a new blade in his razor and began to shave his tanned face. Well, Freddy's reappearance had served one useful purpose: it would get him out of his recent habit of sitting by the telephone and waiting for Hope to call. He would have his breakfast in more stimulating surroundings and get an early start at the office. Then, later on, he would call Denise, the girl from Paramount, and ask her if she was interested in a late-afternoon cruise on the sea, and dinner, maybe, if she'd gotten rid of her pimpled boyfriend, and whatever might develop after that. He must change the monastic routine of the last ten days. He hadn't come to the sunny south to be on his own.

He found a parking space on one of the tree-lined streets of the old residential part of the town and set out on foot in the direction of the main plaza. He was conscious of the heat as he walked along in the shade of the ancient trees. Most of the small white villas he passed were shuttered, and he knew they would remain that way until the hour of the evening *paseo,* at which time their owners would open all the windows and the doors in order to let in the cool evening breeze while they sat on their verandahs and watched the young people of the town stroll by. There had always been large groups of girls and boys, moving independently of each other, with an occasional pair of lovers walking arm in arm, and Brandt wondered if things had changed since the establishment of the democracy and the new sexual freedom that had come with it.

He had grown up in a town similar to this one, a seaside community in Southern California, and he was always reminded of his early youth when he walked through these streets. The sycamore trees were the same, their roots buckling the pavement, as were the cluttered front yards of many of the houses, with an abandoned toy or tricycle lying in the driveway. What dreams he had dreamed while passing down streets such as these! A surprising majority had been sexual fantasies, he realized now, although almost as frequently as his conquests, he had visualized going off to war and coming home a great hero. Then the war in Korea had ended, and in his new dreams he was a famous foreign correspondent instead of an ace in the Air Force, returning home to rest up between assignments in the arms of whoever his dream girl had been at that moment. *La vida es un sueño, y sueños sueños son,* a Castillian poet whose name he had forgotten had written long ago. Life is a dream, and dreams are dreams.

He turned down an alleyway and went up a broad flight of cement stairs that led to the plaza. An old man in a blue workman's cap was sweeping up the debris of the previous evening, but Brandt knew that the red and black mosaics in front of the warped wooden benches would soon be covered with bits of paper and cigarette butts all over again. Spain was still a country of litterbugs, despite the recent campaign warning its citizens to be more tidy. He stopped in front of the newsstand and bought a copy of *Sur,* one of the two Málaga morning papers. Then he went on past the old Gypsy woman's stall a little farther along, noticing that nothing had changed, that she was still hanging out her wares, the hand-embroidered shawls and tablecloths that he had never seen anyone purchase. He said *"Buenos días,"* and she mumbled something in reply, probably in *caló,* the language of her people.

He couldn't blame her for not returning his greeting, and even her hostile glance didn't spoil his good mood. He was enjoying himself, making the most of the warm, as yet unpolluted air and the distinct pleasure that walking through the empty town had always given him. He had always been at his best early in the morning, optimistic by some inborn instinct, owing to his good health, no doubt. He cut across the reddish gravel, for he realized there was a good chance Weaver was waiting impatiently for him inside the café.

He glanced at the date of the newspaper in his hand: it was the Fourth of July. The realization took him back to his youth again, when the occasion was usually marked by grave lectures from his father on the dangers of firecrackers, rather than a reminder of the historic significance of the date. Still, he couldn't help looking back with fondness on those days and the old virtues of naïveté and overconfidence that seemed so appealing when seen from a distant shore. Well, he would celebrate by buying his dissolute friend an early-morning nightcap in lieu of sending a skyrocket into the summer sky.

Freddy Weaver had grown a beard. It gave his long, thin face an almost pious look, a saint by El Greco dressed in a flowered Hawaiian sport shirt instead of a ruffled white collar. He still wore his hair fairly well trimmed, and although there were traces of gray around the temples, he didn't look much older than at their last meeting. Only his skin, where it was visible, looked pastier even than it had in London. And his teeth, when he smiled, were more yellow.

"What'll you have to celebrate the founding of our country?" Brandt asked, once they were seated at the same table he had occupied with Manning only a fortnight ago.

"What are you having?"

"Coffee and toast. Does that interest you?"

"Not really." Weaver looked up at Paco, the waiter, studying the man's round face. Did he know how to make a bull shot, he asked the man in Spanish.

Paco shook his head. He had no idea what Weaver was talking about.

"I think we've come to the wrong place, if that's the only thing that'll make you happy," Brandt said.

"All right. I'll have a Bloody Mary, then."

Weaver lit a Spanish cigarette and inhaled deeply, then blew the smoke out through his nostrils. "You're looking disgustingly healthy," he said to Brandt. "But you've always been a nature boy, haven't you? As long as we've known each other. Still playing tennis and jogging, I suppose? Don't you sometimes feel you've stretched your boyhood to its natural limits?"

"Occasionally."

"Well, I envy you the result, but that's all. Not the sweating and straining. You're gainfully employed as well, Marie Manning tells me."

"Moderately gainful. Enough to pay the rent. What about you? Rumor has it you've abandoned these shores."

"Yes. I sold my house about a year ago, fell into the familiar trap of making a big profit on the place, and then being confronted with the fact that I couldn't replace it. Anyway, the town's lost its charm for me. So I moved across the water."

"Tangier?"

"No. A place called Kénitra, a little way down the coast."

Paco brought Brandt's breakfast and a slightly greenish-looking Bloody Mary. They had squeezed fresh tomatoes to make the juice, he explained, and a few hadn't been quite ripe.

Brandt raised his coffee cup and said: "Well, happy Independence Day, Freddy. It's nice to see you again."

"Absolutely. Although I wish I were the bearer of better tidings."

"What's the trouble?"

Weaver's dark eyes were on Brandt's face as he buried the rim of the glass in his graying beard. "Guy Manning's been involved in an accident," he said.

"When? What kind of accident?"

"The usual thing. He and Marie were coming back from Málaga at about nine in the evening, and a truck pulled out of a side road about five miles east of town, and Guy lost control of his car. They'd been to Málaga for one of Marie's treatments. He wasn't drunk or anything like that, nor was he speeding. The beat-up old VW he drives won't do more than about sixty."

"Where is he now?"

"In the local hospital. The one opposite the *gasolinera.* He hasn't regained consciousness."

"How did you hear about it?" Brandt asked, remembering Guy's rather unflattering remarks about Freddy Weaver. "You weren't particularly friendly, were you, you and Guy?"

"No, we weren't," Weaver said, thoughtfully. "I think Guy disapproved of me. Of the kind of life I lead. He's fairly straight, you know. Then, I chartered his boat once, and we had a few problems about that, too. Marie told me last night that you'd taken her for a month or two. That's how I got your number."

"Did you see her after the accident?"

"Yes. She called me. I was supposed to meet them for a drink at the port at ten-thirty, for a little business meeting." He shook his head. "Ironic the way things work out sometimes. Here she was, going in twice a month for cancer therapy, and she walks away from the accident with nothing more than a little scratch."

"Did she call you from the hospital?"

"That's right." He looked up quickly and frowned. "You sound as if you don't believe any of this."

"I believe you. It just seems strange to me that Guy was planning to meet you for a drink and didn't let me know. I told him I was anxious to find you."

"He probably didn't have time," Weaver said. "I only contacted him yesterday morning to see if he'd let me have his boat. Anyway, Marie called me from the clinic, and I drove over there right away. Guy was in a deep coma."

"Were you involved with Marie?" Brandt asked.

Weaver roared with laughter. "Marie Manning! You must be joking. How long has it been since you've seen her?"

"I've never met her."

"Well, if you had, you wouldn't ask that question. She's no kid. I reckon she's a couple of years older than Manning. And even thirty years ago, I don't think she was exactly a beauty. No, he was browned-off because I broke one of the conditions he put on my charter. A pal of mine had a bar in town here, and he was short of Scotch, so I took *Lulubelle* to Gib and filled her to the gunwales with White Label. One night Guy was in a local gin mill, and somebody told him that it was his own booze he was drinking, and that didn't make him particularly happy."

"I can see where he might have been less than pleased."

"Anyway, I heard that he was in trouble financially, so I thought he might not be quite so fussy now. That's why I called him. I didn't know *you'd* taken her."

"Have you been to see him at the hospital this morning?"

"Nope. Last night was about as much as I could take. I went out and got drunk after I'd spent about an hour there. Then early this morning I decided to call you."

"Just to wake me up?"

"Yeah, that's right," Weaver said, grinning. He finished his drink and made a face. "I thought I'd call my old buddy while I still had your number. I also thought you might be interested in my proposition, now that Guy's laid up." He caught Paco's eye and raised his empty glass, signaling to him that he wanted a refill.

"Are you going to have another one of those?" Brandt asked. "I was under the impression that you didn't enjoy the first one."

"I didn't," Weaver said, "but I feel certain that anything that tastes that bad must be good for my health."

Brandt laughed and shook his head. Weaver had retained his most likable quality: whether he was a prosperous lawyer or a crook out to hustle an old friend, he had a sense of humor. "What's your proposition?" Brandt asked. "I suppose you want to borrow *Lulubelle,* fill her up to the gunwales with booze in Gib, and then bring her back again. For the benefit of a friend, needless to say."

Weaver said, "That's not exactly what I had in mind, pal."

"No? Well, enlighten me a little more."

"The margin of profit on whiskey is only about a hundred percent."

"What's wrong with that?"

"Do they risk six million dollars when they make a movie just to double their money?"

"No. But they're quite often very satisfied when they do. It's better than losing the six, any day."

"I'm only planning to invest five thousand," Weaver said evenly, "and just making ten wouldn't be worth taking a risk."

Brandt said, "I understand," and finished his coffee. "You're planning to bring in a little hash, I suppose, or something equally commercial."

"Don't tell me you have scruples," Weaver said, using the same tone of voice Richard Grey had used when he had asked him if he had any objections to Arab money. Both had had the same disdainful expression on their faces, it occurred to Brandt, as if taking any kind of moral stand was outlandishly old-fashioned. "Smoking pot's no worse than having a drink," Weaver added.

"I know. I've heard all that crap. Pot's easier on the liver, and it makes people friendly. What it does to your brain, nobody knows. Or cares, I guess. In any event, my scruples don't stand in the way. Not as far as smoking pot goes." Paco had come over to the table with Weaver's refill. It had a healthier color: orange instead of green. Brandt waited until he had left before continuing. "However, when it comes to peddling the stuff, I'm a little less apathetic." He didn't want to sound stuffy or righteous, so he chose his words more carefully than usual. "You see, in a fairly long life I've never really stepped outside the law," he went on. "I'm not boasting when I say that. It's just always seemed to me that unless you're really desperate, it's so much simpler to play it straight. Do you know what I mean?"

"I certainly do," Weaver said amiably. "You're comfortably off, money's not that important to you, so why take a chance."

"Well, I'm not *comfortably off,*" Brandt said, disregarding the heavy overtone of sarcasm in Weaver's voice. "But I have enough to keep me going for a while, and I don't want to blow it all on trying to get out of a Spanish jail. Lawyers' fees are high, even here. Besides, I have a lot of friends in this country, who, though they probably smoke a *porro* every once in a while, would think it a little strange that I'd decided to make it as a pusher."

"Okay," Weaver said. "I just thought I'd ask. Guy would probably have turned me down a lot less politely. And he needs the pesetas more than you do."

"He certainly does, the poor bastard," Brandt said.

Weaver lit a cigarette and said, "Well, there are other boats in the harbor."

"There are indeed." He would go to the hospital to see Marie Manning on his way to the office, Brandt thought. He watched Weaver as he sipped his drink, and tried not to appear impatient. His friend had changed; there was no doubt about that. He was as affable as he had always been, but there was an air of detachment about him, as if his mind were roaming far ahead of his words while he was talking.

"Tell me about your job," he said now, after he had wiped his beard clean with the back of his hand. "Is it enjoyable? Do you stand a chance to make some serious bread? They tell me that the property business on this coast is booming again. So you've come back at just the right time."

"I'll let you know how things are going in a month or two," Brandt replied. "I'm not into property yet."

"Well, I hope to see you a lot sooner than that. We might have dinner together some night."

"Call me," Brandt said. "I'm always home in the evening around nine o'clock. Or early in the morning."

He went back to his car, feeling not quite as pleased to be out in the cool, early morning. There was something about Weaver's sarcastic tone of voice that stuck in his craw, that canceled out any possible replay of his earlier nostalgia. It seemed as if his youth was a dream he had left behind a long time ago. He drove through the tangle of one-way streets until he was back on the main highway. Five minutes later he arrived at the clinic. It was just after eight-thirty, yet there was no space in the parking lot in front of the main entrance, so he turned down the narrow street on the far side of the small gray building and left his car on the quay of the fishermen's port. There was no sign of life in any of the sheds facing the battered sea wall, some of which served as repair shops for the town's fishing fleet.

There were quite a few people waiting outside the front entrance, and he went past them, knowing that as a foreigner he would probably be allowed in, although visiting hours, the sign on the glass door read, did not begin until ten o'clock. The young man behind the reception desk seemed to have no record of a patient named Manning, and sent him to the main office at the end of a narrow, littered hallway, where he was told to go to the third floor and ask for the nurse in charge of the emergency ward. But the nurse, when he finally located her, was in the midst of a heated conversation on the telephone. From what he could make out by listening to her excited Spanish, she was trying unsuccessfully to get a doctor to come up and look at a patient who was *gravísimo,* which probably meant that he was dying.

Then he saw Marie Manning seated at a window not more than fifteen feet away. He knew at once that it was she, because she looked so unmistakably English, a thin woman in a print dress, with gray hair and spectacles. She was perched on a metal folding chair, staring dejectedly out at the gray sea and the distant sweep of the coastline, like a prisoner in a foreign jail, longing for the green hills of home. He went over to her, and said: "I'm David Brandt. Freddy Weaver told me the bad news."

She looked up at him with her faded blue eyes. She was smoking an English cigarette, the smell of which was pungently foreign, an aroma that didn't belong in this place any more than she did. "It's very nice of you to have come," she said. "Guy was talking about you just the other day."

"Is there anything I can do?" Brandt asked.

She shook her head. "I don't think so. I don't think there's anything anyone can do. He still hasn't regained consciousness."

"What do the doctors say?"

"That we have to wait, that's all. They can't tell if there's any serious brain damage until he comes to. He's being fed intravenously." She took a crumpled handkerchief out of the small straw basket in her lap and blew her nose. "There is one thing you might be able to help me with," she added. "If you have time, that is, later this afternoon, perhaps you could come to the police with me. They're insisting I make a report, and I don't speak the language all that well. Not that there's a lot I can tell them. I was asleep when it happened. I think a truck pulled out of a side road, but I'm not even certain of that." She was grasping the crumpled handkerchief with such force that the veins stood out on her hand.

Brandt said: "Of course I'll go with you. Do you want me to pick you up here?"

"That would be very kind. At five o'clock?"

He nodded and touched her bony shoulder, thinking of Weaver's raucous laughter when he had suggested that Manning's dislike of him had perhaps been caused by jealousy. "Guy will be all right," he said, trying to sound as if he believed what he was saying. "I know he will."

She looked up at him and tried to smile, but she didn't quite bring it off. "If he would only open his eyes," she said. "I can't bear to see him like this. In all the years we've been married, he's never been ill . . . not even for a day. *I* was always the problem child."

Brandt wanted to tell her to be brave, but he knew she was being as brave as was humanly possible. "I'll see you at five," he said, and went down the hallway past the nurse in the starched white uniform, who was still talking on the telephone.

As he stepped out into the bright sunlight, he almost ran into Freddy Weaver. "Ah, we meet again," Weaver said. "Have you been up to see Marie?"

"Yes. She's on the third floor, sitting outside his room."

"Still no change?"

"No. He hasn't regained consciousness yet."

"Poor bastard." Weaver sighed and rubbed his beard. "Well, there's no use my bugging his wife. I'll call by later."

It occurred to Brandt that Weaver had perhaps not given up hope on getting his hands on *Lulubelle*. And if ever Marie Manning was apt to listen to his kind of proposition, now was the time. Yet it might also be that he was truly concerned, although that seemed fairly unlikely. Brandt jerked his head in the direction of the building behind them. "Not a good place to be on the critical list," he said.

"There are worse," Weaver replied. "They've got some good doctors here. And he probably carried the local medical insurance."

"I hope he did," Brandt said, and glanced at his watch. It was almost nine-thirty. So much for getting up early and having breakfast with an old friend. He felt as if he needed a shower, but it was too late to go back to his apartment and start the day all over again. What would happen to Marie Manning, he wondered, if Guy were to die or be crippled for life? She was a cancer patient, had no money, and didn't even speak the language of the country. Hope Clarendon's problems suddenly seemed fairly insignificant. She was still residing in a comfortable house, had a rich pseudo-husband and a lover. As of last week.

"You don't have a match, do you?" Weaver asked. He had stuck a cigarette in his mouth and was searching his shirt and trouser pockets without success.

"You're lucky. Today I happen to have some." He had started carrying matches for Hope's benefit, knowing that she often misplaced her lighter. "Keep them," he told Weaver.

"You know, my proposition isn't nearly as hairy as it sounds," Weaver said, inhaling deeply. He blew a cloud of smoke out through his nostrils. It hovered for an instant in the warm summer air. "They drop the stuff near a reef off San Pedro and mark it with a buoy. I need a boat just to make the pickup."

"And bring it in to the beach, right?"

"No. Most of the time we just go out a little ways and transfer our cargo to a fishing boat. The risk is minimal. And the rewards . . ." He grinned happily. "You'll have to sell a lot of villas to make that kind of loot."

Brandt said: "Don't try to tempt me, Freddy. Anyway, if it's that easy, you should have no trouble finding a taker."

"That's true enough. Only the boys I usually work with have two of their launches tied up with engine trouble."

"Well, my charter runs out in three and a half weeks. Maybe by that time Guy'll be on the mend, and you can approach him again. And if not, there's always Marie. Though I don't think she's quite the type to take on that kind of a job. Maybe if she's desperate enough . . ."

"Yeah, you never know," Weaver said, disregarding the sarcasm in Brandt's voice. "Let's keep in touch," he added, and started off in the direction of the gasoline station on the other side of the highway. Brandt watched him as he waited for a lull in the traffic and then ran quickly across the four lanes of asphalt. For a man who had been up all night drinking, he moved with surprising agility, especially over the last thirty feet, which he sprinted, as a BMW with French license plates was approaching at high speed. Once he had made it, he trotted over to an old Seat station wagon parked at the far end of the filling station. He turned to wave after he had unlocked the door on the driver's side, and a little hesitantly Brandt waved back.

Of all the people he had known on the coast in the early days, Brandt thought as he watched Weaver drive off, he was the last person he would have predicted would wind up smuggling drugs. He had always seemed much too intelligent to get involved in anything that foolish. Because in the end he would certainly get caught.

Had he been too complacent with his friend, Brandt wondered. Although a lecture on the fact that crime doesn't pay would undoubtedly have been met with disdainful laughter. Weaver was no misguided teen-ager. He was a grown man who knew what he was doing. And he was probably too deeply involved at this point to listen to anyone. Brandt shook his head and walked slowly past the front of the clinic, then turned down the unpaved section of road leading to the fishermen's port. As it always did, the view of the sea, glistening in the morning sun, made him feel better. It had been a fairly disastrous morning so far, one of the worst Fourth of July mornings in living memory, he reckoned. A wavering scrawl of a graffito on the back of a fisherman's shed caught his eye. *No à Otan,* it read. "U.S. Go Home!" Maybe he'd better plan to do just that, Brandt thought.

Except for Esmeralda, the overweight receptionist, no one had arrived at the office. Brandt asked her if there had been any calls, and she shook her head, not bothering to look up from filing her nails. He went into the men's lavatory and washed his face and hands, making a mental note to bring a towel from his apartment. The local paper towels were not very satisfactory. Then, once he was seated at his desk, he turned to one of the back pages of the newspaper he had bought to check his lottery tickets against the long array of winning numbers published in a box.

He had not won, but the last digit on his ticket tallied with the winning number, which meant he would be reimbursed his original investment, minus the salesman's commission. His well-oiled return to the States would have to wait, he told himself as the telephone rang. He picked it up eagerly, thinking that it might be Hope, but it was only Penny, his favorite Antipodean, as he called her to her pretended annoyance. "I have a question for you," she said.

"Shoot. It's your five pesetas."

"Do you actually sleep in your office?"

"Only during the day. At night I pace the floor of my lonely digs, waiting for you to call."

"Don't you think, if anything, you should call me?" she asked coyly.

"I didn't know you were on the telephone. What's the number?"

"I'll have to think about whether I should give it to you. It might be bad for my career."

"With the company?"

"No. Even beyond that."

"Well, let me know what you decide."

"All right. I will. By the way, the boss said for you not to make a luncheon date. He's buying today. Wants to introduce you to your new associate."

"What a shame. I was going to ask you to accompany me to the port."

"I'll take a rain check," Penny said cheerfully. "So save your pesetas."

The girl had a good sense of humor, as well as a good figure. How much simpler his life would be, he thought, if he had devoted himself to amusing her instead of Ms. Clarendon. Well, it was not too late to start, although she probably lived with a Spanish boyfriend well outside the high-rent belt, in Benávis or Coin, or some small whitewashed village up in the sierra.

"When do you expect the noble Richard?" he asked.

"Oh, he should be rolling in any time now, unless some *drongo* had him out late in the local disco."

"Well, when he does, tell him I'm standing by for further orders."

"Right. Will do."

Australians were cheerful people, on the whole, especially the young ones like Penny, Brandt thought. She certainly brightened up the office, which, after Amir's departure less than a week ago, needed brightening, as far as Brandt was concerned. His Iranian friend and benefactor had been quite pleased to be returning to London and his pretty English wife, rain or no rain. "There are far too many Moslems around here," he had told Brandt, with a sly grin. His going had not only decreased the congeniality of the place, but had been bad for Brandt's tennis, because he had been reduced to playing singles with an athletic German lady who barely perspired while beating him with monotonous regularity.

Penny rang back to report that she had heard from Richard Grey and that he wouldn't be in until a quarter after twelve. He hadn't been detained in one of the "local fleshpots," she added, but had been working late closing an important deal. "Just go on doing what you're doing" had been his message for the staff.

Brandt folded up his newspaper. In that one regard, the property business seemed to resemble the movies. The important conferences and the big deals usually took place in the late afternoon or in the early evening, which was why the top brass, with a few exceptions, used to arrive late in the morning and stay on until seven or eight o'clock at night. He could remember having to hang around the offices of the various executives at Warner's, waiting for some important transaction to be completed so that he could prepare his copy of the announcement and telephone it in to beat the deadline of the morning papers and the "trades," *Variety* and the *Hollywood Reporter,* as well as Joyce Haber and Sheila Graham, the two most feared witches of the press.

A wave of nostalgia swept over Brandt as he sat staring down at his lifeless typewriter. That, too, he knew, was a sign of approaching age, the constant longing for a time that was past and that, actually, he enjoyed only in retrospect. He remembered how much he had disliked his job at the studio. The gray concrete buildings had looked like a prison to him on most mornings, a first impression that was confirmed regularly by the gray-haired cop behind the reception desk, whose job it was to write down the hour of arrival of all employees, since someone in the front office regularly checked on his minions' punctuality. That had been one of the reasons he had quit, had given up a pension, as well as possible promotion to a higher station, such as the West Coast head of publicity.

He had gotten a job almost at once with an independent production company, thinking that at last he would be able to cross over to the creative side of the business. Making films abroad was in vogue in those days, mainly because the law provided that an American citizen who stayed out of the country seventeen out of eighteen months would not be required to pay tax on his earned income. Brandt had been sent to Europe as a publicity man, with the promise that he would soon be transferred to active film-making, as a unit manager. And he had never regretted his decision. Hanging around Los Angeles would definitely not have been as instructive or amusing. Although as far as making a career went, it had probably been a mistake.

But at least he had lived in Paris and London and Madrid. And he had even been able to save some money, not millions of dollars like the big stars and directors, but more than he would have saved had he stayed home. As long as he didn't wind up like Freddy

Weaver, he thought, and inserted a sheet of Sun and Sea Realty stationery in the typewriter in front of him. While waiting for Grey he would write a letter to his old boss on the West Coast, a letter he had been meaning to write for weeks. He had heard in London that the man had had a heart attack at the age of sixty-one. That, too, was an American phenomenon. You burned out faster in the smog-ridden haze of Tinseltown, or so he had always been led to believe.

He was just finishing it when Penny opened the door of his cubicle and smiled at him with very white, even teeth, framed in a scarlet mouth. "Richard is here, and beckons."

"That's a shame. I was just catching up on my personal correspondence. What about your telephone number?"

"Later," she said. "Good things are worth waiting for."

He followed her small round behind down the hallway and went through the door she held open for him. There was a handsome young woman seated to one side of Grey's desk, one of those Latin beauties who had always made him wonder why blondes were so much appreciated in this part of the world. She was elegantly dressed in navy blue slacks and an off-white silk shirt, with the usual expensive gold watch on her wrist and the various golden chains and medals, which made him think regretfully of Hope.

The young woman smiled when Grey introduced them, and said, "We have met," in only slightly accented English. "It was at my father's house in Madrid," she added, "a few years ago."

"Then you were still a child," Brandt said, which pleased the young woman and made her laugh.

"Consuela is going to work with us," Grey explained. "Unfortunately, for only a couple of weeks. That's why I wanted you to meet her. She's going to give us a helping hand with our party. See to it that we invite the right people. And that they come."

"I work now, because later my husband arrives with the children," Consuela said, pronouncing the words very carefully as she had no doubt been taught to do by an English nanny.

"David is in charge of our press relations," Grey explained. "You can go over the guest list with him. He'll see to it that the invitations are printed and mailed."

Consuela nodded and said: "Very well. It is the first time I do this kind of work." She went on in her own language to Brandt, "You speak Spanish, don't you, David?"

"I defend myself."

"No. You speak very well."

She turned to Grey and asked if she could use the telephone to call her home. Grey pushed a button on his desk, and Penny appeared. He asked her to take the señora to an adjoining office.

"I approve of your taste," Brandt told Grey once the door had closed behind the two women.

"Yes, she's a pretty girl," Grey said drily. "And she's costing us a lot of money, so don't hesitate to put her to work. Her father is a *conde* or a *marqués.* One of the few who doesn't use his title."

"Is she rich?"

"Of course. That's why she's expensive. She doesn't have to work. She's doing it for fun and pocket money." He returned to the leather chair behind his desk. "Have you thought some more about staying on with us?" he asked, glancing up at Brandt. "You could move into sales as well as handling our publicity. It's not a bad life down here. Not all that inspiring culturally, but you can probably put up with that for a year or two. There's money to be made, unless the country goes sour, and I don't think it will for a while."

"I was hoping to go back to California someday," Brandt said. "But there's no hurry."

Richard Grey made a face. "California," he said. "I suppose that's only natural, because that's where you were raised. But I wonder if you'd be happy there after living in Europe. One of our silent partners, Max Clarendon, has just come back from L.A., and he says it's pretty awful. All they talk about out there is money. And sex, of course, if there's time. And cars. A plastic society."

Brandt asked, "What's he like, Max Clarendon?"

Grey chuckled maliciously. "Max? I'm surprised you've never met him. What's he like? Well, he's a shark. One of the big ones. Of course, I'm delighted that he's put in with us, but he's not the kind of chap I'd like to be working for, if you know what I mean. Intelligent. Ruthless. Ice-cold. His father made a small fortune before the war in aviation. He built the planes; he didn't fly them. Then young Max took over and improved the family holdings. He didn't make a lot of friends while doing so, had to push a few people out of the way to get there. He has a wife back in England and a girlfriend out here, an American woman, I believe. She took his name, to make things look better. That's one of the worst-kept secrets on the coast. I don't know how Max gets away with it, but he does. If you're rich enough, I suppose you can make your own rules."

Penny opened the door and readmitted the beautiful Consuela. She thanked Grey for letting her use the telephone, adding that her call had been to Madrid and that she had been brief.

"I think the company can afford it," Grey said. He turned to Brandt. "I thought it would be nice if we took Consuela to lunch at our hotel," he continued. "One of our Lebanese directors will probably join us. If you're free, that is," he added, turning to Consuela.

She said, "Of course. I am ready to work," and smiled dazzlingly at them all.

The Lebanese director's name was Tobias Tabbal, the Tobias probably chosen by a hopeful mother in Beirut, Brandt reckoned, in case her son grew up to be tall and handsome and became a movie star like Robert Redford. But the euphonic choice of a Christian name had been all for nothing. Tobias Tabbal was small and homely, and to make matters worse, wore a sleeveless undershirt beneath his silk sport shirt, which made Consuela mutter "*¡Qué horror!*" to Brandt. A visible singlet was apparently an assault on her aesthetic sensibilities. But Tobias Tabbal was no fool, it soon turned out. Far from it.

They sat on the terrace of the new Hotel Colón under a green awning, with two waiters and a maître d'hôtel in constant attendance. The presence of Grey, Tabbal, and Consuela Figueras seemed enough to inspire the staff to almost superhuman efforts. It reminded Brandt of the old days in San Sebastián whenever Franco had attended a *corrida.* Whatever talent and valor the bullfighters in the ring may have had, they always exceeded themselves when they saw the Generalísimo and his wife in the flag-draped box at the top of the old bull ring. In the presence of the new directors of the hotel and their guests, the headwaiter and his assistants were making a similar effort.

Tabbal had ordered as a first course a special dish that was made of cucumbers in yoghurt, sprinkled with dried herbs. It was a Lebanese appetizer, he explained, and perfect for the hot weather. This was followed by grilled sole served with boiled new potatoes, and a white Marqués de Riscal that was perfectly chilled. Brandt couldn't help thinking of Marie Manning seated in the hallway of the clinic, waiting for her husband to regain consciousness. He should have stayed with her, he thought guiltily, but then this sort of luncheon was part of his job, although his presence there was certainly not required, since the conversation so far had had little to do with business. Nor did it seem likely that it would ever return to any subject more serious than the gossip of the coast. Consuela was explaining that the rich Arabs who had bought some of the big houses were all known by the names of the erstwhile owners, or at least were referred to in that way by her friends: the Bonfantis' Arab, the Lewises' Arab, or the Garcías' Arab.

Grey laughed politely, as did Tabbal, but they seemed to be only mildly amused. "You think they're bad for the coast?" Grey asked.

"I don't know," Consuela replied. "Bad for the *ambiente,* perhaps; the atmosphere."

"They keep pretty much to themselves," Tabbal said. "And they're pumping in a lot of money. Foreign capital is what Spain needs. And maybe foreign management. I'll give you an example. When we took over this hotel, there were seventeen independent lawsuits being brought by the various employees' unions and guilds. We settled them all, just by giving way here and there. Before, the employers were only interested in fighting the unions, because they were all on the extreme political right, and the unions were all dominated by the left. They were interested in the political struggle, not in doing business. That was bad for the country, too."

"Yes, I'm sure," Consuela said guardedly. "But it is that way in all of Spain even now."

"Except in Catalonia," Tabbal remarked. "There, people are still interested in making money."

"Yes. Perhaps," the girl said politely, and picked at her grilled sole. "My husband says Europe is finished. One must go to America to live, to the United States."

"They have other problems there," Grey said drily. "Crime. Taxes. I'm going to hang on in Europe as long as I can. Salt away a few dollars for when the bad day comes, and enjoy it here for as long as it lasts." He was echoing Hope's sentiments, Brandt thought, and probably Max's, the shark.

"We can't all run away," Tabbal said. "There's not enough room in Beverly Hills *or* in New York. Don't you agree, Mr. Brandt?"

Grey said, "Don't ask him, he's already packing his bags," and laughed.

"Only on certain days," Brandt replied. "I change my mind about going back every week or two."

"What does it depend on?" Grey asked. "Your love life?"

"No, the traffic," Brandt said, and found himself thinking of the Mannings again. What would their reaction be to this kind of a conversation, he wondered. Ironically, Manning, with his Tory convictions, would probably have agreed that it was time to leave Europe. He had left England when the Socialists had come to power, although his luck had changed radically since. Luck determined most things in life, but there were people who still felt that you made your own good fortune. The lucky ones, usually, Brandt thought, not the ones waiting in a littered hallway to hear whether the verdict was life or death.

When coffee arrived, the conversation changed to the topic of where it was best to raise one's children, and Grey was able to score heavily against Consuela. "I still think dear old battered Britain is not a bad place to raise kids," he said. "Beverly Hills would certainly not be my choice. Or New York. Most of my friends there give their children 'mugging money' in case they're attacked on their way to school."

"I cannot believe it," Consuela said.

"I assure you it's true, dear lady."

"I went to school in California," Tabbal said, "and it wasn't like that."

"That's because you were driven to school in your dad's bulletproofed Cadillac," Grey told him. "Anyway, you went to Stanford, which is a little different. And before that you were at Le Rosay, if I'm not mistaken, so your opinion on this subject is not relevant."

"It is decided," Consuela said with a smile. "We go to Chile or Argentina."

"Or South Africa," Grey put in, sarcastically. "There's a country with a great future for you!"

"No, I do not like the blacks," the young woman said emphatically.

Brandt winced. How could such an attractive young woman have such ugly prejudices, he wondered. Although that was to be expected. The liberal and progressive ladies were usually fairly dowdy, with a few notable exceptions. He remembered a joke he had heard in Madrid a couple of years ago: that the Reds, when they came to power, would kill all of the men of the right and all the women of the left. "How do you feel about the Jews and the Irish?" he asked Consuela.

"Please? I do not understand," she said, looking slightly offended. "The Jews and the Irish? I have nothing against them."

"That's very tolerant of you," Grey put in.

Yet she made a point of getting into Brandt's car when it came time to drive back to the office. Once they were on the main road he asked her why she had politely refused Tabbal's offer of a lift. She blushed, and Brandt temporarily forgave her her racism. "I know you better, or I have known you longer," she said.

Brandt laughed. "I met you when you were a young girl," he told her. "That hardly makes for an intimate friendship."

"*Claro,* but you know everyone I know in Madrid. And I am sure you are a gentleman."

"So is Richard. And Tabbal has almost Victorian manners. I don't think either one of them would rape you."

"Of course. I know that. But I find you more *simpático.* Richard is very hard. Cynical. And Tobias sweats too much. We are going to work together, too, and so we must become friends."

The liberated Spanish woman, Brandt thought, afraid to ride in the same car with her boss and a man with slightly darker skin. "I'm not as undangerous as I look," he said. "I also like blacks, or at least I don't think they're any different from us, and although my father wasn't a Jew, he hated Hitler and Mussolini. He didn't think much of Franco, either," he added with a grin.

"Yes. I know that. Many Americans feel that way. Even *my* father was against Franco in the beginning." She paused for a moment. "My father is here now," she continued. "Perhaps if you are free for dinner tomorrow night you could dine with us?"

"I'd be delighted," Brandt said. The unpleasant alternative was another evening alone in his apartment.

"At ten o'clock? You could pick me up at the Marbella Club?"

Brandt nodded. A few hundred yards ahead he saw a tow truck pulling the wreck of an old Volkswagen out of a gulley on the left, and he wondered if that was Manning's car. But he couldn't see the license plates. If it was Manning's car, both he and Marie were lucky to be alive, he reckoned.

"At this time of the year," Consuela was saying, "there are never enough men on the coast. The women have started to arrive with their children, but their husbands are still working in Madrid."

"I hope they stay there forever," Brandt said.

"Not my husband, *por favor,*" Consuela replied. "He is very nice. You will see. You will be good friends."

With Marie Manning beside him, he drove up the main street of San Pedro de Alcántara. It was the hottest time of the day, three o'clock Greenwich time, Brandt calculated, so the sun was directly overhead. There was no shade. The sidewalk cafés were empty, and the shops closed. He turned into the town square. The big, squat, ochre-colored church stood facing the old whitewashed buildings like a mulatto queen with albino courtiers. The spindly palm trees that stood at uneven intervals along the sidewalk were the spear-carriers, the *garde de corps* of her majesty, he thought, the heat and the wine at lunch having their effect on his brain.

"Will the office of the Guardia Civil be open?" Marie Manning asked.

"I should think so. They can't depend on every crook in town taking a siesta."

"They might, you know."

It was the first time Brandt had seen her smile, and suddenly he could guess what she must have looked like as a young girl, very blond and slight, with the birdlike quality that he had often noticed in young English girls.

He said: "I forgot to give you my check this morning for chartering your boat. Here it is." She thanked him and slipped it into her purse. Then he added, "I also forgot to ask you back at the clinic if there were any witnesses to the accident. Did anyone stop to help?"

"Oh yes. I was asleep when it happened. I woke up, and we were in a ditch, and petrol was leaking down on my legs. I couldn't really move at first. Then some men appeared and pulled us both out of the door on the driver's side. Guy was unconscious. He wasn't bleeding, but his eyes were shut, just as they are now."

"Did you get the names of any of the people who helped? The police are sure to ask you that."

"I didn't, I'm afraid. They were all talking excitedly in Spanish, and I really wasn't paying any attention to any of *them.* I was only concerned with getting Guy to a hospital. I was a bit dazed, too."

Brandt parked in the shade of a pepper tree facing the building. *Todo por la Patria* was written in dark green ceramic letters above the doorway. Everything for the fatherland. Slogans of a simpler era, before robbery and theft had become the national pastime. Freddy Weaver's bearded face came floating into his mind. How soon would his friend be led through this archway, or one like it, he wondered, as he went around to the other side of the Peugeot to open the door for Mrs. Manning.

"Well, let's go inside and at least comply with the law," he said, "though I don't think it's going to help much."

There was a photograph of the King on the wall, in olive-drab. Below it a man in darkish green fatigues was seated at a desk, busily filling out a form on the typewriter. He wore a dark shirt and a tie, as well as the kind of peaked cap the Afrika Corps had worn in World War II. He indicated a row of empty chairs standing against the wall in front of him, and Marie Manning sat down, but Brandt remained on his feet, thinking that his refusal to be seated might hurry things along. Finally, when there was a pause in the typing, he explained the reason for their presence.

"Where did the accident take place?" the man asked.

"Between Fuengirola and Marbella."

"Was anyone injured?"

"Yes. This lady's husband."

"Then if the police didn't arrive on the scene, you should make a report to the Traffic Department of the Guardia Civil in Fuengirola or Marbella."

The man was polite but uninterested. He continued his typing while Brandt translated the conversation for Marie Manning. "I should have known that this wasn't the right place," he added. "Who told you to come here?"

"I thought that's what they said at the hospital. I'm so sorry to have wasted your time."

"It doesn't matter." He put out his hand to help Marie Manning to her feet. As he did so, a door opened behind the typist, and Hope Clarendon stepped into the room. Their eyes met, and she stopped. She looked frightened. Then she saw Marie Manning, and that seemed to help her regain her poise. She turned, as if waiting for someone who was to follow her, and Max Clarendon appeared; directly behind him Yves Brouyère.

Brandt recognized Max from the photograph he had seen of him in the bedroom of the Villa Miramar, saw that he was dressed in a similar navy blue polo shirt with short sleeves that showed off his muscular arms. He put his hand under Hope's forearm and guided her on her way. Brouyère was still saying something to someone inside the office from which they had just exited, and he was not conscious at first of Brandt's presence. By the time he, too, had stepped into the room, Hope had disappeared, trailing behind her a waft of her familiar perfume.

Max Clarendon said, "Excuse us," as he went by, and smiled perfunctorily. He passed directly in front of Marie Manning, to whom his words were obviously addressed, his back to Brandt for one brief second. By the time it was Brouyère's turn to move past, Marie Manning was on her feet, looking puzzled, as the Frenchman moved through the narrow gap. He stopped at the door and glanced back. He was grinning, and as his eyes met Brandt's, he winked broadly. There was no mistaking his facial expression. He was enjoying himself hugely.

"I hope it's not a bore for you to take me back to the clinic," Marie Manning was saying. "I feel such a fool for having caused you all this trouble."

Brandt said, "Not to worry." The poor woman would never be

able to guess just how much trouble she had caused, he thought, and neither could he, for that matter. But it obviously would have been better if they had not gone to San Pedro de Alcántara that afternoon.

How many times, he wondered, had Hope's face appeared before him during the last twenty-eight hours? It seemed to him that he had become incapable of thinking of anyone else. Even now, as he drove toward the town through the early-evening darkness on his way to pick up Consuela, he found himself thinking of her, as if she were the heroine in an old-fashioned movie, "the kind they didn't make anymore." Because infatuation was definitely a thing of the past, belonged to the days of *The Blue Angel.* Aging professors merely turned in other directions once they had been rejected by a seductive siren, which thought made him regret once more that he hadn't called Denise Sorel, or Penny, who had left her telephone number in the roller of his typewriter, where he had found it when he had dropped by the office for his messages on the way to the tennis club. She had typed "In case of emergency" across the top of the scrap of paper, either as a wry joke or as a safety measure, just in case Richard Grey or someone else happened to look into Brandt's cubicle.

He drove past the clinic, and for a second his mind was diverted to the small room on the third floor, where Guy Manning was still lying in a coma. Brandt had called earlier in the evening and had been told that there was no change in the condition of the patient, that Manning was no worse and no better. He hadn't asked to speak to Marie, because there was nothing he could say to her, and so he had left his name just to show that he hadn't forgotten his friend. He would drop by there the next morning, or maybe even later on that night, if the party at Consuela's father's house didn't go on too long.

Then, as he sat waiting for the first traffic light on the edge of the town to turn green, his mind returned to the office of the Guardia Civil in San Pedro. Hope might at least have smiled, he thought once again. One often smiled at strangers, in elevators or at traffic signals. But she had probably been afraid that he would speak to her. Yet knowing that Yves Brouyère was following close on Max's heels should have made her realize that it would be much better to stop and say hello, as later she could easily have explained that they had met at a cocktail party or a luncheon. She could even have said that she had gone out in his boat, accompanied by Phyllis Dexter, her friend, which would certainly have been a small lie compared to saying that Hope had spent the night with her after the robbery. But Hope had obviously been too startled to reason it all out that quickly, which made Brandt think she was not all that experienced in adultery, after all. That was the one positive deduction he arrived at, long after the fact.

The car behind him flashed its lights, and he saw that the signal had changed. It was a Mercedes with a green Saudi license plate, he noticed once he had pulled over into the right lane. An Arab prince, no doubt, he thought when a dark face scowled at him as the car roared past, hurrying to an appointment with one of the girls from Chez Madame Claude, or on his way to the port to seek out some of the local talent. But he caught up with the Mercedes again after a few kilometers, because the Arab was turning off into the Marbella Club, too. However, the prince, or whoever it was, drove on down to the Beach Club, while Brandt turned into the entrance drive of the hotel. He asked the concièrge to call Consuela's apartment, and was surprised to see her appear only a few minutes later.

She was dressed in black silk trousers and a scarlet blouse, with a black shawl thrown over her shoulders. She looked too rich for his rented Peugeot, and he told her so.

She laughed and said, "The car is not so important in Spain as the driver."

"The driver is poor, too," he said. "Is this a big party we're going to?" he asked her.

"At my father's house you can never be sure. Sometimes there are ten people, sometimes forty. But why are we speaking English? You speak Spanish perfectly."

"I wish I did. I make a lot of mistakes. The trouble here is that nobody corrects you."

"I'll correct you," she said, "and that way you will learn. But you have to correct my English. Is my accent terrible?"

"No, I like it." He made no reference to her sounding occasionally like a wetback. He didn't know her well enough for that kind of a joke, and she probably had no idea what a wetback was.

She chattered on, friendly but not flirtatious. She told him about her children and the new house her husband had purchased lately in Madrid. Brandt was astonished once again at how insulated the life of her class still was, how as yet untouched by the change that had come to the country. How to keep amused was still her main problem. Summers she spent on the coast, with intermittent visits to Ibiza, which she told him was amusing in small doses. In the winter she went skiing in Gstaad, and in the spring there was the *feria* in Jerez, and the Rocio. They didn't go to Sevilla for the *feria* anymore, because it had changed so much, had been spoiled by politics, like everything else.

"Not a bad life," Brandt found himself saying once again.

"Yes. But how long will it go on? That is why I have decided to work and make money. You never know what will happen someday. 'Someday' is correct?"

"Absolutely."

She indicated the turnoff that led to her father's *finca.* It was the same road with the rusting green street lamps he had taken to Safire's house more than two weeks ago. He drove on in a kind of daze past the arrow marked Las Golondrinas, until the girl interrupted his thoughts by warning him that the next turning to the right was the one they should take. He noticed that there were quite a few lights on at the Safires', so they had apparently returned from Madrid. That was another call he must make the next day, he told himself. It was not a good idea to neglect old friends, and he did owe Safire something for introducing him to Hope Clarendon, although what his debt consisted of, he didn't as yet know.

They turned to the left, and the road followed a broad ridge line that ultimately faced the distant sea. "Look! The moon!" Consuela said, pointing to the broad golden river of moonlight on the water. "It is beautiful, no?" She seemed excited and pleased.

"Very beautiful," Brandt said, wondering if the same view was available at the clinic and the Villa Miramar. They drove through a gate with a small gatehouse directly behind it, and Brandt caught sight of a guard standing inside it, with an old-fashioned bolt-action rifle slung over his left shoulder and the broad-brimmed brown hat that was part of the traditional uniform of the *guardas del campo,* as well as the brown corduroy jacket and the brass badge on a leather belt worn like a sash across one shoulder. The drive beyond the gate was graveled, with a neatly trimmed lawn on each side, leading to the house, a traditional patrician country house, the architecture of which Brandt had always considered to be one of the most pleasing in the world. There were small groups of exotic trees standing on the moonlit lawns, and a plethora of bougainvillaea climbing up the ochre-colored walls.

There were at least fifteen cars parked in the drive, and as it was early, it was quite certain that all of the guests had not yet arrived, so Consuela's estimate of the size of the party had been on the conservative side. "Shall I drop you off at the front door and then park?" Brandt asked the girl beside him.

"Of course not. Leave the car where you like, and I will go with you."

He nodded and drove past the entrance and out toward the front gate again before finding a place. As he did so he saw the Mercedes with the Monaco license plate, and he knew that the Clarendons were among the guests. Had he been alone, he reckoned he might well have driven right out the gate again, but that choice was not possible now. He couldn't very well pretend that he suddenly didn't feel well. It would have been too obvious a lie.

They walked back down the graveled drive in the moonlight. Consuela took his arm, because her high-heeled shoes were not well suited to the deep gravel, as she explained, and they entered the front hall of the house that way. A manservant in a white jacket opened the door for them as they approached. Consuela said, "*Buenas noches,* Nicolas," and Brandt echoed her greeting, feeling reassured by her presence. He would not have enjoyed arriving there alone that evening.

There was a portrait of Consuela's father on the wall, dressed in a *traje corto,* complete with the leather chaps the gentry wore when shooting, and a black Córdoban hat that suited his long, aristocratic face. "*Mi Padre,*" she said, indicating the painting.

"I know."

"Do I look so much like him?"

"You do. But we met before, your father and I, years ago, remember?"

"Of course. When I was just a child," she said, laughing and glancing at herself in a small mirror that hung on the right of the entrance hall.

Nicolas, the manservant, opened a double door leading into a large reception room. There were at least thirty people present, and Brandt found himself searching for a sign of the Clarendons, but they were not in view. Then he saw Consuela's father approaching. He looked a good deal older than in the portrait, yet his tanned face was still handsome, despite his thinning gray hair. He smiled affably and kissed his daughter, who was almost a head taller than he. Then he turned to Brandt, and said, *"Hola. Bienvenido,"* with a pleasant sincerity that was typical of his class and his country.

Brandt mumbled, "Thank you for having me."

"The friends of my children are my friends," Figueras said with a smile. "What will you have to drink? A whiskey? A vodka? You can have whatever you like. A champagne cocktail? *Ocupate de nuestro amigo,"* he told Consuela, seeing that another couple had entered the room behind Brandt.

"I'll have a vodka and tonic," Brandt said to the girl, and she relayed the order to another servant in a white jacket, adding that she would have a glass of champagne. She preceded Brandt into the room to greet some of her friends. Brandt hung back a little, still searching the room, and then took the drinks the servant brought, his own as well as Consuela's. Beyond the crowd he saw that there were French doors leading out into the garden, and that there were more people on the small terrace in the moonlight. He saw a young couple from Madrid he had met on several occasions, whose name he could not recall, and he gave Consuela her glass of champagne and went over to greet them. There were quite a few people there he knew, he was happy to notice, and so he crossed the room feeling less nervous than in the beginning. Thank God it was a big party, he thought, and not a seated dinner of eight people at which he would have to face Max Clarendon across a narrow table.

While he stood talking to the young couple whose name he

could still not remember, he caught sight of Hope on the terrace. She was wearing a dark green dress that showed off her well-formed shoulders, and as he stared at her, impressed once again by her beauty, she saw him, too, and stopped talking in midsentence to the man in front of her, her face at first frozen in the same blank look that he had carried with him in his mind since their meeting in San Pedro, and then she smiled distantly, the way one smiles at a remote acquaintance. The young couple he was standing with suggested that they move into the garden, because of the heat inside the room, and he followed them. He noticed that Hope had reached into her handbag and had taken out a cigarette, which the man with her lit for her, and as there was no use avoiding the inevitable, Brandt crossed to her and held out his hand.

She said, "Good evening," in a low voice, then turned away from him.

Brandt noticed that Max Clarendon was moving toward them from across the terrace. He obviously kept a close watch on his mistress, even at a dinner party. Brandt held out his hand as the man approached, and introduced himself.

Clarendon said, "How do you do," rather gruffly. "We've met somewhere, haven't we?" he asked, after a second glance at Brandt's face.

"We probably have," Brandt replied evenly. "It's a small town."

They sat down to dinner at eleven-thirty. There were three oval tables, one of them presided over by Figueras, which included most of the elderly guests. Teresa, his wife, took charge of the foreigners, having placed Max Clarendon on her right, since he was apparently the most important member of her group; and Consuela, the younger members of the party, advising them one by one that they should make for the table on the terrace. Brandt was flattered and pleased when she put him next to her, on her left, he remarked, because of some slight nod in the direction of an almost nonexistent protocol, as the young man on her right held one of the most illustrious titles in Spain.

"Left or right makes no difference to me," Brandt told her. "I'm lucky to be next to you."

"Left goes better with your politics," Consuela replied, lowering her voice.

"I'm not all that Red. I'm a *centrista,* a liberal."

"Well, for this group that makes you very Red indeed."

"Why? Are they all for the old regime?"

"My father's friends are nearly all 'bunker,' " she said. "Bunker" alluded to Hitler's command post in Berlin at the end of the war, and was the slang term used to lump the far right together.

"Fuerza Nueva?"

"Well, not quite, but almost."

"So I'm not to speak well of the King?"

"You can to me," she said. "I like him, too. But at that other table inside they wouldn't agree with us."

"Where your mother is seated?"

"No. They are all foreigners. My father's table."

Brandt glanced through the open French doors. The guests at Figueras' table didn't look as if they had just emerged from a bunker. The women were all elegantly dressed, and the men were in a variety of fancy silk shirts, open at the neck, that looked anything but conservative. "Don't worry, I won't propose a toast to the King, because I'm a foreigner," Brandt said. "And because my Spanish isn't good enough."

"I am very glad."

Brandt glanced over to where Consuela's mother was seated. Teresa Figueras was a handsome woman in her late fifties, with a slim figure and a narrow face that was excessively wrinkled, probably because she had exposed it too frequently to the sun. Max Clarendon was occupying himself with his hostess, charming her, no doubt, for the woman was laughing politely in response to whatever he was saying. He had the look of a healthy and vigorous man, not at all sharklike, Brandt observed. Only his eyes seemed to indicate a certain ruthlessness of character, for they were small and dark, with an intensity of expression that never faltered. Shark's eyes.

Across the table from him, with her back to the terrace, sat Hope, a black shawl draped around her shoulders. She dropped it over the back of her chair now and turned briefly to make sure that it had not fallen to the ground. For a brief second her eyes met Brandt's, then she turned to the man seated on her right. There was no change in the expression on her face, not even a glint of recognition, and Brandt wondered why it was that she was so frightened of Clarendon. For it could only be fear that would make her so excessively cautious. How damaging could it be that she had met him somewhere? Even if Max were excessively possessive, as an intelligent man he would certainly expect his mistress to have friends and acquaintances. It was probably only because she had a guilty conscience that she was so nervous, he thought, and decided that he would disregard her presence from that moment on, play her game, if that was what she wanted.

He got to his feet. His other dinner partner had arrived. She was young, pretty, with bleached golden hair and a narrow, longish face. She said, *"Hola. Soy Elena,"* while he pushed in her chair.

"Soy David," he replied. He knew that was sufficient for the moment.

Consuela supplied their surnames, explained that Elena was one of her closest friends, that they had gone to school together in Madrid and England. As an afterthought she pointed out Elena's husband, a thin handsome man, with curly brownish hair, seated on the far side of the table, who appeared at that moment to be enjoying the company of an attractive dark-haired girl on his right.

They were a handsome people, Brandt mused, the Spaniards who belonged to this protected and favored class, animated, charming, genuinely friendly to any foreigner who spoke their language, not overly intellectual and therefore less arrogant than the upper-class French, not as decadent as the Italians and therefore not as supercilious. No wonder that they wanted to preserve their society as it had existed for the forty years before Franco's death. He could readily understand that the advent of a democratic form of government frightened them. They had never witnessed at first hand the injustices and horrors of the early days of the dictatorship, had no memory of the photographs of Franco and Hitler together that he, Brandt, could not so easily dismiss from his mind. However, there was no point in thinking about all that now. The thing to do was enjoy himself while he was there as their guest. That was probably why Consuela had kept him close to her, at her table. She hadn't wanted to expose him to the bunker side of the room, and vice versa.

The food began to arrive. It was as lavish as Brandt had expected it to be. The fact that midnight was less than half an hour away did not prevent his host from serving a four-course meal, five if you counted the salad. He ate sparingly, while Consuela and Elena kept him amused with a vivid account of their first week at boarding school in England. It was obviously a reminiscence they often trotted out for their own and any foreigner's amusement. The food, the cold, the games they had been forced to play, all of it sounded like the experiences young men of their age might have had during their military service. The hardships that had been endured were comic, not tragic, and the overall memory served as a source of laughter, in retrospect.

After that subject of conversation had been exhausted, they began to speak of the present, of their lives as young married women in Madrid. Brandt noticed at once that there was a change in their mood. He asked what he thought were the right questions, showed interest in what normally would never have interested him: their domestic duties, their daily lives. Consuela had two small children, he learned, and Elena three. They both had nurses to look after them six days a week, or else they would "of course go crazy." How other women managed without nannies was incomprehensible to them. "They do, you know," Brandt said with a straight face.

"*Si.* But not here, in Spain."

He did not contradict them. They were, after all, only recently made friends. It was when they began to talk about their relationships with their husbands that he knew they were approaching dangerous ground. There were repeated allusions to the *esclavitud* that Spanish women were still being subjected to, but when he asked for proof of their slavery, they were momentarily at a loss for a reply. They were unable to do exactly as they pleased; that was a basic summation of all of their complaints.

"You mean you can't have lovers?"

"No. That is not really the problem," Consuela said with a mysterious little smile at Elena. "It is that we are not so free as the men. If I would like to go to New York for two weeks in October, I must ask Tomás. If I want to buy a new dress, I must ask. If he wants to go shooting in Scotland in August, he does. If he needs a new suit, he buys one."

"Because he earns the money."

"No. I have money, too. Money of my own. But still I must ask. For he looks after it, invests for me. And if he believes what I want to spend is a mistake, he says no, *basta.* And that is the end. No more discussion."

"Then take charge of your own money," Brandt suggested.

"I cannot do that," Consuela explained, "because then he thinks I have a lover. *Los cuernos,* how you say, the horns, that is still the main concern of all Spanish men."

"Well, that shows he cares about you, loves you."

"You are a man. You agree with him, of course," Elena said acidly. "What about our *cuernos?* We should submit, no? A woman without horns is like a garden without flowers."

"I thought the saying was a *man* without horns is like a garden without flowers."

Elena waved a well-manicured forefinger at him. "No, señor," she said adamantly. "The saying is for both, for everybody."

"You think sexual fidelity is so important?" Consuela asked rhetorically.

Brandt laughed. "That depends on whether you're on the giving or the taking end."

"I don't understand," Consuela said.

"I do," Elena informed her friend. "And it is true, what he says. The trouble is that men think infidelity matters more to women than it does to them. But that is not always so," she concluded pointedly.

"It depends on the woman."

"And the man," Elena said firmly.

"I suppose so. For both men and women it can mean very little at times, and at other times it can mean a lot. As the act of love is the most intimate physical thing that can happen between two people, it's preferable that if strong feelings are involved, there should be something exclusive about sex, that the two people who share it should be exclusively devoted to each other. Do you know what I mean?"

"Of course I know," Consuela said almost angrily, moving to her right and giving up her barely touched plate of food to one of the servants. "But for Spanish men it is only the horns that matter. They are not as much interested in sex as in their own pride. That is why they are not good lovers."

"*All* Spanish men?"

"I cannot say all, because I have tried only one so far," Consuela said, blushing.

"I say all," Elena said. "Ninety-five percent."

Her husband was watching them from across the table. "I wonder what you are talking about?" he said with a grin.

"*Nada. No te preocupes,*" she told him. "It does not concern you."

"We are discussing the war between men and women," Brandt said. There was no use making an enemy of a man he hadn't even met.

"I am not surprised," the young man replied. "But it is a war nobody wins."

"And you?" Elena called over to him. "What is it you are talking about?"

"Something more important," he said. "*El amor.*"

After dinner most of the guests moved out onto the terrace. Brandt sauntered down the steps near his table to stand for a moment on the thick Bermuda grass and look up at the moon. Pablo and Elena joined him. He seemed to be a most pleasant young man, not at all the strict husband his wife had made him out to be during the dinner conversation. He was attentive and polite to her, lit her cigarette, went to look for her handbag, which she had left under her chair, and smiled patiently when she continued with her complaints about the lot of Spanish women. He asked Brandt if he played golf, and agreed with him that tennis was a more amusing game. He and his friends played paddle tennis, he explained, and he invited Brandt to join them any afternoon at the courts in Guadalmina, which was where they lived, in an apartment with their children. Brandt told them that he had chartered a small boat for the summer, and invited them to go out with him whenever they felt like it.

"It is not a good coast for a boat," Pablo said. "There is no place to go. My family has a house in the north, near Santander. There a boat is a real pleasure."

"But it rains all the time," Elena said, making a face.

"A boat here is nice to swim off and to go fishing," Brandt replied.

"You have found fish?" the young man asked.

"Well, I haven't this year, but there used to be quite a few." Brandt was conscious that someone had joined their group, and realized that it was Max Clarendon.

"What kind of fish do you catch?" Clarendon asked. He was smoking a cigar, recently lit.

"Bottom fish," Brandt said, stepping back to include him in the conversation. "Not very big ones, but they're good to eat."

"Nothing you would be interested in, Max," the young Spaniard said. They had obviously met before, and knew each other quite well.

"I know there's a boat that goes out after shark," Clarendon said, "but I've never heard of any real sport fishing around here." He stopped abruptly, disregarding the presence of the others. "I know where we met," he said to Brandt. "It came to me during dinner. It was yesterday, in the *cuartel* of the Guardia Civil, in San Pedro. Yesterday afternoon."

"Yes. I was there," Brandt acknowledged. "A friend of mine had a serious automobile accident. His wife was under the impression that she had to make an official report."

Clarendon nodded and pulled on his cigar. "What was your name again?" he asked quietly.

Brandt told him. He was about to put out his hand, but Clarendon had already turned away. There was an awkward silence.

"You were not introduced?" Pablo asked.

"No. Not really."

"I don't like that man," Elena said. "He's not polite."

"Elena! Please!" her husband remonstrated with her.

"It is true," the young woman insisted. "There are people who come here and never learn the language. They stay among their own kind. Like that man. I don't know why Consuela's father always invites him."

Pablo shrugged. "What does it matter," he said. "We will go out fishing with you someday, David. But first you must come and play paddle tennis with us."

"Any afternoon after six. I'm a wage slave."

"Tomorrow?"

"Fine. At what time?"

"Seven-thirty? At Guadalmina."

"I'll be there."

Brandt was watching Max Clarendon as he moved restlessly from group to group, making a leisurely tour of the garden and the terrace. He had the mannerisms of a tiger, not a shark. He had that particular hungry look about him which Brandt had often encountered in the movie business. "Hungry, but they can't eat," a local wit had said about their kind long ago. Max was undoubtedly a dangerous enemy, and Brandt regretted his facetious remark about it being a small town, Marbella; it would have been better to have said that they had seen each other in the *cuartel* of the Guardia Civil on the previous afternoon, as Clarendon was obviously a man with a good memory for faces.

"You want I show you the *baño?*" Pablo asked.

"That's not a bad idea." He followed the young Spaniard across the terrace and into the living room. The bunker group was still seated inside, deep in serious discussion. Consuela's father smiled at them as they went past. Pablo led the way through a lavishly furnished bedroom and indicated the bathroom beyond it.

"Do you think there'll be another coup?" Brandt asked the young man while he waited for his turn to use the toilet.

"No creo," Pablo said. "It is not the time for that sort of thing now. There are many people on the right who are unhappy with the government. And the economy is very bad. But a military coup would make it impossible for us to come into the Common Market. The left is just as frightened. So I think things will quieten down. I hope so, anyway," he said with a smile as he went to the wash basin to wash his hands. "I'll see you in the garden," he added when he had finished. "You can find the way, no?"

Brandt nodded and closed the bathroom door. When he was

done, he started back the way they had come. As he was leaving the bedroom, he caught sight of Hope coming toward him down the narrow hallway. He stopped, having made sure that they were alone.

She looked anxiously over her shoulder. "I can't talk to you here," she said.

"But that's ridiculous. There's nobody around."

She shook her head and went on. For an instant he was tempted to follow her into the bedroom and confront her. But her panic was apparently very real. Or perhaps it was all over as far as she was concerned, had ended the morning she had left his apartment to drive to the airport.

He felt depressed. He made his way to the living room and went out onto the terrace. He saw that a group of flamencos had arrived, three men in black silk suits and white shirts without neckties, and two young women in the long polka-dot dresses that were the traditional costumes of the dancers. Two of the men were carrying guitars. The men had the pale, greenish faces of people who worked at night, although the women were tanned. Some of the guests, aided by the servants, were moving chairs out onto the lawn, leaving the terrace as a kind of makeshift stage for the entertainment.

Consuela waved to him, and he joined her and her group on the lawn. "You like flamenco?" she asked, indicating the vacant chair beside her.

"I wouldn't be in Spain if I didn't," he replied. Hope didn't, he remembered from their first meeting at the Safires', and he was not surprised to see that even before the dancers had started their first flurry of *sevillanas,* she and Max Clarendon had disappeared. Well, perhaps it was better that way, he thought, and took a deep breath.

It was four-thirty in the morning before he was back in his small apartment on the other side of the town. By that time the moon was very pale in the early-morning sky, but the fishing boats were chugging away, the sound of their engines inaudible because of the onshore breeze. He closed the shutters on the terrace and blocked out the picturesque scene. Then, with the staccato sound of the *palmas* still echoing inside his head, he took off his clothes and went to bed. He felt suddenly very tired, but he found that he couldn't sleep. When he finally dozed off, he dreamed of sharks milling around in clear blue water while he sat alone in an open boat under a blazing sun. It was a strange dream, for after a time he noticed that Pamela was in the boat with him, seated in the bow, wearing a transparent blue nightgown. It was the first time she had appeared in one of his dreams since he had arrived on the coast.

"You know I like you," Penny was saying. "You seem like a nice man. Not like the rest of the *drongos* who hang around here. But I don't want to go down in history as the office tart. D'you know what I mean?"

"Indeed I do. But what brought all that on? I just said that if you're ever real lonely in the evening . . ." Brandt paused and smiled.

"I know what you said. I'm not real stupid, you know. I know what you meant, too. So I wanted to get things straight between us. I'm a *modern* woman," she added, making fun of herself. "I don't go all scarlet if somebody asks me if I'd fancy a fuck."

"I didn't ask you that."

"Not yet, you haven't," the girl said.

He had taken her to the Puerto Banús for lunch, as promised, and they were seated out on the terrace under the blue awning of Antonio's fish restaurant, looking out at the yachts moored in the large marina. The young Swedish girl who did abstract paintings had passed by their table, and the thin young man who sold fine golden chains and bracelets, and now the blind Gypsy was approaching with his guitar to sing for the early customers, the tourists, for the Spaniards never arrived before three in the afternoon.

As the old Gypsy began to strum his guitar, Brandt had the distinct feeling that he had stumbled onto the set of a musical comedy, that the white-washed buildings to his right and left were backdrops, that the whole port had been temporarily erected, that even he and Penny were there only to act out their brief scene and then move on. He had often had the same sensation, that he was merely passing through this landscape on his way to a more permanent location. He wasn't going to die on the Costa del Sol; he felt fairly certain of that.

Penny must have read his mind, for she looked up suddenly, and

Brandt could tell by the expression on her face that she had decided to let the subject of sex rest for a while. "I like it here," she said, "but it's awfully plastic, isn't it? Every once in a while I say to myself, Penny, it's time to have one last plate of fried fish, and then move on. Do you ever get that feeling?"

"Every day. But where do we go? Back to Australia?"

"Australia's nice. I wouldn't mind a little house in Manly, and start settling down. The climate's not bad, and the people are more for real, and the beaches are beautiful," she said, giving the last word too much emphasis. "Not a bad place to raise kids, either, if you're into that sort of thing." She glanced over at him. "You're not, are you?"

"I'm not what?"

"Interested in having a family. Were you listening to me?"

"Sure I was listening. I just don't think the way the world looks today makes one want to rush out and start multiplying. Don't you agree?"

"No, I don't. But that doesn't matter."

"I'm too old, anyway. I've missed the boat for that."

"That's what they all say. 'Take your pill, darling. I'm not ready for the big move yet.' Well, I am. 'Fancy a fuck' has lost its charm for me." She looked at her wrist watch, not a golden Rolex, Brandt noted, but a small, stainless Japanese job, the kind poor working girls wore. "I have to be back at the plant in twenty minutes," she went on quite cheerfully. "Richard's expecting an important call from London, and since he's not going to be in until four, I've been elected to take the message. Are you going back, too?"

"I thought I'd go by the other port and check on my boat," Brandt said. "But I'll take you."

"Don't be silly. I'll grab a taxi." She opened her handbag and produced a small mirror. "Minor repairs are in order," she announced.

"The taxi is on me," Brandt said. "I don't want to take advantage of you."

"Please. I have my pride."

He kissed her on both cheeks, gave her behind a small pat, and watched her move down the quay on her high heels, her straw handbag slung over one bare, brown shoulder. A man could do a lot worse, he mused. But how long would it be before the Australian accent would begin to grate on his nerves, he wondered, especially after a long day at the office. Still, a cottage near the beach at Manly, a long distance away from the fallout, had its virtues. Although in the back of his mind he knew he would prefer to return to the States. With Ms. Clarendon, if possible. "What an idiot you are," he muttered to himself, and went back to the table under the awning and ordered a second coffee. "With anis seco on the side," he told the waiter, "as well as the bill." The blind Gypsy was singing a sad Mexican love song.

"Ya no estas mas a mi lado corazón . . ."

He would take *Lulubelle* out for an hour or two, he decided. Perhaps that would make him feel better. He had plenty of time. If he appeared at the office at four or four-thirty, it would be soon enough.

Someone called out his name, and looking down the wharf, he saw a young woman wrapped in a diaphanous silk scarf approaching his table. He had no idea who she was, but he got up politely and pretended that he had recognized her, because from her cheerful greeting he was fairly sure she was an old friend, or thought she was, anyway.

She had sun-bleached blond hair and freckles that appeared to cover her small, well-formed body. "My God, David!" she said. "What on earth are you doing here?"

"What are *you* doing here?" he countered, playing for time. Then he recognized her. It was Constance Henderson, one of the young women who had worked for Pamela. He had always found her to be rather dizzy; she was married to a stocky young Englishman who worked in the City of London as a merchant banker, a well-bred Brit who seemed pleasant enough, but had always seemed vaguely distant. His first name was Charles, Brandt recalled now, and they had a flat in Chelsea and a house in Oxfordshire, in the stockbrokers' belt.

She was there on a boat, she explained, a big motor-sailor that she had signed on as a part of the crew for a lark. They were delivering the yacht to Antibes, had come straight over from Hamble without a stop, four days in the Bay of Biscay, riding out a storm, and then down the Portuguese coast and into the Med. "We stopped in Gib for a few hours to refuel and take on provisions, booze, mostly, and cigarettes, from what I could see. I'm delighted to be on terra firma, I can tell you that," she added as an afterthought.

"And where's Charles?" Brandt asked.

"I don't know and don't care. We broke up a fortnight after you and Pamela parted company. He wasn't the right man for me. You must have noticed that."

"I didn't, but I'll take your word for it. Will you have a drink?"

"Yes, *please.* A gin and tonic. A big one. You can't imagine what it's like being on board ship for a week with seven men."

"Just the job, I should think, for a recently separated young woman."

"That's what I thought, too, but it really doesn't work out that way. If you give in to one, then you're stuck with him, and all the others hate you. And you can't have them all."

Brandt ordered the drinks. "Have you eaten?" he asked the ebullient Connie.

"I've done nothing else for days," she said. "I signed on as the chef, you see. Do you know what it's like, cooking for seven men who stand watches and are always ravenous, every four hours, twenty-four hours a day? I want a drink, maybe even two drinks, and a shower, and just to be with one man for a whole afternoon, not an entire randy crew. We take off again tonight, so I have to make the most of my shore leave."

Brandt laughed. "I was in the Navy for a couple of years," he said. "I know what it's like. Except we had no female chef on board."

"The shower is very important, too," Connie said, giggling. "Our skipper insisted on hoarding fresh water, so it was a bucketful every twenty-four hours, and that's all. I haven't washed my hair for over two weeks."

"I have a shower at home," Brandt said, "but not too much hot water."

"I like you," Connie said. "I always did, you know. Even when you belonged to old Pamela. Couldn't make my real feelings known, of course, because Pam and I were pals."

"We never talk about casualties in the mess," Brandt told her.

He was feeling much better. He ordered two more drinks, one for Constance and another for himself. Things were looking up, he couldn't help thinking.

"Where's Freddy Weaver?" the girl asked. "He lives down here now, doesn't he? He was a friend of yours, I seem to remember."

"He's around. Not quite the Freddy we used to know. A little too heavy on the grass."

"Oh, God, don't tell me that. Just the man we need, don't you think? To complete the afternoon?"

"I don't think I can find him that quickly," Brandt said. "The gin and tonics and the shower will have to do you." He didn't want to admit to the girl that he was a square, that he had never gone in for that kind of thing. It might have spoiled her plans for that afternoon.

He opened his eyes and looked up at the ceiling. The same lizard he had first noticed the morning he had spent the night with Hope was back again, upside-down and motionless, halted in his tiny tracks while on the way to devour a spider or the egg of a fly. Strangely enough, he hadn't seen him since that morning, almost a fortnight ago.

"That goddamned lizard is a voyeur," Constance said sleepily. "He hasn't moved during the last twenty-five minutes." She lifted her freckled, suntanned arm off Brandt's naked chest and turned over on her back. Her breasts were freckled too, so much so that the nipples almost disappeared in their natural camouflage. She had obviously had time for naked sunbathing while cruising south.

"Have you been watching him that long?"

"No," she said with a grin. "I noticed him before and after. Good thing he doesn't know how to talk."

"He wouldn't have much to tell."

"No! That's a shame. Not that I believe you. Still, I like you for saying so. You're nice and old-fashioned. A romantic!"

"I'm glad." They had driven to the apartment and had gone for a swim in the sea at Connie's insistence, because she had told him that had been another of her many frustrations: riding on a boat that wouldn't stop for her to take a dip all the way down the coast of Portugal. Then she had reminded him of the promised shower, especially since she had noticed a bottle of her favorite shampoo on the shelf in his bathroom before her swim. Brandt had waited for her to finish "washing her wig," had stood out on the balcony, experiencing a strange combination of guilt and eagerness. In his slightly drunken state he wasn't sure if he was being unfaithful to Pamela or to Hope, or about to be unfaithful, he reckoned. All signs certainly pointed in that direction.

Then Constance had put an end to the suspense by calling for him to join her in the bathroom. "We're running out of hot water" had been her complaint once he arrived on the scene. "Hurry up and get in here," she had told him, "and help me rinse out my hair."

Brandt had obeyed. There were certain commands he told her that he never argued with, such as joining a lady in the shower at her request.

"Well, that's a point in your favor," she replied. "But do you always wear your bathing suit in the shower?"

"Only in the summer."

"It's winter in here. Thank God it's hot outside, or I'd catch pneumonia!"

For some strange reason she had insisted on not drying off completely before getting into bed. It was one of her hang-ups, she explained, letting the breeze dry her. But in the heat of the afternoon that hadn't happened, for their lovemaking had made them warm again, so warm that another shower had been required, after which they had returned to the bed to rest.

"I always thought she was a bit silly, old Pam, and now my opinion's been confirmed. To leave all this."

"We never talk about past loves in bed, either," Brandt told her.

"I'm so sorry. You have so many rules. It's like being back in school with the nuns."

"I'm glad you feel at home, sweetheart."

She sat up and reached for her wrist watch. "Oh, Christ," she said. "My shore leave's expiring."

"Jump ship."

"I can't. I have all my earthly belongings on board. And I haven't been paid my wages. Why don't you come to Antibes and be waiting on the dock?"

"I have a job."

"And a girl?"

"No girl."

"Poor David." She jumped up and went into the bathroom. Brandt pulled the bottom sheet off the bed and took it out onto the terrace to dry in the sun. He felt disoriented. It was almost five-thirty. The telephone rang. He went back into the bedroom and sat on the edge of the sky-blue mattress to answer it.

"It's me," a woman's voice said.

"Who is it?"

"It hasn't been *that* long, has it?" Hope Clarendon said.

"I never thought I'd hear from you again," Brandt replied, watching the bathroom door open and the naked Connie make her way toward him. She went around to the other side of the bed and dropped herself on the mattress and began to rub the small of his back.

"Are you alone?" Hope asked suspiciously.

"I am."

"It doesn't sound like it."

"I have to recover from the shock of your reappearance."

There was a long pause. Then Hope said: "Max is leaving for Paris on Friday, I *think*. He'll be gone for three days. In case you're still interested."

"Then call me Friday," Brandt said. "Either here or at the office."

"I called the office earlier."

"I took the afternoon off."

"Are you sure you want me to call you again?"

"I wouldn't have said it if I wasn't sure."

"All right. You'll hear from me on Friday." She hung up quickly, as if someone had come into the room from which she was calling, although Brandt knew that was not the reason.

"Who was that? Your secretary?" Connie asked.

"No. An old flame."

"It sounded burned out on your end."

"Did it?" He felt ill at ease. He had never been a very good liar. So it wasn't all over, he thought. It was on again.

Connie said: "Well, this sailor has to get back to his ship. It's all very sad. Such a brief liberty. But a nice one."

"You'll have to get dressed, I reckon."

"*That* won't take long."

She was right about that. She slipped into her dry bikini, after retrieving it from the balcony, and pulled the Indian shawl around her body. All there was left for her to do was put on her Japanese sandals. "I feel better," she said, "thanks to your kind hospitality. A little peckish, I'm afraid, but there's sure to be something in the old tub's larder. Shall we bugger off?"

As they drove west toward the port again, he remembered that he had a date to play paddle tennis at Guadalmina, five miles farther up the coast. And he had never made it back to the office. Well, he would go and watch the others play, pretending that he had a bad back. And as for Richard Grey, if he was suddenly overcome by a desire to see his public relations counsel, he would have to wait until the following day. But he would stop in at the clinic before dinner. That was a more important chore. How many guilts could one man acquire?

"No Antibes, I guess," Constance said, putting her feet up on the ledge over the dashboard. "No familiar face waiting on the shore."

"You never know what might happen," Brandt said. But that was just another lie. He had enjoyed making love to Constance, but as the old Spanish saying had it, hunger is the best cook. And her strange notions about kissing had not been altogether pleasing. She had seemed intent on devouring him. And her hang-up about coming to bed soaking wet would undoubtedly not turn out to be a lasting joy. And the skin on her body was not the smooth, endlessly touchable skin that still clung stubbornly to his memory, although, to be fair, it had been almost unbearably hot in his little apartment at that time of the afternoon. Yet even on a hot night Hope's skin had felt pleasing to his touch. Perhaps there was something to the notion of American skin, after all? Or perhaps it was just his own intense longing that had created the illusion. *La vida es un sueño, y sueños sueños son.* Perhaps that was what the old Castillian poet had been trying to say. Life is a dream, and dreams are dreams. Perhaps he, too, had been in love when he had written those words. Or *encoñado.*

Part Three

Weaver said: "I approve of your always having breakfast here. It makes me feel that at least someone I know is leading a normal, well-regulated life."

"I don't always," Brandt replied. "You're in luck today. I often have breakfast at home."

"Well, home or at El Faro. That's good enough for me. Most of my other friends usually miss breakfast altogether. You, I always know where to find."

"What's your proposition today?" Brandt asked, and indicated to Paco that he would like a second cup of coffee. "A little gun-running? Or smuggling in a few illegal aliens? Or are we still only interested in pot?"

Weaver grinned and sipped his tea. "You're a little edgy, David," he said. "Needlessly so, I might add. Today I have no proposition. Only good news. First of all an invitation to dinner next Sunday night. Lew Safire, who I ran into at Banús, said he's been trying to get hold of you for days. He's cooking some Dago food, as he likes to call it, and he was wondering if you'd be interested. He said he hadn't seen you for weeks."

"Sunday night?" Hope had said she would be calling him on Friday, but then it was quite possible that she wouldn't, if Max decided to stay for the weekend. "Sunday's fine," Brandt said. He had decided that he was tired of waiting for her like a pet dog, eager for its owner's whistle.

"You can bring anyone you want," Weaver said. "A girl, your pet snake, a young Chinaman. I'm quoting Lew, of course. He was into racial jokes yesterday."

"How are his new teeth?" Brandt asked sourly.

"Fine. They looked like a perfect fit to me. Of course, if he's serving pasta, that might mean he hasn't broken them in yet." Weaver lit a cigarette, a Marlboro, Brandt noticed, so he was obviously more solvent now. "Then I have some more good tidings. Guy's much improved. He was able to sit up and gossip yesterday afternoon. His right side's still paralyzed, but at least there's a light at the end of the tunnel."

"I know. I went there yesterday morning."

"Then you know the whole story. The doctors think he'll be perfectly all right with time. Money is the only problem now. His insurance covers most of the medical expenses, but he has no car, and there's no cash flow, as I believe it's called."

"So you offered to charter his boat, right?"

Weaver's eyes narrowed. "What's your problem, David?" he asked. "You running for sheriff?"

"No. But I don't think it would help the Mannings if their boat was confiscated."

"I don't think there's any danger of that happening," Weaver said evenly. "Anyway, she's yours until the end of the month. What happens after that is no skin off your arse."

"I might want to extend the charter," Brandt said. He had decided a few days ago that he would give *Lulubelle* up at the end of the month. He had hardly used the boat, and it was a considerable expense, even if Grey raised his salary, which was unlikely.

"Well, that's up to you," Weaver said. "And Manning, of course. I was hoping to use her now for a week or ten days, and that by adding on the extra time, you could have her in August."

"Does Manning know what you intend to do?"

"No, and neither do you, really."

"You made it pretty clear the last time we met."

"Oh, come on, David. I was pissed when we had breakfast here, whenever that was. I was putting you on. You think I'd risk getting tossed into the local slammer? You must be kidding."

"You weren't that pissed."

"Okay. Forget it." He got up slowly and dropped his lighted cigarette into his teacup. "It's strange. I was under the impression that we were friends," he said. "What do I owe for my tea?"

"It's on the house," Brandt said.

Weaver nodded. "I'll see you around," he said.

Brandt watched him walk out of the restaurant and turn right once he was out in the street. He passed the window opposite which Brandt was seated without looking in. Well, he was an enemy now instead of a friend, although Brandt had the strange feeling that he would hear from him again. *Lulubelle* was obviously important to his plans.

Brandt paid for his breakfast and drove to the clinic. Guy Manning was propped up in bed, reading an old copy of the London *Times.* Marie had gone into town, he said, to buy a few provisions. The food at the hospital was barely edible.

"You've got your appetite back," Brandt told him. "That's a good sign."

"I suppose it is," Manning said uneasily. "I'm more concerned with Marie than with myself. It's all turned into a nightmare. I don't know what made me decide to come down here. I should have stayed in England. None of this would have happened."

"You can have an automobile accident in England, too."

"I know that. But it's not the same thing. When you get past fifty, you should stay where you belong. Your own people, your own country. Mind you, I don't think being a patient under the National Health Service is any sort of a lark."

"I hear they take care of you pretty well."

"I suppose they do," Manning said. "Being old and poor is no good anywhere." He paused. "I don't know why, but dying in your own country seems preferable, somehow. Among your own kind."

"You're not going to die. You've turned the corner. And once you've fully recovered, you can go back to England."

"How?" Manning asked. "On what? I can't even sell that bloody boat. She's under British registry. And how many Englishmen come out here wanting to buy a used cabin cruiser? The ones with a little money want something modern, and the rest will beat you down so much that it's not even worth selling her." He glanced over at Brandt. "I'm sorry to bore you with all this, but I'm rather in a bind."

"You might be able to get fifteen thousand pounds for her," Brandt said. "If you can wait."

"I can't wait," Manning said. "I need money now. Marie's treatments, and all this." He waved his left hand at the small room. "I'm at my wits' end, David. I don't know what to do."

"Freddy Weaver's been to see you, hasn't he?" Brandt asked. He hadn't wanted to discuss all that, but there seemed to be no avoiding the subject now.

"Yes, he's been here," Manning said. "The miserable bastard. I know he's a friend of yours . . ."

"He was. Up to about half an hour ago."

"He's offered me a thousand pounds for a week's charter. I told him she was yours until the end of the month, and he said he'd work it out with you. That you were his pal."

"Do you know what he wants her for?"

"I can guess. He doesn't want to take the sun, that much is certain."

"If they catch him, they'll confiscate the boat."

"I know. But they probably won't. His kind gets away with murder."

"I wouldn't be too sure."

"Well, what choice do I have? Tell me that, will you? I need the money now, yesterday, last week. And Freddy's a slick operator. He doesn't take too many chances. Maybe he *won't* get caught."

"If you want to let him have her, it's all right with me," Brandt said slowly.

"I knew you'd say just that." Manning closed his eyes wearily. There was a faint knock on the door, and Marie came into the room. She was carrying a plastic bag that gave off an odor of roasted chicken.

"How's my patient?" she asked cheerfully. "Not talking too much, is he?"

"No, he's fine," Brandt said. "I'll be going now, anyway." He patted Manning's foot at the end of the bed. "I have to get to the office." He turned at the door. "Whatever you want to do is perfectly fine by me," he said to the pale man lying on the white metal bed.

Manning nodded and raised his good hand. "Come back soon," he said.

Brandt drove to the office in a rage, disregarding the speed limit as if he were Spanish by birth. When he was halfway there it occurred to him that giving up the boat for a week now was actually to his advantage. That would extend his charter into August, when he would probably have more time to use *Lulubelle,* and with any luck, Max might be gone. The thing that had angered him most was that Weaver was getting his way. Then he began to wonder why he suddenly felt such resentment toward his old friend. It was his superior manner, he decided; as if anyone who respected the law was a hopeless fool. In any case, it was nothing to him if Weaver should get caught.

But Manning was probably right: Weaver was too smart to stick his own neck out. The most irritating part of the whole thing was that he would probably make a bundle by loading *Lulubelle II* to the gunwales with Moroccan hash and dropping it off for some poor local fisherman to bring to shore. He glanced up at the rearview mirror. Two motorcycle policemen were following him, and he recognized the brown leather uniforms of the Guardia Civil. One of them flashed his lights, and Brandt pulled over into the summerway.

"*¿Tiene usted mucha prisa?*" the taller of the two asked quietly, after he had saluted.

He had apparently been influenced by the dialogue of American movies. Yes, he was in a hurry, Brandt admitted. His only excuse was that he didn't know the rented Peugeot would go that fast.

The man's face remained immobile. His eyes behind the dark glasses gave no hint of possibly forgiving the infraction. He complimented Brandt on his Spanish and wrote out the ticket. It could be settled at once, or he could make an appearance in front of the judge in Fuengirola. It was up to him to decide.

Brandt paid the two thousand pesetas and nodded when the man told him that they were being lenient because he was a tourist. The fine could be much higher, considering the speed at which Brandt had been traveling. He had also neglected to wear his seat belt. "A compatriot of yours was almost killed not very far from here several days ago," the Guardia told him.

He was probably referring to Manning, Brandt thought, and he was tempted to tell the man that it hadn't been his "compatriot's" fault. But there was no point in prolonging the conversation. He thanked the officer for his "clemency" and drove off. Freddy Weaver would have laughed had he witnessed the scene, he thought to himself after strapping himself in. The Guardia Civil had been lenient, there was no doubt about that, as well as polite. Not wearing a seat belt was worth another two thousand pesetas by the book. The incident cooled his anger. He arrived at his office somewhat chastened, but relieved to discover that he was still the first one there, despite the various delays.

He sat at his desk and read the morning paper. The news about Poland occupied half the front page. The other lead article was about Tejero, and described the conditions the rebellious colonel was enjoying in his prison cell in Galicia. The rest of the paper seemed devoted to football, pages and pages of it, complete with photographs of the various Wednesday night games. On the last page Brandt found a story about the arrest of a group of smugglers who had been caught with a cargo of hashish near the port of Málaga. He would cut it out and bring it to Safire's house on Sunday night, he decided, in case Freddy Weaver showed up for dinner.

He was about to go and borrow a pair of scissors from Penny when the telephone rang. A woman with a deep voice identified herself as Phyllis Dexter. "I'm calling for Hope," she said evenly. "She would like you to meet her at eight tonight, if you can."

Brandt asked, "Where?" He found that his heart had started beating a little more quickly, and he wondered whether the reason was nervousness or anticipation.

"Are you free?" Phyllis Dexter asked.

"I can be," Brandt said. "Where am I to meet her?"

"Take the road to her house, but instead of driving in the gate, continue on down the dirt road to the beach. She'll be waiting there for you."

Brandt was about to ask whether Max had left for Paris, but then decided not to. If they were to meet anywhere near the Villa Miramar, it was quite obvious that he had gone.

"I'll be there," he said. By the sound of the woman's accent, she was English or maybe Irish. After he had hung up he sat for a long while looking down at the front page of the newspaper he had already read. Why not the villa, he wondered, and if the villa was dangerous, why so near the house? They could easily have met at a restaurant or a bar in the port. And why hadn't Hope called herself? Well, he would go, Brandt decided, just this one more time. And it wasn't only because he was curious. He knew that much, without giving it more thought.

Richard Grey called to tell him that an American photographer from the magazine *Town & Country* had arrived on the coast, and that it was most important to persuade the man to include their new development in the picture story he was doing on the south of Spain. He suggested that Brandt contact the man at the club and take him to lunch at their hotel.

"I'll do my best," Brandt assured him.

"He's a compatriot of yours, so it shouldn't be all that difficult. Get Consuela and some of her friends to join you. The beautiful people always make good copy."

There was no doubt about that, Brandt told his boss, glad to have an assignment that would fill his day. It would make the hours before he was to meet Hope pass more quickly.

She was walking up the beach with a dog when he caught sight of her, and he remembered her telling him, the first night he had taken her home, that she owned one and that it was at the vet's. It was a German shepherd, a big one, and whatever had been wrong with the animal was apparently cured, for it was chasing a stick she had thrown with an abundance of energy, splashing through the shallow water along the shore.

The dog saw him, dropped the piece of wood, and came loping down the beach toward him, barking fiercely. She called it to heel, but the dog paid no attention to her. It stopped about fifty feet from Brandt before turning back to rejoin its mistress.

He waited for her to approach. She had taken off her shoes

and was carrying them in her left hand. The bottom of the faded jeans she was wearing were wet from her wading in the foam of the small, spent waves, and he noticed that they were cut wide at the bottom, in the style of the ones he had worn so reluctantly in the U.S. Navy. As she drew near he could see that the white T-shirt she had on had something printed across the chest. ONE OF A KIND he read in spite of the glare of the setting sun. Then the dog trotted over to him and began to sniff at his shoes and trousers. He reached down to pat its moist coat. "Does he bite?" he asked her.

She shook her head and said, "Only strangers and tradesmen."

"How about ex-lovers?"

"What does that mean?"

"Only that you might have called before."

"I tried to a couple of times, but you were never at home. I was afraid to call your office, because they know my name there."

"You could have told me that at the party."

She shook her head. "I was scared," she said. "Max has a sixth sense, or maybe he suspects everyone, I don't know which. After we ran into you in the office of the Guardia Civil, he asked Yves who you were."

"And what did Yves say?"

"Oh, he made some silly crack about having seen you around in the fleshpots. That you were one of the local layabouts. Then when you first spoke to me at the party, he thought it strange that I didn't introduce you and that I hadn't spoken to you earlier that afternoon. He noticed that I was nervous, and he mentioned it when we got home." She paused briefly. They were walking in the direction of the villa, moving over the moist strip of sand, just out of reach of the sea. "Did you leave your car on the dirt road?" she asked.

"Yes. That's what I was told to do." He was aware that she had changed. She seemed less sure of herself than before, excessively nervous.

"I'll meet you there in five minutes," she said. "The servants are still at the house. I'll take Bozo back and change into some dry clothes. Come on, Bozo," she called out to the dog, and slapped her thigh to make it obey. Reluctantly, Bozo abandoned the search for its stick and started to follow her.

Brandt walked back in the direction of the sunset to the narrow trail that led through the brush and bamboo to where he had left his car. In the early evening light the distant mountains beyond the foothills had the look of purple cutouts once again, flat and without any contours, and, as always, they reminded him of the mountains of Southern California. But for once he had the distinct feeling that nostalgia was a mistake, that he was better off where he was. His lunch with the American photographer and Consuela had made him realize how difficult it would be for him to return home. His compatriots had often had that effect on him. The man had been pleasant enough, helpful and intelligent; yet he had made Brandt feel that he was somehow a visitor from a foreign planet and that he had been away too long. It was difficult, in any event, to go back and start over again. It was somehow an admission of defeat.

He was leaning against the front fender of the Peugeot, emptying the sand out of his moccasins, when Hope reappeared. She had changed out of her T-shirt and the bell-bottom jeans and was wearing a summer dress that made her look younger than the uniform of the young she had worn before. "Why do you look at me like that?" she asked, coming to a halt in front of him on the dusty road.

"I don't know. I suppose I can't believe that I've got you back." He tried to take her into his arms, but she pulled away from him. "Don't be so goddamned scared," he told her angrily. "Nobody can see us. We're out in the boondocks."

"This road leads to the *cortijo* where the servants live."

"All right. Then let's get the hell out of here." He opened the door of the car for her and went around to the driver's side and got behind the wheel.

"Do you remember the morning at your apartment?" she asked, "when you saw the freighter heading for Gib? Do you remember what you said?"

"Sure I remember." He started the engine.

"Well, do you still feel that way? Do you still think it would be nice if we were on a ship, heading for the hills of home."

He glanced over at her. The motor of the Peugeot was the only sound in the quiet of the summer evening. Why had she suddenly decided that she wanted to return to the States, he wondered. Two people rarely wanted the same thing at the same time, except maybe going to bed together. He put the car in gear and backed out into the road. "Why do you ask?" he said.

"Because everything has changed, and it's not such a far-out idea anymore."

"Why? What's happened?" He hesitated before driving on, with the car facing in the direction of the villa.

"Max has changed. I have the feeling he wants out. He hasn't said so, but I can tell."

"How?"

She paused. "He hasn't tried to make love to me. I think he's found someone else. He's just as suspicious as before, but in a different way. He doesn't seem to care a damn about the robbery. Yves *made* him go to the Guardia Civil in San Pedro. He would have been quite happy to forget all about it. He said it was dumb of me not to have put everything into the safe at the bank."

"And the Guardia Civil? What did they say?"

"They were about as interested in the case as he is. Oh, they took the names of the servants and said they would watch their movements. But that's about all. So I'm poor," she said with a smile, "and perhaps about to be free."

"Well, there are worse things."

"So I hear."

"Where do we go now?" Brandt asked.

"I said we'd have a drink with Phyllis up at Benávis. There's a bar there and a restaurant. She said she wanted to meet you."

"Okay." He was still annoyed with her for her cowardice. He turned up the road and drove slowly back down it, following the tire tracks, with the weeds in the middle scraping the bottom of the car. In the distance he saw a young man and a young woman coming toward them on foot. Hope slid down low in the seat, turning her back to the window as she did so. "The servants?" Brandt asked.

She nodded. Brandt caught a glimpse of the young woman's face as he drove past the couple. They were walking in single file along the side of the car tracks, the woman in the lead. She was pretty, with long dark hair and dark eyes and a very erect figure. She smiled at him, the friendly smile of the village beauty who doesn't mind an admiring glance from a stranger. Her husband was equally good-looking. He was still wearing his white serving jacket with its high collar. It gave him the look of a sailor, a Latin Billy Budd, with a clean-shaven face. Hope straightened once the young couple was out of sight.

"I don't think they're the people who stole your jewelry," Brandt said.

"How do you know?"

"Just by looking at them."

"Are you such an infallible judge of your fellow men? That all it takes is a passing glance?"

"I can be wrong, of course, but I've usually been right. About girls, that is."

"Is that a fact? I'll try to remember that." She laughed and lit a cigarette. They drove past the garden wall of the Villa Miramar, with the purple and orange bougainvillaea very bright against the whitewashed plaster. Then once they were out on the main road, she rolled down the window on her side of the car and sat quietly in the warm rush of air. After a while she put her left hand on his knee, and left it there in a gesture of gentle possessiveness.

She said: "You haven't answered my question."

"Which one?" He wasn't playing games with her. He had a pretty good idea what she was referring to, but his thoughts were a few thousand miles away. He was visualizing the hamburger stands and gasoline stations that he always made himself think of whenever he tried to cure himself of his homesickness.

"Which one?" she repeated irritably, aping him. They were making their way inland through the dry stubble fields of the plain. The light was failing. It was almost dark near the hills, as the ridge line on their left cut off the reddish glow of the setting sun. "Never mind," she said after a while, and removed her hand from his knee. "It wasn't really an important question."

He said: "You mean about our sailing home together, back to the States? Is that what you're referring to?"

"How perceptive you are."

"I didn't think you were serious, that your question really required an answer."

"I suppose it didn't," she said.

After the traffic of the main highway, he was enjoying the deserted country road and the summer smells that filled the car. He was back in Spain again. He glanced over at her. She was looking out the window on her side, had turned away from him. He knew that she was upset.

"Hope! For God's sake," he said. "I really didn't think you were serious."

"And I wasn't, of course," she replied. "I was testing you just for fun. And you failed the test, as was to be expected. Not to worry. It doesn't matter. My trouble is that I remember what people say to me. I suppose you were being polite. I'd just gotten up out of your bed and was about to drive off to the airport, so you wanted me to feel better about having to go, and you saw the ship heading for Gibraltar, and it seemed the right thing to say at the time. It wasn't something you really meant!"

"Sure I meant it."

"You meant it at the time. Is that what you're trying to tell me? Now, upon mature reflection, you're not all that keen to take me back to God's country. Well, at least you're being honest."

"Don't put words in my mouth," Brandt said. "Don't tell me what I've decided 'upon mature reflection.' " After all the days of his waiting for her to call, to be with her again, they were quarreling, were already estranged. And he wanted her; that was what was most surprising. She had moved as far away from him as was possible in the confines of the car, was sitting with her back against the door, like a cornered animal, and all he really wanted was to go to bed with her, take her back to his sad apartment and make love to her. Even that seemed a remote possibility now. "I like to be with you," he began to explain in a low voice. "I'm happy when we're together. And that's quite apart from what happens when we're in bed together."

"Oh, really?" she said mockingly. "And I was suddenly under the impression that I was your favorite fuck, and that's all."

"Hope! Please."

"Do I offend you with my language? It's not my style, really. But I can't help thinking that's what you'd say if you really spoke your mind."

"You're not my favorite fuck," he told her, thinking that might make her laugh.

"Oh, really? Not even that. Just a convenient fuck."

"Stop it. What's the matter with you? Just because I failed to say what you wanted me to, you want to destroy everything? Is that it?"

"Destroy what?" she asked. "What do we have that's so great? Or that we shouldn't destroy?"

"Look," he said, "we haven't seen each other for two weeks. It takes time to adjust. When I saw you again, it was as if we'd never met. Give us a chance, will you?"

"I explained all that to you, that I tried to call, and that you were never home. Watch the road, will you? It won't help us if we have an accident now."

He turned on the headlights. The road was climbing up into the hills. There was an abandoned farmhouse on the left, a small rectangular whitewashed *cortijo* with a caved-in roof. "The reason I didn't answer your question was because I'd had a change of heart," he said. "Not about you, but about going home. I'd decided back there, near the beach, that you were probably right. That it was better to stay on here. And part of the reason was that you've always been so adamant about liking this place."

"You could have told me so."

"You never gave me a chance." He put out his hand to her. She didn't take it at once, and when she finally did, the gesture was mechanical rather than forgiving. At that moment an animal crossed the road in front of them, a small dog or a cat. He didn't have time to brake, or even change the direction of the wheels. There was the sound of a bump, and he felt the car run over some small object, fragile flesh and bones. He said, "Oh, Christ! We've hit something." He stopped and jumped out, leaving the engine running.

There was just enough light for him to see a smear of blood on the road. But in the dense shrub to the left of the macadam he could find no trace of any animal. He stood listening. There was a distant sound, an injured cry, a cat probably, slinking off to die somewhere in agony. He felt angry with himself, with his own carelessness. He heard Hope's footsteps behind him.

"What was it?" she asked.

"A cat, I think."

"Did you see it?"

"No, but I heard a cry, out there somewhere." In the distance the lights of a car appeared, moving toward them on the road from Benavis. "We'd better go on," he said. "There's nothing we can do now."

She followed him back to the Peugeot. They drove off. The approaching car flashed its lights, and the driver gave them a blast of his horn as he passed.

"If it was a cat, there's not much you could have done about it."

"I could have put it out of its misery," Brandt said.

"I suppose it's all my fault. For being difficult. But I wasn't in the best of moods when we met."

"It wasn't anyone's fault," Brandt said. Although he did blame himself. He hadn't been watching the road, had looked over at his passenger too often. "It's one of the things I most deplore about this country. The way they leave the highway strewn with dead animals. Now I've behaved like one of them. I might as well become a permanent resident."

"It was unavoidable, David," Hope said in a more gentle voice than she had used before. "I just hope it wasn't a *black* cat. That would mean bad luck on top of everything else."

"Not if I killed it," he said grimly.

Phyllis Dexter listened sympathetically to the story of their misadventure. She was more attractive than Brandt had expected her to be; in his experience, pretty women usually had much less pretty women as their best friends. She was also much younger than he would have guessed by the sound of her voice on the telephone. She was Anglo-Irish, a tall blonde with well-formed hands and arms, and under her faded denim shirt there was the suggestion of a thin but muscular body. She was a heavy smoker, and yet the constant use of nicotine had had no effect on her eyes and skin, which were very clear. She had a sensual mouth, he noticed as he watched her sip her drink or eat one of the vinegar-cured anchovies that the small bar had served them, gratis.

"How awful for you," she said to her friend, disregarding the fact that Brandt had been driving, and that the shock of running over the small animal had affected him more than Hope. There was an obvious complicity between the two women that he had often encountered when he had been introduced in the past to the "best friend" of one of his paramours, a show of solidarity in the face of the common enemy, the lover. It was also a secret signal that the best friend was not in competition, not interested in the man. But she knew that she was attractive, which was probably why she felt she had to make her loyalty to Hope clearly known.

If he hadn't just recently shared Constance Henderson's shore leave, Brandt thought, he would have been more inclined to take the woman's attitude toward him at face value. But "dear Connie" had been a close pal of Pamela's, and she, too, had always made a point of addressing all her opinions and jests to Pam, which, as it turned out, was a hoax. Phyllis seemed less genuine than Connie, was obviously a smarter bird, shrewd, observant, controlled. "Let's forget the cat," Brandt said, "and think that she died quickly, *una buena muerte.*"

"Una buena muerte," Phyllis repeated sarcastically. "Is there such a thing?"

"When you get nearer the end, you realize that there is," Brandt said.

"Oh, really? I wouldn't know," Phyllis said sarcastically. She turned to Hope. "How are things at the villa?" she asked. "Did Max get off all right?"

"I presume he did. Yves drove him to the airport."

"When will he be back?" Phyllis asked.

"In a couple of days, I think."

Brandt felt excluded from their conversation. He looked around the bar while the two women chatted on. It was a fairly typical village restaurant, with a few tables in front of the long bar at the back of the whitewashed room. The walls were decorated with old bullfight posters, and Brandt read the names of the matadors featured in big letters, remembering a better time, when Antonio Ordoñez was still fighting, and Paco Camino and Diego Puerta.

He heard Phyllis Dexter ask Hope if she had had any news from the Guardia Civil, and his attention turned once again to the conversation of the two women facing him. "You were there, weren't you, David?" she asked.

"You mean when Hope *discovered* the robbery?"

"Of course that's what I mean," Phyllis said, slightly flustered.

It had been such an obvious joke that Brandt was surprised by her reaction. Perhaps the woman had no sense of humor, he thought to himself, although she didn't appear to be all that square. "Did Hope tell you how we swam ashore, and that Yves came by the house just as we were about to leave?"

"Yes. She told me the whole story."

"Did I?" Hope said. "I don't remember much of anything about those two days. But I must have told you."

"Unless Yves told her," Brandt said, in much of a matter-of-fact voice.

"I don't know Yves Brouyère that well," Phyllis said, and Hope looked over at her with surprise. "Of course I *know* him," she added hurriedly, "but we never exchange confidences."

"Do you think Max knows that I was at the villa with you that afternoon?" Brandt asked Hope.

"He's never mentioned it."

"Would he have, if Yves had told him?"

"Well, I would think so."

"What are you getting at?" Phyllis Dexter asked aggressively.

"Only that if Yves confided in you, he might well have confided in Max, as well."

Hope said: "I don't see that that follows. I told you that Yves is more of a friend of mine than of Max's."

"Yeah, I know," Brandt said. "But in times of stress, people discover they have different loyalties than when everything's going smoothly. Anyway, it really doesn't matter all that much. Another drink, ladies?"

"No, I'm afraid I'm late for dinner," Phyllis Dexter said. "I'm meeting some English friends in Estepona, and they haven't yet adapted themselves to Spanish hours." She put out her hand to Brandt, who took it and got to his feet. "I'm glad to have met you," she said, looking him very directly in the eyes. "And I hope I'll see you again soon."

"I'm sure you will," Brandt said.

"And look after my friend."

"I will."

They watched her move across the restaurant. Her departure caused a stir among the men at the bar, the tourists as well as the Spaniards, the village locals, who, although they were used to seeing the invaders from the coast, were not so jaded as not to appreciate a better than average foreign beauty.

"Would you like to have her?" Hope asked him, with a false little smile.

"She's attractive, but she comes on a little too strong for my taste."

"That's only because she's protective of me."

Brandt shrugged. "You really don't remember telling her that I was with you at the villa that afternoon?" he asked, pointedly.

"No, I don't. But how else would she know if I hadn't told her?"

"That's what *I* want to know. Only Yves could have told her. Unless she spoke to one of his dogs."

Hope said: "I'm tired of the whole story. Where shall we eat? There's a Greek restaurant down the street that's nice and cosy. Have you ever been there?"

"No. But I'm always willing to try a new place. With the right sponsor, that is. Any old place, too."

"Does that include the hills of home?"

"It does," Brandt said. "Definitely."

She suggested that they go back to the Villa Miramar after dinner, because the servants would be gone and it was closer than his apartment. He told her that he didn't like going there. It was too much a part of her other life, the bedroom with the photographs and the big double bed she had shared so recently with Max, whether he had made love to her or not. She reminded him gently that it hadn't bothered him before.

"That was a different time," he told her. "Anyway, it makes me nervous. And if what you tell me is true, that Max has found someone else, he might come back unexpectedly. If he wants to find an easy way out, that is."

She was unconvinced by his arguments. "Max doesn't operate like that," she told him.

"But if we go to my apartment there's no risk at all. If he calls and you're not at home, you can say that you were having dinner with Phyllis."

"I was planning to do that anyway," she told him. "Your apartment is so far away, and I hate to drive back alone."

"I'll take you," Brandt said. "And I'll make a tour of the premises. That's always been my job," he reminded her.

"All right. If you insist."

"Does it make you feel that you're poor again, my apartment?" he asked her. They were driving down the narrow road from Benavis, had already passed the place he had run over the cat.

"No, not really," she said. "A little maybe."

"I've lived in worse places," he said. "And might well have to again."

She sighed. "All right. You've convinced me," she said. "Poor isn't all that important. Or is it?"

"I don't know. You tell me."

They drove on in silence. "I think I should take my car as far as the port," she said after a while. "In case he *is* checking on me."

So they stopped by the villa, and Brandt waited in the Peugeot while she went inside to get the keys for the Mercedes. Then he followed her to the parking lot of the port. She was quite cheerful again once they were together, as if she had dismissed all of her worries from her mind, and he made an effort to join her in her mood.

He watched her get undressed in the light of the oblong moon that floated in the clear sky above the fishing boats; then he made room for her in the bed.

There was the first shock of contact when he took her in his arms. It hadn't been like that with Connie, he found himself remembering, guiltily. Skin was definitely something mysterious, inexplicable, he found himself thinking, was connected with emotion most of the time, but not always. Someday somebody was going to make a study of it, or take a poll, and get rich on the findings.

"I wonder if that lizard is still up there, watching us?" Hope asked.

"You didn't mention him the last time you were here. I didn't think you'd noticed him."

"I don't say everything that crosses my mind."

"I've noticed that."

"Anyway, you're lucky the lizard doesn't know how to talk."

Brandt laughed self-consciously, and thought of Connie. "Even if he could, he'd have nothing much to say," he replied.

She was lying back on the pillows, and she reached down and ran her fingers through his hair. Then she took a handful and pulled. The telephone rang, as if it had been chronometrically timed to coincide with her caress, or whatever the act of pulling his hair was supposed to be. He sat up and reached across her to answer it.

"Let it ring," she said. "You're not expecting any calls at this hour, are you?"

He hesitated. The phone rang on and on. Then it stopped. Brandt lay with his shoulder touching her side. The ringing started once again, and he sat up quickly and picked up the receiver. It was Freddy Weaver.

"You weren't asleep, were you? Not at this early hour? Or were you otherwise engaged?" Weaver asked.

"I was in the shower," Brandt said warily. "What's your problem?"

"Guy Manning's dead. I thought you ought to know. The funeral's tomorrow afternoon."

"What? I thought he was out of danger. What happened?"

"A relapse. It can happen when there's been brain damage. A blood clot, or something like that. We're not much, you know. 'As flies to wanton boys, are we to the gods,' I think is the quotation. 'They kill us for their sport.' "

"That poor woman," Brandt said. "Was he a Catholic?"

"I don't think so. But that doesn't seem to matter. If you pay, they let you into their little cemetery."

"What time tomorrow afternoon?"

"Five-thirty."

"Okay. I'll see you there." He hung up. Hope had pulled up the top sheet and was watching him.

"Bad news?" she asked.

Brandt nodded. “A friend of mine has died. Guy Manning. The man who owns *Lulubelle,* or used to own her.”

“I’m sorry.”

“He wasn’t a close friend, but I’ve known him for a good many years. He came down here, and everything went wrong for him. He had an automobile accident near Fuengirola.”

“That awful road. When are they going to do something about it?”

“Never,” Brandt said. He lay back on the bed again. He felt used up, drained.

“Shall I get us a drink?”

“I’ll do it,” he said. He got up and went out to the kitchen. He made a vodka and tonic for Hope and poured himself a strong Scotch and water.

“Shall we get dressed and go for a walk along the beach?” Hope asked as he carried their drinks back into the moonlit room.

“No. Let’s stay here.”

“If we’d gone to my place, the call would never have reached you,” she said. “People are always in a hurry with bad news. It could have waited until morning.”

“What time do you have to be home?” he asked her.

“Oh, one o’clock or so. In case Max calls. Unfortunately they’ve repaired the telephone.”

Brandt sipped his drink. The cool breeze from the south lifted the white curtains behind the French doors that led out onto the terrace. *Levante,* he thought to himself. The sea would be flat the next day. Good weather for Freddy Weaver’s charter. He turned over on his side and studied the face of the woman lying next to him in his bed. The moonlight slanting across the bed made her dark hair stand out against the white of the pillow. She smiled at him a little sadly. “We’re not here for very long, are we? That’s what makes it so silly to live unhappy lives.” She put out her hand and touched his cheek. He drew her to him and kissed her.

“Making love is not a requirement, you know. We can just talk.”

“I know that,” Brandt said. He felt a tenderness for her that he had never really felt before. He didn’t want to lose her, no matter what might happen. For in the back of his mind, he had the vague suspicion that everything was starting to go wrong. Manning’s accident had been a turning point. Or maybe the robbery at the Villa Miramar, which had preceded it. He didn't believe in portents or omens, had always scoffed at mystic superstitions. People died as a result of violent mishaps every day, especially in Spain. *España, todo peligro,* was a saying he had heard on one of his first visits. Everything was dangerous in this country.

Hope was settled firmly inside his embrace. This is what we have as a defense against death, he thought; a little desire. And it was not so little once he was able to put Manning, lying dead in his hospital bed, out of his mind. But later, when they lay spent on the disheveled bed, the even sharper realization of the pain Marie Manning was experiencing at that moment came back to haunt him, and he found himself wondering if any of his friends would be making love on the night of his own decease.

"What are you thinking about?" Hope asked in a whisper.

"Life," he said, trying to sound suitably lighthearted. "Our own sunny little vale of tears."

"How old was your friend?"

"I don't know. In his early fifties."

She turned to face him. "I love you," she said. "Do you know that?"

The familiar words startled him. He took her hand in the darkness. "I'm glad," he said. "That's the way I feel."

It was about the only place left in town that was still typically Spanish, Brandt thought as he walked through the wrought-iron gates of the cemetery. The white gravel walks and the whitewashed tree trunks of the cypress trees, and the white marble tombs were as Andalusian as the narrow streets of the old quarter had been long ago, before the tourist bars and curio shops had taken over. It was hot. Even in the shade, the air was heavy with heat, as the sun was still high in the cloudless sky.

There were not many people on hand for Guy Manning's last journey. Brandt recognized some of the members of the British community from San Pedro, all standing together in a small group. Opposite them there was a small gathering of locals, Spanish waiters from the failed restaurant, Brandt guessed, as well as Manolo and about half a dozen sailors from the port. Brandt nodded to them and went to stand behind them in the shade of a palm tree. He was a little early. He felt uncomfortable in his blazer and white shirt complete with necktie, which he had put on for the occasion. The blazer was the only half-formal item of clothing he had brought with him from London, in case someone he knew got married. He had never imagined he would be going to a funeral while he was on his holiday.

He felt a hand on his left arm. It was Freddy Weaver. He, too, was dressed in a navy blue blazer with golden buttons, only he had been clever enough to wear an open white shirt. "I'm glad you made it," he said.

Brandt nodded. "Have you seen Marie?" he asked Weaver in a low voice.

"No, I haven't. I thought I'd wait until tomorrow and go by the house. I'm not much good at this sort of thing."

"Who is?" Brandt asked.

Weaver shrugged. His grip tightened on Brandt's arm. "Come on over here for a minute," he said.

Brandt followed him down one of the narrow walks to a family tomb behind a cypress tree. Weaver lit a cigarette. "The boat's all yours again," he said.

"You've finished with her?"

Weaver nodded. "All finished for now."

"Successful op?"

"I have no complaints." He grinned, the cigarette hanging from his bearded lips. "I'm going to make a little extra contribution to the widow," he told Brandt. "Instead of a thousand, I'm going to pay her a little more. She probably won't want to take it, so I thought you might extend your charter for the month of August, and I'll give you the money."

"Without strings?"

"Without strings."

"That's a nice gesture. It's a shame you didn't think of it earlier."

"I had no idea my little exploit would be so rewarding," Weaver said, grinning.

"Why don't you charter *Lulubelle* for the month of August?"

"I'm not that crazy about the sea. And I thought it would look better to Manolo if you kept her. I can always borrow the good ship from you if the need arises."

"I hope that won't turn out to be the case." Even in the presence of eternity, Weaver was looking after his business interests. And making use of others as a front. Still, he was trying to be decent, in his own crooked way. The Robin Hood of the pushers. "Do you think Manolo is on to what you used the boat for?" Brandt asked.

"Oh, he may have a vague idea," Weaver said. "But I gave him a big *propina* the next day, after my moonlight cruise. He grunted and said *gracias,* so I don't think he'll go to the police." He indicated the main gate of the cemetery. "We'd better join the others," he said. "I think they're about to bring in the 'mortal remains' of our poor friend." He turned back to Brandt for an instant. "I'll see you tomorrow night, in any case," he whispered. *"Si Dios quiere.* If there is a God watching us."

"You probably will," Brandt said. It all depended on whether Hope would be alone or not. He could, of course, bring her to the Safires' and brazen the whole thing out, put an end to all the hiding and intrigue. He followed Weaver back down the narrow path, glancing at some of the names on the headstones as he went. The luxury of having a family tomb was an exception. Now they shoved what was left of you into a small cement locker and left you there as long as there was someone around to pay the fees the town charged as rental. He was damned if he was going to have any part of that. He wanted to be cremated and have his ashes dropped in the Med. That is, if he died here, in sunny Spain. It was probably better than dying in Southern California and being buried near one of those big freeways, with the traffic roaring past all day and all night. The noise won't bother you, pal, he said to himself.

He looked to his right and saw that Marie Manning was coming down the main path of the cemetery. She was dressed in black, with a veil, and she was crying quietly. On both sides of her were two women of her own age, both of them unmistakably British. They were dry-eyed, but there was genuine sorrow on their faces. Two men in dark suits, probably the British consul from Málaga, Brandt thought, and the vice-consul.

The procession turned off to the left and followed one of the narrower lanes to where the casket was waiting. The grave had been dug, and the local gravediggers were there as well, both of them characters out of Shakespeare, comics, at first glance. One of them was short, and the other one very tall. They were wearing dark gray uniforms that didn't fit them very well. A man who looked like the vicar from the local chapter of the Church of England was standing behind them. He was a tall, bony-faced Englishman with reddish hair, and he was sunburned the way the Brits always were, the sandy-haired ones, anyway.

Brandt felt a tug on his sleeve and, turning, saw that Phyllis Dexter had stepped over to him. She was wearing gray slacks and a white blouse, not quite the right attire for the occasion. Still, her hair was hidden under a black scarf, and she was not wearing any make-up.

"Max is back," she said in a low voice.

"I hope you didn't come here just to tell me that," Brandt replied. He didn't know why this woman automatically brought out the worst in him. He hadn't liked her from the first moment of their meeting in Benavis, and he didn't like her any better now.

She looked offended. "Of course not," she said. "Marie has been a friend of mine for years."

"I'm sorry. I wasn't trying to be rude," Brandt replied. He noticed that she was still glaring at him as they came to a halt in the sunshine on the near side of the grave. Then she shrugged and moved nearer to the widow and the British contingent behind her.

The vicar said, "Let us pray."

Brandt glanced down at his dust-covered moccasins. If only he believed in prayer, he thought. He had as a youngster, while under the influence of a Catholic nurse from Silesia who had looked after him until he was thirteen. He had fallen in love with her, he remembered once again, because she was pretty and affectionate. Until the age of eleven she had allowed him to get into bed with her on Saturday mornings, when there was no need to get up early and get ready for school. Strange that her image should return to him at this unpropitious moment. Death and desire, he thought for the second time in twenty-four hours. He felt beads of sweat beginning to form on his back, now exposed to the direct rays of the sun. He forced his mind to go to the body inside the coffin. Poor

Guy. He would undoubtedly have been shocked if he had been able to guess what was going through his friend's mind.

He glanced over at Phyllis Dexter. She had her handkerchief out and was drying her tears. Maybe I misjudged her, Brandt thought; maybe she's not as tough a lady as she appears to be. In any case, she's learned to weep on the right occasions. Then suddenly the memory of the day he had gone swimming with Manning off the stern of *Lulubelle* came back to him, and he felt a sudden hatred for useless death. It was all so pointless, so stupid. He started to recite the Lord's Prayer, and found that he could remember it only in German.

The back road near the cemetery was choked with traffic once the funeral was over. He wanted to get to the office before seven to see if there were any messages. But the main road looked hopeless. People were returning from the beach, and there were a lot of cars with construction workers going home from their jobs. He turned right on the *carretera de circunvalación,* thinking he would take one of the small roads that led through the center of the old town and beat the traffic that way. But he took the wrong turnoff and found himself facing one-way traffic, with an ancient truck moving toward him, its driver gesticulating furiously.

He put the Peugeot into reverse, and backed into the parking lot of one of the new high-rise towers that had been built near the municipal market, and waited for the truck to pass. The driver was shaking his head as he went by, cursing him, no doubt, and Brandt waved to the man and smiled. There was no use trying now to make it to the office before they closed the place, so he parked his car and went into a small corner bar. He felt thirsty. A beer was a better idea than trying to get back to the office. There was little chance that Hope had called, anyway, since she had sent Phyllis to warn him that Max had returned.

"Una caña," he told the barkeep, a squat little man in a stained white shirt and black trousers.

"¿Algo mas?" the man wanted to know. The bar was empty, and at the end of the counter there were half a dozen plates with the hors d'oeuvres the barkeep was obviously anxious to sell before the flies ate them.

"Nada, gracias."

The barman brought him his draft beer and left a small tab under the cardboard coaster. Brandt sipped his drink. He was staring off at the entrance of the building in front of him when he saw a woman and a man pull up in a Mercedes. It was Phyllis Dexter. She had taken off her veil. Her streaked blond hair was shoulder length. The man with her was Max Clarendon. He looked around nervously before following her into the entrance of the apartment block.

"Death and desire," Brandt muttered to himself, and the squat little man at the other end of the bar looked over at him, puzzled. *"¿Tiene usted un teléfono?"* Brandt asked him, searching in his wallet for the number Hope had given him on the previous evening, after warning him never to use it while Max was in town.

The man shook his head sadly. *"No hay,"* he said. *"Lo siento."*

It didn't matter, Brandt thought. Bad news could wait. It was also quite possible that Max and Phyllis had gone into the apartment house to visit a friend or a business associate. Just because Max had appeared to be nervous was hardly enough evidence to assume that they were lovers. And even if they were, it seemed most unlikely that they would have chosen that precise moment to make love. That death stimulated desire was a theory that he had become obsessed with because of his own behavior of the previous night. In any case, he didn't relish playing the part of the informer, especially as Phyllis was Hope's best friend. It was better to wait, Brandt decided. If Clarendon was planning to get rid of his mistress, he would make his move soon enough. And if Phyllis was his accomplice, it was better that Hope should discover the unpleasant fact of her friend's duplicity by herself.

He glanced at his watch. It was almost six-thirty. He would have to hurry if he wanted to arrive at the office before it closed. Although Saturday was usually a busy day because of the arrival of prospective buyers from England, Grey closed up shop punctually at seven.

But Esmeralda was still at her desk in the reception hall when Brandt arrived. She was reading the current issue of *Holá,* keeping up with doings of the well-born and famous of her native land. "Any calls for me?" he asked the girl.

She shook her head without looking up from the magazine. The door of Richard Grey's office was open, and he called out to Brandt as he went by.

"How was the funeral?" he asked. He was leaning back in his leather chair, his hands clasped behind his head.

"Not much fun."

"Occasions like that rarely are," Grey said drily. "A chap with a beard came looking for you a few minutes ago," he added. "I told him that you'd probably gone home."

"He didn't say what he wanted?" Brandt asked.

"Nope. Not a word. I didn't ask him, either. He didn't look like a prospective buyer." He paused. "Pull the door shut, will you, David?"

Brandt stepped inside the room and did so. He was puzzled. Grey was not usually careful about conversations carried on in English within hearing of the Spanish-speaking staff. "Something wrong?" Brandt asked.

"No. Not really," Grey said. He leaned back in his leather chair. "Max Clarendon dropped in this afternoon. He doesn't usually do that, especially on the way back from the airport. He'd just come in from Paris. Said the weather was lousy up north. But I didn't think that was all he had on his mind." He paused briefly. "He asked about you," he went on. "Wanted to know what sort of chap you were. How long I'd known you. How long you'd been with the company. I asked him why he was so interested, and he said he'd met you at a party and that he was just curious. You didn't have words with him, did you?"

"No," Brandt said. "We were introduced, and that was about all. The conversation was about fishing, and he said that there were no fish left in the Med. That was the only contact we had."

Grey nodded. "All right. That answers my question. He never interferes in our business as a rule, although he *is* a partner. Still, it's a good idea for you to keep on the right side of him. That is, if you're really planning to stay with us. Should he take a dislike to you for some reason, he could make it difficult for us to keep you on. I just thought I'd let you know."

"Thanks, Richard."

"Your pal Amir called today from London, too, and sent you his regards. He's all for your coming in with us on a permanent basis. But even that wouldn't help much if Clarendon had a gripe against you. Do you follow me?"

"I do."

"That's it, then. You'd better get on home and meet up with your bearded friend. Weaver, I think he said his name was."

"Could be," Brandt said. Something had definitely gone wrong at the Villa Miramar, but it was too late to call there now. And why had Weaver come looking for him? He had just seen him at the funeral, not more than an hour ago.

"By the way," Grey said, "that American photographer was quite impressed with our project. He took a lot of pictures. Said he hopes his editors will give it a good play. That would be a help. We could use a few American buyers. When we run out of Brits." He got to his feet and stretched lazily. "Well, have a good weekend, David, or what's left of it."

"You too, Richard." He started toward the door. Grey followed him slowly.

"Sometimes I envy you being single," Grey said. "A married man never has as much fun. I suppose there are other compensations," he added. "The chances of getting into trouble are greatly reduced."

"Are they? That's not what I hear."

"Happily married, is what I had in mind," Grey said, and laughed good-naturedly. "Well, good hunting."

"Get a good day's rest," Brandt replied as he went through the door.

Weaver was waiting in his car when Brandt drove up. He had taken off his blazer and rolled up the sleeves of his shirt, and he looked a little the worse for wear as he stepped over to the Peugeot. "I'm sorry to trek you down like this, David," he said, "but something urgent has just come up."

"Trouble?" Brandt asked.

"Well, not really trouble, but the makings of trouble, if you know what I mean. Can I come upstairs?"

"Sure. I'm not doing anything this evening. I was thinking of having a swim before it gets dark, but that can wait."

"I won't take much of your time," Weaver said.

"Join me in the swim."

"No, I don't think I'll do that. Maybe just hit you for a drink, that's all."

They went up in the small elevator together without exchanging a word. Brandt opened the front door of the apartment, and Weaver followed him inside. The faithful Carmen had closed the shutters leading out onto the balcony, but had left the French doors open, so it was reasonably cool in the living room. Brandt hung his blazer over the back of a chair and went out into the kitchen for some ice. Weaver had unlatched the shutters by the time he returned, and was standing looking out at the sunset.

"Not a bad little pad," he said appreciatively.

"No, it's not bad," Brandt said. "I keep meaning to buy a few old paintings at the *rastro* to cheer up the place a little, but I never seem to have time. What'll you have?"

"Anything that's easy," Weaver said. "A Scotch, or a vodka."

"You name it."

"Scotch. With ice and a dash of plain water."

Brandt made himself the same thing and carried the two drinks out onto the terrace. A trio of windsurfers were struggling with their colorful sails in the mild evening breeze. Germans, probably, Brandt thought, making the most of the long day. Nobody else would be out at that hour. "Now then, what's happened?" he asked Weaver.

"The best laid plans of mice and men . . ." Weaver began, and knocked off half the contents of his glass. "One of the boys who works with our group has got himself busted."

"Really? That doesn't sound good."

"He wasn't actively engaged in our enterprise at the time," Weaver said. "He got in a fight over a girl. There were harsh words, and he pulled a knife on his opponent. The fellow he was arguing with may not pull through. A typically Spanish incident."

"When did you hear about this?"

"Just now. His father and mother were waiting for me at my hotel when I got home from the funeral."

"And how does that affect you?"

"Well, I don't quite know, but the cops have him, and the chances are they'll work him over. Of course, they have to watch their step a little more than they did in the old days, but when a man's facing a murder rap, he's apt to lose his cool."

"He might talk, is that it?"

"He might," Weaver said. "Stranger things have happened." He didn't seem excessively worried, but he wasn't as relaxed as he had been at the cemetery. "Anyway, I think it's a good moment for me to return to Kénitra."

"When do you plan to leave?"

"I don't know. Tonight, or maybe tomorrow. I hate to miss Lew Safire's party, but on the other hand, I'd just as soon not be too available for a couple of weeks."

"Do the police know where to find you?"

"No, but they might get lucky, just this once. All of which really doesn't concern you, I venture to say. Nor should it. But I did want to make sure Marie Manning got her money. I owe her for the week's charter, and then there's the extra thousand I mentioned to you." He reached into the pocket of his trousers and brought out a wad of five-thousand-peseta notes. "I thought I'd give you the two hundred thousand I owe Marie Manning, and let you pay her. If you don't mind, that is."

"I don't mind," Brandt said slowly, "but what do I say? How do I explain that I'm paying your charter?"

"You tell her the truth," Weaver said. "That I had to leave town and gave you the money."

"Suppose your knife-wielding friend gives the cops the name of the boat you used? What happens then?"

"Oh, I don't think he'll do that. Anyway, the transfer was made at night, and he may never have had a look at our stern."

"Does he know your name?"

"No, I don't think so. He might have heard somebody refer to me as Federico, and he wouldn't have any trouble describing me. I've thought of shaving off my beard, of course. I was even going to ask you if you'd mind letting me use your facilities. I hate to go to a barber shop. There's not a clean establishment in the whole town, except maybe the Don Pepe, and I don't want to go there. They know me too well." Weaver was counting the money he had taken out of his pocket. He had a fairly good amount of money left after he had counted out the two hundred thousand pesetas.

"Wouldn't it be a better idea to go home and start practicing law again?" Brandt asked.

"Undoubtedly," Weaver said, and grinned. "But I hate all that smog in L.A., and my partners wouldn't be all that anxious to have me back, I believe. Who needs a fifty-five-year-old hippy who's been out of circulation for damned near a decade? And the kind of cases I really enjoy handling don't pay all that much. I was a public defender, you know, when I first started."

"I'd heard that," Brandt said. "You were one of the good guys."

Weaver laughed. "I still am," he said. "Now stick all these bills under the mattress, or wherever you hide your cash, and show me where the bathroom is, and I won't bore you anymore with my problems."

"I hate walking around with that much cash," Brandt said, but he picked up the money and followed Weaver into the living room. "I'm not crazy about being your paymaster, either. I've got problems of my own."

"I know you have, but this'll take your mind off them. You can go by the house tonight and give Marie the money. You should make an appearance there, anyway."

"Suppose she doesn't want to accept it? Guy probably didn't tell her about your arrangement."

"That's the whole point, for God's sake!" Weaver exploded. "You're chartering her goddamned boat! In all likelihood she doesn't even know how much Guy was charging you. You're coming out ahead, too. You get the boat for the month of August while she takes a trip back to England and gets herself straightened out."

"Unless, of course, the cops seize *Lulubelle* first."

"There's no chance of that, none whatsoever." He started to take off his shirt. He had a long hairless torso. His body was completely untouched by the sun. It looked slightly obscene to Brandt. "What kind of a razor do you have?" he asked.

"I have a Gillette," Brandt said. "But you'd better think again before you shave. Your jaws will look as pale as your belly. Not exactly a great disguise, it seems to me."

"I hadn't thought of that. You're right for once." He studied his face in the mirror over the wash basin. "To hell with it," he said. "I'll keep the beard and take my chances. Mind if I wash up a little?"

"Go ahead."

Weaver opened both taps. While the water ran into the basin, he lit a cigarette. Brandt went to the bathroom cupboard and handed his self-invited guest a clean towel. "I know a little about your problems, too, my friend," Weaver said cheerfully, "and they're not really very serious." He soaped his hands and his chest, and dabbed a little soap under each arm. "I only have one little bit of advice," he continued. "Never take a girl away from a rich man. It won't work. No matter how crazy she is about you at the moment, the sad day will come when she'll realize that she's made a big mistake. Because there's nothing like being poor for killing a romance. Take my word for it!"

Brandt said, "I don't know what you're talking about."

"Oh, come on. Lew filled me in on what's going on. This is a small town; you ought to know that. Everybody's wise to everything. Anyway, I never give advice. I quote the rule book and the odds. That's all." He rinsed off his chest and his armpits. Then he started to dry himself. "There's another factor you ought to think about," he said. "You've been on your own for years. You were attached to Pam, but that was different. She was an independent lady. She had a job, and you both lived in the same town. That's not like setting out to keep house for real. *She's* going to get tired of doing the dishes, and *you're* going to get tired of coming home to dry them." He chuckled to himself. "That's the good thing about the habit. Once you're on the stuff, you very rarely feel horny. At my age, that is. So that keeps you from making a horse's ass of yourself."

"You don't say."

"Because, finally, your pecker can get you into more trouble than any other part of your body." He grinned at himself in the mirror. "You haven't got a pit stick, have you?" He scanned the shelf in front of him and found the deodorant. "I feel like a new man," he told Brandt. "All thanks to you."

"What exactly did Safire tell you?"

"Nothing specific. Just rumors. And if he's on the wrong track, all the better." He left the bathroom and collected his shirt off the bed. "You'll be seeing him tomorrow night. You can ask him yourself." He unzipped his wrinkled trousers and stuffed his shirt inside them without bothering to button it. "Now, then, if you don't hear from me for a little while, don't worry. Give the widow the money, and keep your nose clean. And I'm glad you're no longer pissed-off at me. I hate losing a friend."

"I hate losing friends, too. Especially to the law."

"Well, you don't have to worry about me. The quick and the dead. Isn't that what they used to say in the war? I learned that lesson the hard way."

He crossed the room to where he had left his glass. "One for the road?" he asked. "Do you have time?"

"I have time," Brandt said. "I can always go swimming in the dark." Weaver was already helping himself to the whiskey. The telephone rang. He went quickly to answer it. It was Consuela. Her husband had arrived from Madrid; they were going to dinner at the club with some friends, and she wanted Brandt to join them.

He agreed at once. It would be a relief to be among Spaniards for a change. He could drop in on Marie Manning on the way; he wasn't supposed to meet the others until ten-thirty. He put down the receiver. Weaver was sprawled on the couch, drink in hand.

"You're a popular fellow," he said. "Especially with the ladies. I don't quite know what they see in you. You're not particularly handsome. I guess it's the wholesome quality you exude. David Brandt. A nice, clean-cut American boy. Not rich, but honest. It's a shame you've never figured out how to cash in on your virtues."

He sat on one of the low couches, with his back to the sea, watching the crowd in the flickering lights that were concentrated on the small, rectangular dance floor, wondering what the hell he was doing there. The discothèque seemed to him to be some sort of torture chamber, invented by Torquemada's successor, and yet his Spanish friends all went there, night after night. It was as if they expected something extraordinary to happen to them, although it never did. The women always complained about how tired they were at the beginning of every evening, but they always agreed to go for just one drink. Then they stayed on for hours, until four or five in the morning. And they would continue to do so for the entire month of August, to the end of their vacations, following a pattern that for some reason they were unable to change. They slept until one o'clock in the afternoon of the following day, dragged themselves to the beach for an hour or two of sun, then went to lunch and collapsed after the meal for their siestas, after which it was time to go to the hairdresser or plan the evening's activities. And it was only the middle of July now. Six weeks of the same grueling routine lay ahead.

He thought of Marie Manning in the small house behind San Pedro de Alcántara, and the hurried half-hour he had spent with her. She had looked rather bewildered when he delivered the money. As expected, she had known nothing of Weaver's arrangements with her dead husband. Brandt had lied rather clumsily, explaining that Weaver had taken over a part of his charter. She had nodded and thanked him. She seemed stunned by everything that had happened. The doctor had given her some pills to sleep, she explained, and she had already taken a couple. It was nine-thirty, and she planned to be in bed by ten. Suddenly her eyes had filled with tears. "You're very kind," she said. "I really shouldn't accept the money, but I do need it." He had denied that it was charity, had insisted that he and Weaver were getting a bargain at that price. She shook her head, weeping quietly, her hands trembling as she held her handkerchief to her eyes. He had wanted to leave, and yet had felt guilty to be going off to a dinner party. She had read his thoughts. "Please don't feel you have to stay here. I'm all right on my own," she had assured him.

More people were arriving at the discothèque, the men in silk shirts and the women dressed up in the fashionable and expensive rags of the day. Consuela waved to him from the dance floor, moving gracefully to the beat of the loud music. She was dancing with her husband, and Brandt knew that she was worried about him sitting there alone, because all the others in their party were also on the dance floor. She beckoned to him to join them, and he raised both of his hands in a gesture of mock horror, having already explained to her that he was a terrible dancer. He waved to her and blew her a kiss. An instant later he found Safire standing in front of him with Wilma, who was all decked out in a sky-blue kaftan trimmed in gold.

"Look, darling," Safire said to his wife, "the wandering lover boy."

Brandt got to his feet and was hugged by both of them. Wilma rubbed the lipstick off his cheeks after she had kissed him. "Where the hell have you been hiding?" she asked. "You dropped clear out of sight."

"Don't ask embarrassing questions," Safire told her. "Can we sit down for a minute while José finds us a table?"

"Of course." He wanted to tell Safire off about his gossiping, but it didn't seem the time or the place. "I've been working," he said to Wilma, who had already turned away from him and was watching the dancers.

"It's tough duty here in July and August," Safire said in a low voice. "Tonight we're with the usual small party of eighteen, some of them intimate friends of yours." He jerked his thumb in the direction of the bar and the entrance of the discothèque beyond it.

Brandt could see a large group moving toward them. He caught sight of Max Clarendon and Phyllis, and quite a long distance behind them he saw Hope, followed by Yves Brouyère. There were a few other people he remembered having seen at the Figuerases' dinner party, the non-Spanish contingent that had been seated at Consuela's father's table and to whom he hadn't been introduced. One of them was apparently repaying the hospitality, Brandt reckoned, for he saw that Teresa and Figueras were bringing up the rear of the party. They were both greeting friends at the various tables they passed, and had become separated from the main body of the expedition.

"I've heard that you've been doing a little gossiping," Brandt said to Safire under his breath. "That's not what I expect from an old friend."

Safire looked startled. "Me?" he asked. "Who told you that?"

"What difference does it make?"

"Well, I'd like to know. Because it's a lie."

"I think Freddy Weaver's too far gone to lie."

"Oh, you've been talking to Freddy. Well, that's different. I wasn't gossiping with him. We were talking about you, that's all.

Two friends discussing an old buddy. And I guess I did repeat a rumor I'd heard. As a matter of fact, I told Freddy that I felt sort of responsible, since I'd introduced you to the lady."

Max and Hope Clarendon were moving past the table, leading the procession. Brandt gripped Safire's knee as a warning to be careful, but he had already seen them. Wilma rose and joined the other guests as they moved on to an adjoining table. "What rumors?" Brandt asked Safire once they were out of earshot.

"What do you care?" Safire replied. "You don't know the guy, and you're not the first lover the girl's had."

"I care," Brandt said, "for several reasons, and the least important one is that her husband is a big investor in the company I work for. I've already been warned by my boss. But fuck that. That's only a job. I don't want to cause the lady anguish, that's reason number one. It doesn't matter to me how many men she has on her list. I don't want her to have any trouble on *my* account. Does that seem so amazing to you?"

"No. Of course not," Safire said, flushing despite his suntan. "And that's what I said to Freddy. One of us ought to warn you. Or warn *her.*" He started to get to his feet, but Brandt pulled him back onto his chair.

"Where did the rumors come from?" he asked. "I want to know."

"Oh, various places," Safire said, evasively. "Yves dropped a hint the last time I saw him. And Phyllis Dexter, though she was more concerned with *your* reputation. She thought maybe you were in on robbing the lady of her jewels. The inside man on the caper." He grinned. "Of course, I straightened her out on that score, told her that probably the one big glaring fault you'd always had was being too goddamned honest. Especially for the movie business."

"That was sweet of you."

"Not really," Safire said. "I was protecting my reputation, too. You met the lady at my house." He got to his feet. "If you did pull the job," he added with an impish look on his face, "I hope you won't forget to fork over my cut. The finder's fee, as it's called in Tinseltown."

"I think the lady would like to give you that herself . . . for your gallant recommendation."

Safire looked back, alarmed. "You didn't quote me, did you?" he asked. "That would really have been a shitty thing to do."

"I've always been too goddamned honest. You said so yourself," Brandt replied. He noticed that Safire had started to sweat.

"I'll talk to you about *that* tomorrow night," he said to Brandt. "One on one."

"I hope I can make it."

Safire looked back once again before he had reached the neighboring table. He didn't look pleased. He shook his head and glanced up for an instant at the ceiling in feigned horror.

Brandt noticed that Max was watching them, but he didn't care. As a matter of fact, he didn't give a goddamn, he decided. He suddenly felt liberated. Clarendon, Grey, Safire, the whole bunch of them could go to hell! What a nest of vipers the place was! The foreign colony, anyway.

He saw Consuela and her husband approaching. As they came nearer the table, she caught sight of her parents and went over to embrace them. Brandt got to his feet and was introduced to Figueras and his wife yet once again. The old man didn't remember him, for which Teresa chided him in wifely fashion.

"But David has been at our house," she said. "Not only here, but in Madrid."

"You must forgive an old man who has had too many whiskies," Figueras said. "And this place, *este inferno.*" He waved a sun-blotched hand in the direction of the dance floor. "It creates havoc with the mind."

Consuela winked at Brandt. "We dance?" she asked.

"It's not my thing," Brandt said. "I've already warned you."

"It doesn't matter. They are playing a slow."

He followed her to the dance floor without a backward glance at Hope's table. Consuela turned to face him and opened her arms. She had a great figure, there was no doubt about that, Brandt thought. But he felt slightly ill at ease. He was reminded, for some strange reason, of his first year in college, when he had been forced to dance with some date he had acquired during the big-game weekend at some awful hotel in Boston. Dancing cheek-to-cheek with a girl you hadn't gone to bed with had seemed absurd to him ever since, probably because it reminded him painfully of his brief attendance at that Ivy League college.

Consuela said: "It's hot. And I have seen at least twenty people we must still invite."

"You better write down their names before you forget."

She laughed. "And Marta, the *novia* we have brought for you? What do you think of her?"

"She's charming. A little young." He had barely spoken ten words with the extra girl, a dark Andalusian beauty from one of the best Málaga families, of course. She had been more interested in one of the young men from Madrid, who was there with his wife, rather than in talking to Brandt.

"But she is *guapa,* no?"

"Yes. *Muy guapa.*" That seemed to be very important, that the girls be *guapa,* beautiful.

"Pero un poco fría. You say 'cold' in English, too?"

"You bet we do."

"But I believe you prefer American ladies."

"Not necessarily." Was she in on the gossip, too, he wondered. He noticed Hope over on the far side of the floor, dancing with Yves. They were talking animatedly. He turned Consuela to the left and saw that Max was dancing with Phyllis. He was holding her close, and she had her eyes closed. She probably thinks that she's at the local hunt ball, Brandt remarked to himself with malice. "You want to sit down?" he asked Consuela. "It really is too hot to dance."

"As you like."

He asked, "What makes you think I prefer my own kind?"

"Nada." She laughed self-consciously. "I have heard that you are very much in love with a *gringa.* I forget who told me."

"It doesn't matter."

"No. Of course not." She paused. "You think somebody could fall very much in love with *me?*"

"I would think *so.* Why do you ask?"

"Because I am curious about your opinion."

"I'm sure you won't have any trouble," Brandt said. "Though

your husband looks like a fairly strong fellow. That might scare off some of the boys."

"Oh, he is," she said, and laughed again. "And very *posesivo.*"

"Well, I'll watch my step."

"But you are not interested," she said. "I know that. But I am happy to have you as a friend."

"I'm glad," Brandt said, and meant it. "Let's go and have a drink."

They went back to their table. Most of the others had returned as well. A "slow" was obviously not too popular with the younger customers. Brandt poured a whiskey and water for himself and one for Consuela. There were three bottles on the table, with a large bucket of ice. Brandt downed half a glass of his drink. He was thirsty, and he had decided not to worry about the drive home. They were destined to stay there for hours, he felt certain, and he could always switch to plain water on the next round.

He looked up. Hope was moving past the table without her dancing partner, and suddenly, without even thinking of what he was doing, he rose and took her by the arm. She looked startled. "Let's dance," he said, and pulled her off in the direction of the crowd on the dance floor. He didn't feel drunk, but he didn't feel entirely sober, either.

Hope said, "I'm not sure this is a good idea."

"I am," Brandt said. "It's the only good idea I've had in years."

They danced in silence. The next tape brought them Julio Iglesias, the poet and the lover with the velvet voice, whose face was on every magazine in Spain at least once a year. Times had changed, Brandt mused. It was no longer a scarred *torero* who was in vogue. The valiant had yielded their place in the limelight to the romantic. "*Cansado de querer, cansado de esperar* . . ." the seductive voice sang while they danced on. Brandt said: "That's exactly how I feel. Tired of loving, tired of waiting . . ."

"What did you say?"

She hadn't understood. Her Spanish wasn't that good. "Nothing. Not to worry, as you're fond of saying."

"But I am worried," she told him.

"Why? Because I asked you to dance? Is that such a crime?"

"We'll soon see."

"*He's* dancing cheek-to-cheek with your best friend."

"I know."

"I wonder if she's his best friend, too . . ."

"I've wondered about that, too. I'm not a total idiot, you know."

They made a tour of the floor. Everybody was there, all the rich residents and the summer crowd from Madrid, as well as a few Arabs; the local German princes were on hand, and a few well-heeled Italian refugees from terrorism and crime, and Richard Grey at the British table, and the local gentry, and the real estate hustlers, and the faded feature players of yore, and the newly arrived tarts from Paris, all of them ready for the month of August; and the crowd that used to go to Biarritz in the summer, and a few retired ambassadors, and the usual group of Peruvians and Argentinians, and quite a number of defectors from Soto Grande, the ones who couldn't stand the good life of golf and bridge and children any longer. "You know what I'd like to do now?" Brandt said. "I'd like to take you home and make love to you."

She didn't reply at once. It was as if she needed to consider his proposition seriously. "I wouldn't mind that," she said after a while, and smiled.

"Well?"

"It might turn out to be rather a final move."

"But you said yourself he'd found somebody else."

"He has. My best friend."

"Right. I saw them this afternoon, after the funeral."

She shrugged. She obviously wasn't interested in the sordid details. "I wish them luck," she said.

"In bullfighting, when a *torero* takes the bull away from one of his companions who is in danger, they call it making a *quite.*"

"Oh, really? How interesting. Well, I've had it coming to me, the *quite,* or whatever it's called."

"Does it bother you?"

"Nope." She sounded cheerful, had fallen in with his mood. "What about your friends?" she asked. "Will they miss you?"

"I don't think so."

"And you won't be sorry, tomorrow morning?"

"About what?"

"Your sudden folly. Or ours, to be more exact."

"They won't put us in jail for it."

"No. I suppose not."

"Instead of leaving right now, would you rather return to your table and tell them you've got a headache, and that you're going to take a taxi home?"

"It would look better. Help him save face."

"All right. I'll meet you in the parking lot in twenty minutes. I'll be waiting in my car in case you're delayed."

"Are we going to catch a boat tomorrow morning?"

"Yes. *Lulubelle.*"

"All right," she said in a voice that sounded like a little girl's voice, and he released her, and she went quite calmly along the edge of the dance floor to rejoin her party. Max was still dancing with Phyllis Dexter, Brandt noticed as he went back to join Consuela and the others.

He stood for what seemed a long time beside the Peugeot, thinking she might have trouble finding him in the crowded parking lot. Although it was nearly two o'clock in the morning, more and more people were arriving. Several of the larger groups turned back after conversing briefly with the doorman. That there was no more room inside should have been apparent by the number of cars, Brandt thought. He glanced at his watch. A few minutes more than half an hour had elapsed since he had left Consuela's table. Perhaps Hope had had a change of heart. Then he saw her step through the half-open door of the discothèque. He was just about to wave when he realized that Safire was with her. She turned and kissed him quickly on both cheeks. Safire was saying something to her, and she was shaking her head, and then he looked up and saw Brandt. He nodded slowly and went back inside the nightclub.

Brandt started the engine and pulled up in front of the entrance of the discothèque. Hope hadn't moved off the tiled terrace, and he reached across and opened the door for her. She got in, and he drove off at once. "I thought you'd changed your mind," he said.

She shook her head. She seemed slightly nervous. "Lew insisted on driving me home," she said. "He wouldn't hear of my taking a taxi. Then he saw you."

"And Max?"

"He didn't say anything."

"Was he angry?"

"No. He didn't appear to be. He went off to dance with our hostess."

"And what did Lew say after he saw me?"

"Nothing much. Just that he hoped that I knew what I was doing."

"And do you?"

"Yes," she said brightly. "I'm going to your place, and we're going to make passionate love." She put her hand on the back of his neck and kissed him gently on the cheek.

They had reached the main highway. He turned to the right once there was a lull in the heavy traffic. "It's as simple as that, is it?"

"Absolutely. Unless you've changed *your* mind?"

"I haven't," he said. "But, then, I don't owe anybody any explanations."

"Neither do I. Not anymore."

They drove on in silence. Brandt could feel his heart pounding inside his chest, as if he were off on some dangerous exploit, as if the next turn in the road would reveal a police patrol car that had been sent to stop them. What's the matter with you? he asked himself. You act as if you were about to risk your life.

Hope switched on the radio. The sound of a *fandango de Huelva* filled the car. It was hardly her favorite music, Brandt realized, but she didn't turn it off or change the station.

He lay awake for a long time after they had made love. Women were supposed to be the ones who were plagued by insomnia after sex, he thought, while men went immediately to sleep. It was probably all the whiskey he had consumed, and the loud music, and his accelerated heartbeat. There was also the little matter of his going off with Ms. Clarendon, for although they had taken the precaution of leaving the discothèque separately, it was unlikely that they had fooled anyone. All Max had to do was go to the telephone and dial the number of the Villa Miramar to check if his wife had arrived home. Or send Phyllis to call her "best friend," pretending that she was worried about her. Probably Max hadn't even bothered. He had only had to look over to the adjoining table and draw the obvious conclusion.

It was his asking Hope to dance that had decided the issue. He had acted on a sudden impulse, prompted a little by the whiskey; yet he realized that it had all been building up inside him for some time. All the pretending and the hiding and, worst of all, her fear of Clarendon; he had suddenly had enough of it, enough of being the subject of local gossip. Then, too, he had suddenly realized that he wanted her badly enough to make his move without waiting for the judicious moment, which would in all likelihood never arrive.

He remembered Freddy Weaver's warning, that it was always a mistake to take a woman away from a man who had money. That, too, had prompted him to act. And Safire being worried about him. They were all afraid of Max because he was rich. To hell with them all, Brandt thought, his defiant mood rising up inside him again. There were moments in a man's life when he had to stand up on his feet and be counted. And it wasn't much of a show of courage, at that. So why was he having trouble going to sleep? Hope was apparently less worried about the consequences of their actions than he was. Then he remembered something somebody had told him in the Navy, an old salt, a veteran of the submarine service, who had described to him how some of the enlisted men had crawled into their bunks during a depth-charge attack by a Japanese destroyer and had gone to sleep at the moment of greatest danger.

He glanced over at the tousled head on the pillow next to him. Hope's eyes were tightly shut. She looked untroubled, contented. For an instant he was tempted to wake her with an affectionate kiss, a wordless confirmation of his feelings for her. It was better to let her sleep, he decided; she was going to be taking most of the flak on the following day. That was one of Pamela's favorite expressions, part of the RAF slang she had inherited from her father, who had been a minor hero during the Battle of Britain. How would she react to the news that he had found a new love, he wondered; would she experience a slight pang of jealousy? He dismissed the thought. It was pointless. He knew that she had never worried about the past nor expected her former lovers to be eternally faithful. She had never even called him, once she had decided to end their relationship. And although the finality of her behavior had wounded him, he had secretly admired her decisiveness.

He, too, had finally learned to act with decision. It was about time. He closed his eyes. He heard Hope sigh, felt her move. Her hand reached out and found his shoulder. Very gently, she moved nearer to him. Her skin was warm and soft where it came into contact with his back. He felt content, at peace. He was no longer alone. A tree frog croaked outside the window of his bedroom, the only audible sound in the warm light.

He was not sure what it was that had awakened him. He could see that the sky outside the bedroom window was already a paler shade of blue. He had forgotten to close the shutters before going to bed. He was about to get up and do so when he heard the familiar creak of the bathroom door. He sat up. Hope was standing in the doorway of the bathroom in her bikini-like underclothes. She said: "I think I'd better go home. Will you take me?"

It was not the way he had expected this particular night to end. "Do you have to go?" he asked her.

She nodded and went to the chair on her side of the bed, where she had left her dress, the red Indian-muslin gown he had admired and yet slightly disapproved of, because it was a little too revealing. "I want to get back before the servants appear," she said. "I don't fancy arriving in this get-up and having a row in front of them." She turned her back toward him. "Will you zip me up?"

He got up and slipped on his shorts. "Why do you have to go back at all?" he asked, and closed the zipper carefully so as not to pinch her skin.

"You can't walk out on twelve years without an explanation of some kind. I think it's more civilized to say goodbye nicely. Or try to, anyway."

"When will I see you?" he asked.

"I don't know. Later in the afternoon. I'll call you."

He said, "All right. I'll be here around five," and kissed the back of her neck. They hadn't made any plans, hadn't discussed their next move. Would she be bringing her things back to his apartment, he wondered, remembering her walk-in closet at the villa, filled with clothes. There would be no room for even a small part of her wardrobe, he thought, and recalled Freddy Weaver's warning once again.

"That was a nice kiss," she said, and went back into the bathroom.

"Are you worried?" he asked, watching her in the mirror. He suddenly felt that he didn't know her at all, had no idea of what she was thinking; she appeared to be so calm, so very much in control of her emotions.

"No, not worried. Scared. I hate scenes. I suppose that's why we've stayed together all these years, Max and I. I've always been frightened of him."

"Is he apt to be violent?"

She shrugged. She was doing her eyebrows, darkening the sun-bleached hair with an eyebrow pencil. She obviously didn't want to answer his question.

"Has he ever behaved violently in the past?" Brandt insisted, watching her more closely, although her face was distorted in the glass. She was concentrating on her eyes.

She said: "It happened before, but it's not going to happen now. He has Phyllis. People aren't likely to get violent when they no longer care."

"I'll go with you," Brandt said.

"I don't think that would be a good idea. You're not really involved, except sort of as a catalyst. I should have left him long ago."

"But you didn't."

"No, I didn't," she said, turning away from the mirror. "That's why I have to face it now." She went over to Brandt and patted his cheek. "Everything will be all right," she said. "Not to worry."

He pulled on a clean shirt and slipped into his moccasins. It was getting light very quickly. He stepped out onto the balcony. The fishing boats were still riding the surface of the placid sea, but they had put out their lanterns. Hope joined him. She lit a cigarette. "Do you always smoke before breakfast?" he asked her, tensely.

"Only when I'm nervous," she said. "And today I have every right to be. Don't you agree? Shall we go?"

"If you feel you must." What else could he say? Once again he had a sense of foreboding, of helplessness.

The sugar cane was like a green wall on his side of the car, a dense vivid green, although the sun had not as yet come up. Brandt glanced at his watch. It was five-forty, not too disreputable an hour to be returning home, as far as the mores of life on the coast were concerned. But if you were bringing someone else's wife home to her husband, it was a little late. She's not his wife, he reminded himself, his eyes on the narrow dirt road ahead. There was a turn, and suddenly he was confronted by another car. It was the Mercedes. Max Clarendon was behind the steering wheel, and Phyllis Dexter was there beside him, slumped down low in her seat.

For an instant they all stared at each other, the radiators of the two cars not ten feet apart. It was such a ridiculous situation that Brandt found himself grinning inanely at the other couple facing him. Neither one of them smiled back. Finally Brandt turned and backed the Peugeot down the narrow lane to where there was a small verge on the side of the narrow track. The Mercedes roared past before he had stopped, leaving a cloud of reddish dust behind its spinning rear wheels.

He heard Hope laugh. "I've told him a hundred times that he should widen the road," she said. "That might have ended up as a nasty accident."

"Well, at least we've avoided a confrontation. If we had been a few minutes earlier, we all might have met on the front porch."

"That might have been more interesting."

"I would say so," Brandt agreed. He put the car in gear and drove on until they reached the main gate. Then he turned slowly onto the white gravel of the driveway. The Villa Miramar lay shuttered and silent in front of them. After they got out of the car, he said, "Do you want me to wait with you until he comes back?"

She shook her head. "He's not going to make a scene now," she said. "I'll bed down in the guest room until the dust has settled a little." She seemed strangely unperturbed. Her earlier nervousness was gone.

"I wonder why he brought her home with him," Brandt said. "Why didn't they go to her apartment?"

"Maybe they were just having a nightcap and waiting for me."

"That doesn't sound like a logical explanation to me."

She laughed drily. "You don't know Max. He probably wanted her to act as a witness to my disgrace. And as a cover-up. That's the way his mind works. He's devious. Ask anyone who's ever done business with him. He was probably delighted when I left the discothèque. He must have known that I was going to meet you. It was the one wrong move he was waiting for me to make."

"Then why did you agree to go? Why didn't you just say that you thought it was a mistake for us both to leave?"

She patted his cheek the way she had done back at the apartment, when she had told him not to worry. "Because I didn't give a damn whether it was the right thing to do," she said. "It was your idea. That's what counted. And still does," she added, and kissed him gently on the lips.

That was why she had been able to sleep, he thought, while he had lain awake with the lizard watching him; that is, if the lizard was still interested. "Yes, it was my idea," he said. "But I didn't know how he was going to react."

"Does it matter?" she asked and, rising on her toes, kissed him again. "The only thing that matters is that it's done. The ball's in his court now, to use one of his favorite expressions. He's not going to shoot me, or anything equally drastic."

"I was always more worried that you might shoot him."

She grinned mischievously and said: "Don't think I haven't thought of that, too. But I don't like the idea of doing ten years in a Spanish jail, though I'm told I'd probably only do four or five. But you needn't worry. I'm not going to shoot anybody."

He nodded. "I know that. The French say, *'Les histoires de fesses se règlent toujours.'* And they're usually right about that sort of thing."

"And what does that mean?"

"That stories having to do with tail always sort themselves out."

"How typically French! And how unattractive! I do think you'd better go now. In case he *does* come back." She put her arms around him and held him for a long time before letting him go.

Brandt looked back after he had gone down the marble steps.

She was watching him, smiling to herself, as if she found it all rather amusing.

"I love you," she called out in a cheerful voice.

He felt less than reassured. He drove slowly down the narrow dirt road, not wanting to meet the Mercedes again on one of the blind curves. He stopped at the junction with the main highway. There was virtually no traffic. He felt tired and hungry, but he knew that at that hour of the morning none of the cafés in town would be open.

When he arrived back at his apartment, he closed the shutters on the bedroom windows and took off his clothes. He was still hungry, but he decided that he'd better get some sleep. It was Sunday, so the office was closed. Thank God for that, he said to himself. How long, he wondered, would it take Max Clarendon to call Richard and complain about his employee? Well, he wasn't going to worry about that one. He had never expected to make a career in the property business, even if it was the only game in town. He got into bed. His pillow still smelled of Hope's perfume, but unlike the first time after she had spent the night there, it didn't keep him from going to sleep.

The telephone woke him. He looked at his watch. It was half past nine. He picked up the receiver, expecting to hear Hope's voice, but it was Connie Henderson. She sounded as if she were very, very far away.

"Where are you?" he asked.

"In Saint Tropez. You know something? There are too many beautiful girls in the world, and half of them seem to be right here."

"You don't say."

"I quit my job," she said. "I couldn't hack it anymore."

"All those men?"

"That and the sea. I've discovered I like to sit at the edge of the water, not on it."

"What are you going to do now?" he asked. He didn't want to sound too friendly, and yet he wanted to be polite.

"I don't know. Hang around here until my money runs out. I might even come back to Spain and see you."

"Yes, well, it's pretty crowded here in August, too."

"Have you met another sailor in the port?"

"Not a sailor, no."

There was a long pause. Then she said: "I see. Well, I might come back anyway. I'm getting used to competition. I'm beginning to like it."

"Call me if you decide to do that," he said.

"I will," she said wistfully. "I won't get in the way, I promise."

"I'll be here," he told her, and hung up. He felt weary. It was getting too warm to sleep. He got up and opened the door leading into the living room. Then he went slowly back to bed. It was probably pretty hot in the submarine, too, he thought, while the depth charges were exploding around it, and here, at least, he had no depth charges to worry about. Not yet, anyway.

It was a quarter past one in the afternoon when Hope finally called. Brandt was making his breakfast, a full-sized, American one.

Her voice still sounded very calm. "He hasn't come back," she said.

"Did you get some sleep?"

"Yes. A few hours. There's a man here from London to see Max. An insurance assessor from Lloyd's. He's sitting in the living room having a beer."

"Did he say what he wanted?"

"It's something to do with the burglary," she said in a low voice. "It seems Max took out a policy after all. Several years ago."

"That's interesting," Brandt said. "So what are you going to do?"

"Stay here, I guess. What are your plans?"

"I don't know. I was thinking of going out on *Lulubelle.* Does that interest you?"

"Well, it would, normally. But I think I'd better hang on here for a while, don't you agree?"

"I really don't know. Do you want me to come over?"

"No, I don't," she said quite firmly. "Are you going to the Safires' tonight?"

"That depends on what you're going to do."

"Well, I'm not sure yet. I'll call you later. Then I'll know more. I have to see how things go."

"I'll be home by seven," Brandt said. "Call me then."

"I'll try."

"What do you mean, you'll try?" He couldn't control his annoyance. It was as if nothing had happened, as if they were back to hiding again. "He's not going to lock you up in a room," he said.

"No, of course not. But if I can't call, I'll join you at the Safires', all right?"

"Whatever you say."

"Don't be angry with me."

"I'm not. I don't want you to let yourself be bullied, that's all."

"I won't. I love you," she added hurriedly.

It sounded like a customary sign-off, akin to saying "Have a good day" or "Take care." Brandt cursed after he had hung up. For an instant he was tempted to call Penny and ask her if she wanted to go out in the boat with him. But it was probably too late to reach her at home, he decided. Undoubtedly she was already on her way to the beach, to some *chiringuito,* where, amid the odor of frying sardines, she would be exposing her well-formed breasts to the rays of the afternoon sun.

He was just about to cast off the stern lines when he looked up and saw Phyllis Dexter standing on the dock, watching him. She was wearing a red bikini, with a towel wrapped around her shoulders as a small concession to decency, and despite his bad mood and the animosity he had felt toward the woman from his first meeting, he found himself admiring her figure. Max Clarendon was not lowering his standards; that much was certain.

"Are you going out alone?" she asked.

"No, I've got a young boy hidden in the cabin so people won't talk," Brandt replied, not very proud of his wit after he had said it. The two diesels were ticking over slowly, emitting clouds of gray smoke, and he didn't feel like making conversation.

Phyllis Dexter's mouth formed a thin red line as she hesitated before answering him. "I wanted to talk to you," she said. "But it doesn't have to be now."

"Why not now? Come aboard." Brandt picked the boat hook off the floor, pulled the gangway back off the edge of the dock, and fastened it in place. "You want to talk here, or do you want to go out for a tour of the coast?" he asked the girl, modifying his unfriendly tone somewhat. She hadn't done him any harm, he reckoned, aside from suspecting him of being a jewel thief, and that might have been quite a normal reaction, based on the general deportment of some of the male singles who hung out on the coast.

"I haven't got much time," she said. "I'm meeting someone here in half an hour."

"Well, we're in Spain, aren't we? So you're fifteen minutes late."

"All right. I suppose it *would* be rather hot sitting here."

"We'd fry."

"But you *will* bring me back in forty minutes, won't you?"

"Absolutely. Kidnapping's not my line. Nor is theft, as a matter of fact." He pulled in on the starboard stern line, and lifting the gangway with his right hand, deposited it back on the dock.

"Are you meeting Max Clarendon?" he called to her over the noise of the engines, once they were under way.

"No. I was meeting a girlfriend. She was going to pick me up at the port and take me to the new *chiringuito* at Cabo Pino. Have you been there?"

"No. But I hear it's a nice beach. One of the few," he added, easing the twin Morse controls forward. "You have a lot of girlfriends, don't you?" he said.

"A few." She disregarded his tone of gentle sarcasm and came into the wheelhouse to sit beside him. "Have you got a cigarette?"

"No, I don't smoke. I'm sorry."

"I left all my things in the car," she explained. "My purse, and my change of clothes, everything. Were you really going out alone?" she asked, as if she were expecting him to lie.

He nodded and said, "Hope couldn't make it today, surprisingly enough."

The sea was a very dark shade of blue, with the only movement on the surface of the water caused by a few schools of sardines feeding on plankton. They disappeared as *Lulubelle* approached, and Brandt marveled once again at the radar devices the small creatures had been endowed with by nature.

"That's what I wanted to talk to you about," Phyllis Dexter said, putting her feet up on the handrail in front of her, just as Hope had done on the day of their ill-fated cruise. Well, that was what Guy

Manning had told him a boat was for: to help catch the birds. Although he wasn't really interested in catching this one. After a pause, Phyllis said: "I'm very fond of Hope. She's been one of my best friends down here since the day I arrived. I don't want her to wind up hating me."

"You should have thought of that earlier," Brandt said. "Or in any event, long before letting Max take you back to the villa last night."

"I went along to the villa with him because I was worried about Hope. She told the people we were with that she wasn't feeling well. When we got there, Max had a nightcap. Then he realized that she hadn't come home at all. Because the dog was still in the house."

"What time was that?"

"About an hour after Hope left."

"You didn't see me go?"

"Yes. But Max didn't. Anyway, he wouldn't have thought anything strange about that. And I certainly had no intention of telling him that she'd probably gone off with you. We just sat there and waited. It wasn't much fun, as you can well imagine."

"I take it Max wasn't pleased."

"In the beginning he was more worried than anything else. He wanted to call the police."

"So you had to enlighten him."

"Look, it isn't as if I betrayed Hope's confidence," Phyllis said sharply. "Nor did I steal her husband. Before last night, I'd never even discussed any of her personal problems with Max. As a matter of fact, Max and I were nothing more than friends for quite a long time. Because I was involved with somebody else. Seriously involved."

"That figures."

"What do you mean by that?"

"Well, you're an attractive girl. It'd be pretty odd if you were unattached."

"Exactly. But the person I was involved with went back to England, and Max wasn't exactly deliriously happy, either, and so the inevitable happened."

"Was that before I arrived on the scene?"

"It was."

They were at least a mile and a half out, and he pulled back on the throttles and shut off the engines. As with Manning, on the day they had taken the boat out for a trial run, he was getting tired of making himself heard above the noise of the diesels. "So what do you want to talk about?" he asked.

"Nothing, really," Phyllis Dexter said, with a forced smile. "Except that I think you and I should try to do everything we can to keep things civilized. I don't mean that we should all be friends and go out to dinner together. That would be a bit much."

"It all depends on Max, doesn't it?"

"Not altogether."

"I think it does," Brandt said. "He has more muscle than she does, to put it crudely. He can be generous, or he can behave like a shit."

"You mean throw her out without a penny?"

"Yeah. Exactly. I don't think Hope has any *legal* rights of any kind, nor do I think she expects to be 'paid off.' But it would help, I should think, if he treated her fairly. After all, she's been his common-law wife for quite a few years."

"What's fair, in your opinion?"

"I don't know. It's not really my problem. You suggested that we should do our best to keep things friendly. That *was* why you wanted to talk to me, wasn't it?"

"Yes. Of course."

"Well, then don't put me in a position where I'm made to sound like a divorce lawyer. Or worse, a venal lover. I don't care what he finally gives her. I want her to walk away from the entire set-up. Take her few belongings and leave. But I'm not inside her head. I also don't want to urge her to make a decision that she's going to regret one day."

"Obviously not," Phyllis Dexter said. She was watching a water-skier who was passing between *Lulubelle* and the shore. The man was making graceful turns across the wake of the boat that was towing him, both of his feet planted firmly on a mono-ski. "But I do think that, since they have no children, Hope can't really expect an awful lot. She hasn't been a particularly good wife, or pseudo-wife, or whatever you want to call it. It's only because Max is a rich man that we can expect him to be generous at all."

"*I* don't expect him to be generous," Brandt said. "Nor do I think there's a hope in hell that they'll stay friends," he added, and laughed at his own unintended pun. "Nor do I care, really. So it's been nice talking to you, as they say in my country, unfortunate as that may sound."

"You don't think there's any point in trying to persuade Hope not to press too hard?" Phyllis Dexter asked.

"I don't get what you're trying to say."

"Well, the house, for instance."

"It's in his name, isn't it?"

"Yes. But he'd have a hard time making her get out. Then, too, I think he'd like to avoid a scandal, if possible."

So that was it, Brandt thought, they were afraid of losing the Villa Miramar. "I don't think Hope would insist on her 'squatter's rights,' or stand off the Guardia Civil when they come to remove her from the premises," he said. "If that's what's worrying you."

"I'm not worried about anything," Phyllis Dexter replied. "Nor have I discussed any of this with Max. I do have a pretty good idea of what it costs to run that place, however, and I don't think you and Hope . . ."

"Look, don't get way ahead of yourself," he interrupted her. "We haven't even decided to keep house, and you're already talking about our maintenance costs."

"You mean to say you haven't even talked about whether you're going to live together? Come on! I can't believe that."

"Well, it's the truth."

"What *do* you talk about when you're together?"

"We don't talk all that much," Brandt said evenly, watching the woman's face to see if she was going to pretend that she was shocked. But she didn't change her expression of vague disbelief; merely laughed drily.

"You mean you only make love? How nice for my chum," she said with heavy sarcasm. "I can see now why she lost her head."

"She hasn't, yet. Even as we sit here sunning ourselves, she and Max may have already decided to get back together again and give it another try."

"I don't think that's likely to happen!"

"You've got him thrown and tied? Is that it?"

"I don't think you know Max Clarendon, or you wouldn't put it quite that way."

"I've been filled in on his reputation."

"Yes? And how was he characterized?"

"As a shark."

"That sounds like Richard Grey," Phyllis Dexter said. "Well, shark or lion or bull . . . if he makes her a fair offer, I suggest she take it."

"What kind of a fair offer?"

"Oh, a settlement of some kind. A flat sum that will give her the chance to start life elsewhere on her own."

"Get-out-of-town money?"

"If that's what you want to call it."

"Christ, lady . . . you have a pretty low opinion of your friend, if you think that's what she's after."

"You were the one who said potential acrimony between the two parties depended on Max. What else does that suggest *but* a settlement?"

Brandt said: "Look, we're not getting anywhere, honey. Why don't you just take a swim, and I'll transport you back to the harbor, and we can both forget that this conversation ever took place. All right?"

"That's fine with me." She rose, and gathered up her hair in a pony tail, and slipped an elastic band around it.

She was a pretty cool cookie, Brandt thought. He wondered if Max had suggested they have this little chat, or if it had been her own idea. He watched her as she stood in the stern, looking down at the water, trying to decide if and when to jump in. There was a splash, and she was gone from view.

"Don't swim too far away from the boat," he called to her. "There are sharks out here, too."

She laughed. "You're really a thoroughly disrespectful man," she said. "That's probably the reason that I'm beginning to quite like you."

* * *

She sat drying herself in the sun, her towel spread out under her narrow behind. She said: "It's very pleasant out here. I must convince Max to get a boat."

"Charter this one. It comes complete with a skipper, Navy-trained."

"I don't think that would do. This boat is just a little too small for four people. Or three, even."

"Yeah, I suppose so." Brandt went forward to start the engines. "We'd better get you back to your friend," he said.

"There is no friend. That was a lie. I was waiting for Max to call me."

"At the port?"

"Yes, he always calls me at the bar I go to. Even when he's in England."

"And you're always there, waiting?"

"Most of the time."

"And if he can't call?"

"Then I hang on until about one-thirty and go about my business."

"I spend a lot of time waiting for the telephone to ring, too," Brandt said, and turned the ignition key on the port engine.

Phyllis glanced at the stainless steel Rolex on her small wrist. "I think I've already missed my call today," she said. "But I'd better go back in any case. I hate lying about where I've been."

"So do I," Brandt said. "But we could both tell the truth for a change," he suggested.

"All right. I did say that I might talk to you if the opportunity presented itself."

"And the idea of a cash settlement? Was that yours, or did Max suggest it?"

"He might have mentioned it."

"Okay," Brandt said. "I guess the important thing is to keep in touch, and not allow negotiations to break down altogether."

"I agree." She smiled up at him, a genuinely friendly smile.

"You no longer suspect me of having been in on the robbery, do you?" he asked her.

"No, I don't."

"I don't like being poor, but I'm not a thief."

"I know that."

"Well, inform your leader, will you?" Brandt said, and took his place at the wheel. It hadn't been an altogether useless outing, he felt, though what the end result would be, he wasn't at all certain. He swung the bow of *Lulubelle* around and headed back toward the skyscrapers of Marbella. Phyllis remained seated in the stern, her eyes closed, her face tilted up toward the sun. After a while she got up and joined him inside the wheelhouse.

"You're sure you haven't got a cigarette hidden away somewhere?"

"Pretty sure. If you'll take over, I'll go down and have a look." He went below. There were no cigarettes on any of the shelves on either side of the cabin. He opened the door to the head and had a look around. Inside the mirrored cabinet over the toilet he found an old package of Murattis. "This is all I could find," he said, standing in the hatchway. "They look to be pretty stale."

"Any port in a storm," the young woman replied. "Now who in the world that you know smokes this brand? Certainly not Hope."

"They probably belonged to the owner."

"I hope he won't mind my having one."

"He won't. Because he's not with us anymore."

"Oh? That sounds rather ominous."

"This was Guy Manning's boat," Brandt said.

"Poor Guy. I didn't know you'd chartered from him. Was he a friend of yours?"

"A good enough friend." He didn't feel like elaborating on Manning's fate. He indicated for her to take the helm again, and went below to get the package of matches he remembered seeing in one of the drawers of the galley.

"I worry about Marie," Phyllis said, after Brandt had lit her cigarette for her. "My God, we think we have troubles. That poor woman."

"That's why I thought you might try to convince Max to charter this boat. To help Marie Manning. My deal with her expires in a couple of weeks. And then there's September, the best month of all."

"I can suggest it," she said. "I don't think it'll do much good. But I can try."

She seemed to be making an effort to be friendly. Perhaps he had misjudged her, he thought; perhaps she wasn't quite as tough as she had at first appeared. Not quite as tough, but tough enough, just the same. That she was concerned about Guy Manning's widow was probably nothing more than window dressing. She had gone straight from the funeral to meet her lover. And what about yourself, pal? Brandt queried his conscience. It didn't take you long to recover from the shock of your friend's death, either. Turning to Phyllis, he said, "I wonder what's happening back at the villa."

"I wonder, too." She shook her head. "Isn't it all silly? You'd think grown-up people could resolve their problems amicably."

"Yeah. You'd think so. But they seldom do."

"If only we all had lots of money," she said. "Everything would be so much easier."

"Maybe not," Brandt said. "Maybe there'd be even more slaughter."

She laughed good-naturedly. They were about a mile from the entrance of the port. Brandt noticed a white power boat with a flying bridge cutting through the calm sea on a course directly opposite his own. The boat looked to be of Italian design. It was crowded with half-naked bodies, especially the sun mattress on the foredeck. He recognized Consuela and Elena among the sunbathers. They waved to him as they went by. Then the skipper of the boat turned sharply and pulled up alongside *Lulubelle*, decreasing his speed as he did so.

"Come and have lunch with us," Consuela shouted to Brandt. "We're going to Cabo Pino."

"I may see you there," he replied, cupping his hands in front of his mouth as he shouted back across the narrow space of water that separated the two boats. Consuela and Elena waved, and the white power boat resumed its original course.

Brandt was conscious of Phyllis Dexter's questioning glance.

She probably expected him to invite her to come along, he thought. But he wasn't that eager to spend the rest of the afternoon with her. He felt instinctively that it wouldn't help matters.

Hope said: "Where have you been? I've called you at least four times."

"Out on the boat. As scheduled," he told her.

"All afternoon?" She obviously didn't believe him. Women, too, had a special radar, he thought, provided by nature for their self-protection, like the impulse that made the sardines leave the surface of the sea before the boat could reach them.

"No, I wasn't alone. I met with some of my Spanish friends and had lunch with them." A lie of omission that he would rectify later. "What happened with Max?"

"Nothing as yet. He took the man from London out to lunch, and when he came back suggested I have dinner with him. He's taking a nap now."

"No recriminations? No scene?"

"No. Nothing like that." She sounded distant, annoyed, which was understandable. She had probably not had a very pleasant day. "What are you going to do tonight?"

"I don't know. That depends on what you're doing. I told you I was supposed to go to the Safires'."

"We're invited, too. But we're not going."

"Well, you can call me there, as planned, remember . . . If you get through dinner early enough." She didn't reply. He waited for a while, then asked, "Are you still on the line?"

"I am."

"Hope, for God's sake, I didn't think there was any point in my waiting around here all afternoon in the apartment." If he told her that he had seen Phyllis, she was bound to get angry. He sensed that she felt victimized, as if he had failed her at a crucial moment. "Look, I'll wait for you at the Safires'. When you finish dinner, you can come by there and pick me up. And if that's difficult, you can call me, and I'll meet you at my place."

"I'll see if I can."

"What would prevent you? He'll probably want to see Phyllis after dinner."

"How do you know? Is that what she said? Have you seen her? You're hiding something from me."

"No, I'm not. Look, it's ridiculous to have this sort of conversation on the telephone. I'll wait for your call at Lew's house."

"Have you seen Phyllis? Please tell me, if you have."

"Yes, I've seen her. She was at the port. She feels just as we do, that there's no point in pretending any longer."

"Why didn't you tell me that right away?"

"Because I don't want to go into all that on the telephone. Come on, have a little faith in me. Faith, hope, and charity, remember?"

But she didn't appreciate his little joke. "I'll call you at the Safires'," she said brusquely. "If I can."

He said, "Come on, darling. Relax." But she had already put down the receiver. The dial tone rang in his ear. He went out on the terrace and sat down in one of the deck chairs. It was almost nine o'clock, but it was still light. He knew that dinner at Las Golondrinas wouldn't be until ten-thirty. He had plenty of time to shower and get dressed.

He felt ill at ease, and at the same time he was overcome by a strange lethargy. It all seemed much too complicated, suddenly. He disliked the cold tone of suspicion that she had adopted so readily with him. She had lived a life of deception so long that she was incapable of trusting him even now. And she was probably scared, too, knowing that she was committed, that she had turned a corner in her life, and that she might come to regret it. He knew that was how she felt, because he was experiencing an identical feeling. Everything was simple when they were together, and even more so when he desired her. He had no doubts about the future then. Now he was physically tired, burned out by the sun, and being alone was somehow reassuring, for he felt no responsibility to anyone, could do as he pleased.

If she reached some sort of settlement with Max over dinner and decided to stay on, make her peace with him, how deeply upset would he be, he wondered. He was sorry that he hadn't asked Connie for her telephone number or her address so that he could reach her in case he wound up on his own again. "If only we all had lots of money," Phyllis had said, and she had been right, of course; money simplified everything. But, then, if that was true, perhaps he wasn't really in love with Hope. Or was he capable of love at all? What the hell did he feel? Make no decision when you're tired, he told himself, and went to get himself a drink. That had been a sound bit of advice he had learned early in the game, but, unfortunately, he had usually disregarded all of his own rules.

He went back to the deck chair and sipped his weak Scotch and water. The Mediterranean was a flat lake in the failing light. The fishing boats would not be going out as it was Sunday, as even the fishermen observed the Sabbath, now that democracy had come to Spain.

It was a big party. He realized that as soon as he had arrived, for there were tables in the garden as well as inside the house. He knew hardly any of the people who were already there. "Come, I'll introduce you," Wilma Safire said, after she had kissed him and wiped her lipstick off his cheeks, as was her habit.

"Don't bother," he told her. "I'll wander around and get myself a drink."

"All right, honey."

"Where's Lew?"

"In the kitchen, where he belongs," she said, and floated off in her white kaftan.

He found the bar, which this night had been set up in a corner of the library under a varnished Toulouse-Lautrec poster, and waited his turn to be served a drink by the white-jacketed barman. Someone pinched his back, and, turning, he was confronted by Freddy Weaver. He almost didn't recognize him, for Weaver had shaved off his beard after all.

"What hell are you doing here?" Brandt asked.

"I might ask you the same question. Lew said he didn't think you'd come, that you'd be hiding out somewhere."

"I don't know what made him say that."

"He suggested you were in the middle of a personal crisis, that your love life was boiling over."

"Well, he was wrong, as usual." He ordered a weak Scotch and water and followed Weaver out onto the terrace. The Spanish guests were arriving now; it was nearly eleven o'clock, their usual hour for making an appearance. "What about you?" he asked

Weaver. "Did you decide that you were safe once you'd shaved?"

"I did, as a matter of fact. But even that was unnecessary, as it turned out." Weaver grinned mysteriously. "The goddamndest thing happened," he continued in a low voice. "There was a fire in the jail, and it was about four o'clock in the morning, so nobody could find the key, and my young Spanish associate choked to death in the smoke. Isn't that some twist? They couldn't get the poor son of a bitch out of his cell, so they sprayed the place with water, and that was the end of their star witness." He shook his head and laughed. "It's pretty awful, really, but he'd probably have gotten twenty years for manslaughter, so what the hell!"

"Remind me not to get put in jail in this charming town," Brandt said.

"Well, don't knife anybody, if you can possibly avoid doing so." He looked off in the direction of the garden gate. "There's Yves with his new girlfriend," he said. "She must be all of eighteen years old. Ah, the Frogs! When they get down here in the sun, they get charged up with all kinds of energy."

She was quite pretty, the tall blond girl who had entered the compound with Brouyère. Her hair was shoulder length, and she was wearing a blue, diaphanous dress that, even at a distance, showed off her girlish body. Her face had the vacuous look of a starlet, or maybe she was merely dazzled by the size and splendor of the gathering. Yves was steering her in their direction, as neither the host or the hostess were in view. He bowed sarcastically to Weaver and Brandt, and introduced the girl as Señorita Nielsen, his "new fiancée." "You look naked," he said to Weaver, "and about fifteen years younger."

"That's the kindest remark you've ever made to anyone," Weaver replied. "You know David, don't you?"

"Yes, I've met Mr. Brandt here and there, but we've never conversed." He paused. "I hear you're a good tennis player, as well as a yachtsman," he said. "I can't remember who told me that, but maybe we could have a game someday, doubles preferably."

"Any time," Brandt said guardedly.

"And the yacht?" Brouyère asked. "Is she still afloat?"

"Very much so."

"I'm not a good sailor," Brouyère said, "but Miss Nielsen loves the water. Actually, she's a champion windsurfer."

"You sail?" the girl asked Brandt.

"I used to," he said. "But I have a power boat now."

She made a face. "I like only to sail," she said, apparently not interested in continuing the conversation.

"Well, then we'd better sail away," Yves Brouyère said, taking the girl's arm and leading her in the direction of the living room.

Freddy Weaver observed their departure with vague interest. "That must be one of the prettiest behinds in town this summer," he observed. "Or any summer, for that matter."

"I didn't know you cared anymore."

"Well, curiously enough, since I've shaved the hair off my face, I've suddenly become horny. So it seems that the mask behind which we hide does influence our character. Or our glands, anyway."

"It's probably because the heat's off you," Brandt told him.

"That, too, is a possibility." He looked off in the direction of the garden gate. "Now there's a pretty girl," he said appreciatively. "And alone, too."

Brandt turned in time to see Hope come onto the patio. She was wearing navy blue slacks and a white blouse, with a brown serape over her shoulders. She obviously hadn't expected the party to be as lavish an affair as it was, and she hesitated an instant, no doubt looking for her host or hostess.

"She's a friend of mine," Brandt said, and moved off before Weaver could reply. He kissed Hope on both cheeks, noticing that her hand was strangely cold. "Are you all right?" he asked her.

"Sort of. I had no idea this was going to be such a big shindig," she added in a low voice, "or I wouldn't have come."

"I'm glad you did."

Wilma Safire joined them. "I'm so glad you could make it," she said. "Where's Max?"

"He had another date. He hopes you'll forgive him," Hope said evenly. "Does that foul up your seating arrangements?"

"No, of course not. We have too many men tonight, for a change, so it doesn't matter at all. Can I get you a drink?"

"I'll do that for you," Brandt said. He took Hope's arm and steered her in the direction of the house. More guests were arriving, and Wilma Safire went off to greet them.

Brandt asked the barman for a vodka and tonic, and led Hope into the living room, which was still empty of guests, because it was cooler outside.

"What happened?" he asked her.

"I'll tell you later," she said. "Do you think we have to stay for dinner?"

"It'd be rather difficult to leave now."

"I know. I should have called first."

Safire entered the room. He saw them and came over to embrace Hope. "Better late than never," he said. Then, turning to Brandt, he added, "I hope you don't mind my kissing the lady." He held her at arm's length. "You look more beautiful than ever, sweetie pie." He sighed dramatically. "Ah, yes. It's true, isn't it? Love makes the world go round."

"Love and money," Brandt replied.

Safire said: "That's a very cynical remark, David. Only the rich have money problems. You know that. Better than anyone, I should think. We who are poor have only problems of the heart." He kissed Hope again. "Are you hungry, angel?" he asked her.

"Starving."

"Then you'd better come into the kitchen and nibble on a carrot. Dinner won't be for quite a while. David can go and mingle with the guests. If you can bear to be parted."

"I think we'll survive," Hope said.

Safire took her hand and led her out of the room. He obviously wanted to talk to her alone, Brandt thought, and made his way back to the terrace. Wilma came over to him. "Do you want to meet one of the most beautiful girls in the world?" she asked him. "Rich and single, to boot, or recently divorced, to be more accurate."

Brandt said, "If you think I should," and let himself be led out onto the lawn. He didn't want to meet anyone. He wanted to get out of there as quickly as possible. What was Safire up to, he wondered. Was he going to apologize to Hope for having been a shit? It was hardly the time or the place to explain his caddish remarks.

Wilma forgot about her promised introduction to the divorced beauty, whoever she was, and left Brandt to survey the various groups of guests on the lawn of the patio in front of him.

He caught sight of Weaver standing with a group at the far end of the terrace. They were all men, a majority of them Spaniards. One of them was holding forth, so no one bothered to introduce Brandt when he joined them. The one who was doing all the talking was tall and thin, with dark hair brushed straight back on his narrow head, which made him look like an old-fashioned *torero.* It was immediately apparent that he was talking about politics, and that the point of view he was expressing was an unusual one, to judge by the skeptical look on the faces of his listeners.

"Any regime that is in power for forty years brings certain benefits," he was saying. "Stability is a boon for any country. But what has the old regime left us with? An economy that is an unqualified disaster. An uneducated people. Cities that are centers of discontent and crime. A countryside that has been emptied of agricultural labor, and a regionalism that is blind. The Basques, the Catalans, the Valencianos, the Andalusians, and the Gallegos all want their own governments. Without paying for it, of course. That is what forty years of Franco have brought us. That and inflation. Our only healthy industry is tourism. So what will we become? A nation of waiters and barmen, of whores and translators and real estate speculators. That is the legacy of a dictatorship that lasted twenty years too long . . ."

"But the rest of the world is no better off, Luis," someone interrupted him.

"And what comfort is that?" the man asked rhetorically. "We go to our doom with the Italians and the Greeks and the French. We drift into socialism or atomic war along with the rest of Europe."

Weaver took Brandt's arm and led him away from the group, just as a chorus of protest engulfed the young man. "A very serious discussion," he said, and grinned. "No place for you and me."

"Speak for yourself," Brandt replied. "By the way, who was that guy?"

"A young lawyer from Madrid. I think he's a little high, or he wouldn't be spouting off like that."

"What he had to say didn't sound so far-out to me," Brandt said.

Weaver shrugged. "The obvious cry of despair always contains a little truth. But to give the right solution to a problem is something else again. The country is in a mess, but it's still more pleasant to live here than any other place I've been, including home-sweet-home. So what the hell's the use depressing everybody at a party where they've all come to have fun." He scratched his jaw, a habit that was undoubtedly a leftover from his bearded days. "I need another drink," he said. "Idealists always depress me."

"Well, at least the fellow speaks good English," Brandt said as they started toward the house.

"He should. He studied in America. Then came back here to go to law school."

"Reminds me of Freddy Weaver when he was a young man in L.A."

"Is that right? Who the hell was he?" Weaver said, and took a drink from a tray that a servant in a white jacket was offering around. He tasted it, made a face, and shrugged. "Spanish champagne! Well, what the hell, it won't kill me." He lit a cigarette. "You know, you're right, David," he continued. "I used to be a big liberal. 'A premature antifascist,' as it was called in the old days. Then I came here, and I wasn't crazy about the regime, but nobody was starving, and the streets were safe at night, and all the rest of it. And then the old man died, and we had democracy. You think it made anyone any happier? Wages went up because they had unions again, but prices went up, too. Inflation was the next step. Strikes. Crime. Pornography. Endless political speeches on the television. Okay, they get the forty-hour week, and the workers can make it home by six-thirty, *if* they still have a job. An improvement, I suppose. How much do you think the Generalísimo could have stolen every year? A million dollars? Or maybe two, even, or three? But how much does it cost to send the King on an official visit to Washington, or any other place he has to go? Ten times that, at least. So the nation's not so much better off, or it's a debatable point, in any case. I don't know. I just get tired of watching it all. So I say to myself, 'Let them figure it out. You just take care of Freddy, and see that he has a nice time.' "

"Not a particularly admirable point of view," Brandt said, "but I suppose, inevitably, a lot of people wind up thinking that way. Fortunately, not everybody," he added.

Weaver shrugged. "Let the young take over. I'm too old and too beat-up to care. Maybe if I lived in my own country I'd feel different."

"Maybe. But I doubt it."

"Do I detect a note of mild contempt in your voice?"

"Contempt? I don't think so. What right would I have to be contemptuous? My father was a better man than I was. He was concerned with the future of the world right up to the end of his life. But things didn't look as black in those days." He wanted to get away from Freddy Weaver. And from all of the others. The social scene on the coast was not for him, he had decided once again. "I'm going out to the kitchen to retrieve my girl," he said. "If she wants to be retrieved, that is."

"Va usted con Dios," Freddy Weaver said. "Go with God. And if your girl is interested in a joint, come back and see me."

He wandered into the kitchen, but his host was nowhere in sight. And neither was Hope. There was a young woman standing in front of the stove, stirring the spaghetti sauce with a wooden spoon, and at the sink off to the right an old woman was washing pots and pans. *"¿Donde esta el señor?"* Brandt asked the one who was acting as assistant cook, but she merely shrugged her shoulders, as if her stirring demanded all of her mental powers and had thus left her speechless.

"Se fue," the old woman said, and shrugged her shoulders as well.

It was too hot for Brandt to remain there, especially since it didn't look as if he was going to get much information from the staff, so he went back through the living room and out onto the terrace again, where he stood for a while, his eyes passing over the crowd of guests. From a distance it looked like a hell of a party, he thought; from a distance! He felt a hand on his arm. It was Consuela, more tanned and beautiful than ever.

"Have you seen Lew or Wilma?" she asked him, after he had kissed her brown cheeks.

"I'm looking for them myself," he said. "Where's your husband?"

"Getting us a drink." Consuela said. "Have you been here long?"

"It seems like it," Brandt told the girl.

She smiled mechanically. "Perhaps Lew is in the kitchen?" she said.

"No. I've just come from there."

"There are a lot of people."

"There are indeed."

She excused herself, because she had seen her friend Elena somewhere in the crowd. Brandt went back into the house and recrossed the living room. He stepped through the swinging door into the pantry just as Safire entered from the back patio. He said: "You know, you really were a shit to tell that girl what I told you in confidence."

"It was unavoidable."

"Oh, come on. There must have been something else to talk about."

"I made the mistake of asking her if she'd had an affair with you."

"What the hell for? What difference did it make to you? I didn't say *I'd* been her lover. Anyway, you must have known I was pissed that night, or else I'd never have made that kind of remark. Now she hates my guts, and I can't really blame her. You're a great pal."

"Why did you bring it up?"

"Well, I had to say something. I couldn't just let it ride."

"Why not?"

"*I* don't know," Safire said. "I just think you behaved like an asshole."

Wilma came into the kitchen. "The natives are getting restless," she said. "I think we'd better feed them."

"I'll be ready in fifteen minutes, baby," Safire told her. "You can keep everybody happy for that long, can't you?"

"I'll try," Wilma said, and went out through the swinging door again.

"Where did Hope go?" Brandt asked Safire once his wife had left.

"I have no idea. We exchanged a few unpleasant words, thanks to you, and then she just fucked off. I tried to make a joke of the whole thing, but she was in no mood for gags. I followed her out the back door. She didn't even have a car. She came here in a cab, I guess. The last I saw of her, she was going out the servants' entrance on foot. Christ, what a way to start an evening!"

"I'll try to find her and bring her back," Brandt said, although he had not the slightest intention of doing so.

Safire said, "Well, lots of luck!" He opened the door of the big American refrigerator in the pantry. There were several wooden salad bowls inside it, and he took out two of them and carried them into the kitchen. "Tell Wilma to send in the waiters we've hired for the night. On your way out, that is."

"Will do," Brandt told him.

"And remind me never to introduce you to any of my friends," he called after Brandt. "Or anybody else, for that matter."

He drove very carefully down the road leading to the main highway, his headlights on high beam. But there was no sign of anyone, only the unlit green street lamps and the scruffy forest of pine trees bordering the pockmarked macadam. Then as he approached the intersection, he noticed that a small yellow Seat was blocking the entrance to the main thoroughfare. There were three young men inside it, he saw at a glance, and Hope was standing nearby, and they were quite apparently trying to pick her up. He gave the horn of the Peugeot a brief tap, and the youth in the back seat made a rude gesture, the victory sign or the finger, Brandt couldn't tell which, but he pulled on the hand brake and got out of his car, knowing that it was dangerous to do so, because he was outnumbered. But he had no choice. He called out her name. Still she made no move in his direction. She had her back to him, her head turned to the right.

The man behind the steering wheel of the Seat opened the door on his side. He was obviously the bravest of the trio, a tall thin youth with long straight hair. Just then another car turned into the side road and stopped. That decided the issue. The driver of the yellow Seat got back into his car and drove off.

Hope pulled her serape around her shoulders and walked up the road toward Brandt. He opened the door for her, trying to control his annoyance. "What's the matter with you?" he asked. "What made you go off like that?"

"I'd just had it," she said defiantly, "so I thought I'd leave."

"You might have told me."

"I didn't know where you were, and I didn't feel like looking for you."

He walked around the back of the Peugeot and got in behind the wheel. She was looking through her handbag for a cigarette. "I don't suppose you have a light," she said.

"No, I don't. Do you have to smoke?"

"Yes, I do," she said angrily.

"Then perhaps you should have gotten into the other car. They'd have given you a light and, who knows, maybe something more."

"Well, you rescued me from that," she said sarcastically. "I'm grateful."

"Where do you want to go?" he asked her. "Are you hungry?"

She said: "Home, I guess. I certainly don't feel like sitting in a restaurant."

"Where's home? My place or the Villa Miramar?" He felt tired. He wanted to make peace with her, was tired of all the tension.

"Not your place," she said. "I'm depressed enough as it is."

"All right. I'll take you back to the villa. You can have a night-cap with Max."

"He's not there," she said, her face set in a sullen expression he had not seen before. "He caught the late plane for Madrid. He's going to Monte Carlo for a couple of weeks. To give me time to pack my things."

"To pack your things?" He waited for a lull in the traffic, then pulled out into the highway.

"Yes. It's his house. I don't own any part of it. I told you that long ago." She looked over at him suspiciously. "What did Phyllis have to say on the subject?"

"Nothing much."

"Then what did you two talk about?"

"She suggested that she and I exert our influence to keep things civilized. Not stir things up."

"That's sweet of her. Did you have lunch together?"

"No, I met some friends and had lunch with them."

"Did Phyllis say anything about the house?"

"Only that Max didn't want to throw you out. She said that he was anxious to avoid a scandal."

"Of course. He wants people to think he's a gentleman. That's very important to him. He suggested I look for an apartment. He intimated that he would buy one for me."

"What else did he say?"

She sighed and said: "Oh, the usual things. That he was disappointed in me. That I should have told him that I was unhappy long ago. That the least I could have done was treat him as a friend." She paused thoughtfully. "I suppose he's right in a way," she continued in a low voice. "I didn't behave very well. Because I was frightened of him."

"Did you tell him that?"

"Yes, I did. I told him that he never included me in his thoughts or his plans. That he treated me like a mistress, not a wife. He denied that, as I expected he would. He asked me to give an example, so then I told him that it was rather strange he had never bothered to tell me that my jewelry was insured after all, that I only discovered it when the man from Lloyd's showed up." She laughed briefly and shook her head. "Of course he had a ready answer to that. He said that he had wanted it to be a pleasant surprise, and that he planned to tell me himself."

"Good old Max. I suppose the other pleasant surprise was that he was going off with Phyllis."

"He denied that, too. He said she was just a friend. He finally admitted that he went to bed with her, but only because he sensed that I didn't want to have anything to do with him anymore."

"Phyllis was a little more honest," Brandt said. "She even admitted that their affair had started before I arrived on the scene. Because she didn't have anyone else, and because she knew you and Max weren't deliriously happy. She also told me that she didn't want you to wind up hating her."

"Did she now? Well, you can tell her that she doesn't have to worry. The next time you take her boating, that is." She flicked her cigarette out of the window. Brandt looked into the rearview mirror, and saw the sparks land in front of the car behind them. "What is it the French say? That problems having to do with tail always sort themselves out? Well, maybe ours won't," she added.

"Does he want you back?"

"He didn't say so. He was strange, though. I've never seen him like that before. He said he wanted to meet you and find out for himself what kind of a man I was involved with. That he didn't want me to make a terrible mistake. He was kinder than he's been for a long time."

Brandt kept his eyes on the road in front of him. "He was trying to make you feel guilty," he said.

"I suppose that was it. I asked him if he wanted to go to the Safires', and he said no, that he was catching the plane to Madrid and going on to Monte Carlo in the morning. He said that he would call me later tonight."

"Is that why you wanted to go to your place?"

"No, not only because of that. I feel a little lost, suddenly. I don't know why."

The traffic had thinned out once they had passed the Puerto Banús. He took her hand. "Are you sure you're not hungry?" he asked her.

"That sounds as if you are."

"Well, it always helps to eat when you're sad. It always helps me, anyway." He waited for her to laugh, but she didn't.

"I'll fix you something at the house," she told him. "We may as well make use of the place as long as we can."

As he approached the main gate, he saw that the house was in total darkness, which he thought was strange, and he told her so.

"I suppose Max was under the impression I was going to spend the night with you," she said, and got out of the car. He kept the engine running and the headlights on while she opened the front door and turned on the lights in the front hall. Then, as he switched off the ignition, another car turned into the drive. It was a red Ford Fiesta, and it stopped directly behind the Peugeot. A small man in a blazer and gray flannels got out. He had wavy blond hair and a face that had obviously been overexposed to the sun that day, for it was bright crimson. He moved uncertainly across the white gravel, almost as if he were slightly tipsy.

He said, "My name is Hoskins, Ralph Hoskins," and, fumbling inside his blazer for his wallet, brought out a card. "Is Mrs. Clarendon in?"

Brandt was about to ask the man what he wanted when Hope appeared. She said: "Yes, Mr. Hoskins. I'm here. What can I do for you?"

The man turned away from Brandt and went up the marble steps, his movements a little more controlled. "I'm sorry to bother you at this late hour," he said, "but I called earlier, and there was no answer. I'm off to England in the morning, and I did want to have a word with you before leaving."

"That's all right," Hope said. "Come in, won't you?"

Brandt looked questioningly at her, but she motioned for him to join them, so he followed Hoskins up the marble steps and went into the house.

The three of them stood in the entrance hall. It was quite apparent that Hope was puzzled by the man's visit, although she obviously knew him. "Will you have a drink?" she asked, doing her best to make the offer sound genuine.

"I've already had quite a few," Hoskins said with an apologetic smile. "But I suppose a beer wouldn't hurt me. If it's no trouble, Mrs. Clarendon."

"No trouble at all. What will you have, David?"

"A glass of water. Or a Coke," Brandt said. "Whatever is easy."

"A Coke would probably be better for me, as well," Hoskins said, "but I don't like the stuff. It only makes me thirstier. It's this heat, I suppose. I'm not used to it."

"We have plenty of beer," Hope said. "Why don't you take Mr. Hoskins out on the terrace, David?"

Brandt led the way through the living room and opened the sliding doors. As they stepped outside, the man took a deep breath and unbuttoned his double-breasted blazer.

"This is a nice place," he said. "But it's too warm a climate for me. I'll be glad to get back to the rain of our English summer."

"You have to get used to it," Brandt told him. "Why don't you take off your jacket and your tie?"

"You don't think Mrs. Clarendon would mind?"

"I'm sure she wouldn't."

He watched Hoskins take off his tie and his blazer. There were large rings of sweat under each armpit. He took out his handkerchief and mopped his face. It was a well-meaning face, Brandt decided, a little swollen by the sunburn he had inflicted on his fair skin. The eyes were blue and uncomplaining, and the mouth under the stubby nose was rather full, almost girlish. It would be impossible to mistake the man for anything but what he was: middle-class English. "Be careful of this cool breeze," Brandt said. "It can be as treacherous as the sun."

"It's very pleasant here," Hoskins said. "My hotel room is like an oven."

Hope came through the open sliding doors, carrying a tray with the drinks. She put them down on the glass-topped table in front of the white couch and chairs. Hoskins watched with happy anticipation as she poured his beer into a tall glass.

"This is very kind of you, Mrs. Clarendon," he said. "I didn't mean to put you to all this bother."

"No bother," Hope said calmly. "Now, then. What is it you came to see me about?"

Hoskins took a sip of his beer. He looked nervously over at Brandt. "It's a rather private matter," he said. "Perhaps it would be better . . ."

"Mr. Brandt is a very close friend," Hope said. "I have no secrets from him."

"That may well be," Hoskins replied, wiping his face with his handkerchief again. "But you see, I'm a little out of my depth here."

"I can take a walk on the beach," Brandt said.

"I'd rather you stayed," Hope said. She sounded adamant. "Is it about the insurance claim?" she asked Hoskins. "Because Mr. Brandt was here on the afternoon of the robbery. He might even be able to help."

"Well, it is and it isn't," Hoskins said. "You see, Mr. Clarendon was rather annoyed this morning because we'd had our little chat. After you went to your room he accused me of being indiscreet.

'Unprofessional' was the word he used. I don't want to make the same mistake twice."

"There's no danger of that," Hope told him.

Hoskins took another swallow of his beer. "All right, if you insist," he said. "In for a penny, in for a pound." He straightened in his chair. "I only wanted you to know that the claim is a pretty straightforward proposition. The police report will have to be translated, and all that. But I see no reason why the company should hesitate to reimburse you." He stopped and took a deep breath. "That is not the reason I came."

"What is it then?" Hope asked. Her tone of voice was sharp, indicating that there were limits to her patience.

"Well, this policy of Mr. Clarendon's," Hoskins began. There was the sound of a door opening inside the house, and he stopped and got quickly to his feet. As he did so, Bozo trotted onto the terrace from the living room. The dog barked briefly, then went over to Hoskins and sniffed at the cuffs of his flannel trousers.

"He won't hurt you," Hope reassured the Englishman.

Hoskins patted the dog's head. "Didn't half frighten me," he said. "Well, as I was saying, the policy covering the stolen jewelry seems to be quite in order. I'm quite certain the underwriters will make good the claim. However, the terms of the policy make Mr. Clarendon the beneficiary. Even though the jewelry may have been your property, we will be reimbursing him."

"I understand," Hope said quietly.

"That could be why your husband was so exercised this morning. After talking to you, I realized that you had no idea the jewelry was covered at all. So I thought that it might be helpful if you were acquainted with all of the facts."

Hope said, "That's very nice of you, Mr. Hoskins. Would you like another beer?"

"No, I'll just finish this one, thanks awfully." He picked up his glass and drained its contents. "I trust I haven't kept you up too late." He smiled. "They have different hours in Spain. Never seem to go to bed at all. Well, I must be off."

"I'll see you to the door," Brandt said. He did so and shook the Englishman's hand. "Have a good trip home, Mr. Hoskins."

"I'm sure I will. I'll be glad to get back. England's not such a bad place, you know." He bobbed his head. His blue eyes misted over for a second. The mention of England, Brandt thought, or perhaps the relief of getting out of there was probably the cause of the sudden surge of emotion. He had, after all, behaved in a rather strange manner, had skated on thin ice on the hottest night of the summer, *his* summer, in any event. As Brandt turned away from the front door, there was a loud knock and, reopening it, he discovered that Hoskins hadn't left after all.

"Forgot my blazer," he explained. "This is definitely not my day." He preceded Brandt out to the terrace, retrieved his jacket and his tie, and hurried off.

Brandt waited until he heard the front door slam shut to make sure the man was really gone. "Well, what did you make of that?" he asked Hope.

She shrugged. "Max obviously made another friend," she said caustically. "Hoskins' revenge." She wandered out toward the pool, then came slowly back to the terrace. "It doesn't come as a surprise to me that Max made himself the beneficiary of the policy. I've often wondered if he didn't stage the robbery himself. To clip my wings even more. Although that theory seems a doubtful one now. I don't think defrauding Lloyd's is really his bag. He likes to stay well inside the limits of the law." She went over to the glass-topped table and made herself another vodka and tonic. "I suppose he'll reinvest the insurance money in a few baubles for his new girlfriend." She poked at the ice cubes in her drink with her manicured forefinger. "You're fortunate, you know," she said to Brandt. "Not being rich, you've always been loved for yourself alone. You should feel good about that."

Her mood improved noticeably. The insurance man's visit had relieved her of any feeling of guilt about Max; that much was immediately apparent. Although she made no further mention of the intelligence Hoskins had given her. Brandt stood in the kitchen, watching her operate her modern and complex electric fixtures, until, in order to relieve the tension, he asked her how many hours of dual instruction she had needed in order to fly solo.

She smiled and said: "Not too many. About half a day. I'm not just a pretty face, you know."

"So I've gathered."

She was making him scrambled eggs and chicken livers, a package of which she had taken out of the deep-freeze compartment of the refrigerator. The microwave oven thawed and cooked them in a matter of minutes, as it did the Provençale tomatoes she cooked as a side dish.

"Are you going to join me in this feast?" he asked her, seeing that she was putting half a dozen slices of white bread in the long chrome toaster.

"Indeed I am. Mr. Hoskins' visit has revived my appetite."

"You really think Max is planning to keep the money if they do pay off the claim?"

"Of course he'll keep it. He would never have dreamed of turning it over to me. Under any circumstances. I'm his slave. I always have been. He paid the bills and took care of me. But that's all. He never gave me any more money than I needed for the day-to-day running of the house. As long as I behaved, he would have gone on doing so."

"As long as he *thought* you behaved."

"Exactly." She turned a dial on the oven, opened it, and placed two plates inside it, as well as an aluminum-foil pan that contained the buttered toast. "Would you like to eat out on the terrace?"

"Any place you say." He caressed her back as she got a tray out of one of the cupboards. She smiled briefly at him, the busy smile of a housewife whose mind is on her chores.

He followed her out onto the terrace and cleared the table of the glasses that remained as reminders of the insurance man's late visit. Then they sat down to eat. But she got up after only a few seconds.

"What would you like to drink?" she asked Brandt.

"I don't know. What have you got in mind?"

"I'd like some champagne. I feel like celebrating."

She went off and returned a few minutes later with a bottle of Moët & Chandon. Brandt struggled with the cork. It popped finally, and he poured for both of them.

"I'd like to propose a toast," she said. "To the new me."

"All right. Although the old you was good enough."

"No, it wasn't," she said. "The old me was docile, obedient. Maybe I didn't behave like the perfect wife, but he didn't know that. The new Ms. Clarendon is going to fight. Struggle for her rights, and all that. Women's lib has come to the Costa del Sol."

"How's that going to affect us?"

"I don't know yet. You're not the one I'm most concerned with at the moment."

"You're not going to move out of the Villa Miramar?"

"Certainly not right away. I'm not going to leave this place so that he can move in with that tart and sleep in my bed." She raised her glass. "To Mr. Hoskins," she said. "I hope he's enjoying a good night's rest. He's earned it."

"He certainly has." Brandt touched glasses with her and drank. The wine was cold and refreshing. "I'm not sure *I'd* like to live here," he said. "Even with you."

"We'll cross that bridge when we come to it. There are no boats sailing tomorrow, you know. For the land of the free or any other place I'd like to go. Even with you." She sat back in her chair and sipped her champagne. "You know, I've been a dummy for a long, long time."

Brandt got up and went over to kiss her on the top of her dark head. He put his hand inside her shirt. "Then you don't think the meek will inherit the earth?" he asked her.

"No, I don't," she said. "Not anymore."

After she had placed the dishes inside the dishwasher, she asked him if he wanted to see a movie. "Always," he told her; "I'm a cinema buff," and put his arms around her while she worked her computerized appliances.

"No, I'm serious," she said. "Something to take our mind off things . . . this whole mess."

"What have you got to offer?"

He followed her into her den, and she went over to the video set and selected a tape of *Ordinary People.* Brandt wandered around the room, noticing that nothing had changed. No one had as yet bothered to move the personal details of the décor, he thought, probably because the issue was still in doubt. He took off his moccasins so as not to soil the white rug and sat down in one of the armchairs.

She joined him after she had lit a cigarette. The film began. It seemed well directed to Brandt, and the acting was real enough. But it was a story about neurotics, and when the psychiatrist appeared, he found himself losing interest. She noticed that he was watching her instead of the screen.

"What's the matter?" she asked.

"I have a thing about stories involving shrinks," he told her. "I'm sure it's a good movie, but it's not for me. Not under the present circumstances."

"You've been away from the States too long."

"Could be."

"All right. We'll turn it off. What else can I offer you?"

"How about a walk on the beach? Or a swim, even."

"Have you got a bathing suit?"

"It's in the car."

He went to get it. By the time he had let himself back into the house, she had already changed and was waiting for him with a towel wrapped around her shoulders. He went into the guest bathroom and put on his trunks. They walked out onto the terrace and crossed to the pool. Bozo was asleep by the glass-topped coffee table, unconcerned with their movements.

She said: "The beach is full of tar and jellyfish. Why don't we go in the pool?"

"If you prcfer." He was puzzled by the change that had come over her, her distant manner. It was as if they werc strangers again. He watched her dive into the clear water, lit by the submerged lights. She surfaced and pushed her wet hair back into place.

"Aren't you coming in?"

"Of course I am." He dove in and came up beside her. When he put his arms around her, she averted her face. "Is something wrong?" he asked her. "Do you hate all men tonight?"

"No, of course not. I'm just not in the best of moods. That's understandable, isn't it?"

"Absolutely." He released her and swam to the shallow end. He watched her climb up the swimming ladder on the side opposite where he lay submerged in the warm water. She got her towel and dried her head and legs. Then she went into the house. She returned an instant later with a bathrobe obviously intended for his use. Bozo was watching them drowsily now. All the splashing had awakened him.

"Would you like a drink?" Hope asked Brandt.

"No, thanks."

"What about a little pot?"

He was surprised at the offer. "I didn't think you used that stuff."

"I don't, as a rule. But when I'm nervous the way I am tonight, I find it helps. Better than a sleeping pill, any day."

"Have you got some?" He wanted to make love to her. It was, he thought, the only way to break through the barrier she had erected between them. And if smoking pot would help, he was quite willing to try it.

She nodded and said: "I always keep some on hand for Max. Or I used to, that is. It was the only way I could get him to sleep when he would come back from one of his exhausting trips, nervous and full of jet lag."

"I'll try anything once," Brandt said. "Within reasonable limits."

She smiled and shook her head. "You are Mr. Clean, aren't you?" she said. "Who would have thought it?"

"I'm not, really. I've just found that there are better ways to get sleepy."

"But the combination is much more effective," she said, and went back through the open sliding doors into the living room. Brandt wrapped the bathrobe around him and kicked off his wet bathing trunks. Then he lay down on one of the sun mats beside the pool. She joined him a few minutes later. She had put on a toweled robe like the one she had given him, and she knelt beside him on the mat. She had a couple of paper tissues in her hand, and when she opened them, Brandt saw that they contained a mangy-looking cigarette, the kind he used to make as a kid with the tobacco he and his friends had collected from old cigarette butts.

"I hope Max won't mind," Brandt said.

"I don't think he will. He has other things to worry about right now." She lit the joint and stretched out on the mat. "Just inhale a little at a time," she said.

He did so, and coughed. "It really doesn't do much for me," he told her.

"It won't right away, you silly ass."

He looked down at her as she lay beside him. She took a puff and held in the smoke. He leaned over and kissed her, and she released the smoke into his mouth.

"Inhale it. Don't blow it out right away."

But he had already done so. She shook her head and lay looking up at him. "To think I've tossed everything away for a dumbbell like you," she said.

He tried to kiss her, but she moved away and took another pull on the cigarette, so he took her by the hair and forced her to kiss him. The smoke tasted like old straw, but she responded to his tongue. Then she sat up and looked over at the dog. It was sound asleep again, its muzzle down flat on the marble tiles. She glanced up at Brandt, seemingly reassured, as if Bozo might have been eavesdropping.

"You know who you look like?" she said. "The Reverend Mr. Davidson in the original version of *Rain.* I saw it on television the last time I was in New York. I never thought then that I'd actually meet his double." She grinned. "Do you really think of me as a wicked girl who's leading you into sin? Because I'd like that."

"There's no more sin nowadays," Brandt said, "short of killing somebody."

"I've thought of that, too."

"You've seen too many movies, dear girl."

"I don't mean that I'd ever really do anything like that. But I find myself thinking what it would be like if his plane crashed on the way to Monte Carlo. And then I find myself wishing that it would." She drew on the moist stub of the wrinkled cigarette. "It's not a very nice feeling when you realize that you're capable of wishing these things."

"It's not that difficult to leave him." He thought that he probably did sound like the Reverend Mr. Davidson.

"It's difficult to leave all *this,*" she said and waved a hand, trailing a wisp of smoke, at the villa and the pool before she took another puff. She had the look of a naughty child, or a spoiled young woman, rather, Brandt corrected himself. It was having an effect on his desire, he discovered, either that or the smoke he had swallowed.

She said: "When you've had real leather, it's hard to go back to plastic. Some actress is supposed to have said that first . . . when she came back to Hollywood after making a movie in England. Well, I know what she meant. Can you imagine my going back to live in Ventura County? Now will you kiss me, please?" He hesitated, and she laughed at him. "Kiss me," she said again. She dropped the moist, used-up cigarette on the white marble beside the mat and pulled him to her.

He did as he was told. She tasted of burned weeds, which he found an improvement over stale tobacco. He put his hand inside her bathrobe, but she pushed his arm away. "What's the matter?" he asked her.

"I'm not in a big hurry, that's all. I think I've been too easy a target for you, anyway. Too willing. I'm going to revert to the great American tradition and play hard to get." She kissed him hard, and then pulled her mouth away from his mouth. "Don't you think most murderesses must be lousy lays?" she asked him.

"You weren't talking about killing your husband. You only wished him dead."

She grinned and said: "That's true. And I'd probably feel terrible if it did happen."

"Probably. Especially if you discovered that he'd left the house and most of his money to Phyllis."

"I hadn't thought of that." She paused. "I doubt he would, you know," she said upon brief reflection. "That would involve making a will, and I know Max doesn't like to contemplate the ever-after. He used to get annoyed with me when I'd ask him whether he wanted his body sent back to England when the time came, or whether we should both be buried in the little graveyard up on the back road. He doesn't like thinking about death. Or talking about it. So I doubt he's made his last will and testament. When he dies, all of the money will probably go to his wife and his two daughters, and Phyllis and I will be back to square one. Or I'll be with you, square two," she said, and laughed happily at her own joke.

Brandt pulled open her robe and kissed the nipples of her brown breasts, and at last she responded to him. "Let's go to bed," he whispered in her ear, and kissed it.

She shook her head. "No. I want to make love here," she said in a firm voice. "Remember when we went out in your boat, and I told you that I didn't like copulating in public?" She giggled to herself. "That still goes, but I never said I didn't like fucking out of doors."

"I remember," he said. "Grass makes you very talkative, doesn't it?"

"A little. Do you mind?"

"No. It was just a random observation." He pulled open his bathrobe, and their bodies touched finally, and she opened her legs to receive him. She gasped, and he said, "God, what a lot of time we've wasted."

"No, we haven't."

His mouth found her mouth again, but only for a moment. Then he kissed her body, her breasts, her arms. He wanted to please her more than he ever had wanted to before. Her arms locked around his body with surprising strength. He had a brief realization that the mat was harder than the bed and that he might hurt her, and then there was the clear sound of a voice in the still night.

"Señora," the voice said. It was a woman's voice, and it came from the lawn beyond the pool.

They froze, and then he rolled free of her, his knee striking the cold marble of the tiles. Hope was on her feet an instant later, pulling her bathrobe around her as she did so. "Who is it?" she said, and then, "What do you want?"

Brandt saw a young woman in jeans and a white shirt standing on the lawn on the other side of the pool. It was the maid. He recognized her at once, although he had only seen her on the road the evening he met Hope on the beach. Behind her, standing inside the gate that led out onto the beach, was her husband. He was smoking a cigarette, the end of which glowed in the darkness. Beyond him, on the dark blue expanse of the sea, were the lights of the fishing boats. "God Almighty," Brandt muttered to himself, "what idiots we are."

"*¿Qué quiere usted?*" Hope asked, and Brandt was surprised that she had enough self-control to ask the intruders what they wanted in their own language.

"Nada, señora," the young woman replied, in a voice that trembled a little. *"Nada, nada."*

Hope remained standing there long after the young couple had disappeared through the gate leading to the beach. It was as if the shock had immobilized her, had cemented her to the white marble under her bare feet, and for a second Brandt found himself admiring her beauty, the disheveled hair, and the naked legs that the hastily adjusted bathrobe didn't quite hide. He went over to her and took her in his arms. He said: "Forget it. It's over. Come inside."

Then, in a voice that was partly muffled by his embrace, she began to rage. "He sent them," she said, sobbing quietly. "He sent them to spy on me. He paid them off. That's why they came up the beach. Because they've never done that before. Never, never."

"We were idiots to stay out here," he told her. "It's quite possible they were taking a walk and saw that the pool lights were on."

"Oh, come on! Rosalia hates the beach. She's told me so. She doesn't even walk on the beach in the daytime."

He said, "Come into the house," and took her hand and led her into the living room, then pulled shut the sliding doors. He didn't bother to pick up the shriveled joint lying beside the mat, but made a mental note to collect it later. As if hiding the evidence mattered now, after they'd been caught in the act!

She took a cigarette out of one of the silver boxes on the end tables of the couch, and he lit it for her. She appeared to have calmed down a little. At least her tears had stopped. She wiped her eyes with the sleeve of her bathrobe. She was no longer high; that much was certain.

He followed her into the bedroom, and she crossed to the bed and sat down on the white bedspread. As she did so, the dog scratched on the glass door from the terrace. Hope said, "Let him in."

Brandt undid the catch and slid open the door. The dog came into the room and flopped down at the foot of the bed. "It's surprising he didn't bark," Brandt said.

"He wouldn't. He knows them too well."

"I forgot about him. He probably went off somewhere while we were lying there on the mat."

She managed a bitter laugh. "He was probably embarrassed by his mistress's behavior. You don't like to watch, do you, Bozo?" she said to the dog. He looked up at her with sad eyes when he heard his name. "Well, at least Max won't try to get *him* to testify," she said.

"I think you're jumping to conclusions. What makes you so sure Max has paid off the help?"

"Because I know. Oh, he didn't send them over here in order to catch us making love. He probably suggested they come by the house at night and see that everything was all right. It would sound to them like a reasonable request. And he probably told them to come in through the beach gate, but they never said anything to me about it."

"If he left after you did tonight, he probably gave them their instructions then."

"That may be. Juanito was going to drive him to the airport in the Mercedes. That's why I took a taxi to the Safires'. The thing that makes me suspicious is that Juanito didn't leave the Mercedes in front of the garage when he got back. That's what he usually does, in case I want to use the car early in the morning to go and play golf."

"Maybe he was going to do that later."

"After he'd come up here on foot? That doesn't make sense."

"You think he left the car at his house and came up the beach in order to spy on you?"

"Max probably told him to. He wanted to find out if you were coming back here with me. He asked me about that, if I'd ever had you here at night. As if that was somehow a worse betrayal than my staying at your flat."

"I must say, I understand that. I never liked coming here, either."

"But you pushed through, all right."

"Yes, I did."

"What does the place have to do with it? If you're going to sleep with somebody, what difference does it make where you do it?"

"It makes a difference to some people."

She put out her cigarette in the ashtray that lay on the cover beside her. "I can't fight him," she said in a calm voice. "I don't know why I thought I could. He's smarter than I am. And more unscrupulous."

"Scruples don't have much to do with it," Brandt said. "When you're jealous and suspicious, you don't worry about the rules."

"Oh, really? Tell me more."

The telephone rang. She put her hand on the receiver and let it ring several times more before she picked it up. Then she nodded to Brandt and pointed at the mouthpiece with her left forefinger. "Where are you?" she said into the phone. "Madrid?" She paused. "I got home about an hour ago. There were too many people, and I wasn't hungry." She listened for a while and nodded her head. "You're coming back tomorrow? Why, if I may ask? To talk to me! But we talked today, didn't we? All right, I'll tell him: he's to meet the four o'clock plane. Are you sure you can get on it? Fine. I'll be here. Good night." She put the telephone down slowly, making sure that it was secure in its cradle. Then she looked over at Brandt. "Well, we won't have to wait very long to find out what he's going to do. That's a blessing, isn't it?"

"It's better to get it over with," Brandt said quietly. He had acted like a damned fool. You had to be a damned fool to make love at the side of a swimming pool when there was a perfectly good bed available. Actually, he should have insisted that she come back to his apartment, or he should have taken her to the villa and left her there. The evening had been a shambles, right from the beginning. It was as if he had lost control of his own free will, as if he were suddenly incapable of obeying the dictates of his own common sense and was being dragged along by her fear of the situation she had suddenly found herself in, her panic at the uncertainty she now faced.

He said: "I guess I'd better go home. Do you want to come with me?"

She shook her head. "No. I'm going to stay here."

"Do you want me to stay for a little while longer?"

"What's the point?" she asked.

"I don't like to leave you like this."

"I'm all right," she said.

"Shall I call you in the morning?"

"If you feel like it."

"That's a silly thing to say."

"I guess I'm just silly, that's all." She took another cigarette from the package on the bed beside her. "I'll take you to the door," she said.

"You don't have to bother."

"I have to lock it, anyway."

Brandt went into the guest bathroom and put on his clothes. Bozo followed them both into the entrance hall. He watched them with a bored expression on his noble face as Brandt kissed his mistress good night.

"Don't worry. It'll all work out."

"I know. It's an old French saying."

He knew that he should tell her that he loved her. But the words stayed in his mind. So he said, "Take care," realizing it was a trite and ridiculous farewell, at best.

"I think it's too late for that," she replied, and closed the door behind him. He heard the metal latch close as she turned the key. Then he walked slowly across the white gravel to his car. As he started the engine, the garden lights went out. He drove out of the gates and down the unpaved road, with the sugar cane a green wall beside the car.

As he neared the Puerto Banús the traffic increased again, and at the actual entrance to the port there was a long line of cars waiting to turn left. Sunday night, he said to himself, and drove on. They were all out on the town, the tourists and the locals, and the people down from Madrid, and the self-exiled rich from Soto Grande, who came down the coast to finally have some night life besides their in-grown parties; and the Jererzanos and the Malagueños, those who could afford it, all out to pick up a foreign blonde, or one of their own kind, now that the constraints no longer were effective; all God's children out to dance and eat and parade along the quays of the port, or just stare at the strange-looking foreigners, or hustle them. But the general idea was to get your fill of food and drink and noise and action, as it was called, and then maybe, if you had enough energy left over, to climb into the sack with your beloved, recently found or long-grown-accustomed-to, and if it wasn't too late, or she wasn't angry at you for dancing with someone else, the final coupling was in order, fancy or restrained, brief or long drawn out, with the aid of a joint or too much booze, so that your sun-baked body could drift off to sleep during the cool of the late-morning hours, with your crotch sated, limp, quiet, dead. That way you could wake up to greet the blazing midday sun with just the right amount of bleariness, brought on by alcohol or fornication or drugs, or all three together, and then you could go to the beach and stumble along the dirty sand to your favorite *chiringuito* and start the whole process over again.

Well, he wasn't one of them tonight, Brandt thought, and he probably wouldn't be the next night or the night after that. For his luck had run out, on this coast anyway. That was fairly obvious.

He passed the local Holiday Inn, and soon the recently completed mosque came into view, lit by floodlights, on the left-hand side of the road. It had the appearance, he realized once again, of one of the minor attractions of Disneyland, all white and shiny and new. What a place to build a church! And yet, in a perverse way, perhaps there was some sense in the choice of the location. It was probably not a bad idea to remind the faithful of the wisdom and strength of Allah, and to do so as close to the sources of sin as possible. If you still believed in that sort of thing, he thought, and recalled his own recently expressed dictum, that really the only sin left was murder.

PART FOUR

Brandt stood leaning on the iron balustrade of the Paseo Marítimo as if he were one of the ancient pensioners who spent their evenings looking out to sea. It was still light. The sun hung over the edge of the horizon, casting its orange light on the bronze statue of a water-skier that stood on the farthest point of the main sea wall. It was a pleasant sculpture, he thought; a young girl skimming over the surface of the Mediterranean represented the spirit of the place better than any statue the town might have put there.

To the right of him lay the old port, with its low, whitewashed buildings. It really did look like a tourists' paradise, which was undoubtedly what the architect had intended. If you didn't let your eye wander inland, but kept it focused on the quays and the yachts and the buildings along the main pier. Beyond that, it was Miami Beach, as Guy Manning had remarked to him less than a month ago. Yet if you hadn't seen it the way it was before, Brandt mused, you might be quite satisfied. But then no place he knew had changed for the better, so there was hardly anywhere he wanted to go back to, which made moving on rather pointless. But he would be forced to move soon. He was fairly certain of that. Max Clarendon would see to it that before long he would be on his way.

Unless, of course, Freddy Weaver came to the rescue, which was highly unlikely. When he had called that morning to ask why they had disappeared so suddenly from the Safires' party, it had occurred to Brandt that it might well be worthwhile inviting him to lunch in order to ask his legal advice. Weaver hadn't practiced law in the States for a long time, but he obviously knew more about the rights of a common-law wife than anyone else around. At least anyone they could trust. And despite the fact that their friendship was not exactly in full bloom, Brandt felt certain that Weaver would at least lend a sympathetic ear.

But he couldn't have lunch, because he had "a previous engagement," as Weaver had put it rather self-mockingly. He was perfectly willing, however, to have Brandt buy him dinner. That is, if he could wait until after the bullfight, for that was all part of the planned "fun and games" for that afternoon. "You still go to those things?" Brandt had asked with surprise.

"I do when somebody else pays for the tickets."

"I suppose that makes sense," Brandt had replied. "Although a bullfight in Marbella might make me hesitate to accept even a bona fide invitation."

"That's because you're purer than I am."

"I don't know about that."

"Well, we can discuss it at dinner," Weaver had told him. "But I still don't know why you finked out on the party last night. Lew was pretty upset."

"I'll explain at dinner."

"Will you be alone?"

"I will."

"That's a shame," Weaver had said and, after they had agreed to meet in the old port at nine-thirty, hung up.

Brandt glanced at his watch. It was ten minutes after nine, and he was still early for their appointment. He wandered slowly down the sidewalk, enjoying the warm summer evening. From the beach below came the familiar babble of Spanish voices and the pungent smell of sardines being grilled over an open fire. The poor enjoy themselves more than the rich, he thought, even if they have to pay for their pleasure later. He noticed two young girls in jeans sitting on a bench farther along. They were both redheads, sisters quite obviously, and probably Americans, to judge by the orange backpacks leaning against the railing in front of them. Brandt greeted them with the customary "Hi," which brought smiles to their freckled faces.

It turned out that they were from Bend, Oregon, and were spending the month of July hitchhiking through Spain. They had been to Pamplona, as was to be expected, which they had found to be disappointing because of the crowds of French tourists, but they had nothing but praise for the rest of the country. "Only one thing," the prettier of the two said. "The men are really strange. You can't go anywhere at any time of the day without somebody following you or speaking to you in the street. It really gets to be a bore."

"They're Latins," Brandt replied, "and they've been denied the pleasures of the flesh too long. Also, we have a reputation of having less stringent morals."

"I don't know about *that,*" the girl said, and laughed. "I only know they really come on strong."

"I said we have the reputation, that's all." She was really quite pretty, with a direct manner that was thoroughly appealing. What a blessed race they were, the young from the unspoiled regions of North America. The fable of Marxism hadn't touched them, so they still looked at the world with generous and interested eyes. Nor had the majority of them been perverted by dope or the twisted mentality of the big cities on both coasts, which seemed to demand slovenliness as a basic passport with which to move freely among their own kind. But he was generalizing again, he warned himself, drawing instant conclusions that lasted only a short while, until some other random meeting reversed them.

He suggested to the girls that they might try El Faro for dinner, or if they liked spaghetti, the Italian restaurant where he was planning to meet Weaver. He had no ulterior motive in doing so. He was in no mood to pick up anyone, pure or impure. Then he wandered on.

He had gone only a hundred yards more when he heard the sound of horse's hooves on the pavement behind him and, turning, saw a carriage approaching. The horse had the usual small parasol attached to its head stall, which gave it the ridiculous look of a circus horse fallen on poorer days. The Gypsy driver pulled harshly on the reins, and the carriage came to a stop opposite Brandt.

Freddy Weaver was seated on the white canvas-covered cushions in the back, grinning self-consciously. "Join me, David!" he called out to Brandt. "There's no extra charge."

The driver got down off his box and opened the small, varnished door, and Brandt settled down next to Weaver, aware at once of the strong smell of alcohol on his friend's breath. It disappeared only when the carriage had resumed its forward movement. "What did you do with your car?" Brandt asked.

"I left it at the bull ring," Weaver said grandly. "I couldn't wait for them to untangle the traffic. You would have been sitting in that Dago restaurant by yourself until at least ten-thirty. And of course there wasn't a taxi in sight."

"What about your host?"

"Oh, they were going on to some cocktail party at the club, and I think they were glad to be rid of me. You see, I struck up an acquaintance with the man sitting behind us, and he had a bottle of Fundador, so I may have disgraced myself slightly."

"I get the picture. How was the fight?"

"Godawful," Weaver said. "The senior matador had dyed hair, and the bulls spent more time on their knees than he did. You were wise not to attend."

"I warned you."

"I know you did. Anyway, the ride back from the plaza with my Gypsy friend here has turned out to be the most pleasant part of the afternoon. That and the free brandy. I hope you don't expect too much brilliant dialogue from me during dinner, however, because I'm fairly pissed."

"A plate of spaghetti will sober you up," Brandt said. He didn't tell Weaver that he hadn't expected brilliant dialogue, was more interested in some free professional advice.

"I don't really want to sober up," Weaver said. "I just want to forget the ugly spectacle I was forced to witness for two long hours. There weren't even any pretty girls to look at. Only a lot of sunburned Germans. The old elegant days are gone forever, I'm afraid. The world is full of ghastly trippers, it seems." He yawned and lit a Spanish cigarette.

Brandt was grateful for the odor of black tobacco drifting his way. The driver turned his scrawny gray into the main entrance of the port. A long-haired youth on a noisy motorbike made a U-turn in front of them, but the horse didn't seem to mind. The loud noise of the bike was like the blast of a Tommy gun.

"There ought to be a law against those goddamned things," Weaver said.

"I believe there is."

"Well, they ought to enforce it."

"They ought to enforce a lot of their laws," Brandt replied. He wasn't looking forward to his meal with his drunken companion. He directed the driver to the small restaurant on the main pier and helped Weaver out of the carriage. The place was crowded, and they had to wait at the bar for a table. Weaver ordered a Scotch and water in order to get rid of the sweet taste of the brandy in his mouth. It was going to be a long evening, Brandt reckoned, but he really had nothing else to do, as Hope was dining with Clarendon. He had the feeling that he was suspended in a strange kind of limbo, a lull before the storm.

They had tomatoes with mozzarella cheese, followed by spaghetti Bolognese, and Weaver sobered up enough to listen to Brandt's story of his love affair with Hope Clarendon. There was a party of English tourists at the next table, so it was relatively easy for Brandt to avoid going into the intimate details Weaver asked for from time to time, grinning malevolently as he posed his indiscreet questions, as if he were a divorce lawyer who was trying to decide the merits of a case before agreeing to defend a client.

"What difference does it make where we went to bed together?" Brandt finally asked him, keeping his voice low so as not to be overheard by the young woman seated to the right of them.

"No difference at all," Weaver said. "I'm just a curious old bastard. Forgive me. What is it you really want to know?"

"I want to know what rights this woman has; that's about all."

Weaver smiled. "Well, that's easy," he said. "She has no rights whatsoever. We're in sunny Spain, and the principals involved are all foreigners. No Spanish court would want to hear the case. And even if the lady were to claim Spanish residence, that wouldn't help her, because in this country, a woman who cuckolds her husband is a dead duck. And your friend isn't even married. The man owns the house, and all the rest of their goods and chattels, and he can just tell her to get lost, and that's the end of it."

"What about England?"

"Well, he has a legal wife there, doesn't he, so again Ms. Clarendon is out in the cold. The man, under British law, especially if he's the injured party, holds all the cards."

"And in California?" Brandt asked.

"Ah, California's a little different. There's the case of Lee Marvin that furnishes a precedent, but even then the woman didn't get beans. If I were the lady's lawyer, I might try to sue for services rendered as a housekeeper, a caretaker of the estate, or something like that. But as neither part is a resident of the U.S., there's not a court in our fair land that would accept jurisdiction. Clarendon could just ask that the case be thrown out of court, and that's exactly what would happen. Just like the Spanish courts, American ones have enough cases to worry about without taking on extra work."

"There's nothing she can do, then?"

"Well, I think the only thing she *could* do is change all the locks on the doors and sweat it out. He'd probably have no trouble getting an ejection order, but it's unlikely that he'd want the Guardia Civil going down there to evict her. So maybe that way she could get some kind of minor settlement, a few bucks to avoid a scandal. Just as if I were *his* lawyer, I'd advise him to take possession of the place and change the locks to keep *her* out. See what I mean? Legally, she's a dead duck, as I said before. A pretty dead duck, but a dead duck just the same."

"That's what I thought."

"She should try for an amicable settlement," Weaver said, wiping his mouth with his napkin. "He's a rich man, and I feel pretty sure he doesn't want to make waves if he can avoid it. Also, he's going to get the money from the insurance company, so he can afford to be fairly generous."

"That's his, too?"

"Absolutely. The jewels were hers, but he paid the premiums on the policy and made himself the beneficiary, so that's the end of that." He paused to sip his wine. "Why the hell did you get caught?" he asked. "That, too, was a dumb move."

"We didn't get caught. Not by him, anyway."

"Well, the servants saw you fornicating by the pool. And even if they don't talk, you'd already done the next best thing on the previous evening. Of course, the lady could have said that she found out about *his* extracurricular activities, and was hurt and didn't want to stand in his way. So she spent the night at a flamenco, and stayed pure as the Virgin Mary."

Brandt laughed and said, "It's no good; she hates flamenco," and lit Weaver's afterdinner cigarette.

"Well, then she deserves to be penniless." Flamenco's kind of like tomatoes. If you hate it, you shouldn't live in Spain."

"Well, it doesn't look as if she will for very much longer."

"Ah, come on. Don't be a pessimist," Weaver said. "The way out of this situation is to stay friends. Apply the pressure of helplessness. Try to awaken the man's pity. Beg forgiveness. We'rc all human, she tells Max, all prone to the same failings: greed, lust, jealousy, fear."

"What do I say?"

"Sweet fuck-all. You get lost. You come to Morocco for a couple of months. You tell me hash does nothing for you. Well, you'll learn to love it once you get into the good stuff."

"I doubt *that,*" Brandt said.

A large group of young men in black eighteenth-century costumes came into the restaurant, carrying a variety of instruments: guitars, mandolins, and tambourines. They were all very cheerful as they took their places between the tables of diners and began to play. They then burst into song. The noise was deafening inside the low-ceilinged room. Weaver leaned across the table toward Brandt with a pained look on his face.

"Students!" he shouted. "Supposedly! The trouble is, I've seen these same assholes panhandling around here for five years."

"Don't be so hard on the young," Brandt shouted back above the strains of "Granada."

"I'm not, as a rule. It's just that I've been folkloricked out of my tiny mind today. First the bulls, and now these strolling players. Get the check, and let's split, as I believe they still say in old Beverly Hills."

On the crowded quay outside the restaurant, they ran into the two girls from Bend, Oregon. "We couldn't find your Italian restaurant," the prettier one, who was obviously the leader of the expedition, told Brandt.

He pointed to the entrance of the place behind them and said, "It's right there."

"Oh, for goodness sakes," the girl said, and giggled.

Brandt realized that he hadn't heard anyone use that particular expletive without sending it up for a long time. "Where'd you eat?" he asked, aware of Weaver's appraising scrutiny of the two girls.

"At the Faro," the other girl said, and made a face.

"Was it bad?"

"Well, maybe we ordered the wrong things. I guess it's a fish place, and we ordered steak."

Weaver said: "Meat in this part of the world is to be avoided. Except, of course, human meat. I'm surprised David didn't tell you that. Anyway, the important question is: What are your plans for the rest of the evening?"

Brandt gave him a tired look, which even in his drunken state Weaver recognized as a reproach. They were children, and he disliked the idea of picking them up. "They're going to find someone their own age or go home," he said.

The girls laughed. "I think we're just going home," the first girl said. "Our Spanish isn't good enough to defend ourselves against the locals."

"Well, you've just hit on two locals who speak English," Weaver told them. "And you won't have to defend yourselves against us, because David here is in love, and I'm impotent, as of the last census taken."

The girls thought he was very funny and agreed at once to his suggestion that they take in the local flamenco parlor. They introduced themselves. The prettier one was called Peggy, and her sister's name was Patsy.

"Now where did you park your car, David?" Weaver asked, taking over the arrangements. "Or have you forgotten."

Brandt told him, and they walked up to the Paseo Marítimo together, with the two girls between them. "I thought you'd been folkloricked out of your tiny mind," he said to Weaver once they were all seated in the Peugeot.

"That was an hour ago," Weaver said. "I've just made a remarkable recovery. I feel young and vital again. The result of hearing a female voice speaking my own tongue, no doubt."

They drove up into the old town and parked the car in one of the back streets. Then Weaver led the way to a small *tablao-flamenco,* hidden away in the corner of one of the old plazas. It was a typical tourist trap, with bullfight posters on the wall behind the narrow, wooden dance floor that served as a stage for the entertainers. The owner was a plump lady in her forties in a tight red dress that bulged in most of the wrong places. She appeared to remember Brandt from somewhere and, after wiping the perspiration off her brown cheeks, kissed him affectionately. Then she kissed Weaver, too, as well as the girls, and led them to a table facing the floor. Peggy and her sister ordered Cokes, and Weaver, after overruling Brandt's protests, asked for two sol y sombras, a fairly lethal mixture of sweet and bitter anis.

Although the place was far from crowded, the show started almost immediately. There were two guitarists in black suits with white shirts open at the collar, and two rather skinny Gypsy women in the traditional polka-dot dresses of flamenco dancers. After the usual concert of *palmas,* the entire ensemble danced a round of *sevillanas,* the graceful, innocent kind of number that never failed to lift the spirit, Brandt thought as he watched the women turning and twisting with two male Gypsies who had been waiting at the bar for the act to begin.

Despite Brandt's initial reticence, he found himself enjoying the evening. The show was corny, but the two girls from Oregon seemed delighted with it. After the *sevillanas,* one of the men danced alone, pounding the wooden floor with his high-heeled shoes, his face twisted in the passionate grimaces that the dance apparently required. More people were arriving all the time, filling up the empty tables, and the plump proprietress greeted them all like long-lost friends.

Weaver leaned forward and said: "The man who opens a branch of Dr. Scholl's in this town need never look back," and the two American sisters giggled appreciatively.

Then after another concert of *palmas,* from the entire ensemble, more drinks were served, and the two guitarists launched into a *rumbita,* which was the sign for the proprietress to do her solo. Despite her figure, she danced with astonishing grace, and after a while was joined by the taller of the two male Gypsies. She retired to the bar to towel off her face, and the young Gypsy crossed to Brandt's table and pulled Peggy out onto the floor. The girl blushed and protested, but finally consented to join him in the dance.

She had no idea of what was required of her, but the Gypsy showed her how to move her hands, and after a few inhibited movements, she responded to the music. Brandt had often witnessed foreigners making fools of themselves at various flamencos in Madrid and on the coast, but the young girl was so innocent and graceful that it was pleasant to watch her. She had a sense of rhythm, and her young body was well formed, and when she finally made the usual departure from the floor, her performance was greeted with a wave of enthusiastic applause from the Gypsies and the other patrons of the establishment.

It was her sister's turn next, and then the Gypsy danced with a tall Swedish lady, who barely moved at all, and only managed to look like an embarrassed monument around which the dark-skinned young man danced in what looked like some strange mating ritual between alien races. It was the proprietress's turn after that, and she dragged several protesting Englishmen out under the lights, to the delight of their sunburned wives or girlfriends. Brandt felt the time had come to leave, but just as he was about to suggest they ask for the check, Peggy and Patsy excused themselves and disappeared into the ladies' room.

"They're cute," Weaver said as he watched them go. "Nice and wholesome. I'm going to ask the one called Peggy if she'd like me to go down on her. With no ulterior motive in mind, of course."

Brandt shook his head and said, "Sometimes your charm escapes me, Freddy. I mean it."

"I don't see why," Weaver said. "I offered her a little Moroccan shit, and she didn't seem at all offended. Just said, 'No, thank you,' as polite as can be."

Brandt controlled his annoyance. He knew that Weaver was drunk, but that really didn't seem to be an excuse. To make that kind of a gross remark after watching the girl dance charmingly was so offensive to him that he knew he could easily get angry. Yet he knew, too, that by the unwritten rules of male good fellowship, he was expected to accept it as a joke. Like Safire's vulgar remark about Hope.

But in his drunken state Weaver wouldn't let the matter rest. He said, "You're shocked, aren't you, Davie boy."

"No. Not really."

"What then? Disgusted? I believe that's the word for the look on your silly face."

Brandt took a deep breath. "I think you've turned into a pretty miserable specimen, that's all. But what the hell," he added. "Who am I to criticize?"

"That's right," Weaver said evenly. "I was just getting to that. Who the fuck do you think you are, anyway? I see you as a kind of stepped-up pimp. 'What rights does the lady have?' you ask me. The 'lady'! For whose benefit you take me to dinner because you think I can steer you onto some kind of gravy train at her husband's expense. And then you act like the parish priest when I make a sexy joke."

Brandt got slowly to his feet. The ensemble was back to doing *sevillanas* once again, but he made himself heard above the clapping and the castanets. "If you weren't pissed, and bombed out of your mind, I'd take you outside and stick your head in the gutter, where it belongs," he said.

Weaver's face was twisted with anger, his small dark eyes bloodshot and narrow. "Don't worry about my being pissed, pal," he said. "I can handle you easy." He got up unsteadily.

"Oh, go fuck yourself," Brandt said lamely. Out of the corner of his eye he saw the two girls approaching. He turned away from the table and took them both by the arm. "Come on. The party's over," he told them. "I'll take you home."

"Why? What's happened?" Peggy asked, but she didn't try to resist him. They went outside into the street.

"Nothing's happened. I'm going to take both of you back to your hotel."

"But what about Freddy?" Patsy asked.

"Forget Freddy. He's drunk." He guided them across the small square, then released his hold on their bare arms.

"But we haven't even thanked him," Peggy said. "I mean, he was very nice, even if he was a little tipsy." She stopped on the sidewalk and looked back anxiously to see if Weaver was coming.

He appeared an instant later, swaying slightly and stuffing change into his trouser pocket. "Brandt! You're a shit!" he shouted. "A cheap shit and a coward," he added after a small white car had swerved to avoid hitting him. He seemed unconscious of the near mishap, and stepped in front of Brandt, glaring fiercely at him. "Well, here I am," he said drunkenly. "What are you going to do about it?"

Brandt noticed that his fists were clenched, although Weaver hadn't raised his arms from his sides, and he stepped forward quickly and grabbed Weaver by both shoulders. "Don't be an asshole, Freddy," he said, but Weaver shook off his hold and swung at him. The blow caught Brandt in the chest and knocked him off balance. Almost as a reflex he struck out at the other man, and felt his left fist connect with Weaver's head. His hand hurt more than the punch he had received, and he saw that he had cut Weaver's mouth. A second later he felt someone grab him from behind, and realized that it was the doorman from the restaurant across the street. Weaver started to rush toward him, but two other men intervened. One of them was a taxi driver he had known for years and who had driven him to the airport on several occasions. "Señor Brandt! *Por Dios!*" the man shouted.

Weaver was offering no resistance to the men who had grabbed him. He put his hand to his bleeding mouth, and turned away. The men released him, and he staggered slowly down the narrow street. The people around Brandt were all talking at once, asking what had happened, but he didn't bother to reply. The two girls were nowhere in sight.

The taxi driver said something to the effect that he had better leave before the police arrived, and Brandt nodded and started up the street to where he had left his car. From a doorway a bedraggled Gypsy woman holding a small child in her arms put out her soiled hand. *"Por caridad,"* she mumbled, but he was in no mood for charity of any kind. He shook his head and hurried on his way.

He stood under the shower and rubbed his aching hand. He felt sick to his stomach. The whole thing was his fault. He had known that Weaver was drunk, so why had he reacted so violently to the man's tasteless remark? People had said worse things to him, and he had let them pass. It was the girl, he realized; Peggy. There was a look on her face that had reminded him of the painting of Hope at the Villa Miramar, a look of guileless expectancy that the painter had caught, and that the girl from Bend, Oregon, still possessed.

But that was hardly a reason to pick a fight. It was his own childish remark, he remembered painfully, that had led to the brief brawl. He had been an idiot to say he would take Weaver outside and stick his head in the gutter, because Freddy was drunk enough by that time not to know what he was doing.

The telephone rang. Brandt turned off the shower and looked at his watch. It was one-thirty in the morning. Perhaps it was Weaver, he thought, and, grabbing a towel, hurried into the bedroom. But it was Hope. In contrast to his own mood, she sounded in good spirits. "Did I wake you? I'm sorry," she said. "But I had to talk to you."

"That's all right. I was reading," he lied.

"That's good," she said cheerfully. "I'm glad you're improving your mind." She paused significantly. "Everything is much better here," she went on. "We've had a long talk, and Max was most reasonable. His only real complaint is that I should have trusted him, but he admits that he didn't exactly behave well, either."

"Where is he now?" Brandt asked.

"He's gone out. Probably to see you-know-who. But that doesn't matter. If that's what makes him happy, what the hell! He wants us all to get together. He's insisting on that. I said that I didn't think that was such a good idea, and he asked me why not, was I ashamed of you? So I said all right, if you want to see David, I don't mind. Then he said that he wanted to have a look at *Lulubelle.* I guess Phyllis put him up to that. She wants him to help Marie Manning by chartering her boat. Her good deed for the day, I suppose."

"When does he want to do that?"

"Oh, any time. Tomorrow, if you like. Or the next day. Whenever it's easy. He said we might meet at the port, look at the boat, and have a chat. I suppose it makes sense."

"What about all the rest of your problems?"

"You mean the house and the insurance money and all that? Well, he suggested we each get a lawyer and try to make some 'equitable arrangement.' I was thinking we might call your friend Freddy."

"I don't know if that's such a good idea," Brandt said. "I think we'd do better with a Spanish lawyer, somebody who doesn't know us all socially."

"All right. It was just a thought. I'll call you in the morning."

"Do you want to come here?" he asked her.

"You mean now? No, it's too late," she said without hesitation. "I think I'll get some sleep. I haven't had much of that lately. You, too. You could use a little rest."

"All right. Call me before nine-thirty, if you can, or after ten at the office."

She laughed and said: "I'll make a note of that. Before nine-thirty, or after ten at the office. You're not 'pissed-off' or anything, are you, David? Because I really couldn't call earlier. We were having the first civilized talk we've had in ten years."

"No, I'm not pissed-off," Brandt said. "Just tired."

"I know. Well, go back to sleep. Dream happy dreams."

"You, too," he said and hung up. Despite the warm night, he suddenly felt chilled. He got back under the shower, but the hot water had run out. Instead, a lukewarm stream played on his back. He turned it off, cursed the Spanish plumbing, and rubbed himself dry with a fresh towel. He didn't feel sleepy. He should have insisted that she come to see him. He needed her. Not carnally, he thought, but to comfort him and tell him that he hadn't been a goddamned fool. But if he told the story of his evening on the town, she might not show all that much sympathy.

He wished that he had a sleeping pill of some kind, and went over to the chest of drawers and got out his shaving kit to see if by any chance he still had one of Pamela's in stock. But he hadn't. All he found was a few British coins and a slip of paper with Connie Henderson's London address and her telephone number, scribbled in a childish scrawl.

The morning was hot and humid. There was no wind. The only cloud in sight sat perched like a featherbed on the summit of the Sierra Blanca. "Vacation weather," Brandt muttered to himself, as he stood watching Manolo polish *Lulubelle*'s windshield. Hope had called at ten-thirty, sounding just as relaxed and cheerful as she had in the middle of the night. Was he ready for the big confrontation, she had wanted to know. Max was leaving for Monte Carlo on Wednesday, really going this time, as he couldn't put off his business meeting any longer. So perhaps it *was* better to get it over with. Max had suggested that they meet at Guillermo's in the Puerto Banús at two o'clock so that he could have a look at the boat "and inspect the new man in her life." It was easier than meeting in town, since there was never any place to park, and the bars in the old port were even more crowded.

Reluctantly, Brandt had agreed to the arrangements, as he had his doubts about Clarendon's sincerity; there was no reason to suppose that he had had a change of heart and was willing now to act in a civilized manner. A man who took out a secret insurance policy on his mistress's jewels with himself as the beneficiary was unlikely suddenly to behave like Daddy Warbucks. Yet Brandt knew that he had no choice but to comply with Hope's wishes. Although he was in no mood for another clash like the one he had had with Freddy Weaver; he felt "clapped out," as the British were fond of saying, which was not the best frame of mind in which to face his rival.

Manolo grunted and moved aft along the narrow companionway in his stubby bare feet. The morning rubdown of *Lulubelle* had been completed. He squinted suspiciously up at Brandt with his small, bloodshot eyes. "*¿Usted va salir?*" he asked.

Brandt nodded and explained that he was going to the Puerto Banús to meet some friends.

"*¿Al Puerto Banus?*" There was a hint of disapproval in the sailor's voice, as if going to the adjoining port four sea miles away was an adventurous undertaking that involved risking life and limb.

Brandt said that was exactly what he had in mind, and Manolo told him that in that case he would come along. There was some sense in that, Brandt realized, because docking the boat alone might present a problem. He asked Manolo if he had eaten, and the sailor replied grumpily that he wasn't hungry and was willing to wait and have lunch later on.

Brandt took off his shoes and went on board. While Manolo cast off the stern lines, he started the engines. It would have been much simpler to meet Clarendon in the old port, at the bar where Phyllis usually waited for his call. But there was no use speculating on all that now. Nothing that involved Clarendon was ever going to be easy, he thought, and cursed the man. His mood improved, however, once they headed out to sea.

The water was flat and a very dark blue, and looking aft at the white wake the boat left behind her, Brandt knew that it was just this kind of a day that had enamored him of this part of the world and this particular body of water. There were scores of small craft out, cruisers and sailboats and pedaloes, as well as dozens of windsurfers, although there was no wind. It was quite obviously a day designed for man to play.

After the engines had reached the correct temperature, he set the throttles at cruising speed and turned the helm over to Manolo. Then he went forward and lay down on the mattress in front of the windshield and watched the familiar landmarks slip by: the new skyscrapers west of the town, the club, the Oasis, until the sea wall of the Puerto Banús came into view. He sat up then and, like a recently arrived tourist, gaped at the huge yacht lying a quarter of a mile off the entrance to the port. He had seen the same ship before during the previous summer, knew that she belonged to an Arab who had made his fortune selling arms and pumping oil. As Manolo steered *Lulubelle* impudently past the tall, white monster yacht, there was the sound of a rapidly approaching aircraft, and the owner's private helicopter appeared above them, hovered over the stern for a moment, and then clattered down onto the pad behind the ship's raked smokestack.

Brandt said, *"Mi nuevo barco,"* and Manolo grinned. One of the yacht's officers was leaning on the varnished railing of the crew-deck, fifteen feet above *Lulubelle*, and Brandt waved to him. The man didn't wave back. Instead, he made some remark to the dark-skinned woman standing next to him that made her laugh. Brandt gave them the victory sign and walked aft along the companionway. It wasn't his week to make friends, he thought, or even hang on to the old ones he had acquired long ago.

They turned into the port. Manolo pulled back on the throttles, and they planed in on a small wave of their own making. Brandt saw a sign on the far end of the fueling dock that read MUELLE DE ESPERA, and he pointed it out to Manolo, indicating they should tie up there. A sailor in a white T-shirt and white trousers came out of the small hut behind the fuel pumps and caught the line Brandt tossed him. He wanted to know how long they planned to stay there, and Brandt told him they would not be more than half an hour. A customs officer in a dark blue uniform appeared. Manolo informed him they had come from the old port, and the man nodded and went off with his clipboard tucked under his arm, obviously glad not to have to fill out the forms that were mandatory for any boat arriving from a foreign country.

Once they were securely tied up to the pier, Brandt asked Manolo if he wanted to go get something to eat, and the sailor grunted and said that he preferred to wait on board. It was just as well, Brandt thought. That way he had a good excuse for cutting short his meeting with Clarendon. He collected his shoes and stepped ashore. The sun beat down on his head and shoulders as he stooped to slip them on. *"Hasta luego,"* he called out to Manolo, and started off on foot in the direction of the main pier. He was truly in the land of the very rich, he reckoned, as he moved past the yachts moored to his right. He felt nervous. He hadn't had enough sleep.

He passed the corner bar that was the favorite of all the tarts and the layabouts, and walked on in the direction of Antonio's fish restaurant, where he had lunched so often with Pamela. One of the waiters waved to him and shouted a friendly greeting. He knew more waiters than any other American in Spain, he thought, in the Basque country in the north, in Burgos and Madrid and Sevilla, and the Costa del Sol. He waved back and went on. Then he saw Hope coming toward him. She was smartly turned out, as usual, in white trousers and a white and blue–striped French sailor's tricot. Despite the heat, she looked cool and well groomed, her hair ruffled slightly by the breeze that had come up. She smiled at him as they met, and offered her cheeks to be kissed.

"Are you all right?" she asked. "You look a little hot and bothered."

"Well, it's a hot day," he replied. "And I'm not looking forward to our meeting."

"Don't be silly. It'll be all right," she said. "Your new friend Phyllis has come along. To make things easier."

They had arrived at Guillermo's Bar. Clarendon and Phyllis were seated at a table in the sun, and Clarendon rose slowly as Brandt joined them. He nodded. They shook hands. Brandt was conscious of the other man's appraising glance, the alert eyes studying his face, as if they had never met before.

"I'm sorry I'm late," Brandt said. "I came in the boat, because I was told you wanted to look her over."

"You're not late," Clarendon said. "We were early. We had a look at another power boat, which turned out to be *precintado* by the customs people, why I don't know."

"The papers are probably not in order," Brandt said. "That's usually why they put a seal on the controls, so that the boat can't be used." He looked around for a chair. The terrace of the bar was crowded. He smiled at Phyllis and shook hands with her, too. "Wouldn't you be more comfortable inside?" he asked her.

"It smells of fried fish in there," Phyllis said. "It's either sweat or suffocate," she added. "What we could do is move on to some other bar. Or why not go out on *Lulubelle* and have a swim? If you have time, that is."

"I have time," Brandt said. "But I only have beer on board."

"Is it cold?" Clarendon asked. He had dropped back in the wicker chair again, his tanned face turned to the sun.

"It's not cold," Brandt replied. "But I could easily pick up some ice at the petrol dock."

"All right," Clarendon said. "If it's not too much trouble." He had closed his eyes against the bright glare. Apparently he had finished appraising his rival, had seen all he wanted to see.

Brandt said, "No trouble at all." He looked questioningly at the two women, and they both nodded, as if they were all conspirators together. "Then we might as well get started."

Clarendon got to his feet and gestured to the waiter that he wanted to pay. "I have to be back home by four," he said. "I have an overseas call coming in that's important. I presume we can manage that."

"No problem," Brandt said. "There's nothing much to eat on board, except some sardines and crackers and a couple of cans of baked beans. But that should do for a snack."

"I never eat lunch," Clarendon said. "Breakfast and dinner is usually all I have time for."

"And the ladies?" Brandt asked.

"Don't worry about us," Phyllis Dexter said. "Sardines and crackers is our favorite meal."

Once they were clear of the Arab's yacht, Brandt headed *Lulubelle* back in the direction of the old port. While walking toward his rendezvous with Clarendon and the two women, he had noticed that a light breeze was starting up. It was stronger now; there were minute ripples on the surface of the sea, which as a rule were reliable indicators that the weather was about to change. That accounted, too, for the extreme heat of the day. It was always hotter when there was a west wind, although it came from the cold Atlantic, and cooler when the wind was from the east and the warm Mediterranean, paradoxical bits of information he had picked up from Manolo.

But Brandt kept his recently acquired knowledge to himself. His passengers had not come along for a nature lecture. The ladies wished to take the sun and swim, which was quite apparent, as they had brought along their skimpy bathing suits. They were already bedded down on the sun mattress, lying side by side, seemingly at peace with each other. Women were obviously more forgiving of disloyalty than men, Brandt decided, or at least more sensible about not holding a grudge, especially when it was in their best interests to make peace.

Brandt turned and glanced aft. In one corner of the cockpit Manolo was leaning against the railing of the stern pulpit, smoking a cigarette and looking out at the coastline. Max sat down in the opposite corner, raised his feet onto the cushioned bench, and closed his eyes. He had put on his swimming shorts. He was in good shape for a man his age, especially one who worked as hard as he did, from Hope's accounts. His shoulders were well formed, and he had only the trace of a paunch. He probably went regularly to a gymnasium or played squash, Brandt thought, inspecting the older man's physique. It was strange that his physical relationship with Hope had come to an end, since he still had the outward appearance of a well-conserved male. Clearly there was no logical explanation for attraction or desire.

He looked up now, probably sensing that he was under observation, stretched his long body, and got slowly to his feet. "How far are we going?" he asked Brandt once he had joined him inside the wheelhouse.

"As far as you like," Brandt replied. "The water's usually cleaner on the other side of the town. If the girls really want to swim, that is."

"It doesn't look too dirty here," Clarendon said, looking out the open window on his side.

"But not too clean, either," Brandt replied, and pointed at a thin line of brownish weed on the surface of the water.

They stood in silence for a while, the steady drone of the engines serving as a kind of background music for their thoughts. "It's not a bad little boat," Clarendon remarked. "Does the man come with it?"

"Manolo? Well, he keeps her clean, and if you want him to, he's quite willing to go out on most days. You have to pay him extra, of course."

Clarendon nodded. "I'd need him," he said. "I don't think I'd like to take her out alone, and while I'm gone . . ." He stopped in midsentence, obviously not wanting to commit himself as to who would be the mistress of *Lulubelle* should he decide to charter her. "Your charter expires fairly soon, I'm told, and then Mrs. Manning, or whatever her name is, would be without a customer. Although I shouldn't think it'd be too difficult to find someone to take the boat in August and September," he added.

"It's not that easy, either," Brandt said. "*Lulubelle* flies a British flag, so that makes chartering her illegal. She would have to find someone who's a friend . . . and a foreigner, of course."

"That should influence the price," Clarendon said.

"It does."

"How much does she get?"

"About twelve hundred dollars a month," Brandt said, upping the fee a little. "If the boat flew a Spanish flag, the price would be three thousand, if not more."

"I see," Clarendon said. "Well, I'll have to think about it. What does the sailor get?"

"I suppose if you took him on as a steady hand, you'd have to pay him fifty thousand pesetas a month."

"What do you pay him?" Clarendon asked.

"Much less," Brandt said. "But he only puts in two hours a day." Richard Grey's description of Max Clarendon came quickly to his mind, although he knew from past experience that the rich were always careful about money. "If you like boats, it's not a big expense," he told Clarendon. "A couple of meals in one of the better restaurants, and you'd spend that much and more."

"I suppose so," Clarendon said drily. He turned away and started to climb out on the companionway in order to join the two women on the sun mattress.

"Mind the little hooks there on the deck," Brandt warned him, leaning out the window on his side. "You can stub your toe quite easily."

Clarendon nodded. He didn't say thank you or anything like

that, and for an instant Brandt regretted having warned him. The two women made room for Max on the mattress, and he lay down between them. A strange outing, Brandt thought, as he stood watching them. Then he was conscious of Manolo's presence beside him.

"Esta cambiando el tiempo," the sailor said gruffly.

Brandt looked off at the horizon beyond *Lulubelle*'s wake. A heavy cloud bank was moving in from the west. The man was right. The weather was definitely changing. The cold wind from the Atlantic was bringing a fog with it to the warm coast.

"Niebla," Manolo said, and frowned.

It would be a while before the fog reached them, Brandt reckoned, and there was always the chance that the heat of the sun would burn it off. Yet he pulled back on the controls, and the boat's bow settled low in the water. They were about four miles to the east of the town. There were groves of pine and eucalyptus trees along the shore, and the water was unmarked by refuse or plankton of any kind.

"Swimming party report aft," he called out to his guests on the mattress.

The two women sat up, each clutching the small bra of her bikini. Phyllis Dexter looked sleepy. She had had a full night, Brandt reckoned; the victor collecting her well-earned spoils. He noticed that the heat was intense now that the forward movement of the boat had stopped. He shut off the engines. Manolo was still looking off at the distant fog bank that was as yet at least fifteen miles away. He shook his head.

"*¿Anclamos?*" Brandt asked the sailor. He had learned in the Navy that a command always sounded better if put in question form at the lower levels of the seagoing hierarchy. Especially if the command was a dubious one.

Manolo shrugged. There was no use dropping the anchor if they were only going to swim, he told Brandt, as there was no current and hardly any wind.

Clarendon stood beside him in the cockpit, watching the two women as they swam slowly toward the shore. Whatever thoughts were going through his mind, he was keeping them to himself for that moment. Brandt glanced over at him, thinking that if they were going to talk at all, now was perhaps a good time. Although he really didn't know what was expected of him. He was under the impression that Clarendon had wanted to meet him, that the outing had been planned as an audition, with him trying out for the role of Hope's new companion. Or perhaps Clarendon had only really wanted to have a look at the boat? It was difficult to figure the whole thing out.

He studied the man's face. In a rugged way, Clarendon was quite handsome. Yet there was a duality about his features that brought to mind some of Picasso's paintings of his fellow men. One side of the face was almost kindly, but the other side had a harsh, predatory look. The mouth was determined, and the brow under the bald top of his head was furrowed. He didn't have the appearance of a man who had been tortured very often by doubt. He turned now and walked back into the shade of the wheelhouse, apparently having decided to put off diving into the sea. "You know, this wasn't my idea," he said, sitting down on the bench behind the helm.

"It certainly wasn't mine, either," Brandt replied.

"It was Phyllis who thought of it. I suppose there's some sense in it. Just to relieve the possible embarrassment of running into each other at a party." He paused. "That is, if you're planning to stay on here," he added.

"We've made no plans," Brandt said, and noticed that the "we" had a certain effect.

Clarendon nodded; to himself, so it seemed. "It's not really a town a man like yourself should settle down in," he said. "How old are you? Too young to retire, I'd say, even if you had the means. And to make a living here, if you're not a hustler or an investor, might prove difficult. That's why this whole situation is pretty absurd."

"I don't quite follow you," Brandt said quietly. "What situation are you talking about?"

"This whole mess . . . which is probably my own damned fault to some degree. A man shouldn't leave his wife on her own for too long, I suppose. Especially in a place like this, a summer resort that offers all kinds of temptations, causes women to mingle with people they normally would never meet."

Brandt was tempted to laugh out loud, but he controlled himself. "I think we might even have met in a city," he said with a smile. "Paris, London, New York, Los Angeles. I've lived in all of them, and my acquaintances were never restricted to any one class. Nor do I really feel she fished me out of the gutter," he added.

"I didn't mean to imply that. You're an American, as is she, and presumably in your great country there are no class differences." Clarendon's eyes narrowed. "But that's not the point I was trying to make. Hope, mainly through her connection with me, has lived the life of a wealthy woman. For her to change her life style now, in middle age, will prove to be quite a task."

Brandt said: "An acquaintance of mine has already pointed that out to me. That it's always a mistake to take a woman away from a wealthy protector."

Clarendon frowned. "It's not the way I would have put it, but nevertheless I think that's true," he said. "Nor do I think that your financial situation is likely to change."

"You never can tell," Brandt said with a smile. "I might win the lottery."

Clarendon gave a bitter little chuckle. "Well, yes, there's always a chance of that," he said. "But a fairly remote chance, I'd say. Not a thing you can count on. Nor would I count on Hope's 'expectations.' You see, there's one sort of fellow that's always annoyed me, and that's the chap who wants a free ride. Tries to climb on your back in a business deal and come out with a profit for himself. Or marry money. I've always done my best to stick a spoke in that chappie's wheel."

"I don't think we'd better go on with this conversation," Brandt warned him.

"*I* think we might as well, now that we've started," Clarendon said. "So that there are no false illusions. For either one of you. Of course I'm not going to let Hope sink into 'squalor.' I'm too fond of her to let that happen. But I'm not going to feather her nest for your benefit, either."

"I don't really give a goddamn what you do," Brandt said. He felt that he was about to get angry, and he wanted to avoid that, if possible. They were too far away from port for an unpleasant scene. "Why don't we join the ladies?" he suggested, sarcastically.

"All right," Clarendon said. "I've had my say."

Brandt turned away and went into the wheelhouse to get himself a towel. When he started back aft, he saw that Clarendon was standing on the small deck area over the transom, preparing to dive into the water. He looked more like a bird of prey than a shark; an aging hawk.

"Just one more thing," Clarendon said. "It's my view that there are people who are destined to spend their lives living in shabby rooms, eating poorly cooked food, and riding around in cheap cars. I want Hope to have a taste of that kind of life for a while, because she thinks it doesn't matter right now."

"And then when she's paid the price for being disloyal to you, you'll step in and save her? Is that the plan?" Brandt asked. He was past being angry. It was all too ludicrous, really. "It must be great to be able to play God," he said and, stepping past Clarendon, dove into the water.

The sea was cool. Just the right temperature, he thought, to wash away his irritation with himself for having agreed to meet Clarendon at all. He turned over on his back and swam away from the stern of *Lulubelle.* He watched Clarendon dive in, and waited for his bald head to surface before he swam on in the direction of the beach.

It would be funny if the old bastard had a heart attack about now, he thought, but apparently that was not to be. Clarendon was swimming with powerful strokes toward the bow of *Lulubelle.* Brandt caught a glimpse of Manolo standing just forward of the sun mattress. The sailor was staring off at the cloud bank on the horizon with a worried look on his face. It was time to get the two women back on board, Brandt decided, and put an end to this ridiculous boat ride.

But it would take too long to swim to the beach, he realized, and then swim back: *Lulubelle* was lying at least a hundred and fifty yards out. Brandt waved his arms, but neither Hope nor Phyllis saw him. They were walking along the shore, picking up stones and skimming them across the flat surface of the sea while deep in conversation. He thought of calling out to them, but knew that his voice wouldn't carry that far, so he turned and swam back to the boat.

He was slightly winded when he arrived at the base of the swimming ladder. Clarendon was lying on the sun mattress on the foredeck, his face buried in one of the faded blue cushions. Manolo was already standing inside the wheelhouse, waiting for the command to start the engines. Brandt joined him after drying himself off. The fog bank appeared to have reached the entrance of the Puerto Banús, although the white buildings behind it were still in sunlight, as were the mountains behind the port. *"Vamonos,"* Brandt said, and the sailor made a face.

"¿Y las señoras?"

"Las recojemos mas cerca de la playa."

The man nodded. He didn't look happy, but he turned the starter keys, and the diesel engines came noisily to life. Brandt waited beside him, hesitating whether to take over the wheel, but the sailor stood his ground. He obviously preferred to take the boat in close to the shore himself. Brandt did not interfere. He stepped out onto the companionway. Clarendon sat up abruptly.

"Where are we going?" he asked.

"In closer to pick up the girls. There's a fog coming in from the west."

Clarendon nodded and lay down again. The fact that the fog might present a serious problem had not occurred to him. It was just as well, Brandt thought. There was no point in worrying any of his passengers.

Manolo steered the boat to within fifty yards of the beach and then pulled the controls back into the reverse position. Brandt whistled and waved to the two women. They looked puzzled, both of them shading their eyes against the glare. "Come on! We have to go!" Brandt called out to them.

Hope nodded. She turned and said something to Phyllis. They were still lingering at the edge of the water. Hope was the first to put her feet in. Phyllis seemed undecided whether to follow her. She cupped her hands in front of her mouth. "Can't you come in a little closer," she called out. "I'm tired!"

"It's pretty shallow," Brandt called back.

"All right." She moved slowly into the water, wetting her arms and stomach first. Brandt went aft with a dry towel and, when Hope arrived, helped her climb up over the transom.

"Well, did you have your little chat?" she asked him.

"We did indeed."

"Not a very friendly one, I take it?"

"No, it wasn't."

"Oh, really? And why is that?"

"He suggested that I was looking for a 'free ride.' That that was the only reason I took up with you. He thinks I'm after your money, or *his* money, to be more exact."

"Is that why we're going in early?"

"That and the fog." He pointed to the white mist that was still moving toward them. Only the top of the Sierra Blanca was visible now. The remainder of the coast was wrapped in a thick cloud.

Phyllis was drawing near the stern. She turned over on her back and floated the last few feet.

"I'm not in very good shape, I guess," she said once she was standing in the cockpit.

"Too many cigarettes," Brandt told her. "Watch it, we're about to get under way." He nodded to Manolo, and the sailor pushed the controls gently forward.

Phyllis slid down onto the cushioned bench in the stern. She toweled off her legs and chest and then turned over on her stomach. "It was so nice on the beach, I hated to get back in the water," she said. She closed her eyes. "Where's Max?" she asked drowsily.

"Up forward."

The light had changed, Brandt noticed once he joined Manolo. The sea was a silvery gray. An instant later the fog closed down on all sides of them. Manolo muttered to himself and pulled back on the throttles, reducing their speed to eight knots. A film of moisture covered the windshield, and Brandt flicked on the wipers. But Manolo was a little too short to be able to see out of the space the wipers had cleared. He ran a stubby hand through his thick black hair, muttered to himself, and leaned out the window.

As he did so, he almost collided with Clarendon, who had risen from the mattress and was moving aft along the companionway. Manolo ducked inside for an instant to allow the man to pass, and then stuck his head out the window again. The rush of moist air made him squint.

"Bloody cold up there now," Clarendon said, stepping down into the cockpit. The floorboards creaked under his weight. "You haven't got a jacket or anything like that on board, have you?"

"I believe there's a blanket in one of the cupboards below," Brandt told him. He wasn't going to fetch and carry for the old bastard when all eyes were needed on the sea beyond *Lulubelle*'s bow.

Clarendon went below and reappeared a moment later with a section of the tarpaulin that was used to cover *Lulubelle*'s cockpit in the winter. "Couldn't find the blanket," he said, "but this'll do." He moved into the stern, where he stood looking down at Phyllis for a moment or two. She had spread two towels over her body and was lying face down across the width of the cushions, apparently fast asleep. Clarendon wrapped the tarpaulin around his shoulders and frowned out at the gray sea. Then he seated himself on the padded coaming of the transom.

The fog was getting visibly thicker. Manolo pulled back on the throttles, and they cruised along at about five knots. Brandt heard the chug of a diesel engine off to the left of them, and a small fishing boat came into view, heading in the same direction as *Lulubelle.* The two men standing aft of the engine had put on their yellow slickers. The one at the tiller shouted something to Manolo, and he shouted back, an unintelligible curse.

"It's dangerous, isn't it, this fog," Hope said. She had moved forward and was standing on Brandt's left.

"It's not the best weather for yachting," Brandt told her, and smiled grimly.

"Are you going to try to get back to Banús?" she asked. She seemed very calm.

"If we can," Brandt said. He stepped over to the window on the starboard side and leaned out. He could see only about twenty feet ahead of them, and then suddenly there was an open space, and directly ahead of them he caught a glimpse of a stone jetty. He shouted a warning to Manolo, but the sailor had seen the section of breakwater at the same time as he had. He spun the wheel hard to port and pushed the throttles forward. *Lulubelle*'s bow rose in the water as her speed increased, and an instant later they were clear of the obstacle, heading out to sea.

Hope gasped and stumbled back, thrown off balance by the sudden surge of the boat. Brandt managed to grab her arm and keep her from falling. He pulled her forward so that she could get a grip on the handrail, and then he turned to face the stern. Phyllis Dexter had not moved, but there was no sign of Clarendon.

He shouted, "*¡Para!*" and pushed Hope out of the way in order to get within reach of the controls, but Manolo had already ducked back inside and was pulling down on the throttle levers in order to reverse the engines. He glanced over at Brandt. He still had not understood what had happened. Then he, too, looked aft. "*¿Donde esta el señor?*" he asked, turning to face Brandt, although he had obviously realized by that time that Clarendon had fallen overboard.

Brandt didn't bother to reply. He moved quickly into the stern. As he did so, Phyllis Dexter stirred under the towels she had spread out over her body. She sat up, as if someone had awakened her in the middle of a bad dream.

"Where's Max?" she asked, apprehensively.

Brandt said, "I don't know," and stepped up onto the cushioned bench. There was no sign of Clarendon in the gray water to the rear of the boat. The engines were turning over slowly, the exhausts spitting out sporadic streams of sea water. Brandt braced himself and stood staring off into the mist, listening intently for some cry of help. At that moment the woman behind him started to scream.

He jumped down into the cockpit and grabbed her by the shoulders and shook her. She stopped screaming almost at once and stared at him, like a child who has been reprimanded by a complete stranger. As they stood there, facing each other, there was the flat, hoarse sound of a foghorn off to the left of them. Manolo pushed the throttles forward, and the deck lurched under their feet. Brandt managed to keep his balance, but he couldn't prevent Phyllis from falling as her legs buckled under her. Her head hit the deck with a dull thud.

He reached down to help her. She had started to tremble. He

noticed that her eyes were closed. Her whole body was shaking now. He looked up, but both Hope and the sailor were staring out through the windshield. A ketch was bearing down on them, a ketch with a navy blue hull, and Brandt realized that Manolo's quick maneuver had saved them from a collision. An instant later the ketch had disappeared into the fog. Manolo pulled back on the throttles once again, and *Lulubelle* lay rolling from side to side in the mild wake of the sailboat.

"Me cago en Dios," the sailor said, and looked over at Brandt as if he expected to be rebuked for the blasphemy.

Hope released her hold on the handrail and stepped over to where Phyllis Dexter still lay motionless on the deck at Brandt's feet. The expression on her face had not changed since the initial moment of danger. She was making an effort to control her nerves, that much was obvious, yet she did not appear to be excessively frightened. She leaned over and took Phyllis by both ankles. "Let's take her below," she said.

Brandt nodded, and together they carried Phyllis down the narrow ladder. They put her down gently on the bunk behind the varnished, rectangular table in the main cabin, and Brandt propped a pillow under her head. Hope was panting a little from the physical effort.

"Max will be all right," she said in a flat voice. "He's a strong swimmer, and we couldn't have been very far from the beach when he went overboard."

She seemed so positive that for an instant Brandt felt reassured. "Did you see him fall?" he asked.

"No, I was watching the jetty. I thought we were going to hit it."

The woman on the bunk moaned and turned on her side. She put her face against the back rest and drew her knees up to her chest, shivering convulsively. Brandt pulled open the bottom drawer of the cabinet facing them and found the blanket he had offered Clarendon a few minutes earlier. He shook it out, then wrapped it tightly around Phyllis' body. He was suddenly conscious of Hope watching him. Their eyes met. She nodded in sarcastic approval.

"Take good care of her," she said. "We may need her."

"What the hell are you talking about?"

"She saw Max fall off the stern. She knows we didn't push him."

It was such an absurd remark that he knew at once it could only have been prompted by jealousy. He looked down at Phyllis to see if she was listening, but her eyes were still tightly closed. "You said that he'd be all right. That he was a strong swimmer."

"He might have hit his head on the side of the boat when he fell. I didn't think of that."

It was her tone of voice that troubled him more than her words. Was she wishing that the worst had happened? He said, "We'd better find him," and started toward the hatchway. He heard Phyllis moan again, but he didn't stop. He climbed quickly up the ladder.

Manolo was standing at the helm, waiting for orders. Apparently he had decided that the boat was his only responsibility, that the safety and welfare of the passengers were not his problem. Brandt told him to head back in the direction of the jetty. The sailor nodded, and they got under way. Brandt realized that he had no idea of where they were. He had lost all sense of direction. They had turned out to sea when they had sighted the pier, but they had turned again in order to avoid the ketch. He noticed that Manolo was checking the compass.

"Does he know where he's going?" Hope asked. She was standing in the cabin, pulling on the tricot she had worn on board. She ran her fingers through her hair, patted it into place, an automatic female gesture.

"I think he does," Brandt said. He felt weary. He swung one foot onto the companionway and found the handrail that ran along the top of the cruiser's wheelhouse. Then he moved forward. Once he was standing on the foredeck, he put both of his hands on the chrome railing of the bow pulpit. He would have a better chance that way to see anything in the water in front of them. The fog seemed to have gotten even denser. The palms of his hands were sweating. He glanced back for a second. Hope was standing in front of the co-pilot's seat on the starboard side. The windshield wipers cleared the mist that covered the glass in front of her grim, pretty face. Brandt saw that she had lit a cigarette. Manolo had his head out the open window, his eyes screwed up so that they formed two narrow slits in his weatherbeaten face.

Brandt gazed out at the flat sea through which they were moving. "It was an accident," he found himself muttering under his breath, as if he were rehearsing an alibi.

There was a sudden gust of wind, and the shore was visible a hundred feet ahead. The beach they were approaching was revealed to him through the swirling fog. The sky was still low and gray, as was the surface of the water. The strip of sand beyond it was gray, too, only a lighter shade, and the vegetation beyond the far edge of the beach was a dirty brown.

Manolo shouted something to him, and he looked up and saw that they were approaching the pier. He hurried aft along the narrow companionway and stubbed his toe on one of the hooks on the deck. Disregarding the pain it caused him, he swung his body down into the wheelhouse. They had arrived at the exact spot where Clarendon had fallen overboard. Brandt said, *"Muy bien,* Manolo," and patted the sailor's shoulder.

"It's not deep enough to drown here," Hope said, ducking her head back inside the window. "There's only about six feet of water."

Brandt nodded. "It's lucky we didn't run aground," he said. He had noticed that *Lulubelle*'s wake was full of churned-up sand.

Manolo steered the boat in a long, curving arc back out to sea. The fog had lifted all along the shore. In the distance they could see the concrete towers of the town, a wintry-looking modern city, hovering on the edge of a flat stretch of gray sea. The sun seeped through the mist to the east and shone briefly on the remnants of an olive grove, dotted with white houses. The speed of the boat increased, and the sea wall of the old port came into view.

Brandt was about to ask the sailor what he thought they should do, when a noise behind him made him turn. Phyllis Dexter had appeared in the hatchway, wrapped in Manning's old blanket. Her wet hair hung down to her shoulders. Her eyes were bloodshot. "I want you to take me back to the Puerto Banús," she said in an ominously flat voice. "Right away."

"Do you feel a little better?" Brandt asked her.

She disregarded his question. "I want to go back *now,*" she said pointedly. "I know what you're doing," she went on. "You're pretending to look for him."

"We're not *pretending,* Phyllis," Hope replied acidly. "Don't act like such a goddamned fool."

"I'm going to the police," Phyllis Dexter said. "You should have turned back the moment he fell. It's too late now."

Hope said, "What are you talking about? We did try. And then the other boat came bearing down on us." Brandt could tell that she was controlling her temper.

"We'll take you wherever you want to go, honey," he said gruffly. "And you can do whatever you want to do. But I think you'll find that Max is probably back at the villa by the time we dock."

Phyllis Dexter stared at him with contempt. "Just take me back to the port," she said, and backed down the ladder. They could hear her coughing violently inside the cabin.

"*Vamonos a Banús,*" Brandt told the sailor.

Manolo grunted, and looked out to sea. The fog was still hanging low over the water to the west. *"¿A Banús?"* he said, repeating the command with disbelief.

"Si," Brandt said. *"La señora tiene su coche alli."* She had her car there, he thought, and she knew the police in San Pedro better than the police in Marbella. He turned to Hope. "Max had better be alive," he told her, "or we're going to be in for a hard time."

"Don't worry about him," she replied. "He hasn't drowned. The Clarendons die hard, or so he's always told me."

Halfway to the horizon there was a silver river running west through the grayish-blue sea. The sun had found its way through the swirling mist and was marking a course for them to follow. In the distance, near the shore, the white buildings of the port were already in view, looking less like a picture postcard than usual because of the absence of the sun. Their little afternoon drama, Brandt realized, had taken place in a few square miles, not even out of sight of land on a normal day. A similar thought must have occurred to the woman standing beside him. Hope shook her head, her eyes on the not-too-distant shore.

"I'll bet we'll laugh about all this once it's over," she said, and reached for the package of cigarettes lying on the varnished wood behind the glass of the windshield.

"I hope you're right," Brandt said, "but it's not over yet." He had never really liked her Christian name, he decided, would certainly never have saddled a child of his own with it.

Later, when they were about to turn into the entrance of the port, and the silver river was nearer, he asked Manolo what was causing it. *"El corriente,"* the sailor replied, as if he were answering a child.

The current, of course, Brandt thought. That was the reason for the fog, too; the pressure from the Atlantic meeting the warm air from the east. He noticed that the rich Arab's yacht was no longer anchored outside the breakwater. She was probably on her way to Saint Tropez or Ibiza. If they had crossed her path in the fog, they might not be alive now, any of them, Brandt mused grimly.

They tied up at the *muelle de espera,* promising the sailor on duty once again not to remain there for more than a few minutes. Phyllis Dexter waited until *Lulubelle* was tied securely to the dock before she ventured out of the cabin. She had put on her clothes and carried her bikini rolled up in a towel. She stood for a moment, blinded by the light of the afternoon sun, then turned to face Brandt. "You wanted him dead, didn't you?" she said in a low voice. "Even if it was an accident, it was what you wanted."

Brandt said roughly: "Come on, Phyllis. Pull yourself together. You'll find Max safe and dry at the villa when you get there. Don't talk nonsense."

"If he's not there, I'm going to the police," she said. She raised her hand to the back of her head, to touch the place where she had struck it on the deck. "There is such a thing as criminal negligence, you know. You were in command. You should have gone back to look for him at once."

"We did just that," Brandt told her. "I had to take care of you, too. And protect the boat."

"Thanks for nothing," she replied.

She didn't even look at Hope. She moved slowly across the cockpit. Manolo helped her up the steep, cement steps off the port side. Once she was on terra firma, she reached into the pocket of her skirt and took out her sunglasses. She put them on, and went off in the direction of the imitation Moorish tower that housed the port authorities.

"You'd better go with her," Brandt said to Hope, "and at least make sure she calls the villa before she begins stirring up trouble."

Hope nodded quietly. "As long as I don't have to talk to the bitch," she said. "Are you going to wait here?"

"I'd better," Brandt said. "They might try to make Manolo move off if he's on his own." He waited for Hope to find her shoes, and helped her up the steps. "Don't be too long," he told her. Then he joined Manolo on the foredeck. It wouldn't hurt to have a friendly word with the man and pay him a few thousand pesetas extra for his help. *"¿Tiene usted hambre?"* he asked him while they stood warming themselves in the sun.

The sailor shook his head. He wasn't hungry; thirsty perhaps, but that was all. Brandt went below and got a couple of bottles of beer out of the plastic container. Phyllis Dexter, he noticed, had left the blanket he had wrapped around her lying on the deck in front of the main bunk she had occupied. He tossed the blanket onto the varnished table and joined Manolo on deck.

The port was crowded with sightseers walking up and down the quays in order to gape at the rich on their big yachts. Manolo was still staring up at the sky, still concerned with his main enemy, the weather. *"¡Qué lio!"* Brandt said to him.

"Si. Un lio gordo."

He was not convinced, then, that Clarendon had made it to the beach, else he would not have qualified the *lio,* the mess, as being a fat one. Brandt ventured to say that unless Clarendon had hit his head on the way down, he should have made it easily to the shore, and the sailor replied with surprising certainty that *el sẽnor* had not touched the boat once he had fallen. They would have heard the noise, and there had not been a sound.

"*Y ¿las helices?*" Brandt asked.

"Las helices, nada," Manolo said almost angrily. It would have been impossible for Clarendon to be caught by the propellers, because he had fallen aft while the boat was moving forward.

Hope called out to Brandt from the dock. He went back into the cockpit and helped her come on board. "He's not at home," she said quietly. "And they haven't heard from him, either."

"Would he have called home, knowing we were still on the boat?"

"He was expecting an overseas call at four. He said it was important, and knowing him as I do, I think he'd have had the servants pick him up. If he made it to the beach, that is . . ."

"What about Phyllis?"

"I don't know what she's up to. But I'm not going to follow her around like a pet dog."

"Don't you think one of us should stay with her?" Brandt asked. "Just to make her a little more careful about her accusations."

"I don't think it would help," Hope said. "Anyway, she's probably gone by now."

Manolo was standing on the pier, talking to another sailor, and he nodded now and came over to where Brandt was waiting in the stern of *Lulubelle*. *"Ya no hay niebla,"* he announced.

Brandt nodded, sensing that there was something else on the sailor's mind beside the weather. Would it matter very much if he didn't return to the old port with them? the man asked. The question was put in a rather laconic way, and yet it was apparent to Brandt that it had been carefully phrased. His friend, the sailor explained, was driving to La Linea, and had offered to take him along. That way he could visit his family and be back the following day.

"No me importa nada," Brandt replied, although it did matter to him. He would have preferred to have the sailor with them for the trip back, in case Phyllis had succeeded in prodding the police into action with her false allegations. There was just a chance that they would be on the dock waiting for *Lulubelle*'s arrival.

"Ya no hay nada que hacer," Manolo said, adding a little logic to his request, that there was nothing more he could do, that his presence wasn't needed to get *Lulubelle* back to her home port.

"Bueno. Hasta mañana," Brandt said coolly.

"Pues . . . hasta mañana," Manolo mumbled, and went off with his friend. They didn't even wait to help cast off the lines by which the boat was still attached to the pier.

Brandt gave their retreating figures a last doubtful look and went forward to start the engines. Then he moved aft and undid the nylon rope with which *Lulubelle* was tied to the pier.

"What about Manolo?" Hope asked. "Is he jumping ship?" She had climbed back up the cement steps and was standing by to cast off the line in the bow.

"He's getting a ride to La Linea to see his family. I told him he could go. We don't need him anymore."

Hope made a face and said, "Rats leaving the ship that didn't sink," and, once she had undone the line forward, stepped back onto the companionway.

Brandt watched her push against the pier with her right foot as if she had handled small boats all of her life. She appeared to have put all of their problems out of her mind, was very much her normal self again. He waited for her to join him in the wheelhouse before getting under way.

Once they were clear of the port, he set a course for the skyscrapers of the distant town. Now that the fog was gone, the air was surprisingly clear. The mountains towered over the port beyond the boat's wake. He would swing in closer to the shore, Brandt decided, and pass near the site of the accident once again. That way he could check precisely how far from the beach they had been when Clarendon had fallen overboard.

Hope settled back onto the co-pilot's seat on the starboard side and put her feet up on the handrail. "What a mess I've gotten you into," she said. "But Max seemed so reasonable last night . . . I guess it was stupid of me to trust him."

"It was my fault as much as yours. If I hadn't asked you to dance . . ."

"There's no point in going over all that again," she said. "And no matter what Phyllis tells them, it wasn't our fault that he fell overboard."

"I don't think we'll hang," Brandt said ironically. "If he *is* lost, which I think is most unlikely. Anyway, let's not assume the worst until we know for sure."

"The worst?" she replied, and shook her head. "It would have been much worse for me if I'd lost you." She was looking off at the distant horizon, her face turned away from him.

He said, "Come sit here," and made room for her on the helmsman's bench beside him. He took her hand. Her fingers were cold. The news that Clarendon was not at the villa had obviously unnerved her, although she had given no outward sign that she was frightened. "You know that I'm crazy about you," he told her. "No matter what happens."

"That's nice to hear," she said, and tightened her grip on his fingers. "The funny thing about you is that I don't think you ever really made up your mind about me," she went on. "That's what made me wonder if I hadn't made a mistake. I don't mean going to bed with you, and all that. I was just beginning to think that I'd taken the whole thing too seriously. Not in the beginning, but later on, when I found out that Max was having an affair with Phyllis. Like the afternoon we met on the beach, and then went to have a drink with the about-to-be new Mrs. Clarendon."

"I remember that afternoon," Brandt said. "We hadn't seen each other for a long time, so we were both nervous. Then the cat crossed the road in front of my car, and I hit it. It must have been a black cat, after all," he added.

"Let's not assume the worst until we know for sure," she said, imitating him. She managed a nervous laugh.

He said, "You're right," and let go of her hand. The stern of the boat was rising with each wave of the following sea, and he turned the wheel so that they would not plow into the waves in front of them once the boat had stopped surfing. The windshield was covered with spray. He turned on the wipers. They were about a mile and a half down the shore from the port, and at the far end of a small beach he recognized the stone jetty they had swerved to avoid a couple of hours earlier. There was a lot of debris on the surface of the water. The westerly wind was driving it onto the shore. He saw a log directly ahead of them and altered his course to avoid it. He noticed that there was a round object floating near the log that looked like a ball. Then he realized that it could be a man's head. He pulled back on the throttles, and as *Lulubelle* rolled from side to side in the swell, he saw that it was Max Clarendon's head resting like an abandoned brown soccer ball on the surface of the sea.

He looked over at Hope. She, too, had seen Clarendon, was staring out at him through the space the wipers were clearing on the starboard side of the windshield. She turned to look over at Brandt. "Is he dead?" she asked.

Brandt reversed the propellers. The man in the water in front of them hadn't moved. The following sea was driving the boat toward him with alarming speed. Brandt felt his stomach tightening. He cursed himself for having let the sailor go, and pulled back on both throttles. Take your time now, he counseled himself. By gently advancing the starboard throttle, and pulling back some more on the lever opposite it, he swung the stern of *Lulubelle* around so that they were drifting stern first in Clarendon's direction. A wave splashed against the side of the boat. Brandt brought both throttles back to the neutral position, making sure that they were in the right place and that the propellers had stopped turning. He glanced over at Hope. She was clinging to the handrail in front of her.

"What can I do?" she asked.

"Nothing. Don't touch the throttles, and come into the stern." He scooped up the nylon rope he had left lying on the deck when they had pulled away from the dock, attached one end of it to a cleat, and climbed down onto the swimming platform. Max Clarendon and the log he was holding on to were less than twenty feet astern of *Lulubelle.* He stared up at Brandt with glazed, panic-stricken eyes.

"Help me," he called out, his voice barely audible above the noise of the idling engines.

Brandt dove into the water. A couple of strokes brought him within arm's length of the drowning man. He looked back toward the boat. It was still drifting slowly in their direction. He grabbed Clarendon's right arm, and the other man's weight dragged them both below the surface. He kicked hard, struggling to get his head clear. There was a good chance that they would both drown, he thought, and cursed himself again for having been too soft with Manolo. Then he took a deep breath and went under again in order to loop the rope around Clarendon's chest. He managed to tie a knot, although his lungs were beginning to ache. He surfaced, and swam for the swimming ladder.

Clarendon wasn't moving, he saw as he pulled himself up onto the wooden platform, was still clinging to the log. Brandt got to his feet and grabbed the nylon line. Very slowly he took up the slack. Then he realized that the boat now presented a greater danger to the man in the water than the sea. He made the line fast to the railing in the stern and dove back in again.

He felt the edge of the swimming platform against his back and, locking his left arm around Clarendon's shoulders, grabbed for the ladder with his right hand. As the boat rose with the next swell, he felt his elbow straining under Clarendon's dead weight, and then as the boat dropped, he managed to pull Clarendon in closer to the boat. Suddenly the weight grew lighter, and he realized that Hope had pulled in the line. Clarendon's body was secured now to the tubular frame of the ladder, bobbing up and down with the stern of *Lulubelle.*

He got both of his hands on the edge of the wooden platform and hoisted himself up on it. With Hope pulling on Clarendon's arms, they hauled his limp body up onto the afterdeck. Hope draped a towel over Max's shoulders and started pounding his back with the flat of her hand. Clarendon began to cough. He was spitting out sea water and saliva, his chest racked by spasms. Then he started to shake. He rolled over and lay face down on the afterdeck, looking like a fish that had been hauled up out of the sea. A shark, Brandt thought, of a new species. He almost laughed out loud with relief. The shark was alive.

He went forward into the wheelhouse to take over the helm. *Lulubelle* was rolling from side to side, the short, choppy waves slapping against the hull. Brandt eased the throttles forward and turned the chrome wheel. He glanced aft. Hope had managed to drag Clarendon down onto the bench in the stern. She was standing over him, her feet braced against the movement of the boat. Then she straightened and stood leaning against the padded transom. Her eyes met Brandt's for an instant. She managed a weak smile. The drama was over.

Brandt made certain that they were headed in the right direction, and went down into the cabin to get Manning's old blanket. When he came up on deck, he noticed that Hope had taken over the wheel. He patted her on the back. "Don't worry. She's all right on her own. Runs straight back to port," he said.

"I wasn't sure."

He handed her the blanket. "Better wrap this around your friend. He's been in the water for quite a while."

She nodded and yielded her place to him. "Do you think he'll be all right?" she asked.

"I think so. Didn't you tell me that the Clarendons die hard?"

"I didn't say that. He did."

"Well, he proved it," Brandt said. He pushed the throttles forward to get the bow higher up out of the water. Hope had gone back to spread the blanket over the man lying in the stern.

They had been lucky, Brandt thought, goddamned lucky. If he hadn't decided to follow the coastline in order to pass near the jetty again, Clarendon would undoubtedly have drowned. It was unlikely that he could have lasted much longer. There were several small fishing boats heading back in the direction of Estepona, but they were all passing at least five hundred yards away from where Clarendon had been floating in the choppy sea. Brandt remembered the story of a fisherman who had fallen overboard during the previous summer and had kept himself afloat for nine hours before he was rescued. But Clarendon, no matter how tough he was, was older and less physically prepared for that kind of ordeal.

He was sitting up now, his elbows resting on his knees, staring down at the deck. Hope was wiping his face with a towel. Very slowly he raised his head and looked over at Brandt. Then he said something to Hope. Was he thanking her, Brandt wondered, or was he registering some complaint? Brandt stepped back into the cockpit. The alert eyes stared at him unwaveringly. Yet it seemed to Brandt that the man's facial expression had changed. The animosity was still there, but the disdain was gone. "What happened to Phyllis?" Clarendon asked in a weak voice.

Hope said, "She insisted on being taken to Banús so that she could go to the police." That was all. She obviously didn't think that any further explanation was necessary.

Clarendon looked puzzled. "The police," he repeated. "Whatever for?" Neither Hope nor Brandt replied. Clarendon shook his head. "Don't tell me that she suspected foul play," he said, with a grin. He chuckled maliciously. "Isn't that just like her to behave like a character out of Agatha Christie," he went on. "Although,

I must say, the thought crossed my mind when I hit the water."

"Why didn't you yell?" Brandt asked.

"I did, once I caught my breath. You weren't more than about a hundred yards away. I couldn't see you, but I could hear the engines. Then another boat came by, a sailboat with a blue hull, and I yelled at them, but they didn't hear me either. Or if they did, they probably thought I was some nut swimming around in the fog, yelling to keep from being run over."

"We thought you'd swim to shore," Hope said.

"Yes. Well, I thought of that, too, but I wasn't sure of the direction. By the way, what made your man accelerate without warning? That's what I want to know."

"We were about to run into a jetty," Brandt said drily. "We were only about fifty yards from the beach."

"Why didn't you shut off your engines?"

"What? And wait to get run into without being able to move?"

Clarendon nodded. He put his hands up to his face and rubbed his eyes. "I suppose I was an idiot to sit back there," he said. "Where's your boatman now? Don't tell me that he ran off with Phyllis, thinking I was dead?" He managed to grin. "Stranger things have happened," he said.

"No, he left us at Banús," Brandt replied. "Probably didn't want to face you, in case you made it to the beach."

"He's no fool," Clarendon said weakly. "I'd push him into the sea if he were here right now." He took a deep breath and coughed. "You wouldn't have any drinking water on board, would you?" he asked. "My mouth is all swollen from the salt. Or a beer, if you have no water."

"I'll get you some," Brandt said, and went below. Clarendon was behaving pretty well, considering the close call he'd had. When he returned to the cockpit, Clarendon was chatting quite calmly with Hope, although he was still shivering. "Then you'd given up the search," he was saying, "and were heading back to port, right?"

"More or less," Brandt replied. "I thought I'd pass near the place you went overboard, and then we sighted you in the water."

Clarendon nodded. "I guess I owe the fact that I'm still alive to your tenacity," he said. "And the log I found floating around out there. There was a strong current once the fog started to clear, and I didn't have the strength to swim against it. I decided my best chance was just to hang on and hope somebody would find me." He drank all of the water in the glass Brandt had handed him, coughed, and spat on the deck. "They say a man's whole life passes before his eyes when he's drowning. That's all rubbish, I want you to know. All you can think about is how much longer you can hang on."

"Well, you did the right thing, as it turned out," Brandt said. "And you were lucky. So were we," he added.

"I'm not so sure about you," Clarendon replied, with a sardonic grin. "I hadn't as yet changed my will, you know," he said, turning to Hope. "You'd have been quite pleased, after you'd recovered from the initial shock. Of course Phyllis might have stirred up a little trouble for you." He chuckled maliciously. "Good old Phyllis," he said. "Still, with a good lawyer, you'd have been all right in the end, I reckon." He spat again, this time over the side.

Brandt went back into the wheelhouse and took over the helm. He didn't want any part of that conversation, he decided. He shook his head. You had to admire Clarendon for being a tough old bastard, but that was all. He had probably never heard of gratitude. Nor was he endowed with a great amount of tact. For an instant Brandt regretted his decision to pass near the jetty on their way back to the port. Yet he knew that he had done the right thing. Aside from the scandal Phyllis Dexter would have provoked, he would always have felt guilty about not having one more look for his guest. Maybe now Clarendon would be a little more generous with Hope. It was unlikely that he would forgive and forget, but the two hours he had spent in the water might have chastened him a little. In any event, Brandt consoled himself, *his* problems with Max Clarendon were over.

There was a man with a black beret on the back of his head sitting on the edge of the pier, reading a newspaper, Brandt noticed as he backed *Lulubelle* into her berth. The man didn't look as if he was connected in any way with the port, but he got to his feet, picked up a line, and waited for Brandt to step into the stern before he tossed it to him. Then he tossed out the starboard line, as well, and helped lift the gangway into place.

Brandt thanked him in Spanish, and the man smiled and waved. He had a round, good-natured face, the kind you often saw in the bars of small towns in Castille. He had a little bit of a paunch; the skin on his bare arms was white, so he was probably a shopkeeper from the north on vacation.

Hope came up out of the cabin as Brandt shut off the engines. "I'd better see to it that Max makes it home," she said in a low voice.

"Probably not a bad idea, though you could put him in a taxi."

"I really feel I should go with him."

Brandt nodded. She was right, of course, although he would have preferred her to stay with him. Clarendon came up into the wheelhouse. He still looked a little pale, but appeared to have recovered somewhat from his ordeal. "I'm not going to thank you for a pleasant outing," he said. "Nor do I think I want to charter your boat for the rest of the summer."

"It's not my boat," Brandt told him.

"Well, anybody's boat," Clarendon said. "I've had quite enough of the sea for a while." He took a thick wad of five-thousand-peseta notes out of his pocket. Brandt watched him peel off one and shove the rest back into his trousers. "You think this is a big enough tip for your man?" he asked. "It's about twenty quid."

"That's up to you. You don't have to give him anything if you don't want to."

"Well, he put me into the water, but I don't think he did it intentionally. Will you see to it that he gets it?"

Brandt was about to tell him that the tarpaulin that had been lost would cost at least twice that amount, but he thought better of it. "Okay," he said. "I'll give it to him tomorrow."

"Then we may as well go," Clarendon said, turning to Hope. He started aft, moving rather slowly. He seemed to have aged ten years.

Hope said, "I'll call you later."

"I'll be home."

She hesitated a moment, waiting for him to look over at her. "Are you all right?" she asked.

"I'm fine. I've had a lovely afternoon."

Still she hesitated. Brandt went down into the cabin to make sure that his guests had taken all of their belongings. He felt tired. Still, the day could have ended much more tragically, he reckoned. For the second time that afternoon he folded up Manning's old blanket and stowed it away. Then he got himself a cold beer from the plastic container. As he opened the bottle he caught a glimpse of Hope and Clarendon walking slowly down the dock. The little man with the beret was still there, watching the proceedings. Brandt took another bottle of beer out of the container and went up on deck. It was hot in the port, although the sun was hanging low over the horizon. "*¿Quiere usted una cerveza?*" he called out to the man with the beret.

"*Pues si, gracias,*" the man said. He looked surprised but quite happy. He hadn't expected to be rewarded with a beer for his efforts.

Brandt opened the second bottle and went up the gangway to give it to the man. They stood on the pier, watching Clarendon and Hope make their way to the main dock. Clarendon had linked his arm through hers and was moving along rather hesitantly.

"*Esta bastante viejo para tener una mujer tan joven,*" the man in the beret said with a smirk.

Brandt shrugged in reply. He wasn't particularly anxious to continue the conversation, and certainly not to explain that Clarendon had only recently aged so much that he looked like an unfit companion for his escort.

The man took a long drink out of the bottle and wiped his mouth with the back of his hand. His smirk turned into a broad grin.

"*Mas sabe el diablo por viejo que por diablo,*" he said. "*Es un viejo refrán español.*"

Brandt had heard the old Spanish proverb before, that the devil was even wiser because he was old than because he was the devil. It was a well-chosen saying, he agreed, and laughed politely.

From where he was standing, Brandt could see the main pier as

Hope and Clarendon arrived in front of the terrace of one of the cafés. Hope had admitted to him, he recalled, that she had often wished an accident would remove Max from the scene. But she was greatly relieved, now that they had reclaimed him from the sea. Or did she believe that the experience would perhaps bring about a change of heart and make Clarendon less vindictive? He was being unfair to her, Brandt decided. Forget it; be grateful everybody's alive, he counseled himself, and went back on board *Lulubelle* to change his clothes.

The man in the beret waved to him as Brandt stepped down into the cockpit. *"¡Gracias!"* he called out. *"¡Vaya usted con Dios!"*

Brandt parked the Peugeot in its usual place in front of his apartment house and took the elevator upstairs. It was still stuffy and warm in the passageway that led to the entrance of his apartment. He was looking forward eagerly to a shower and a rest on the terrace with a cold drink. He turned the corner of the hallway, fumbling in his pocket for the key. Then he realized that someone was seated on the tile floor opposite his doorway. He caught a glimpse of long, tanned legs that were abundantly freckled. It was Connie Henderson. She was sound asleep, her back resting against the plaster wall, her head tipped forward, her blond hair hiding her face.

He stood looking down at her. Christ, he thought, another problem to deal with. Very gently, he touched her bare shoulder.

She groaned and looked up at him. "Oh, hello," she said with a smile. "Do you remember me? I'm the sailor-girl who left you behind."

"I remember," Brandt said. "What the hell are you doing here?"

"I came to borrow a shower. Couldn't find a decent room in the whole bloody town. But not to worry. I can sleep on the terrace, or right here if the terrace isn't available." She struggled to her feet. A light green zipper bag was on the floor beside her, and a folded-up blue dress on a hanger.

He kissed her on both cheeks. "Why didn't you call?" he asked her.

"I did. All afternoon. But there was no answer. I even called from the airport. That was about one o'clock."

Brandt said, "I was out on the boat." He inserted the key in the door, and she followed him inside with her belongings.

"Have I arrived at the worst possible moment?" she asked. "That's usually what happens to me. But I couldn't warn you, because I only made up my mind to leave France this morning. Couldn't take it anymore. You know they really don't like us Brits, the bloody French. Common Market be damned." She paused briefly. "Are you not even a little bit glad to see me?"

"Don't be silly. I'm delighted. Only my life isn't as simple as it was a couple of weeks ago."

"I didn't think it would be. That's the trouble with being a sailor-girl. But honestly, I won't get in the way. A drink, a shower, and maybe with the help of your telephone we can find a little pad somewhere for a night or two or three."

"I'll see what I can do. You know where the shower is. I'll make us something to quench our thirst. Don't run the hot water too long. The supply is limited."

"I remember," Connie said. She stretched her slim, well-proportioned body. "You can join me, you know. I don't mind."

"I don't think I'd better," Brandt said. "Not just now."

He watched her rummage inside the zipper bag in the middle of the floor until she found what she was looking for: a clean pair of the smallest knickers Brandt had ever seen. "I'll just run the hot water for half a minute," she assured him, and disappeared into the bedroom.

He got out the ice and made two vodka and tonics. Then he called the Hotel Coronado, which was only a few blocks away. There was a chance they might have a room later, the receptionist told him, as one of their guests had not arrived. If he could call back in an hour, they would give him a definite answer. Brandt assured the man that he would, and carried the two drinks out onto the terrace.

The wind was abating, although the sea was still marked by small waves. The sun was about to disappear in the dark blue expanse of the Mediterranean. Suppose Hope decided not to call, Brandt thought, and just dropped by? That would be a fitting end to the day. Connie Henderson came padding out onto the terrace on naked feet, with a towel wrapped around her. She looked, he couldn't help thinking, ridiculously seductive. "There's still plenty of hot water," she said. "I hope."

"I hope so, too," Brandt replied. Hope again. He wondered what she was doing at that very moment. Putting Max to bed? Making him a hot drink? Listening to his complaints or his promises? He got up and went into the bathroom and stripped off his shirt and jeans. He felt slightly tipsy. The moist floor seemed to be moving under his feet, as if he were still on board *Lulubelle.* Then he turned on both the cold and hot taps, and stood with the lukewarm water cascading down on his shoulders. *"Les histoires de fesses se réglent toujours,"* he said to himself drunkenly. It had been a day for proverbs and sayings. And providence from the Almighty. Yet he couldn't help wondering if he'd been all that fortunate, after all.

He slipped on a clean pair of slacks and a white polo shirt, and went out to join Connie on the terrace. It was almost dark; the street lights were on in that part of the distant town which he could see from where he was standing. The warm evening air made him think of the first few times he had taken Hope to dinner. How could he have guessed the complications that would result? And yet he had always had the feeling, right from the start, that their romance would not be smooth sailing.

He crossed back to the deck chair Connie had left vacant beside her, and sat down wearily. She was still wearing his bath towel, wrapped around her like a sarong. "Do you think I might have another drink?" she asked. "No, don't move. I can help myself."

She tightened the towel around her chest and went off humming to herself. Brandt made a mental note to call the Hotel Coronado again in twenty minutes. Although he was quite glad she was there at that moment. Sitting alone, waiting for Hope to call, would be a lot less pleasant.

"Want me to freshen up yours?" the girl asked from the doorway of the living room.

"No. I'm fine."

She disappeared, then returned a few minutes later, wearing the dress she had carried with her on the clothes hanger. "And what have you been up to in my absence?" she asked. "Nothing very constructive, I dare say."

"Don't ask," he replied wearily.

"I won't," she said, and giggled happily to herself. "You know, I haven't had such a good summer, either. The Med's a nice place if you have plenty of money. But if you're short of cash, it can be hell, really. Things got to be so desperate that I finally called Charles. Poor bugger, he was lonely, too, or so he said. Wanted me to come back and have another go, as he put it. I asked him to send me five hundred pounds. He didn't like that much, said he'd rather send me a prepaid ticket on British Airways. So I told him not to be such a stingy sod, and hung up."

"Do you think he'll send the money?" Brandt asked. It didn't really matter to him one way or the other, but it helped prolong the conversation.

"I don't know. We'll see. I'll go to the post office tomorrow morning and hope for the best. If worse comes to worst, I can always try to get another job on a boat. One that's heading in the right direction. That should be possible, don't you think?"

"I don't know. This time of the year most of the big yachts are off to Greece or the south of France."

"Well, let's hope Charles really is lonely. I might even call him again. Swallow my pride and tell him that I miss him, too. Unless, of course, you think you might want a cook and housekeeper?"

"I don't believe that's in the cards."

"Oh?" she said. "Then you really are involved."

"I'd say that was a fair estimate of the situation."

"But then why aren't you deliriously happy? Why are you sitting here alone, waiting for the phone to ring?"

"Because I'm an idiot," Brandt said. He got up and went inside to make himself another vodka and tonic, one a little stronger than usual. Then he called the Hotel Coronado again. There was a room available, the desk clerk told him, provided he could be there within half an hour. He assured the man that he would, and went back outside.

Connie was standing at the edge of the terrace, leaning on the balustrade and looking out to sea. "You know, Charles always used to say that if a man reached the age of fifty without having at least a million pounds in the bank, he was either stupid or damned unlucky. I never paid much attention to him, but he's probably right. That's why I think you should marry some rich girl and settle down. With your talents," she added with a grin, "that shouldn't be all that difficult."

"Thanks for your advice," Brandt said drily.

"No, I mean it. I like you. You're not like most of the other shits I've known. And playing time is sort of running out for you, isn't it?"

"If you say so."

"I'm not suggesting you're an old fart, or anything like that. But in ten years, where will you be? If you go on like this?"

"Still working for a living, I hope," Brandt said.

"Oh, come on," she said. "Work, work, work. What does it get you?"

"Peace of mind," Brandt told the girl, and patted her on the behind. "Come on. Finish your drink. I've found a pad for you. It's not the Ritz, but it's better than bedding down out here on the terrace."

"Very well. You know best. But if your call doesn't come through, you can always come by and pick me up. It's not far from here, is it, my new pad?"

"Two minutes by car."

"Do we have time to finish our beakers?"

"Absolutely."

She took several long sips, her eyes on his face as she did so. "You don't think your 'mystery guest' is likely to show up here in person, do you?" she asked.

"I doubt it. Don't panic." But he was beginning to feel a little nervous, too. "By the way, I've been meaning to ask you . . . where did you pick up that habit of coming to bed soaking wet after a shower? That's one I'd never run into before."

"Oh, that," Connie Henderson said. "Well, I always thought it showed that I was in a hurry to get back to my lover. I hope it didn't turn you off."

"It didn't," Brandt said. "Not to worry."

Only later, after he had deposited Connie Henderson at the Hotel Coronado and had returned to the apartment, did he realize that he had enjoyed the hour he had spent with her. To talk idly with someone with whom you were not seriously involved was a pleasure. It helped that he still found her attractive, but that wasn't the main reason he had enjoyed her company. She was a little daffy, but in a nice way. That she was uncomplicated, or appeared to be, was her greatest virtue. She didn't take life too seriously. With Charles, her husband, she was in all likelihood quite a different person.

Then the telephone finally rang, and it was Hope. Her voice sounded strained. There was a flat sound to it that he recognized by now as hiding an inner tension, especially when she asked him if he could come at once to the villa.

"Wouldn't it be better if you came here?" he asked.

"No, it wouldn't," she said.

There was a long pause. He was tempted to argue with her, try to convince her that they would be more relaxed if she came to him, but he sensed that it would be useless. "Where's Max?" he asked.

"He's not here," she said bluntly. That was all.

He felt weary, but he knew that he had no choice. It seemed like madness, his driving all the way to the villa just to talk to her, with both of them having to worry that Max might return home at any moment. Even if he'd gone off to find Phyllis, he would certainly not stay away for very long. He couldn't have recuperated his strength that quickly. But she was adamant.

It was eleven-thirty by the time he was back on the road. He felt hungry. He thought of stopping in one of the bars in town for a sandwich, but then changed his mind. He would persuade her to go out to dinner with him, since she had probably not eaten, either. Or if she had, she could keep him company at a place he knew of in San Pedro where they served steaks and hamburgers all night long.

As he drove through the gate he saw that none of the outside lights were on. That seemed strange, unless she had turned them off after Clarendon's departure. Then he remembered the night they had driven back after the robbery in order to hide the revolver, how they had made their way into the dark house together, both of them nervous and worried. Their troubles had only increased since that evening, he thought, as he walked across the white gravel to the front door.

It opened as he approached, a space just wide enough for him to enter. The living room and the terrace were in darkness, too. There was a light on only in the bedroom, he realized, which spilled out into the hallway. She took him into her arms and clung to him, sobbing softly. He kissed her damp cheeks. "Hey, what's the matter?" he asked, trying to sound cheerful, although he knew something was seriously wrong.

"I've had such a godawful time," she said, and took his hand to lead him down the corridor to her den.

She had put a movie on the video, a recent film, Brandt realized, recognizing one of the actors. The scene had been shot at night, so that he couldn't see her clearly when he looked over at her after she had closed the door. He realized that the left side of her face was swollen. He pulled her over to a chair and sat down, holding her in front of him. She had changed, was wearing a silk dress of a light color that he could not quite make out in the semidarkness, but that showed off her brown skin.

He asked: "What happened? Did you have a fight? What happened to your face?"

"We had a scene, and he hit me. I guess I should never have come back here with him from the boat."

"I shouldn't have let you," Brandt said quietly.

"But he'd nearly drowned, and after all, we've been together for a long time." She paused. "He was all right at first," she went on in a low voice. "A little subdued, of course, because he was worn out. Then he had a couple of drinks, and I fixed him a tortilla and a salad. We ate out on the terrace, and he was most reasonable. Said he'd misjudged you. That you were a nice enough chap, but not the right man for me." The night sequence had ended on the video screen, and the music and the dialogue grew suddenly louder, so she got up to turn down the sound.

"Why don't you turn that thing off?" Brandt asked.

"Because when it's on the servants think I'm still awake, watching a movie. And that way we can talk," she said patiently.

"All right. So he said I'm not strong enough a partner for you. What else did he have to say?"

"Oh, the usual thing. That I was his, that he still wanted me and would never stand for my going off with anyone else. So I brought up Phyllis, and that only made him angrier. He said that you were probably the one who told me about their affair. In any case, he said, she didn't matter to him, and then he grabbed me. I pushed him away and even tried to laugh him out of it. I told him that he was in no condition to rape me, so he'd better not try. That's when he hit me. I don't think it was with his fist, but he must have caught me with the heel of his hand. It stung, and I almost fell down. I felt I was going to be sick to my stomach. He was clinging to me by that time, asking me to forgive him. He was almost crying. I pulled away from him and ran out of the house." She stopped suddenly. "Let's not talk about all that now, please," she said, dropping to her knees in front of him. "I want to forget it happened."

"All right. If you like. You can tell me about it later."

"Yes, later," she said, taking his hands in hers. "Just not now. You know what I'd like you to do now? Make love to me. Does that sound completely bananas? Because it would help me forget. It always has in the past, you know."

Brandt said, "What about Max?"

"He won't be back. Not tonight, anyway."

"I may not sound very romantic, or macho, but I'm hungry, believe it or not. I haven't had anything to eat all day, and it's been a pretty busy ten hours . . ."

"We can eat later," she said, "*after* we make love. Or are you really too weak to perform?" she asked. She found his mouth with her mouth, and kissed him hard. Brandt thought, What the hell, maybe this is some sort of test I'm supposed to pass; and responded. Then he heard the dog barking in another part of the house and pulled away from her.

"Don't worry," she said. "It's only Bozo. I locked him up in the guest room after I called you." She put her hands under his shirt and ran her fingernails lightly over his back. "I do like your body, you know," she said. "It makes up for a lot of things."

"Like what?"

"Your being uncommunicative. I never liked the strong, silent type until I met you."

She pulled him to his feet and led him into the bedroom. Then, with a quick wriggling movement, she shed her dress. He was impressed as always by her beauty. But when she covered his face with her torso, he was conscious that her skin was slightly damp, even to the touch of his hands as they caressed her breasts. He rolled her over and lay for an instant with his spine arched, looking down at her.

"What's wrong?" he asked.

"Nothing's wrong . . . now that you're here."

"Don't lie."

"I'm not lying. You're just looking for an excuse not to make love, because you're hungry or you don't feel like it."

He shook his head. "I can tell by your skin," he said. "Something's bugging you."

"It's warm in here, that's all," she said, and drew his face down to her body.

The telephone rang. They lay inert while it rang on and on. She lay listening to it, her eyes wide open, as if she could tell by the ring or the number of times it was repeated who it was that was calling. At last she pushed him aside gently and went to answer it. Brandt noticed that the instrument had been moved to the other side of the bed, probably because that was where Clarendon slept.

He turned on his side to watch her. She picked up the receiver and said, "Hello," and then waited, listening. Then she said, "No, he's not here," and hung up.

Brandt sat up. "Who was that?" he asked sharply, half expecting her to lie.

She said, "Yves," and he knew his suspicions had been justified. She wouldn't have been abrupt if it had really been Brouyère.

"Does he know about what happened this afternoon?"

"I'm not sure. I didn't think there was any point in telling him. Not now, anyway." She moved around the foot of the bed, and the telephone rang again.

She went back slowly to answer it. "Hello," she said softly. "Yes. But it doesn't matter. No, he's not here. I'm sorry. I couldn't tell you that. Look, I've taken my sleeping pill, so I'd rather not talk now. We can talk in the morning."

Brandt jumped up quickly to try to intercept her, but she avoided him and, crawling back to bed, pulled the sheet over her.

"Hope . . . you've got to tell me. I know something's wrong."

She didn't reply. She lay still, her eyes on the ceiling. "Is it over between us?" she asked after a while. "You don't want me anymore. Because you can't be that hungry."

"Don't be ridiculous," he said. "I just know you're keeping something from me."

"It can wait," she said.

"No, it can't."

"All right. If you insist," she said. She turned away from him, her head buried in her pillow. "I told you that I made up my mind long ago that I was never going to let him beat me up again. So when he struck me, I ran into the den. I remembered what you told me about not keeping the gun hidden in the bedroom, so I decided to hide it there. I got it out of the suitcase in the garage the night after the servants caught us making love beside the pool. I hid it in the video set, because nobody in this house knows how to operate it except me, so nobody was apt to find it. Of course, he followed me. I tried to lock the door, but he pushed it open before I could do so. Then he struck me again with the back of his hand. 'Maybe this is what you need,' he said. 'Maybe this is what you like.' I begged him to go away and leave me alone. I told him that I didn't want any part of his money or the house or anything. That I wanted out, that's all. But he only laughed at me. He said that's what you'd told me to say. Then he grabbed me and flung me onto the floor. He ripped off my sweater. Here, you can see where it bruised my neck. So I lay still for a moment, and he thought he'd won. He rocked back on his knees to undo his belt. I thought he was going to hit me with it, so I jumped up and got the gun."

Brandt could feel a sinking sensation in the bottom of his stomach. "Oh, Christ," he said. "Why did I ever let you come back here with him alone?"

Hope turned to face him. The sheet fell below her breasts, and she pulled it up to cover her body again. She said: "He was surprised that I had a gun. He couldn't believe it at first. I backed out of the room. He followed me at a distance. I'd decided I was going to the garage and get the car in order to get out of here, drive to your place. He followed me out the front door. He was talking all the time. He told me that I didn't have the guts to shoot him, just as you didn't have the guts to leave him to drown. I warned him that he might be wrong. Then I told him that he would never touch me again. Not as a lover, or to hit me, or anything else. I pushed open the garage door. I knew the keys were inside the Mercedes. He stepped inside and, as soon as I was in the car, pushed the doors shut again. I thought I could back through them, but then I remembered they were metal doors, so I got out of the car again, and he made a rush for me. I pulled the trigger when he grabbed my arm. He looked amazed. He stood there for a moment, his hands on his chest. 'You little bitch,' he said."

The palm of Brandt's hand was moist on her forearm, moist and cold on her moist skin. "Is he dead?" he asked in a whisper that sounded like the whispers of the actors on the screen in the next room.

"I don't know," she said. "And I don't care. We should never have saved him. I kept thinking you might have drowned, trying to pull him out of the sea. And what for? Just so he could despise you for being weak? Just so he could beat me up and rape me?"

"My God," Brandt said. "And you waited until now to tell me."

"Because I wanted you to make love to me again. To wash away all the rest. To get rid of all the hate."

"Who called you just now? I've got to know. It's important." His mind was racing ahead.

"Phyllis," she said. "And then Yves. I guess they were together, making sure that Max wasn't here before they went to the police."

He got up and put on his shirt and trousers. His heart was pounding inside his chest. As if they had just made love, he thought. "What the hell are we going to do now?" he asked her. "Do you have any idea of how much trouble we're in?" It was an absurd question. He was trying to control his nerves, wasn't reasoning. He started to pace the carpeted floor in the darkness.

"There's a way out," Hope was saying. "I know there is." She hadn't moved from the bed. She was lying there, watching him. She reached out for the package of cigarettes on the night table. In the flame of the match, he caught a glimpse of her swollen face. He knew that she was frightened that he would leave her, sensed that that was what he wanted to do. He felt sorry for her, yet estranged.

She got dressed and he followed her through the kitchen into the servants' wing, down a narrow hallway that led to the interior entrance to the garage. He had no idea of what she had meant when she said "There's a way out," but calling the police was quite obviously not part of her plan. That had been his first reaction, outraged as he was by her story. She had a legitimate alibi: self-defense. But as he stood waiting for her to find the right key to the garage door, he realized that had he voiced his feelings, he would have sounded naïve, even silly.

Phyllis would undoubtedly reveal the facts of her close friend's private life, that she had a lover, and had had others in the past. And, if called, Safire and Brouyère would be forced to confirm her allegations, whether they wanted to or not. And a husband who beat his unfaithful wife or mistress in a fit of jealousy would be considered to be behaving in a completely normal manner in this country, as well as most other countries, Brandt reckoned. It certainly didn't give the woman the right to shoot him in cold blood. She hadn't really been in danger of losing her life. The gun had been in her hands. At best, she would be sentenced to five or ten years in jail, and a Spanish jail, at that. By a Spanish court, under Spanish law.

Then it occurred to him that he would probably not escape unscathed, either. It might turn out to be difficult to prove that he and Hope had not conspired to kill Max Clarendon, despite the fact that he had saved the man's life only a few hours earlier. He could prove that he had been with Connie Henderson that evening, but there was the gap of an hour that he had spent sitting in his apartment, waiting for Hope to call. A prosecuting attorney could make good capital out of that hour, as it was precisely during that period of time that the actual shooting had taken place.

The lock clicked open, and they stepped into the garage. She stopped almost at once and left a space for him to pass between the garage wall and the Mercedes. By the light from the hallway he saw what she intended him to see. Max Clarendon was sprawled out on the cement floor behind the rear bumper of the car. His back was against the metal garage door, and his legs were spread out in front of him. His head was tipped forward, his chin resting on his chest.

Brandt knelt down beside him. He was dead. There was no doubt about that. His silk shirt was unbuttoned. A small bullet hole was visible in the left side of his tanned skin. He was wearing some sort of elastic belt under his trousers, and it was tight enough to keep the blood from the wound from seeping down into his crotch, although there was a pool of blood on the floor behind him.

Hope said, “We’ve got to move him. We can’t just leave him there.” She made it sound as if there had been an accident, as if she were motivated by compassion, a helpless compassion, at that.

Brandt’s pulse was throbbing inside his head. He straightened, unable to take his eyes off the dead man on the floor in front of him. “If we move him,” he said slowly, “it’ll look as if we were trying to conceal evidence from the police.”

“The police?” She was staring at him as if he had lost his mind. “If the police find him, we’re lost.”

“You can plead self-defense,” he said, repeating the alibi he had already discarded in his mind, not knowing what else to say.

She shook her head. “They won’t believe me, you know that,” she replied. “They’ll send me to jail. They’ll say I killed him because I wanted the house, because I wanted to live there with you. Phyllis will see to that.”

“What else can we do?” She had a plan. He had none. He was trapped. It was all up to her now. “We can’t say that we just found him here,” he went on. “And try to tell them somebody else shot him. That wouldn’t hold up for ten minutes.”

She said: “It *was* somebody else. It wasn’t me. I know it sounds crazy, but after he hit me I was no longer able to think clearly. It was as if I were standing outside my own skin. I knew that everything I’d tried to do was wrong, reason with him, be kind, pretend that we were still friends. I was driven by an instinct to save myself. That’s why I picked up the gun. I never intended to use it. Before he grabbed me and insulted me, that is.”

Even as he stood listening to her, he realized that if she really did have a plan to dispose of Max’s body, it was a mistake. That what he had said was the only way out for her. She could plead temporary insanity, and even in Spain, because she was a foreigner and because times were changing, she might get away with it, walk out of the courtroom and get into her car and drive off, a free woman. She might, and she might not, he thought. But that wouldn’t really help *him.* Chances were, he wouldn’t go to jail, but he would no longer be the same person, not after the newly liberated Spanish press got through with him. He could forget about going back to the States and finding a job. He would have to change his name and start all over again. Alone. He looked over at Hope, trying to get some hint from her face that she knew just what she was doing, or if she was really telling the truth.

But she was still standing with her back to the light that was slanting in from the hallway, and her features were not visible in the semidarkness. Brandt said, "You told me that there's a way out. I'd like to know what it is."

She said: "There's an old mattress cover in the suitcase where we first hid the gun. I came across it the other day. We could put him in it and take him away somewhere."

"Where? It's not that easy . . ." He stopped. He felt that it would sound harsh if he said "to dispose of a dead body." Why he should worry about how he sounded, he himself didn't know.

"You mean easy to do, or easy to live with?"

"Both."

"I wished him dead, and felt ashamed of myself for doing so, and was relieved when you saved his life. I don't know what I feel now. I only know that I don't want to go to jail." She stopped, then moved around the back of the car, still without looking down at the body lying at Brandt's feet. "I want you to help me," she said in almost a whisper, pleading with him. "You've got to help me. Because you love me, or you did. Or you said so. And because you'll be implicated, too."

"I realize that," Brandt said, and looked at his watch. "I also know that the police might be here in a few minutes."

"I won't let them in. They have no right to come into the house without a search warrant."

"I wouldn't be too sure about that. We're not in California, you know. We're in a country where the police have different habits." He paused, trying to decide what he should do. "But one thing I do know. I shouldn't be hanging around the house when they get here."

She appeared to be frightened, then. "You're not going to leave me to face them alone, are you?" she asked.

"You'll have to . . . the first time, anyway." He glanced over in the direction of the shelf at the back of the garage. "Let's get the mattress cover," he said. "We can't make things much worse by doing that, I suppose."

She went to the suitcase and opened the top; a white cardboard box fell onto the floor, spilling out a lot of old photographs under the front wheels of the car.

He helped her pick them up. Most of them, he noticed, were of her and Max, discarded snapshots of their life together. He didn't bother to look at them, but there were a few of the villa while it was being built, he saw as he crammed them back into the cardboard box, and a few taken at various parties they had hosted together in happier days. Christ, Brandt thought, memory-lane time, tucked away along with what is about to be Max Clarendon's shroud.

She found the mattress cover she had been looking for, and he put the box with the photographs back into the suitcase and closed it. Then she went into the house for the keys of the Mercedes. While he waited for her to return, Brandt noticed that he was sweating, that his shirt was clinging to his body. They were laying the groundwork for their own doom, he felt; was sure that they would never get away with it. But he had no choice. He couldn't run away, because he knew he was in too deep, and behaving like a coward and a shit would only make matters worse for him.

Putting Clarendon inside the mattress cover wasn't that easy, either, but somehow they managed to do it. Then together they heaved the bloodstained white sack into the trunk of the car. Brandt found a chamois cloth, wet it, and wiped the blood off the taillights and the rear bumper. "I'd better get the Peugeot out of the drive," he said after she had locked the trunk. "In case the police *do* come."

She nodded. "I'll let you out the front door," she said. "If you leave your car somewhere among the dunes, you can walk back along the beach."

He followed her back down the white marble floor of the hallway. She opened the front door for him without turning on the lights. Once he was in the rented car, he started to sweat even more. He drove out the main gate and up the dirt road with only the parking lights on.

There was a cleared space a quarter of a mile from the villa near where he had parked before; he headed the Peugeot toward the sea and left it between two sand dunes. Then he took off his shoes and made his way slowly toward the beach. After he had gone about a hundred yards, he stopped to catch his breath. The sand below the high-tide line felt cool under his bare feet. On a sudden impulse, he stripped off his shirt and trousers and walked out into the sea in his undershorts. The cold water refreshed him. He floated on his back and looked up at the stars. The summer night was clear and still. After a while, he straightened and swam back to the shore. He found his clothes, and folded them up carefully, and walked down the beach toward the Villa Miramar.

The garden lights went on when he was less than a hundred yards away from the house. There was an old fishing boat on wooden blocks higher up on the beach, and he ran over to it and knelt down behind it. He could hear Bozo barking furiously, and then suddenly the barking stopped. Someone the dog knew had arrived at the house, and Brandt reckoned that it was Phyllis and Yves Brouyère, or both of them. If Yves had brought his dogs, there was a good chance they would be running all over the place, he thought, and would wind up sniffing the blood under the garage door. Or they might even come down to the beach. But there was nothing he could do about it. He thought of going back to where he had left the Peugeot, but that didn't make much sense, either. The dirt road he had taken led to a dead end. There was no other way to the main road except to drive past the house. And if he went back to wait in the Peugeot, he would not know when to return to the villa, so he decided to stay where he was.

The fishing boat looked as if it hadn't been used for quite a while. He lifted the canvas cover and saw that there was a set of oars inside it, an anchor, and a rusted diesel engine. In the stern there was a rolled-up net that had seen better days. Brandt tried gently to lift the boat, wondering how difficult it would be to get it to the water, and realized at once that it would take at least four men to move it. He had thought for a moment that they could put Clarendon's body in the boat and take him out to sea, tie the anchor to his feet, and push him over the side. So much for that idea, he told himself. Then the garden lights at the villa went out again. There was a faint glow visible behind the beach wall, and he guessed that Hope had left the pool lights on as a signal to him that her visitors had departed.

He decided to wait a while longer behind the fishing boat. He was trying desperately to think of some other way of disposing of Clarendon's body, but his mind refused to function. He remembered the little man in the beret waiting on the dock, getting ready to toss him one of the mooring lines. If he read about Clarendon's disappearance in the papers, and if there were pictures, he might well recall that he had seen Max alive. He hadn't thought about that small flaw in her plan to dispose of the body. The little man's testimony would be enough to hang both of them, or send them away for a long, long time. But now it was even too late to call the police. How could they explain stuffing the corpse into a mattress cover and lifting it into the trunk? And if they lifted him out and carried him into the house, there would still be plenty of evidence that they had done so as a last resort.

Bozo's bark startled him. The dog had come down the beach and was standing on the far side of the boat, wagging its tail. Then he saw that Hope was there, too, fifty feet or so behind the dog. She had changed into a night dress and a dressing gown, obviously in order to pretend that she had already gone to bed when the people arrived, whoever they were. At least she was still using her head, Brandt thought as he moved toward her.

"I turned off the lights so you'd know they'd gone," she said. She seemed quite in control of herself.

"Who was it?" Brandt asked.

"Yves and Phyllis, and some man from the Guardia Civil. He was in civilian clothes, but he showed me his identification."

"Did they search the house?"

"No. They didn't even come into the living room. I told the man from the Guardia Civil that we hadn't been able to find Max after he fell overboard, and that was all. He didn't speak much English, but Yves translated for him."

"What did Phyllis say?"

"Nothing. She just stared at me, and I stared right back. Then the man from the police wanted to know where you live, and I told him I didn't know. After that they left. I suppose Phyllis had plenty to say once they were back in their car, but while she was in the villa, she didn't open her mouth." She paused. "Does Phyllis know where you live?" she asked, suspiciously.

"I don't think so. But they won't have any trouble finding me tomorrow morning. And what do we do now?" Brandt asked. He didn't mention the man in the beret to her. There really was no point in telling her that yet.

She tapped the side of the boat with her well-manicured fingertips and said: "I suppose this thing's too heavy for us to put in the water. But I have another idea." There was not even the trace of concern in her voice, and Brandt wondered if she'd taken a tranquilizer, or if she really had swallowed her nightly ration of sleeping pills.

"Have you taken a Valium?" he asked her.

"I haven't taken one of those things for years," she replied. As he stepped out from behind the fishing boat, she saw that he was in his underwear. "Have you been swimming?" she asked him. She looked as if she were trying to keep from laughing. Then she crossed her arms and held herself and shuddered. But Brandt knew that it wasn't because she felt the cold. The night was as warm and balmy as a mild summer day.

"I needed to cool off," he said gruffly. He gathered up his clothes, and they started off down the beach, with Bozo trying to squeeze in between them.

"You can have a shower in the guest bathroom," she said, pushing Bozo out of the way with her foot. She put her arm through Brandt's arm and took his hand. "Don't hate me, please," she said in a low voice. "Don't be tough and impersonal. We'll be all right as soon as we get out of this mess."

He didn't contradict her. He didn't tell her that he didn't think they had a chance, although that was what had been going through his mind for the last half-hour. "I don't know what we can do," he said in a tired voice.

"Come back to the house and have something to eat," she said. "We have time now to think of something. And I have an idea. I told you that."

He nodded and led her down to the water's edge, where there

were no stones. Then when they were opposite the villa, they went up through the garden gate. The pool lights made the dark house look abandoned, a white mansion nobody had lived in for years.

"I'll get you a towel if you want to wash off in the pool," she told him, and crossed the terrace to let herself in through the glass doors of the living room.

Brandt went around to the shallow end and lowered his body into the still water. The pool was warmer than the night air. He thought of Clarendon lying dead in the trunk of the car, thought of all the times he must have bathed in the pool at night after a party. Then he moved slowly up the steps and stood waiting for her to return.

He took the bath towel she gave him, shed his underwear, and tightened the towel around his waist. "When you got the revolver, did you think of shooting him?" he asked her.

She stared at him for a long time before she spoke. "Of course not," she said. "I wanted to keep him from hitting me again, that's all. I told you that. Why do you ask? Why do you ask me that now?"

"Because that's what they're going to want to know," he said. "The police."

"Not if they don't find him."

"But they probably will," Brandt said.

She shook her head. "No, they won't. Not if you help me."

"I'll try," he said, and meant it. Besides, he had to; he was in it, too. "But you've got to be straight with me," he added.

Tears filled her eyes. "Oh, I suppose I thought of shooting him before," she said in a choked voice. "When he threatened to beat me up, or when he did, and even afterward when he'd cry and apologize and then try to make love to me. Even when I was repulsed by him I'd let him, just so he'd go to sleep and I wouldn't have to listen to his telling me he was sorry over and over again. I'd lie there and try to imagine what it would be like if I did shoot him, if I'd be tortured by guilt, because I was still very much involved with him, even if I didn't love him anymore. Then he'd usually go away, to London or New York, and I'd forget how unhappy I'd been. Finally I went to bed with somebody else. That was after he'd threatened to throw me out of the house and bring his wife here from England. It was the first time I'd ever been unfaithful to him, and I thought I was in love with this other man, and he was the one who gave me the gun. Not because Max had hit me, I never admitted that to anybody, but because I was alone so much of the time."

"Who was it?" Brandt asked.

"Yves, of course. I thought you'd have guessed that by now."

Yves Brouyère, the mysterious Frog, Brandt thought, and walked slowly up onto the terrace. He had never been able to accept the idea that Safire might have been her lover, after all; had believed her that Lew was only boasting. And he had dismissed her going to bed with Brouyère as an accident, the kind of brief affair women stumbled into when they were alone. But now she had admitted that she had been in love with him. In love. What a strange expression. With her pseudo-husband's best friend. She had needed someone, he could see that all right, tied as she was to a man who thought he owned her and could mistreat her because he had money and she was dependent on him. So Yves had provided the gun that had killed Clarendon! And half an hour ago he had come to the villa with Phyllis and the police. Maybe he thought he could protect her.

Hope had followed Brandt up onto the terrace. He saw that she was in control of herself again, although she was still dabbing her eyes with the small handkerchief she had found in the pocket of her dressing gown. She said: "Come inside. I'll make you a sandwich, and tell you my plan. I know it will work. I'm sure of it."

"I'll get my things," Brandt said and went back down to the side of the pool to retrieve his shoes and the clothes he had left on the diving board. Bozo lay watching him, his snout resting on the cool tiles between his sandy paws. He wasn't much of a dog, that was certain, dozing by the swimming pool while his master lay dead in the garage. But then Max had never been his master. He was Hope's dog, and he was beautiful and dumb. Or maybe he was smart. Smart enough not to get too involved with the human race.

They were in the kitchen, and she was making him a sandwich, and when she first started to speak, he thought she was embarking on an anecdote, some incident out of the past that she was prompted to relate at this moment, out of an understandable nervousness. So he only half-listened, watched her put the bun and the frozen sausage into the microwave oven, fill a glass with ice from the ice-maker, and open the bottle of Coke, preparing an American midnight snack, a Coke and a hot dog, with mustard and ketchup.

"The bun might be a little stale," she warned him. "That's why I'm toasting it."

"It doesn't matter," he said. He felt strangely detached, was experiencing the same feeling she had described, as if he were standing outside his own skin, and he thought it was fatigue that had brought it on. This was not happening to him, to David Brandt, he thought, who has never been in any kind of serious trouble, who has been fairly straight with everybody all of his life. Now he was involved in a murder. All right, it had been committed in self-defense, but subconsciously, by her own confession, she had planned it often before.

She was continuing with her story. She had been to a party with this man she was seeing a few summers ago, one of those big, boring parties that she had learned to avoid since, and late at night, because they hadn't wanted to go to a discothèque with the rest of her group, she and her date had decided to go for a drive in the hills. It was the man's idea, not hers. He said that he wanted to show her a piece of property he was thinking of buying and developing, although that was obviously not the only thing he had in mind.

"Our friend Yves again?" Brandt asked, forcing down the stale bun and the tasteless sausage.

"No, not Yves. Somebody else. It doesn't matter who. Anyway, he drove me up into the mountains in his car, and we turned off onto a dirt road in a part of the sierra I'd never been to before, and we could see the coastline down below us, all the lights stretching from Fuengirola to San Pedro, and then he stopped the car, because he realized that he was on the wrong road. But there was no place to turn around, and so we went on for quite a little way, the road getting steeper all the time. Suddenly there was this terrible smell, and we saw that on our right there was a deep valley, and it was the town garbage dump that we'd come to.

"He stopped, and the car filled with flies, and the smell was awful, but we had to go on just the same. We drove for another kilometer or so, and there was a big flat area with a bulldozer standing there in the moonlight, and bits of garbage strewn all over the road, and the man laughed and said this was obviously not the piece of property he had in mind. He said that he was shocked that the town had such a primitive way of disposing of refuse, and that he was going to talk to the mayor or the local priest, because the place was a terrible health hazard. There were rats scurrying around in the dust, and we saw a fox, or a mangy dog, we couldn't really tell what it was, and as he turned the car around, I got a glimpse of this steep valley full of refuse, a whole hillside full of cans and bottles and rotting food, and we rolled up the windows and drove back down the road again." She stopped. By then it was fairly apparent why she had told the story, and she knew that she didn't have to go on.

Brandt drank his Coke. It had gone flat and tasted of sugar, but he drank it anyway, knowing that nothing was going to taste right at that moment. "What makes you think they won't find him if we leave him there?" he asked.

"The police never go near the place. The trucks dump the garbage, and then later, when they get around to it, the bulldozers push dirt down on top of it all."

Brandt said, "It's not my idea of a final resting place, the local garbage dump." He was experiencing the same sensation of remoteness again, felt played out.

"What does it matter where we lie and rot," Hope said. "He might have been floating in the sea if we hadn't found him. Would that be so much better?"

"What about the bloodstains on the floor of the garage?"

"We'll have to wash those away. There's a hose and some cleaning fluid the gardener used to clear away the oil and grease from the cars."

"And the man at the port?"

"What man are you talking about?" she asked.

"The man who tossed me the mooring lines when we brought Max back this afternoon."

"Oh, that man," she said dimly. "I don't know. Maybe he won't remember. Anyway, no matter what, that part of it doesn't change."

"Unless we call the police."

She stared at him and shook her head. "They'll send us to jail," she said, "so what's the use of even discussing that again."

What she said was true. They could go over and over it all, and it would always come down to the same basic fact: there was no way out for either one of them. "All right," he said. "I don't think it'll work, but we might as well try your plan." She didn't reply. Instead, she turned away. The hot dog and the Coke lay in the pit of his stomach. "Can I have a glass of water?" he asked.

"There's a bottle of Lanjaron in the icebox," she said. "I'll go change my clothes." She started to leave the kitchen, but then changed her mind. "Here, I'll get it for you," she said. She took the glass he had emptied, and rinsed it out, then filled it with ice cubes again. He watched her pour the bottled water into the glass. She smiled as she handed it to him, a smile of encouragement that he could have done without. She was stronger than he was. He knew that now.

She was not worried about finding the turnoff from the main road, she had explained to him not long after they left the villa. The party that night had been at the house of some people who lived above the Safires, so that made the first part of their search fairly simple. It was only later, once they were up in the hills, that they might have difficulty finding the garbage dump.

"How do you know they won't be working there tonight?" Brandt asked. They were on the main highway, a few kilometers from the port. Brandt drove carefully, keeping in the right lane. It was just after two o'clock in the morning, one of the worst hours to be on the road, what with the drunks headed for home, and moving on to the next bar.

"I'm not sure the garbage trucks aren't out," she said, "but I'm fairly certain the bulldozer only works in the daytime. It would be too dangerous to operate a machine like that at night."

She was right about that, but he suggested that it would be dangerous if they encountered one of the big orange trucks up there in the sierra. "Hard to explain what we were doing there."

"We could be lost," she said. She lit a cigarette and shoved the used match into the overflowing ashtray. It was no use worrying about minor dangers, her attitude suggested, and again he wondered if she had taken a pill of some kind to calm her nerves.

She had seemed less calm when they cleaned the floor of the garage. It was probably seeing the blood that had upset her, he thought while he had scrubbed away at the stain that would not disappear. She had gone back into the house to turn on the garden lights again so that he could see what he was doing, and she hadn't come out again for almost a quarter of an hour. She was wearing jeans and a navy blue cardigan over a white T-shirt when she reappeared, and she had seemed calmer, pulled together.

Brandt kept his eyes on the road ahead. In the rearview mirror he could see that a car with bright lights was about to pass them on the left. It was a big Seat of a dark color, a fairly new one. The driver tapped his horn several times.

"What the hell does he want?" Brandt said testily. "He's got the whole road to himself." Then he recognized Tomás and Consuela, who had rolled down the window on her side. She waved. Tomás leaned across his wife and shouted to them in order to make himself heard above the noise of the two cars.

"David! *¿Qué tal?*"

Brandt nodded and smiled. "All right. And you?" he yelled back.

"Come and have a drink with us," the young Spaniard called out to them.

"We can't. It's too late."

"*¡Qué va, hombre!*" Tomás pulled ahead of them. At the intersection of a small unpaved road, he turned off.

Brandt stopped the Mercedes behind the other car and got out quickly, trying to decide exactly what he should say. Tomás stepped out onto the road, his manners impeccable, as always.

"One drink, David. It's not late," the Spaniard insisted, as they shook hands. "It's early. Come on. *Una copa.*"

"It's been a bad day," Brandt said. "Some other night."

Tomás' face changed expression. He grew serious. "You have a problem?" he asked. He looked back at Hope. The headlights of the Mercedes blinded them both, but Tomás had obviously seen who was with him.

"Can I help you?"

"No. I'm afraid not. But thank you, anyway."

He said he was sorry, and he probably was, Brandt thought. He touched the young man's shoulder and said, *"Gracias."* Then he walked over to where Consuela was sitting. "We'll get together soon," he told her.

"Of course. Next week," she replied. "At the fiesta." She was all dressed up for the evening, in an extravagant red dress that showed off her good figure. She put the tips of her fingers to her mouth and blew him a kiss.

David walked back slowly to where Hope was waiting for him in the Mercedes.

"What did they want?" she asked.

"To invite us for a drink."

"What did you say?"

"That we couldn't. That we'd had a bad day. In case they remember meeting us tonight when the whole story comes out." He got in behind the steering wheel. The Seat's indicators were flashing, and then it pulled out onto the highway, its wheels churning up dust.

Hope was lighting another cigarette. Pill or no pill, she was frightened now, Brandt thought. He pulled out into the right-hand lane.

"Where will you say we were going if they ask you tomorrow or the next day?"

"They won't ask. They're friends," he said. The kind of friends that would never believe that he was involved in anything like this, he thought. Because in the lives they led, murder was something they only read about in the newspapers. That had been his status, too, up until a few hours ago.

They drove on in silence, past the Puerto Banús and the club, until they found the road that led up to the hills past Lew Safire's house, where less than a month ago they had met.

* * *

She sat with her face up close to the windshield, watching the road ahead so as not to miss the turnoff. They were above the tree line, having left the last big Arab villa behind them, an estate with a high white wall and some unpronounceable Arab name on the gate. For the tenth time, at least, Brandt was reviewing the events of the day, suspecting that there was some other small detail they had both forgotten that would come up later and wreck their story.

"How did you get to the port this morning?" he asked.

"Why? What does it matter?"

"It just occurred to me that it's strange this car was still in your garage."

"Phyllis picked us up. At first Max wanted to take his car to the port, too, and then, while I was getting my handbag, they must have decided between them that Phyllis would drive us in her Renault."

"I see. That's probably why she wanted to be dropped off at Banús."

"I suppose so." She paused. "Slow down now. I think the dirt road we took is on our right."

"You have a good memory," Brandt said.

"We came back the next day with my friend's lawyer to show him the dump. So that he could write to the mayor." They drove on for another hundred yards or so. Then they came to a side road. "This is it," Hope said. "I'm pretty sure."

Brandt put the Mercedes' lights on high-beam. The road wound up through a small valley and then issued out onto a ridge line. There was a fire break on the right side of it that reminded him of California. It looked as if it had only recently been cleared. He got a glimpse of the lights of the coastline in the rearview mirror. Then the road rose steeply in front of them. There was a long curve to the right that brought them to a flat stretch much wider than the road had been before. At the end of it there was what looked like a huge parking area, marked by tire tracks. There were crushed beer cans lying in the reddish dust, and a few scraps of waste paper.

"I think this must be it," Hope said. She sounded doubtful for the first time since they had left the main highway.

Brandt brought the Mercedes to a halt, and they sat in the cloud of dust raised by the car's wheels. After it had passed, he turned off the engine. The air smelled of sage and rosemary and dust. There was not a trace of the odor of garbage. Hope got out of the car, and Brandt joined her. The stars were shining brightly above their heads, asserting themselves against the slim sliver of a moon. They walked slowly to the edge of the canyon, less than thirty feet to the right of them, and stood peering down into the darkness. From far away there came the sound of a dog barking above the minute tinkling of a bell. The warm breeze blowing toward them brought a familiar smell to Brandt's nose. "Sheep," he said. "I guess the priest or the mayor took your friend's complaint seriously."

She didn't answer him for a while. She was still looking down into the valley. "I'm sure we took the right road," she said.

"How long has it been since you've been here?"

"Two years."

"Two years is a long time. They pushed earth down onto the garbage, and nature did the rest." He felt relieved. He had never liked her plan. Down deep he had not agreed with her statement that it made no difference where we rot. Not that he believed in Max's "eternal soul," or even his own, for that matter. But there was also something brutal about flinging a man's body into a *barranca* full of rotting garbage, and he knew it would have come back to haunt him all of his life, even if he had been only an unwilling accomplice.

A fly buzzed around his head. The last survivor of a vanished race, he thought, and shooed it away with a wave of his hand. He turned to look at the woman standing beside him in the darkness. She shivered, just as she had done earlier in the evening, and crossed her arms, clinging to herself for assurance, he thought, because she was just as desperate as he was, now that her plan had turned out to be a fiasco. "What do we do now?" he asked her, not taunting her, but really wanting to know, thinking that she must realize that she had no choice but to give herself up.

"I think we should drive to the port," she said. "Do you have the keys to the boat with you?"

"They're on board, under the cushion in the stern. I never take them with me. That way, Manolo can get into the cabin in the morning."

She nodded and started back toward the door on her side of the car. "What time is it?" she asked him.

"It's late," he said, without bothering to look at his watch. "I know what you're thinking, but it won't work. We can't carry him along the pier with everybody sitting there, having a nightcap on the quay."

"We can go and see." She got into the car and closed the door on her side.

He got behind the wheel. "If we're stopped by the police for any reason whatsoever . . ." he said, and started the engine.

"Well, that's a risk we'll have to take. There are only a few hours of darkness left. Once it's light . . ."

They would have to give themselves up, he thought, finishing the sentence for her. He turned the car around and started back down the road. The lights of the town grew closer. They were traveling in the wrong direction, he couldn't help thinking. He had felt safer in the darkness of the mountains. But she was probably right. If they left their cargo up in the hills somewhere, someone was sure to find it. Later on, in the winter, the natives spent their Sundays in the sierra, with their wives and children and their dogs. Even in the fall they climbed up through the valleys, looking for wild asparagus. If somehow they could manage to drop Max Clarendon's body into the depths of the sea, they might have a chance to save themselves. Or save her, he thought. No, that was wrong. They were both guilty. Anyway, he couldn't abandon her now. That would be an act of cowardice he wouldn't be able to live with, even if he went scot-free. It was too late to turn back.

He found a parking place quite easily near El Faro. He wanted to have a look around the port before taking the car down onto the main pier, he told her. He would be right back.

But she got out of the car and followed him down the cement steps. Quite understandably she didn't want to sit there alone, so he waited for her to catch up with him. At that hour of the morning there were often a lot of *gamberros,* rowdies, as they were called, who did a little purse-snatching. The serious muggers, who had temporarily increased since the passing of the old regime, and who had used knives as a rule, had been dispersed when the police were given back some of their old powers, which were rumored to include taking them up into the hills and administering the old type of correction, a good beating with a rubber truncheon.

They passed through the second row of shops and took an alleyway that led out onto the main pier. Almost all of the bars and restaurants had closed; only the Italian place on the corner was still open, serving the last few customers, who were all seated inside. At the far end of the main quay a waiter was stacking the terrace chairs on the now-empty tables. An old woman was sweeping up the debris left over from the evening's festivities.

Brandt walked on in the direction of the sea wall. He could make out the distant silhouette of *Lulubelle*, her gangway pointing up at the sky, exactly as he had secured it. He started to turn back in order to speak to Hope when he caught sight of a man approaching him. It was the night watchman, a small gray-haired man he had seen once before, late in the evening.

The man said, *"Buenas noches,"* in a voice that was both a challenge and a greeting.

Brandt said, *"Buenas noches,"* and the old man recognized him.

"¿Van a salir?" the man asked.

Brandt replied that they had thought of going out, but were still undecided because of the weather. The old man grinned after glancing over at Hope. There was nothing wrong with the weather, he said. The sea was calm.

"Es un poco tarde," Brandt said, hesitantly.

"¡Qué va! Es buena hora para pescar . . ." It was a good time to go fishing, he said, although he meant something else. He added that he was going to get a bite to eat, which was why he was having a last look around.

They went on to the narrow pier at which *Lulubelle* was docked. Brandt undid the rope holding the gangway and lowered it. Hope stood watching him. Brandt handed her the keys to the Mercedes.

"Get the car and bring it down here," he told her. But she hesitated. Had she lost her nerve, he wondered, now that he had made up *his* mind?

"What about the guard?" she asked.

"He's gone to get something to eat."

"But he'll see us leave."

"What difference does that make? We can say we went out to have another look for Max's body."

She nodded and went off. Brandt boarded *Lulubelle* and found the keys where he had left them. After he had opened the cabin door, he moved aft again and went ashore. He could remember from his time in the Navy an incident that had not occurred to him before. There had been an accident on board the destroyer on which he had been serving. The breach of a five-inch gun had blown out, killing two sailors. They had been buried at sea, he remembered, sewn into their mattress covers and weighted down with lead; had been dropped off the fantail while the crew stood at attention on the afterdeck. The ship's loudspeaker had broadcast the appropriate music, Taps, a recorded version.

What he needed was something to weigh down Max's body so that it wouldn't float and be washed ashore. *Lulubelle*'s anchor wouldn't do, because he would have to explain how he had lost it. The Mercedes' headlights blinded him temporarily as Hope parked the car at the end of the dock. As she turned them off, he caught sight of a small boat-trailer someone had left at the intersection of the dock and the narrow pier he was standing on. A broken section of curbing was jammed in behind one of its wheels. Both would help to do the job, he thought as he stood waiting for Hope to join him. He was surprised at his ability to think clearly at that moment.

The trailer would serve as a caisson for Max's body, and the piece of curb would be his headstone, fifty fathoms deep. There was the risk that someone would see them, but the risk was small. In the section of the port where *Lulubelle* was berthed there were only day-boats that nobody lived on. The bigger yachts were all at least two hundred yards away, and at that hour it was unlikely anybody would be seated out on deck, spying on his neighbors.

He held out his hand, and Hope looked questioningly at him. He said, "Give me the keys. I presume the ignition key unlocks the trunk." He had decided that it was no use procrastinating any longer. There was no other way out for either one of them now.

* * *

The small boat-trailer proved to be quite easy to move, even with the weight of Clarendon's body resting on it. Taking him on board *Lulubelle* was more difficult, but between the two of them, they managed to carry the sagging mattress cover down the narrow gangway and deposit it on the floor of the cockpit. Then Brandt returned the trailer to where he had found it. The fragment of curbing he reckoned to weigh at least fifty pounds once he had lifted it up on one shoulder. Securing it to the mattress cover might present a problem, but when they were out at sea, he knew he would have time to devise a way. The important thing now was to get safely out of the harbor.

The noise of the engines seemed excessively loud when he started them, but once they were running at idling speed, he felt less nervous. He had untied all of the lines before turning the ignition keys, so that he had only to undo the stiff rope in the bow and toss it clear of the path the boat would travel. It had a buoy attached to it with a more flexible length of line, and he remembered that Manning had warned him of the danger of getting the floating rope fouled in the propellers. A little accident like that would put an end to their plan.

Very gently he eased the controls forward, then returned them to the neutral position while the boat glided out into the narrow channel. He couldn't see the buoy in the darkness, and holding his breath, he swung *Lulubelle* around and pointed her in the direction of the harbor entrance. Ahead of him he could make out the green light at the end of the sea wall, and he steered for it, knowing that he must keep it on his port side and not pass closer to it than four or five yards. Once they were clear of the marina, he breathed a little easier.

He set his course by the line of fishing boats on the distant horizon, aiming *Lulubelle* for the last light in the floating picket line. There was no trace of the west wind that had come up late in the afternoon and had blown away the fog. Yet he knew that they must proceed slowly, as there might still be some debris floating in the water. Once they were well away from the shore, he could increase their speed, although at night there was always the danger of running into a log or a half-submerged oil drum. He switched on the running lights and glanced at his watch. They still had at least two hours before daybreak, plenty of time.

Hope was seated beside him, her cigarette glowing in the darkness of the wheelhouse. He wondered what thoughts were passing through her mind. Max had taunted her, had accused her of being weak, almost as if he had wanted her to act violently in order to justify his own sadistic behavior. If he had known that she kept a gun, he would undoubtedly have been more careful. And if he had known that her weakness had its limits, that once these were reached, she was remarkably strong. Brandt was learning that now.

He noticed that she had put out her cigarette and had shifted the position of her body so that now she was half-facing him, with her back resting against the support of the side window. "What are you thinking about?" Brandt asked above the clatter of the engines.

She raised her shoulders in a shrug that expressed her fatigue. "And you?" she asked.

He didn't reply. "Were you thinking about Max?" he asked her.

She nodded and said: "Yes. I was wishing that we had never met. I suppose that's the way you feel about us," she added in a low voice.

"No. I only wish we had met under different circumstances." That was true, but he realized it wasn't much comfort. He wanted to console her, help her, if he could. "Out there is about as good a place to be buried as any," he said. "No worse than the cemetery on the back road."

"I suppose not," she replied. "How far out are you going?"

"Six or seven miles. If there's time. It'll probably start getting light in an hour and a half." He indicated the helm, and she squeezed past him and took over the wheel.

He went down into the cabin in order to get a knife out of the drawer under the sink. The lights of the coast, he noticed when he came back up on deck, had receded. Then he went aft and found the spare piece of nylon rope they had used for tying up at the *muelle de espera.* He cut off a piece long enough to attach the mattress cover to the chunk of curbing lying on the deck beside Max's body.

Even if he burned the end of it, Manolo was certain to see that it was shorter. He would have to invent some kind of explanation for what he had done, which wouldn't be easy. But with any luck the sailor wouldn't notice it for a couple of days. It would be even more difficult to explain why they had gone out again that night, should Manolo meet the *guarda* in the morning. But there wasn't much chance of that happening, since the night watchman went off duty several hours before the sailor usually arrived at the port.

Then there was the little man with the beret. If he made a habit of hanging around the port, there was always the chance that he and Manolo would strike up a conversation. In that event he might well say something about having seen Max disembark. It was unlikely, but it could happen, Brandt thought, especially if the newspapers made a big thing out of Clarendon's disappearance.

There were quite a few loose ends that could trip them up. But there was no use thinking about any of that now.

Brandt tied the nylon rope securely around the bottom of the mattress cover, and knotted it just above Clarendon's feet. He noticed that the palms of his hands were moist. He would wait until later to attach the rope to the piece of curbing, he decided, once the boat had stopped moving. His mouth was dry with fear. Why had he allowed her to go back to the house alone with Max, he found himself thinking again. He straightened and looked up at the distant stars. The cool night air made him feel better. But he knew the feeling wouldn't last.

The size of the swell had increased. It was as if he were crossing a dark and gently undulating plain, a solitary voyager escaping the shore, although that, too, was merely a wish-dream. He was not alone, and he was doomed to return.

Hope had gone below a quarter of an hour ago, to rest, so she had said, for which he was grateful. Before that the silence between them had begun to tell on him. There were so many questions he was tempted to ask, but that he knew would sound only like accusations. Had she hated him for years, the man she had killed? Why had she never told him the truth about the violence and the indignities she had been subjected to? It would have made him behave differently. He would never have allowed her to keep the gun, because, as it was, he had foreseen the first night she had showed him the revolver that it might end this way. Useless questions, now that they were accomplices. Then he couldn't help remembering repeatedly that he had saved Max's life at the risk of his own. The irony taunted him, grated on his nerves.

It had undoubtedly provoked Clarendon, too: the fact that his mistress's lover had fished him out of the sea. It had angered him once he had regained his strength, had made him act irrationally. He had committed suicide, in a way. Of course, he had not known that she had a gun. That was the only flaw in that line of reasoning. But once he had seen it in her hand, he had not modified his behavior. If she was telling the truth, and there was no reason to disbelieve her story, he had done everything to make her pull the trigger, had ridiculed her, and had finally made a grab for her, all actions of a man seeking his own destruction. If he had reasoned with her, had tried to diminish her fear of him and her anger, had allowed her to leave the villa, he would still be alive.

Brandt turned and looked back at the mattress cover lying in the rear of the cockpit, as if to remind himself that it was not all a bad dream. Beyond the wake of *Lulubelle* the sky was a lighter shade of blue above the eastern ridge line of the mountains. There were no lights visible, now that they were well away from the land, only the flashing of a beacon, the lighthouse in Fuengirola. It would help him return to shore, he thought, so it was better not to proceed too far out, to a point where the beacon was no longer in view.

He pulled back on the throttles and allowed the boat to drift to a halt. For a moment he debated with himself whether to shut off the engines. Then he recalled a movie he had seen many years ago in which a man and a woman had taken the body of her murdered husband to the side of a railroad track and had left it there, to look as if he had fallen out of a train, and then had been unable to start the motor of their car, in which they had planned to escape. So he decided to let the engines idle on, in the unlikely event that he would not be able to start them up again.

He stuck his head into the open hatchway in order to check the fuel supply. Both tanks were still half full. Hope sat up on the bunk behind the varnished table. "Have we arrived?" she asked.

He nodded. They had arrived at no particular destination, but they were out beyond the depth where even the larger fishing boats dragged their nets and might present a risk to their plan.

"Do you need me?" She had gotten to her feet and was standing on the faded carpet, looking up at him.

He nodded. "I'm afraid so," he said. It would all be more easily and quickly done with her help: lifting Clarendon's body up onto the afterdeck and then dropping it into the sea. And it was for her that he was doing all this, so why should he have to do it alone? He was doing it for himself, too, he reminded his tired brain.

He went back into the cockpit and fastened the nylon line around Clarendon's "headstone." Then he tied a double knot and looped it around the jagged edge of the piece of curbing to make sure it could not slip out when they dropped it overboard.

Together they lifted the mattress cover onto the rear bench. The deck rose and fell under their feet. Brandt picked up the curbing and placed it at the head of the mattress cover. He was short of breath by the time he had finished.

"Help me lift him onto the afterdeck," he said. She stared at him, as if what he was asking of her was some sort of penance he had devised. "There's no other way," he told her.

She swayed slightly, as if she were going to faint. "I'll try," she said.

Together they managed to raise the mattress cover up off the bench, but he had to help her with her end, as she appeared to have arrived at the limits of her strength. It made him angry, her faltering now, but he controlled himself.

"You've got to hold the stone," he told her, "and drop it once he's in the water."

"Can't you do it?"

"No. I don't want it to scar the side of the boat."

He lifted it up for her, and she held it in against her stomach, leaning against the railing of the cockpit. He pulled at the mattress cover until it was poised above the starboard side, then pushed it with all his strength so that it fell clear. He saw her try to lift the stone, realized that she wasn't strong enough, and crossed quickly to her side. The weight of Clarendon's body almost jerked the fragment of curbing out of their hands, but he managed to lift it and toss it clear.

The white sack went straight down, pulled by the sinking headstone. In a few seconds it was gone, leaving a trail of bubbles behind it. He looked over at her. There were tears in her eyes.

He understood. She had finally realized the enormity of what she had done. He tried to think of something he could say to her, but his mind was a blank.

"I loved him once, you know," she muttered.

It was not what he wanted to hear at that moment. "I'm sure you did," he replied, realizing that it sounded callous and unfeeling.

He turned away and left her standing there, at the side of Clarendon's grave. Once he was back at the helm, he pushed the throttles forward. The mountains in the distance were dark under the lightening sky. After they had been under way for a minute or two, he saw the flash of the beacon to his right. He spun the wheel to correct their course. Looking back, he could make out the white semicircle of their wake. Hope was still standing in the stern of the boat, her dark hair blowing in the wind. She was gazing off at the sea behind them.

He thought of Freddy Weaver as they drew nearer the port, and how he had turned down his proposal to smuggle hash on board *Lulubelle.* Vaguely he recalled his own words, that in a long lifetime he had never stepped outside the law. Weaver would certainly have the last laugh if one of the loose ends Hope and he had left behind them finally tripped them up. Loaning a friend your boat so that he could do a little drug-smuggling was mild stuff compared with what he was involved in now. Although, in the end, the sentences for both crimes would probably be about the same: a few years in Carabanchel prison, where some of the leading members of the country's society had done time.

Weaver's illegal enterprise wasn't any more risky, either, he reckoned as he steered *Lulubelle* into the entrance of the small marina.

There was nobody in sight. The night watchman was probably asleep inside the office of the port authorities, now that it was light.

All the bars and the cafés were deserted, as was the street behind the port. The sun had not yet appeared from behind the mountains, but the street lamps were out. The only lights he had seen during the last half-hour of their journey were the headlights of the cars on the main highway, people arriving for their summer holidays on the Costa del Sol.

He stopped the boat in front of the small white buoy floating in the water outside their mooring, and went forward with the boat hook to bring the bow line on board. Hope had gone below after they had dropped Clarendon's body into the sea, and had not reappeared. He went back inside the wheelhouse and backed the boat into its berth. There was no one on the quay to toss him a line, he was glad to see, and he did the job quite efficiently by himself, using the boat hook to snare the ropes and the gangway, and after it was all done, he turned off the engines. Then he collected the piece of line he had cut with the kitchen knife and took it down into the cabin in order to burn its frazzled end.

Hope sat up when she heard him open the drawer under the sink. She brushed her hair back with her hands and looked over at him. "What are you looking for?" she asked.

"A match," he told her.

She didn't ask what he needed it for; merely opened her handbag and handed him a box of matches. He held the end of the rope over the stainless steel sink. Turning it slowly, he melted down the telltale strands, managing not to leave any of the burned nylon on the metal.

"Are we back in port?"

"We are."

She went into the head, and he flicked on the water pump. He heard the buzz of the electric pump and the water running into the sink. A drop of melted nylon had fallen on his right pants leg, a few inches above his naked foot. Another tiny item of evidence, he thought, but probably not the one that would send them both to jail.

He waited until she had come out of the head, and then went in to wash his hands and face. The narrow confines of the small toilet still retained the odor of the perfume she had applied, and he remembered having seen the small atomizer she carried in her handbag on previous occasions. She was recovering, he thought. Spraying herself with scent was a sign of normality. He dried himself on the towel that had hung inside the head ever since the day he had first chartered *Lulubelle,* and made a mental note to have it laundered. Then he stepped back into the cabin.

He said: "Shall we go? My car's still parked on the road beyond your house. I'd better get it before somebody sees it." She nodded. Brandt looked quickly around the interior of the cabin while she made her way up the wooden ladder into the wheelhouse. Everything was in its place. Manning's old blanket, the pillows that could serve as life preservers, the various tubes of sun cream that he had also inherited from Manning. He picked up the rope, tested the melted end to see that it was cold, and followed her out of the hatchway.

He was about to stow away the nylon line when he saw the little man with the beret standing at the foot of the gangway. He was grinning at them, the knowing grin of an old reprobate who can still recall his own early sins. Brandt could feel his heart accelerating inside his chest. He pushed the length of rope out of sight. Then he straightened and said, *"Buenos días."*

"Muy buenos días," the man replied as Hope moved along the gangway and stepped down onto the pier. The lascivious grin broadened on the round face under the black beret.

"¿Muy agradable la noche en el mar?"

"Si. Muy agradable."

Hope had already started off down the pier in the direction of the Mercedes. The man in the beret looked her up and down, quite shameless in his appreciation of the view of her behind.

Brandt pulled up the gangway and fastened it in place. He couldn't keep his hands steady. They were doomed, he thought, beyond any doubt.

The man in the beret turned to face him *"¡Qué nos quiten lo bailado!"* he said, and chuckled.

"Si, señor," Brandt replied. He had heard the expression often before. "Let them try to take away that which we have danced" was a literal translation. He repeated it to himself as he unlocked

the door of the Mercedes and opened it for Hope. The little man was still watching them as they drove off.

The white pole across the entrance to the port was down, but the night watchman appeared as soon as they stopped, and raised it.

Brandt nodded to him. Then, on a sudden impulse, he rolled down the window on his side. "*¿Quien es este señor con la boina?*" he asked the *guarda,* pointing back in the direction of the pier.

The night watchman raised his shoulders in a tired shrug. "*¿Este? No sé. No es de aquí.*"

"Who did he say the man was?" Hope asked nervously.

"He doesn't know. He's a stranger."

"That's better than his being a local," Hope replied.

"A little better." It didn't mean that they were home free, he thought grimly. The man, even if he were from the north, might still come forward as a witness against them. Although it was less likely. But then the night watchman might well be mistaken. There was nothing they could do about it. Hope took a deep breath and settled back in her seat. She seemed to be somewhat reassured, as if the worst was over.

They drove past the villa and on down the dirt track to where he had left his car. The sun was already shining on the dark blue sea, with the sky a lighter shade of blue on the western horizon. What breeze there was was cool, relatively cool for a July morning. There were tiny waves, forerunners of the stronger wind the weather report on the car radio had prophesied. The sea smelled of kelp, a smell that the wind was driving inland across the dry shore.

The beauty and peace of the morning overwhelmed him as he stepped out onto the space between the dunes where the Peugeot stood in the clear light of early morning. It was as if the beginning of this summer day were intended for both of them to forget the horror of the night. The thought occurred to Brandt that it had perhaps been a nightmare, after all, but he knew that it hadn't. He looked over at Hope. She, too, had gotten out of the Mercedes and was looking out at the Mediterranean.

They stood in silence, a continuation of the silence they had maintained during the drive up the coast from the port. She didn't appear changed, Brandt remarked; looked deceptively rested. The fresh air seemed to have rejuvenated her. "God, what a night!" she said. "How could it all have happened?"

It was precisely what he was thinking. He said, "I don't know." Although he did, of course, having gone over it in his mind again and again, blaming himself repeatedly for having let her go back to the villa alone with Clarendon. It was almost the only thing he had been able to think of during the last few hours.

She walked slowly around the front of the Mercedes in order to get behind the wheel and drive off, he supposed. But she stopped near him, her eyes searching his face. "You know, almost the worst thing about it is what it's done to us," she said.

He nodded. He knew what she meant. Although she looked as pretty as she ever had at that moment. He wished he had more confidence in his feelings for her. If he had loved her more, he would not have let her go back to the villa with Max. That was it. It had been his failure, his failure alone. Clarendon had won out in the end. "I should never have let it happen," he said. "It was my fault."

She didn't reply at once, and when she spoke, it was clear that she had moved on in her mind, had left the wreckage of their love affair behind. "I think it would be better if we didn't see each other for a while," she said.

"I suppose so."

"Until all this has been forgotten."

He grimaced. "That might take years."

"I didn't mean until we'd forgotten."

He nodded. "There's bound to be an investigation," he said. "This thing isn't over, you know. I have to go to the authorities and report the accident. Either to the Guardia Civil or the police." He paused. "I've been meaning to ask you . . . what did you do with the gun?"

"I've hidden it again."

"That's not good enough. Throw it away. Into the sea. Wait until evening. Swim as far out with it as you can. Or give it to me. I'll do it."

"No. I can manage," she said. "Will you call me sometime?" she asked him.

"When?"

"I don't know. Early in the morning or late at night."

"All right. I'll call you once I've been to see the authorities."

"When will that be?"

"Today, I guess. Or tomorrow. Today is better, I suppose. As soon as I find Manolo. He'll have to go with me. He's a witness, too."

"Will they want to question me?"

"I would think so. And Phyllis."

She sighed. "Then we're really not safe yet?" she asked him.

"No. Not yet."

"Should I get a lawyer?"

"No. Definitely not. Not now."

She nodded. "I think you're probably right," she said. She held out her hand. He took it, thinking that they had never said good-bye like this, like partners in crime. "I love you," she said. It didn't sound all that convincing. "And I trust you," she added. That did.

Trust was sometimes better than love, he thought, especially when it was dictated by mutual need. He leaned forward and kissed her cool cheek. She started to pull away. "Never one," he told her. "Both cheeks when you're saying farewell to a friend."

She got into her car and drove off without looking back. He walked out across the sand dune in order to give her time to arrive at the villa, her villa now. It was seven-thirty; in less than an hour the servants would be arriving. He had to get out of there. They had seen him often enough on this stretch of road.

A few hundred yards before the turnoff to his apartment house, he changed his mind about going home. He decided that he was in no condition to receive the police if they should come knocking on his door at nine o'clock in the morning. Nor did he want to be alone. Not just yet. So he drove on to the Hotel Coronado and called Connie Henderson's room from the reception desk. The night clerk was still on duty, and he appeared to be a little surprised to see Brandt at that hour. But once Connie answered, he handed him the desk telephone without comment.

"It's me," Brandt said.

"My God, what are you doing here?" the girl asked in a sleepy voice.

"I'll explain later. Can I come up?"

"If you don't mind looking at a tangled wreck." She gave him her room number and hung up.

The night clerk went back to his bamboo chair without a word, and Brandt rang for the elevator. The inside of the small, mirrored cage smelled of stale beer. Somebody must have spilled a bottle of it during the night, Brandt thought, and it had dried on the cork floor.

Connie had left the door open for him, and he walked slowly into the shuttered room. The girl was lying naked in the double bed, with the sheet pulled up to her waist. "What can I do for you?" she said. "Or shouldn't I ask?"

"A shower and a little rest is all."

"What's the matter? Is there still no hot water at your place?"

"No, that's not the problem. I didn't feel like waking up alone this morning."

"Oooh, are things as bad as that?" Connie Henderson asked, grinning, as she turned on her side to watch him.

"Bad or good. I'm not sure." He stripped off his shirt and went into the small bathroom. There was a wash basin, a tiled shower, a bidet, and a toilet. The mirror had seen better days, and better-looking faces, he thought. He heard the pad of bare feet behind him and saw Connie's naked torso in the streaked glass.

"Just have to brush my teeth," she announced.

He stepped away from the basin to make room for her. Then he undressed and got into the shower. The water was either scalding hot or freezing cold, a typically Spanish fixture. But he was too tired to mind. He dried himself on a limp, sky-blue towel that was already too moist to absorb much water. But he felt better, stronger, anyway. Then he went back into the bedroom. Connie seemed to have gone to sleep. Her freckled, tanned back was exposed to his view as he slipped under the rumpled sheet beside her. He lay on his back and stretched his legs. He didn't want to think about anything for at least a couple of hours.

"Did it turn out to be just a summer romance?" the girl mumbled from the other side of the bed.

"Something like that." He closed his eyes. He saw the dark expanse of sea again, just as he had seen it when *Lulubelle* had drifted to a stop in the receding darkness.

"Would you prefer not to talk about it?"

"Not this morning, anyway. Or tomorrow morning, either."

"That's all right with me. I hate to listen to other people's problems." She turned to face him, still clutching the sheet, her half of it. "Then you can come back to England with me," she said, "and look in on poor Charles."

"I might do that." He could fly to London, he thought, and from there take the direct plane to Los Angeles.

"Was she a Spanish lady, your summer romance?" Connie Henderson asked.

"Nope. One of my own kind."

"A Yank, no less."

"That's right."

"Difficult ladies, the Yanks. But they do know what they want, the ones I've met." She turned her back to him again and moved closer. "You've always liked English girls best, haven't you, darling?" she asked drowsily.

"I don't know about that. Right now I'm not even sure I like girls at all."

"You're lying. But it's not important."

It was so much easier not to care, he thought. He touched her back with his hand, patted her fondly. "I hope you're not planning to go to the post office too early," he said. "They're open until two o'clock." He closed his eyes. How soon would "hope" once again be just a word, he wondered.

"I can even wait until tomorrow," the girl said. "I'm in no hurry to go home."

Neither was he, he thought, now that he was on his way.

PART FIVE

In his dream he was swimming in a dark sea. He recognized the old jetty near the Santa Monica Beach Club, where he had gone body-surfing every summer while he was still in high school. The familiar California landscape made him realize he was having a nightmare, yet he was unable to wake up and put a stop to the images that were passing through his mind.

A wave broke in front of him, and he dove under it, clawing the sand on the bottom so that the churned-up water wouldn't toss him around. When he surfaced there was another wave facing him about thirty yards beyond where the first one had broken, and he had to swim hard and dive again so that it wouldn't come down on top of him. He was short of breath, but he had to swim on out in order to get beyond the white water of the next wave, and then there was one that he saw wouldn't break, and he let it carry him up its blue crest, and beyond it, as far as he could see, there were more waves coming toward him, an endless line-up all the way to the horizon, breaking farther out each time. He turned to look back at the beach, and there was Hope, sitting on the sand, talking to someone he didn't recognize at first, but who he realized a second later was the man in the beret. He had his shirt sleeves rolled up and was playing with the white sand, scooping it up with his right hand and letting it sift out through his fingers. He wanted to shout for help, but he couldn't make a sound. Then a wave broke on top of him and turned him over and over in a series of underwater somersaults. While he tried to scream.

A voice said, "David! Wake up," and he knew that it was Connie Henderson, and that he was lying in her bed, not drowning, but safe on terra firma in a room at the Hotel Coronado.

"What time is it?" he asked the girl next to him in the rumpled bed.

"I don't know. Nine-thirty, or something like that. You were thrashing around like a beached whale."

Brandt said, "They don't thrash around. They just lie there and die."

"Well, a salmon then, or a trout. You kicked me."

"I'm sorry." He got out of bed and went into the bathroom. He felt weak. He leaned on the edge of the wash basin and stared at himself in the faulty mirror. He had the feeling that he had been asleep for a long time, but since it was only nine-thirty, he knew that it had been less than an hour and a half. The dream had made him lose track of time.

He washed his face with cold water and dabbed it dry with the towel that was still wringing wet. Then as his mind cleared he realized that the sanctuary he had chosen was not a sanctuary at all. It would have been better to go back to his own apartment and face the police, if they came looking for him, as if he had nothing to hide. He had made the wrong decision again, probably because he was tired. Or because once you started down the wrong track, there was no way to make things come right.

"They're rather chintzy about towels in this hotel," Connie called out from the bedroom. "Want me to call down and ask them for reinforcements?"

"No, that's all right. I have to go in a few minutes, anyway."

"So that's the sort of a man you are . . . sleep and run."

"Just today. Can I use your toothbrush?"

"Of course, my dear. We're still friends, aren't we?"

He went back into the bedroom to collect his clothes. Putting on a worn shirt was not his idea of how to start the day. But he had no choice. He wanted to get to the port by ten-fifteen, before Manolo had finished washing down *Lulubelle* and discovered the burned end of the nylon line. It was better that they have a talk before someone else told him about the boat having gone out early that morning. At least that way he would know whether telling Manolo that Hope had wanted to go out to look for her husband's body would suffice as an explanation. The rope, he could always pretend, had been cut and cauterized by a light-fingered neighbor, one of the summer sailors down from the north.

"When will I see you again?" Connie asked from the bed.

"Lunchtime, I guess. About two-thirty. If you can hold out that long."

"I'll do my best," the girl said. "Although I think Spanish hours are most uncivilized. No wonder they can't ever get anything done in this country."

The port was still deserted, he saw at a glance the moment he arrived. The gangway of *Lulubelle* was up, lashed in place just as he had left it. None of the other sailors who worked there were on hand for him to ask if they had seen Manolo. Nor was the man with the beret anywhere in sight. He made his way back to the main street of the port and asked a waiter standing outside the Italian restaurant why there was nobody around. It was a holiday, the man explained, the day of Santiago the apostle, patron saint of Spain. Everything was closed. Only poor waiters, like himself, had to work.

He found a telephone booth and dialed Hope's number. The number rang with its familiar sound, but nobody answered. He hung up and dialed the number again. He let it ring at least fifteen times before he gave up. Either she had gone out, or she had decided not to take any calls. It was hot inside the booth, so he held the door open with his foot and dialed the number again. From where he was standing he could see *Lulubelle*. If Manolo should turn up, he thought, he could at least ask him what they should do. He knew that it was their duty to report the accident to the authorities as quickly as possible.

Then he remembered that Manolo had told him he would see him tomorrow, but that he had said nothing about what time he would be there. He would go to Banús and see the port authorities in the control tower. Even if it was a holiday, there would be someone on duty there, especially as it was the high season.

* * *

The man on duty in the port master's office was one of the new, young, bearded types that democracy had brought to Spain. He stared out the window of the control tower while he listened to Brandt's story and stroked his reddish beard. Was Brandt certain that the man had not returned to his domicile, he asked. Perhaps he had gone to a friend's house to rest? Nodding gravely when the bad news had been confirmed, he made a note of the name of the boat and the time and place of the accident. Brandt would have to go to the Comandancia de la Marina and make a full report, he said. No, not the Guardia Civil or the police. An accident that had occurred at sea in Spanish waters was the province of the Comandancia. Unless there was a suspicion of a crime of violence having been committed. In that case the Comandancia would inform either the police or the Guardia Civil.

No, it had been an accident, Brandt repeated.

The bearded youth nodded again, his eyes still on the placid sea outside his window. The Comandancia, then, he said. Whether they were open on a holiday, he wasn't sure, but he would find out immediately. He picked up the telephone on his desk and dialed a number. For a while he listened impassively, then held the instrument away from his ear so that Brandt could hear the distant unanswered ringing for himself. *Mañana,* he said; the señor would have to wait until the following day. There was probably a sailor on duty, but the office was closed.

Suppose a vessel ran into trouble on the high seas, Brandt asked the young man, what procedure would he follow then?

In that case he would call the Comandancia in Málaga, and even they might well be closed on a holiday, although there was undoubtedly an officer on duty somewhere, in Cadíz or Algeciras. The port itself was not equipped to deal with that kind of eventuality, the young man explained. Nor did the local naval authorities have a boat available for rescue missions.

Brandt thanked the fellow for his trouble and drove home to shower and shave. Then he tried to call Hope again, but there was still no reply from the Villa Miramar. The servants were probably taking the afternoon off as well, he thought, in their master's absence. He felt frustrated, isolated, his nervousness increasing by the hour. He called Connie Henderson at the Coronado.

The post office had been closed, she told him, as were all the shops in town. "However, I'm starving," she said. "Holiday or no holiday, you've got to take me to lunch."

They went to a fish restaurant down the street from El Faro, and the girl downed a five-course lunch. Brandt ate part of the salad he had ordered, and drank some acidy white wine. His eyes ached from lack of sleep, and the smell of fried fish made him feel slightly nauseated.

"You'll waste away if you don't eat," Connie warned him. "Then what'll I do? No husband, no lover."

"Old Charles will come to the rescue," he assured her. "Don't worry."

He felt suspended in time. It occurred to him that he could catch the plane to London the next day, along with Connie, but he knew that flight was not the answer. He would have to stay on for at least another week. He ordered an anis seco, feeling as dissolute as old Freddy Weaver, and even more outside the law.

"Would you like to go to the beach?" the girl asked. She had realized by this time that there was something seriously wrong. "A plunge into the cold sea might cheer you up. And I could take the sun."

"You can do that on my terrace while I take a siesta."

"A solo siesta?" she asked with a fake, innocent smile.

"Yeah, a solo siesta." There was no use trying to explain to her that sex was the last thing he was interested in; she would take it as a personal affront or added evidence of his outmoded morality. Another misconception. His morality was nothing to brag about, a harsh fact she might soon become acquainted with.

"Poor David," she said, patting his hand. "Well, 'tis better to have loved and lost than never to have loved at all. Isn't that what they say?"

"Could be," he replied wearily. "They say all kinds of stupid things nowadays."

Late that night, after he had taken Connie home, he finally reached Hope on the telephone. "Where have you been?" he asked her as soon as she answered. "I've been calling you all day."

"I took a pill, and went to sleep in the guest room. I couldn't face my own bed."

"And the servants?"

"I gave them the day off. Today was a holiday, you know."

"I know that. Everything was closed. I couldn't even report the accident. But what about this afternoon? I called at five."

"I went out with some friends."

"Who?" he asked sharply, realizing as he did so that he sounded like a jealous lover.

There was a long pause. She was obviously debating whether to lie to him or not. "Yves," she said, finally. "And his Swedish girlfriend, the windsurfer."

"What did he have to say?"

"Nothing much. He called England for me. The family solicitor will be arriving here tomorrow."

"I see. What about Phyllis?"

"She's calmed down a little, so he said."

"Do you want me to come and see you?"

There was another long pause. Her voice sounded strained when she spoke again. "I'd like you to, but I'm scared. I have the feeling that we're being watched. I know it's dumb of me, but I'm frightened, David. I don't want to go to jail. I couldn't take that. You were probably right in the beginning, when you said we should go to the police. It probably would have been better."

She started to cry. She was breaking down finally, was losing control of her nerves. "I'll come right over," he said.

"No, don't do that. I'm worried the servants might see your car. Oh, David . . . what are we going to do?"

"Nothing," he said. "We've got to wait and hope for the best, that's all. Take a sleeping pill. I'll call you in the morning."

"All right," she said. "But call early."

"I will. I'll call you at eight." How long would they have to go on this way, he wondered, waiting for what the next day would bring, unable even to comfort each other or share their fears. He said, "Hope. Listen to me," as if he were speaking to a child. "If you go to pieces now, we're lost."

"I know," she said. "I'll be all right in the morning. I don't want to take another sleeping pill, but I'd better, I suppose. Don't forget to call."

"I won't," he said. "Try to get some rest."

Early the next morning, after collecting Manolo at the port, he drove a mile east of the town to the small ochre-colored building that he had passed so often without knowing that it housed the Naval Command. Manolo had scowled when Brandt had informed him that he wanted him to come along. He was not registered as a member of *Lulubelle*'s crew, he said, and therefore had no right to be at the boat's helm. That explained the man's sudden desire to visit his family in La Linea on Monday afternoon. But Brandt had insisted that the sailor accompany him. He had no intention of giving false evidence, and ultimately he would be called to testify, in any case. The sailor had muttered to himself, but ultimately agreed to go.

The desk clerk on duty was an amiable man who asked them to wait until the officer in charge could see them. There was a sailor on guard in the small office, wearing a cartridge belt and a soiled white cap that made him look like one of the actors out of an early Russian movie, and he stared at Brandt with unconcealed curiosity, as if he belonged to a different race. After a quarter of an hour they were taken upstairs and asked to wait in another office, the windows of which looked out on the fishermen's port.

The sea was flat, Brandt noticed, under a cloudless sky. Scores of gulls circled above a fishing boat that was unloading its catch, their catlike cries clearly audible above the noise of the traffic on the road behind the building.

After another quarter of an hour of silent waiting, a naval officer in a white uniform appeared. He was a short, pale-faced man with a pencil-line mustache and a small paunch. His name was Lieutenant García, José García, probably Pepe to his friends, Brandt thought, if he had any. Brandt explained the purpose of their visit once again, and the lieutenant told Manolo to wait, and ushered Brandt into the adjoining office. There was a photograph of the King on the wall and a map of the coast behind the lieutenant's desk. At a small table in the far corner of the office a clerk in uniform was seated at a typewriter, and as Brandt entered, the man looked up briefly and nodded to him. The lieutenant indicated a wooden chair facing him.

Yet it was all over in less than half an hour. It would be necessary to make a full report, he told Brandt rather regretfully, having realized that there was no avoiding the paperwork involved. Brandt was surprised that he was not required to take an oath of any kind, although he noticed later that a sworn oath as to the truth of his declaration had been included in a flowery last sentence above his signature. It didn't matter, as he had not had to lie. He had related exactly what had happened in as much detail as he could remember: the time of their departure, the names of the people on board, the weather, the exact time of the accident, as well as the time of their subsequent return to port. Lieutenant García had rephrased his statements into correct Spanish while Brandt sat listening to the clerk's typewriter clattering on, nodding his agreement to the terser version.

Once his deposition had been completed and signed, the lieutenant asked who owned *Lulubelle.* Brandt explained that the widow of the registered owner had loaned him the boat for a few weeks following her husband's death in an automobile accident. The officer frowned and looked disapproving for the first time since the start of the interview. Was the boat on charter, he asked, obviously more concerned with the legal status of the yacht than with the accident that had occurred at sea. Had Brandt given Mrs. Manning any money? Brandt admitted that he had loaned his friend's widow a small sum, but insisted that the loan had nothing to do with his using the boat. He would have to brief Marie Manning, he realized, so that if she were asked, her statements would coincide with his.

It was quite apparent that the lieutenant didn't believe him. The owner had loaned him the boat as a favor, Brandt insisted. And it was purely an act of friendship that, following her husband's death, he had helped her financially. It would, he knew, have been better had he not mentioned the loan at all, but he didn't want to ask Marie to perjure herself in order to protect him. She was in no condition to withstand questioning.

García made a note of *Lulubelle*'s location. The boat would have to be *precintado,* he declared, until its legal status was clarified.

Under no condition was Brandt to take the yacht out again. Boats flying foreign flags could not be chartered, he added, and Brandt had better inform the Señora Manning of this fact.

Brandt nodded in agreement. Would the other people who had been on board be required to make depositions, he asked.

García shrugged. It was quite possible they would be called, he said, but that was a decision his superiors in Málaga would make. He had never had to deal with a problem of this kind. He got to his feet. He would take the deposition of the *marinero* now, he informed Brandt. His manner was less friendly than it had been at the start.

Would there be any objection to his leaving the country, Brandt asked when they reached the door. Lieutenant García's small, watery eyes narrowed with suspicion. It was all going wrong, Brandt thought. It had been so easy at the start. Too easy. Would the small lie he had told about chartering *Lulubelle* bring about their downfall? Not the man in the beret, nor the burned end of the nylon rope, but the first illegal step he had taken more than a month ago.

As long as there was no charge against the señor, Lieutenant García replied. He wasn't planning to leave the next morning, was he?

Brandt felt the blood rush to his face. He was perspiring, although it was pleasantly cool inside the small office. No, not the next day, he said with a forced smile, but possibly in a week or ten days.

The lieutenant shrugged. A week or ten days should be sufficient for the authorities to conclude their investigation, he said. By that time, in all likelihood, the missing man's body would be washed ashore. But now he wanted to talk to the *marïnero*.

Brandt waited nervously in the adjoining office for Manolo. The only person who might denounce them was Phyllis, he thought, and Hope had told him on the telephone that Brouyère said she had calmed down. But he may only have wanted to make Hope feel better. Phyllis might easily become vindictive again, especially if the man in the beret was heard from, should he recognize Max from a picture in the newspapers. He was still the key to their salvation or their doom.

After fifteen minutes Manolo reappeared, and Brandt drove him back to the port. On the way the sailor made no mention of the complications he had feared would result from his having to make a deposition, made only a disdainful reference to the lieutenant's lack of experience, and fell silent once again.

Brandt gave him the five thousand pesetas Clarendon had left with him as a tip, and added another five thousand of his own. Manolo grunted a brief *gracias* and asked who would pay for the tarpaulin Clarendon had taken with him into the water. Brandt assured him that he would take care of whatever expense was involved in having a new one made, as well as paying the sailor for his month's work.

Manolo said, *"Muy bien,"* and got out of the car. He was subdued, but not much more so than usual.

Brandt sat for a moment, watching him go off in the direction of the sea wall. It was unlikely that he would return to the Comandancia on his own, even if he learned from the night watchman that Brandt had taken *Lulubelle* out in the middle of the night, or when he discovered the shortened nylon line. Or if the man in the beret should befriend him, which was unlikely, as Manolo seemed to be very much of a loner, a fairly ill-tempered man who had not much use for mankind in general, and in particular for anyone who didn't make his living from the sea.

It was his own behavior that troubled Brandt even more than all the loose ends Hope and he had left behind. He was conscious in retrospect that some of the questions he had asked the lieutenant had been superfluous, as had his gratuitous admission that he had loaned Marie Manning money. Was there within him a subconscious desire to cast suspicion on himself, a Dostoyevskian need to get caught so that he could expiate his guilt? It didn't seem possible. He was as eager as Hope to avoid doing time in a Spanish jail.

He was overtired, that was all. His brain was refusing to function normally. And the sun beating down out of the July sky was no help. You'd better get some rest soon, pal, he counseled himself as he drove away from the peaceful seascape of the port and its surroundings.

It was eleven-thirty by the time he arrived at the office. Penny looked at him a little strangely, but she made no mention of the accident, although she had undoubtedly heard the news. "Richard is out," she told him, "but he said he wanted to see you this afternoon at five-thirty."

"Do you know what it's about?" he said to the girl, another useless question he might well have refrained from asking.

"Not a clue," she replied. "He's gone to see the *notario,* and after that he's having lunch with some prospective buyers."

"Any other calls?"

"None that I know of . . . but you'd better check with Esmeralda."

"Will do," Brandt said. "Is everything all right with you?"

"Everything's fine. If only I didn't have to work for a living."

He smiled at her, but she was busily occupied with the letter she was typing. He went to his own cubicle and sat staring at the empty desk. After a while he got up and started out of the building.

"I'm going to lunch," he told Esmeralda.

He drove to San Pedro in the early afternoon to call on Marie Manning. There was an old Rover with a British license plate parked in front of the small house, and he let himself in through the small iron gate and rang the doorbell.

A young woman in a bathing suit came to the door, and an instant later a small child appeared behind her, holding a piece of bread in its hand. The young woman had a long, thin face that vaguely resembled Manning's, although her coloring was quite different. She had dark hair, cut short and tightly curled after the fashion of the day.

"I'd like to see Mrs. Manning," Brandt said hesitantly. "My name's David Brandt."

"She's not here, I'm afraid," the young woman replied. "I'm her daughter. My mother has gone back to England."

"I see," Brandt said. "Will she be coming back soon?"

"Not for a while. Won't you come in?"

"No, thanks. I have to run along." He hesitated a moment. "I was a friend of your father. And your mother, too."

"Is there a message I can give her?" the young woman asked. "I expect to be talking to her in the next few days."

"I'm afraid it's rather complicated," Brandt said. "It's about the boat. I was chartering it, unofficially, of course, and now there's some sort of problem about its registry."

"I wouldn't know anything about that," the young woman said. "I'm just here on holiday with my children. But my mother will be back in six weeks or so. Perhaps you'd like to leave a note for her."

"No, I don't think I'd better do that," Brandt said. "If you could give me her telephone number in England, I'd prefer to call her."

"Of course. I'd be happy to do that." She left the front door open and went into the house.

Brandt stood outside with the small child facing him. It was difficult to tell if it was a boy or a girl. After a minute of staring up at him, the child held out the piece of bread to offer him a bite. He said, "No, thank you," and the child looked puzzled and ran back into the house.

The young woman returned a few minutes later. "I couldn't find a pencil," she said. "I'm sorry to have kept you. Here's my mother's number in London," she added, handing Brandt a slip of paper. "I hope there's no serious problem about the boat. I know my mother wants to sell it. She has no use for it now."

"No, it's nothing serious," Brandt said. "I'll call her tomorrow or the next day."

Grey received him alone in his office. His manner was aloof, as usual, although he seemed to be making an effort not to appear unfriendly. "Bad news," he said, "especially coming, as it does, on the eve of our inaugural fiesta."

Brandt nodded. He said, "We did everything we could to find him," and stopped. What else could he say?

"I'm sure you did," Richard Grey replied. He went to the window and stared out at the eucalyptus trees casting the last shadows of the day on the dry ground. "There are certain malicious rumors floating around," he went on, "that, although I don't think anyone takes them seriously, won't be particularly beneficial to your reputation. It's one thing to have an affair with a man's wife, but quite another to have him disappear off your yacht."

"I wasn't at the helm when it happened. There are witnesses."

"I know all that. It's a most unfortunate incident, the whole bloody thing. But you do have to realize that it puts us in a funny position, as your employers. You weren't too eager to stay on here, anyway, I seem to remember, and this accident, I'm afraid, has decided matters. I'm sorry about that. But as the British press will undoubtedly launder all the dirty linen possible, it doesn't seem to be a good idea to have you continue with us."

"I can see your point of view," Brandt said quietly.

"Well, I'm sorry. What else can I say?" He turned away from the window and managed a frozen smile. "I always thought Max might come to a violent end. He was not a particularly pleasant man."

"He fell off the back of the boat," Brandt interrupted heatedly.

"I know. It's just bad luck the word was out that you were having a love affair with his wife or his mistress, or whatever she was."

"They'd come to a parting of the ways," Brandt said. "All that had been settled. He was involved with someone else."

The frozen smile had returned to Richard Grey's handsome face. He said: "My dear fellow. I'm sure you didn't push old Max into the sea. Especially as there *were* three other people on board."

"Where did you hear the story?"

"Oh, it was all over town last night. I've forgotten who called me. But it seems that Max's new girlfriend was spreading some pretty wild rumors before she came to her senses. But all that doesn't change the fact that he was one of our investors. So, you see, my hands are pretty well tied." His tone of voice was urbane, civilized. He was certainly not one to mourn Max Clarendon's death with any genuine feeling. "Of course, I'm not saying that you shouldn't attend our party, if you feel that not attending would prejudice your reputation even more. However, I must remind you that the press will be on hand. You know that better than anyone, since you invited some of them. And they live off other people's troubles, don't forget."

"I'll think about what's best," Brandt said. "For me and the company."

"I'll have Penny prepare your final check," Grey continued, as if Brandt hadn't spoken, "and drop it by your office." He held out his hand.

Brandt took it, knowing that Grey was certain to notice his cold, moist palm. But, then, when a man is fired, he thought, he wasn't expected to be entirely unmoved by the proceedings.

"Good luck," Grey said, and clasped his own dry hands, as if to rub them clean after the handshake.

"I'll need it," Brandt replied. He felt himself flushing again, and wondered if that was going to become a chronic symptom of his inner malaise. Or would time diminish this manifestation of his guilt? Time and a change of scenery. He walked slowly out of Grey's office, conscious of his own extreme fatigue. He felt the need of a long rest, desired sleep more than anything else. Like the men in the submarine, with the depth charges detonating all around them in the deep.

Connie was waiting for him at the apartment when he got home. She was in a good mood, because her money had arrived. "Good old Charles," she said, after Brandt had kissed her cheeks. "He really has come through in grand style. So, as I'm off tomorrow, I'm taking you to dinner. To the best restaurant in town."

He agreed halfheartedly. But first he had to get a little rest, he told her. He lay down on his bed without taking off his clothes. A mosquito droned above his head, and he got up to spray it with the can of insecticide he kept on his night table. As soon as he had closed his eyes again, the telephone rang. He picked up the receiver, and there was the familiar clicking of a pay telephone. He thought it might be Hope, but instead a young girl's voice said: *"¡Cochino, asceroso!"*

At least whoever it was who had called to insult him had not roused him out of a sound sleep. *"¿Quien es?"* he asked, managing to control his anger.

"Vete a la mierda," the girl said quietly, but with malice, and hung up.

He lay back on the bedspread. His shirt clung to his body, although there was a cool breeze coming in from the terrace. The telephone rang again. He picked it up and said: *"¡Voy a llamar la policía!"* But a boy's voice merely croaked, *"¡Cabrón!"* and the line went dead.

Connie came back into the room, wearing only the bottom half of her bikini. "Why are you shouting you're going to call the police?" she asked. "I could hear you out on the balcony."

"The goddamned telephone," he said. "But it's just some kids enjoying themselves on a hot afternoon."

"Well, take the phone off the hook, stupid," Connie told him. "You look all pale," she added, glancing down at him. She pinched his leg and took the receiver out of its cradle. "Go to sleep, David," she said in a gentler voice, "or you'll be a wreck tonight. And this is apt to be our last date for quite some time."

"I'll be all right," he told her. He put a pillow on top of the phone so as not to hear the dial tone, which had already turned into a steady busy signal. "Wake me up when the sun goes down," he said. He didn't feel well.

They went to La Fonda and sat on the patio at a small table that Brandt promised the headwaiter they would vacate by ten-thirty, since the restaurant was fully booked. Connie wanted to order caviar, but Brandt restrained her. There was no sense throwing her money around, he told her. She might need it when she got back to England. So instead they had cold avocado soup and broiled lobster, as well as a bottle of Moët & Chandon to celebrate the end of the summer. Her summer, anyway.

The restaurant was beginning to fill up as the headwaiter was preparing the crêpe suzettes Connie had ordered for dessert. The people who were arriving were all foreigners. The Spanish crowd would not be in until eleven o'clock, Ramón, the headwaiter, told them, so there was no need for them to hurry. He was making an extra effort to please Connie, who looked her best in the flimsy dress she had brought with her on a hanger for just such an occasion.

Brandt had already called for the check when a party of four was ushered into the garden. From a distance he recognized Brouyère and his Swedish girlfriend. There was a tall man in a blazer and a necktie with them, and as they were being led to a corner table on the far side of the patio, Hope joined them.

She hesitated for an instant, and Brandt started to get to his feet, but she turned away and moved on to where Brouyère and the others were waiting for her. Brandt realized that she had obviously pulled herself together enough to go out to dinner. Brouyère waved casually as he helped Hope into her chair. The Swedish girl stared across at Brandt with a puzzled look on her face.

"Someone you wish we hadn't run into?" Connie wanted to know.

"Yes and no."

"I've never known it to fail," the girl said cheerfully. "You can't get away with anything in this world. I suppose I'd better slip you the money for the bill under the table. That way it won't look as if I'm keeping you."

"It doesn't matter," Brandt said. "She's not facing us." He managed to smile as he opened the fancy box containing the bill for their dinner.

"I'm relieved. I was worried for a moment that it was the blonde. She looks much too tarty for you, you know. Not your type at all."

"Thank you for the compliment."

As they left the patio, Hope turned in her chair, and their eyes met. He pantomimed that he would call her, but he wasn't sure that she had seen the gesture, because she had already turned back to face the others at her table. Brandt felt a pang of helpless regret. There was no point in going over to speak to her. There was nothing he could possibly say in the presence of Brouyère. He would call her later, he decided, and explain.

Connie insisted on taking him to Régine's for a drink and a dance. It was still too early to go to bed, she said, unless, of course, he had decided to abandon his vow of celibacy, she added, pinching his neck.

"Then we'd better go dancing," Brandt told her.

"I thought that was what you were going to say. You know, I had an American beau once who had a theory that every lady he turned down would come to haunt him in hell once he got there. I suppose I should have held on to him."

"You probably should have. But tell me . . . what happens if I go to heaven?" he asked, trying to sound lighthearted so as not to spoil her evening.

"Well, that's a chance we all have to take," she said, and kissed his cheek as they drove on. He patted her leg. He could only think of the troubled expression on Hope's face the first moment she had seen him on the patio of the restaurant. She looked as if he had betrayed her.

Régine's was half empty, which made the music sound even louder than he remembered it from the few times he had been there in the past. What clients were already on hand appeared to be Arabs. They were accompanied, as usual, by the blond, sunburned ladies they favored: Paris imports or German Fräuleins down on their luck. They watched with hostile faces as he danced a slow with Connie to the plaintive voice of Julio Iglesias.

"Until just now, I was beginning to think true love had gone out of style," Connie whispered to him, her bare arm circling his neck.

"I don't think it ever will," Brandt assured her.

"That's bad news," Connie replied, and giggled happily to herself. "Come back to the table and have a little more bubbly," she suggested. "It's on old Charles."

After he had dropped her off at the Hotel Coronado, he hurried home and dialed Hope's number. It rang on and on. She was obviously not home yet, and the servants were fast asleep. It was too early, he thought, or too late.

There was no space available on any of the flights to London until after the first week in September, Brandt discovered when he called the British Airways office in Málaga on the following morning. However, the agent assured him that if Mrs. Henderson reported in an hour before the takeoff that afternoon, she would get a seat. There were a great many no-shows at that time of the year, because passengers often decided at the last minute to prolong their vacations.

Connie seemed quite unconcerned when he gave her the news. If necessary, she could always try again the following day. She would keep the hotel room for an extra night, as it was only a question of fifteen hundred pesetas, and she was rich for once. She had gotten the message, she said, that he didn't want to put her up at the apartment.

He took her to a small *chiringuito* near the old port for lunch. It was a small, temporary restaurant: a battered wooden hut that served as a kitchen, and a concrete slab protected by a roof of palm fronds on which half a dozen tables and chairs had been set up. On the narrow strip of beach in front of the *chiringuito*, there was a row of dilapidated canvas chairs with a few parasols stuck in the sand for the use of the customers who wanted to sunbathe before or after their meal.

When they arrived, Connie was not very impressed with the appearance of the place, but Brandt assured her that the food was good and that she could take a last dip in the Mediterranean before they had to leave for the airport. She shed her clothes once they had ordered, and proudly showed him the new Brazilian bikini she had bought that morning, which consisted of a purple string, a golden fig leaf to hide her "most private parts," and a halter that managed to hide her pink nipples. "Darling, I really am ashamed to tell you what I paid for this little number," she told him, impervious to the astonished but admiring stare of the Spanish waiter who had taken their order.

"I'm glad I didn't take you to the club," Brandt said as Connie lowered herself onto her beach towel.

"That shows you how wrong you can be," she replied. "The best people are wearing these things now. The hicks haven't caught on yet."

While she swam in the calm sea, Brandt lay in the shade of the parasol waiting for her to return. Despite the heat, he didn't feel like going into the water. The waiter brought him an iced sherry, and he sipped it slowly, listening to the guttural sound of the Swedish tourists who had arrived to occupy one of the tables on the concrete slab behind him. He felt listless, used up, despite having slept almost eight hours that night.

After a few minutes, Connie returned to the towel she had spread out beside him, and they lay in silence for a while, each absorbed in his and her own thoughts.

"This is the life, all right," Connie said, turning over on her stomach to let the sun brown her back. "Still, I don't know for how long I could take it. All this sun and salt water. It makes me feel permanently randy."

"Maybe you should bring Charles down here for a long weekend," Brandt suggested.

"Oh, I don't know about that," she replied. "He'd only get terribly burned, and complain about the food. I'd rather sneak away and come visit you from time to time."

"I don't think I'll be here for very long," Brandt told the girl. "And once I leave, I don't think I'll ever come back." Brandt was suddenly conscious of someone standing near them on the gray sand. He looked up and saw the little man in the beret behind him. The man was nodding to himself, enjoying the view of Connie's bare behind, adorned only, as it was, by two sections of purple string. He had recognized Brandt. He raised his hand in a vague salute from behind the parasol.

"La mejor parte del sol es la sombra," he said, happy to share his wisdom with an old friend.

Brandt was unable to reply. His heart had started to pound inside his chest. Finally the man shrugged and ambled on, moving along the beach in the direction of the old port.

Connie raised her head and watched him go. "Who was *that?*" she asked. "Another old friend of yours?"

"I don't know who he is," Brandt said. He had started to sweat. His heart was still pounding hard.

"What did he say to you?"

"He quoted an old Spanish proverb. That the best part of the sun is the shade."

"How little they know, these people," Connie said, and dropped her head back on the towel.

Brandt got to his feet and made his way to the side door of the kitchen shack. An old man in a white chef's hat and a dirty shirt and trousers turned to look questioningly at him. Brandt pointed to the now-distant figure of the man in the beret, strolling down the beach.

"¿Quien es este señor?" he asked.

The chef stepped outside to have a look before he replied. *"¿Este señor? Es un loco,"* he said, pointing a nicotine-stained finger to his head; then screwed it into his right temple. *"Es mi cuñado,"* he added, and laughed hysterically.

Brandt felt as if a great weight had been lifted off his soul. The key witness, the cook's brother-in-law, was a loony, an old nut who spent his days hanging around the neighborhood, quoting familiar sayings. He joined the chef in his hysterical laughter.

The old man stopped after a while to catch his breath. *"Ya pueden comer,"* he said, and went back into his own loony bin to cope with the smell of frying fish.

Brandt went slowly down the cement steps of the shack and joined Connie on the gray sand. "Lunch is ready," he said. "But you'd better put on your T-shirt to eat. I don't think this place is ready for a Brazilian bikini." He found that he was suddenly in a much better mood, almost his old self again. If they had not been pressed for time, he would have gone for a swim.

His euphoria increased as he drove Connie to the airport. She noticed the change that had come over him. "I don't know why you're suddenly so damned cheerful," she said. "Is it because you're getting rid of me? That's not very nice, you know. Doesn't make me feel wanted."

"It has nothing to do with you," he told her. "You've been my sole moral support, believe me."

"I don't, as a matter of fact."

"I'll put it in writing, if you like," he said. It was partly true. Her good-natured prattle had helped him to get through the last twenty-four hours, although now he was quite relieved to see her go. He needed to be on his own in order to come to some final conclusion about what he would do. He had also decided that he should make an appearance at the inaugural party at the hotel, and taking her along seemed a bad idea. He had provoked enough gossip on the coast.

There was very little traffic going in their direction at that hour of the afternoon. Coming out of Málaga there were a lot of cars with French and Belgian license plates, heavily loaded down with luggage and filled with dark-skinned occupants. They were all Moroccan "guestworkers," as they were called, heading south for their summer vacations. Every year the same mass migration took place, bringing with it heavy casualties on the road. On the whole, the Moroccans were known to be poor drivers, and since they didn't have enough money to stop en route, their fatigue made them even more accident prone. They were like the flocks of ducks and geese that headed south in July and August, he reckoned; a good many of them were doomed to die on the way, but that didn't seem to discourage them.

They arrived at the British Airways desk twenty minutes too early, and the man at the check-in counter, impressed by Connie's looks, assured her that there would be room on the plane.

They went to the bar for coffee. A large group of Americans were occupying the tables and chairs in front of the counter, and Brandt found himself staring at his fellow countrymen as if they were travelers from another planet. It was their dress and their manners that set them off from the other passengers. The men looked corpulent in their plaid summer trousers and their brightly colored linen blazers, and the women, with their strident voices and their blue-tinted hair, appeared to Brandt to be walking parodies of the American tourist.

"Your lot," Connie said with a smirk. "Do you think you'll be happy living among them again?"

"I'll get used to it."

"I wonder."

"Soldiers and tourists are never good representatives of their own country."

"I suppose that's true," the girl said. "A planeload of Brits wouldn't make me particularly eager to go back, either." She looked thoughtful. "If you do decide to pass through London, you'll call, won't you? Any weekday morning after eight-thirty. Although if Charles and I decide to patch things up, I'm going to try to be a reasonable wife."

"That sounds like a good idea. Anyway, I doubt I'll be coming back to England."

"Well, we'll see." She raised her cup of coffee in a toast. "Thank you for everything," she said. "It was nice while it lasted."

"You're not off yet," he warned her. But as it turned out, there was a seat available on the flight, and he kissed her goodbye outside the departure gate. "On both cheeks," he instructed her, remembering, with a sudden feeling of longing, his words to Hope.

On the way out of the airport building he passed through the crowded bar again. The Americans seemed even more boisterous, more grotesque-looking. Where the hell do I belong, he wondered. In what country would he finally feel at home? And safe?

The drive back made him realize that he would miss Spain and the coast. Despite the ugliness of the built-up areas along the sea front, there was something about the familiar scenery: the tattered bullfight posters on the crumbling walls of the old buildings, the white villages up in the hills, even the sunburned tourists waiting at the bus stops along the highway; they were all part of the life he had gotten used to during the past month. But he knew that he had no choice. He had to leave. He was without a job and would soon be without a place to live.

He had taken his checkbook along, so he drove directly to the old port to find Manolo. He wanted to get rid of all the chores connected with his departure. He still had to pay Carmen, the maid, and then go to the bank to close his account and convert however many pesetas he had left into dollars.

Manolo was working on one of the other boats he looked after a little farther along the quay, but the moment he saw Brandt stop near *Lulubelle*, he came over to him. The gangway was still up, the cabin door locked against all intruders.

He hadn't cleaned the boat yet, the sailor explained, as he knew the customs people would be coming along soon to put a chain and a seal on *Lulubelle*'s wheel.

Brandt nodded. He felt the small, shrewd eyes watching him suspiciously. *"¿Usted ha salido la otra noche, muy tarde?"* Manolo asked gruffly.

"Si." The night watchman had apparently informed him that the boat had left the port, so it was useless to deny it.

"¿Y porque?"

What could he say? There was no logical explanation possible. *"Para buscar mas,"* he replied. Although he knew it was a ridiculous answer. Why would they have gone out that night to search for Clarendon if they had not been able to find him on the previous afternoon? He added that they had gone ashore to check whether Clarendon had returned to the villa, and then had decided to resume their search.

"¿Por la noche?" the sailor asked, a note of disbelief in his voice.

"Por la mañana," Brandt said. That was about as logical an excuse as he could give, that they had decided to look for Clarendon's body in the first light of day. It sounded strange, he added, but Clarendon's wife had insisted they go.

Manolo grunted. *"¿Y claro, no han encontrado nada?"*

It was a statement, phrased as a question, that, of course, they had found no trace of the missing man.

Brandt nodded. They stood in silence, both of them looking off at *Lulubelle*, lying in the flat water of the port. *"Asi es,"* Brandt said with finality. That's the way things were.

Manolo lit a cigarette. He tossed the spent match in the direction of the boat. *"Es gafe, este barco,"* the sailor said, with some feeling.

She was a jinx, all right, Brandt agreed. He asked Manolo to lower the gangway, and they went on board. In the suffocating heat of the cabin, Brandt wrote out a final check for the sailor's services. He added ten thousand pesetas to replace the tarpaulin Clarendon had taken with him when he had fallen off the stern. He didn't want Marie Manning to have any extra expenses once she returned. And he wanted to make sure that Manolo didn't hold a grudge against him, now or later.

He waited until eleven-thirty to go to the party. He knew that by that time even the most Spanish of the Spaniards would have arrived, as it was known that at a fiesta of that kind the food was usually in short supply. He noticed that the band Consuela had imported from Madrid was already providing the normally deafening music, although no one had yet ventured out onto the wooden dance floor that had been laid down near the shallow end of the large new swimming pool. There was a big crowd waiting for drinks at the bar, and the long buffet was receiving the finishing touches of a small army of chefs and waiters. A few of the older guests were already seated at the twenty or so round tables, making sure that they would not have to eat standing up or sitting on the white wall that surrounded the spacious lawn.

The garden had a festive look, decorated with lights and flags and streamers, and the people, at first glance, appeared to be handsome and well dressed, the women in full evening attire and the men in silk shirts and brightly colored slacks. There were a few men in blazers and ties, but they were mostly the older generation. He recognized no one until he had reached the bar, and then Consuela came over to him, followed a few seconds later by her husband.

They greeted him affectionately, as if nothing at all had happened, and only after Consuela had gone off to get him a drink did Tomás mention the accident. They were both sorry about his troubles, he assured Brandt, and gave him a brief *abrazo*. Pablo and Elena joined them a few minutes later, and the same show of sympathy was repeated. Elena suggested that he join all of them at the table they had staked out, and made a disappointed face when Brandt said he wasn't sure he would stay for dinner.

It wasn't only the countryside he would miss, Brandt decided after they had wandered on and joined their friends; it was the people he would soon regret having left behind. Not that any of them were such close friends, but that didn't matter. It was their warmhearted nature, their good manners, their sense of humor, the rich and poor alike. They were the best thing that Andalucía had to offer, and their charm was worth more than the climate and the other prodigious gifts of nature that the region possessed.

Then he saw Freddy Weaver in the crowd waiting at the bar table in front of him. Brandt raised his hand in a hesitant but friendly wave. Weaver turned away as if he hadn't seen him. One cut, Brandt thought, the first of the evening. But he could hardly have expected Weaver to forgive him quite that easily.

He felt a hand on his shoulder and, turning, came face to face with Lew Safire. Brandt said, "Hello, Lew. I'm glad to see you," which wasn't quite true.

"Glad to see you, too," Safire said, his tanned face serious but not unfriendly. "You've really become the talk of the town, although not for the most flattering reasons." He smiled sympathetically. "I'm sorry," he added.

"Thanks. It's nice of you to come over and say so."

"I felt kind of responsible for a while," Safire continued in a low voice. "Because I introduced you to the lady. But what the hell, accidents do happen."

"They do," Brandt said.

"Well, don't let it get you down."

"I'm trying not to, but it's not that easy."

Safire shook his head and made a pained face. "I knew Max pretty well," he said. "I suppose I even considered him a friend. But to be honest with you, he was pretty much of a son of a bitch." He shook his head. "He was a shit heel when he was sitting on the stern of your boat. I don't know what would make him a saint when he hit the water. Still, you know what people are like. Death has a strange effect on their opinions."

"I know that," Brandt said. "But it's a bad thing to happen when you take someone out on your boat."

Safire said: "Sure it is. But you're not in the Navy now. And from what I hear, you weren't even at the tiller, so why should you have to shoulder all the blame? The best thing you can do in my opinion," he added, "is to give this place a miss for a while. Get it together in some other town."

"That's what I plan to do."

"Go back to L.A., is my advice. They're more likely to forgive a man out there, for accidents and whatever other sins committed along the way. You're young enough to hack it. It'd be tougher for me."

"Thanks, Lew," Brandt said, and meant it.

"Give my best to your lady," Safire said. "She's a good girl." He raised the glass in his hand in a solemn toast and wandered off. Brandt watched him disappear into the crowd at the bar. Then he caught sight of Richard Grey standing near the end of the lawn. He was talking to two dark-complexioned men dressed in white trousers and white jackets. One of them was Amir Rajawi. Grey nodded to Brandt, a distant nod that was anything but an invitation to join his group.

Brandt returned the nod and moved off in the opposite direction. The world, thank God, was a big place, he thought. The fiesta had provided him with ample proof of that.

Amir caught up with him at the foot of the marble stairs as he was about to leave the party. "You weren't even going to say hello?" he asked, looking slightly offended.

"I didn't want to embarrass you."

"Don't be stupid. It's when you're in troubl friends."

"So they say," Brandt replied. "But you've stuck enough for me."

Amir said, "Well, I don't regret it."

"Thanks, pal," Brandt said.

"And if you go to L.A., call my uncle. He's the only the book, I think. Or anyway, he used to be."

It was the kind of offer Brandt never took too seriou was nice of Amir to make it.

He was home by twelve-thirty. He sat down on the bed and Hope's number. She answered after the first ring. Her sounded no different from the way it always had when he had phoned her late at night or early in the morning.

Brandt said: "I wanted to say goodbye. Could I come and you for a few minutes?"

"I suppose so. The servants are asleep." A chill had crept in her voice as soon as she had realized who was calling. "Are yo leaving soon?"

"In a couple of days. But there are a few things I think you should know about as soon as possible."

"You might as well come along, then," she said, after a brief moment of hesitation.

"Would you rather meet somewhere else?"

"No. I'll wait for you here."

"I'll be there in half an hour." Their encounter of the previous night had obviously upset her. But there was no use trying to explain on the telephone Connie's being with him at the restaurant. It was not an invention that had ever lent itself to that kind of a dialogue.

He changed his clothes and drove to the villa. It was a warm night, and he hadn't felt really comfortable in the silk shirt and navy blue slacks he had worn to the party. The garden lights were on, he noticed as he drove through the gate, and the front door was slightly ajar. He closed and locked it after he had entered, almost out of habit.

Hope was waiting for him on the terrace. He kissed her on both cheeks, holding her by the shoulders for an extra second, as was expected of an old lover, he couldn't help thinking. She was wearing a toweled bathrobe that left her arms and shoulders bare, and he noticed that her skin was cool, as if she had just been swimming. "Would you like a drink?" she asked in the same distant voice.

"Yes, if you're making one for yourself."

She made them both vodka and tonics, then sat down facing him on the white couch. "What did you want to tell me?" she asked.

He leaned forward. He wanted to go and sit beside her and take her hand, but he sensed that she would only move away. He said, "Hope. What's the matter with you?"

"Nothing. I'm all right."

"You act as if I were Mr. Hoskins."

"Well, what do you expect?"

"Not that," he said.

"Who was the girl with you the other night?" she asked in a voice that was openly hostile now.

"The wife of a friend."

"Be careful. That could become a habit."

"You weren't his wife, and he wasn't a friend. What about the man with you?"

"You mean Yves Brouyère?"

"No, the other one."

"He's the Clarendon family solicitor."

Brandt sat back in his chair. "Look, this is absurd," he said. "We have enough problems without having this kind of conversation."

"I suppose you're right," she replied, but she did not appear any more relaxed. "Go ahead. You wanted to talk to me."

"That's right. I wanted to say goodbye, and to tell you that I'm very sorry it turned out this way. And that my feelings for you haven't changed. The only thing that has changed are the circumstances of our lives. Because of an accident. That's what it was, finally. Then, too, I wanted to let you know that you might be called upon to make a deposition. I reported what happened to the naval authorities, and had to give your name as a witness. If you tell them the truth exactly as you remember it, I don't think there'll be any complications."

She nodded. "I understand," she said. "Phyllis came to see me and asked me to forgive her for her outburst. She seems to realize that she behaved badly on the boat." She stopped short.

"And Yves?"

"Oh, Yves . . . he hasn't said anything. He didn't like Max, although he pretended to. He recommended I see his lawyer." She stopped again. "What about Manolo, the sailor?"

"I don't think we have to worry about him."

"And the man in the beret?"

Brandt shrugged. "He's a nut. Not the village idiot, but maybe his father."

"How did you find that out?"

"I ran into him at a *chiringuito* near the old port. The people there knew him. He's the cook's brother-in-law. His word wouldn't mean a thing, even if he did remember meeting us that afternoon."

"Are you sure?"

"Pretty damned sure." He hesitated an instant. Then he asked: "What about the gardener? Did he see the stain on the floor of the garage?"

She shook her head. "I took care of that," she said in a low voice.

"How?"

"I dropped some black paint on it that I found in the kitchen."

"I see." She hadn't lost her head altogether, he thought, or at least had recovered fairly quickly in the morning. He looked over at her. She was staring at her hands, folding them nervously. Then she glanced up at him. The expression on her face had softened.

"Then you needn't leave, really," she said. "You could stay on here?"

"And do what? Wait for some time to pass, and then move in with you?" He shook his head. "I don't think that's in the cards," he said. "Not that I wouldn't like to stay with you. But not here. I'd wake up every morning thinking of Max lying out there, where we dropped him. If I could sleep, that is." He got up and went over to her and took her hands in his. "I'll be back," he said, and meant it. "I can't live without you. I know that now."

She nodded. "I feel the same way," she said. "When you walked in just now, I knew that I still loved you. Seeing you again had the same effect on me that it did the first time we met."

Brandt pulled her up on her feet. "I still love you, too," he said. "But that's not enough to wipe out the rest. That's why I have to leave now." She put her arms around him. He held her for a brief while, his hands on the smooth skin of her shoulders. "I'm sorry," he said.

She drew in her breath. She made a sound that might have been a sob, but when he looked down at her face, he saw that her eyes were dry. She smiled a forced smile. "I'm sorry, too," she said.

She took him to the door. Just before he got into his car she raised her hand as if she wanted to detain him or to wave, he wasn't sure which. But instead she put the tips of her fingers to her mouth, as if to stop whatever words she was about to say. He dropped into the seat, started the engine, and drove out through the white gate and on down the dirt road, with the sugar cane blocking his view of the sea. At the junction of the main highway he stopped, although there was no traffic. But he was strong enough not to turn back.

The following Sunday he took the plane to Madrid. He had a reservation on the Iberia flight to New York at noon the next day. From there he planned to continue on to Los Angeles. He had decided not to go via London. It was not a place he wanted to visit, feeling the way he did. He had experienced enough pain there, was not yet ready to feel defeated again while walking down the same streets he had left behind only five weeks ago. And there was certainly no point in looking up Connie and Charles or any of their mutual friends. In any event, there was no use putting off his arrival at his final destination any longer.

There was no point in his staying on the coast for an extra few days, either. He had completed all of his chores, paid the maid, and closed his bank account. There were still two weeks left on his charter of *Lulubelle*, and although the customs people had not yet put a seal on her, they were certain to do so in the next few days. He saw Manolo quite by chance on his last day in town while he was having his breakfast at El Faro. The sailor mentioned the shortened nylon rope. He seemed to assume that some tourist had helped himself to a few yards, and burned the end of it so that it wouldn't be noticed at once. *"Ya estamos en Agosto,"* he said meaningfully, for August was the month when the coast was most crowded with strangers from the north.

The last loose end that might conceivably have tripped them up, Brandt thought as the Iberia airliner roared down the runway. Or at least could have complicated their defense if a few other factors had not worked out the way they had: the man in the beret, Phyllis . . . But he knew he must put all that out of his mind, and the sooner the better.

Yet even as he stared out the small window next to his seat, he knew that this was easier said than done. The lights marking the curved shore of the coast were visible below him as the airliner climbed into the dark sky over the Mediterranean. The pilot seemed to have left his runway lights on a little longer than usual; their bright beams probed the flat surface of the water three hundred feet below, and suddenly, in his mind's eye, Brandt saw the white mattress cover again, as the piece of curbstone pulled it down to the bottom of the sea, and he realized that was a picture he would never be able to forget, no matter how far he traveled on.

He closed the small curtain over the porthole and faced the front of the airplane. When the pretty hostess asked him what he would like to drink, he ordered a vodka and tonic. "A strong one," he told the girl, who nodded and smiled. She noticed the drawn curtain and asked him if he was sorry to be leaving the Costa del Sol. The weather in the north was bad, she informed him. It was raining in Madrid. She made a face and went off to get his drink.

A little rain wouldn't bother him, he thought; it would go well with his mood. He had had enough of the sun to last him quite a while. There was some truth to the old Spanish saying, that the best part of it was the shade. He knew that he would miss the warm evenings more than the hot days.